Killer Line

KILLER LINE

A novel

Dave Bartram

fantom
publishing

First published in paperback in 2023 by Fantom Publishing, an imprint of Fantom Films
fantompublishing.co.uk

A catalogue record for this book is available from the British Library.

ISBN: 978-1-78196-389-0

Typeset by Phil Reynolds Media Services, Leamington Spa
Printed and bound in the UK by ImprintDigital.com

Cover design by Will Brooks

PROLOGUE

May 2011
Fort William, Scotland

'Khalid... Khal... for mercy's sake pick up the phone!' Jonathan was frantic. 'God, this is one unholy mess... Agnes is fighting for her life in Belford hospital! The outboard failed, so I rowed across the loch for more than two hours, against a vicious headwind... A man in a bakery van rushed us to the hospital. Without his kindness she might have died in my arms!' His groggy voice cracked with emotion.

The acrid odour of disinfectant from along the empty corridor pinched at the membrane of his nose, and created a sore, burning sensation in the corners of his eyes. He wiped them with a grubby handkerchief, retrieved from his jeans pocket along with a handful of coins to feed the flashing payphone.

'If the unthinkable happens and she doesn't make it, there's something I need to get off my chest. What I'm saying is, I've not exactly been honest with you... I need to set the record straight. Find me Khal,' he whimpered despairingly. 'You're my only hope!'

The handset crashed down onto its cradle and he collapsed, exhausted, into a chair.

*

One hour later

'Sir... Please wake up... Sir?' The lilting Scottish voice echoed in the hallway, making scant impression on the unconscious wastrel, until a light nudge to the shoulder caused him to stir and he stumbled unsteadily onto his feet.

'Agnes... is she still breathing...?' Jonathan screeched in desperation. 'Please, tell me she's going to be okay?' The nurse recoiled instinctively as

1

his unkempt figure lunged towards her. 'I need to see her... let me see her, I beg you!'

'Sir, if you please... your lady friend's heavily sedated just now, although we're hoping she's through the worst of it,' the Sister said optimistically. At that moment her pager beeped, and her expression swiftly changed as she glanced at the message.

'What is it?' he panicked, pulling at his tousled locks. 'I can see it in your eyes... she's taken a turn for the worse!'

'Take a deep breath and calm yourself, sir, *please*,' the nurse advised firmly. 'Her breathing patterns are strangely irregular, so we need to transfer her to the ICU up in Inverness.'

'Forgive me... I'm knackered, and so, so afraid!'

'Apology accepted,' she replied. 'I suggest you gather up an overnight bag to tide the pair of you over for a few days.'

'But, we've nothing more than the clothes on our backs... no car, or other mode of transport... just a humble fishing boat with a clapped-out motor – and that's moored up against the harbour wall more than forty miles away!'

'How extraordinary, hmm... I'll need to consult my supervisor!' she balked, before turning a nifty pirouette to head back in the direction of the ward.

*

His backside perched on a flip-up seat by the side of the gurney, he gently caressed Agnes's exposed right hand. In the sockets beneath his bushy eyebrows, tears began to well; and it was a few moments before he noticed the yellow-bibbed EMT vying for his attention.

'Pardon me buddy, what's up?' Jon responded, having caught his reflection in the ambulance's blackened window glass.

'At some point we'll need to fill in a few blanks as to the patient's identity. Just how well do you know her?' asked the fresh-faced paramedic, battling to make himself heard against the constant thrum of road noise.

'Well... I know for sure her name's Agnes Ryan, and that she was born in Galway on the west coast of Ireland. I also know she's the most important, beautiful human being I ever laid eyes on!' Jon wiped at his eyes as he spoke.

'Aaah, don't worry – she'll be as right as ninepence once we get her on a ventilator... Do you know her date of birth, or any other personal details which might help us trace her medical records?'

'September the first; she turned forty-two last year. It was a beautiful, starry night…' For a moment, Jon was lost in sentimental reminiscence. 'We got drunk out of our minds, and went skinny dipping in the moonlight!'

'Sounds like the perfect way to celebrate a special occasion!' the medic chuckled, his fingers darting over the keys as he entered the details onto his laptop. 'What about her parents… did she mention them at all?'

'Her mum died when she was in her early teens, of some incurable disease; I'm pretty sure she said it was genetic…'

'Any mention of her father or any other surviving relatives?'

'Nothing to speak of; he upped and left when she was a tot. Her surviving grandmother lives over on the Emerald Isle.'

'So there's no one else you know of?'

'Huh… just an uncle, also from Galway. A pretty dubious character by all accounts; she's always given him a wide berth,' Jon said derisively, clinging onto the handrail to ride a sharp bend with the ambulance's suspension.

'No long-lost brothers or sisters?'

'Nope… she was an only child. A woman in a million… The pair of us have been joined at the hip for the past couple of years.'

'In which case we should name you as the next of kin?'

'Makes perfect sense… The name's Jonathan Jacob M – small c – Gold – rick,' Jon said. 'Otherwise known as JJ…' It had slipped out before he realised what he was saying.

The paramedic looked up in astonishment. 'You're kidding me, right? JJ as in JJ Gold…? The papers said you were dead!'

'Well, they were wrong – I'm the living proof!'

'But you look so… so different!' the guy said, scratching his head.

'A little dishevelled, you mean?'

'Forgive me, but I'm in a state of complete shock! I bought your new album… only last week!'

Now it was Jon's turn to be astonished. 'New album? I haven't been anywhere near a studio in four or five years!'

'*Angel of Death*… the soundtrack to the new Ridley Scott movie?'

'Soundtrack… what's going on?'

'It rocketed to number one, just a few weeks ago… How could you possibly not know?' the medic gasped, shrinking back in trepidation.

'Number one…? *What*…?' Jon boomed. '*THE BASTARDS!*'

PART ONE

ONE

JONATHAN JACOB MCGOLDRICK uttered his first cry in the clammy surrounds of Edinburgh's Simpson Memorial Maternity Pavilion, under the doting, watchful eyes of half English, half Scottish parents Moira and Eddie. He had entered the big wide world in the midst of an unseasonably mild Indian summer, at 0438 hours on Sunday October 8th 1972.

In the spring of 1974 Eddie's job in textiles required the family to relocate south, taking five-year-old daughter Kirsty and the eighteen-month Jonathan to a modest semi-detached house on the outskirts of a small Leicestershire town.

By the age of five, the youngster was precociously spanning his tiny fingers across the yellowing ivories of the family's upright 'joanna'; and it was not long before his prowess extended to the fretboard of a beat-up acoustic guitar, purchased by the delighted boy's admiring father from a second-hand store at the knockdown price of a fiver.

Paying little heed to the brash, largely overrated New Wave movement sweeping early-eighties Britain, the budding virtuoso instead tuned his adolescent ears to the works of savvier composers such as Paul Simon and the Beatles. He quickly found his own feet as a songsmith and took to the streets to showcase an eclectic repertoire of originals and inspired covers to the pricked-up ears of curious passers-by.

One of these was local impresario Liam Burke, who immediately recognised the boy's undeniable potential and stopped to chat. 'I run a couple of live music venues in town,' he explained, 'where we like to feature the best of the region's up-and-coming talent.'

'Any chance you could chuck in a few expenses?' Jon cheekily replied, before agreeing to a regular Thursday-night slot.

*

'Louie, you've got to see this kid... he's dynamite!' Burke said pushily, employing his powers of persuasion during a late-night call to music magnate Louis Kelly – the man he had once referred to as his 'significant other'.

'I'm up to my eyes in it at the minute, Lee; we're working every hour God sends on a new TV talent show set to take the nation by storm,' Kelly wavered. 'Send me a DAT demo of a couple of his strongest tunes.'

'Don't go fobbing me off, Louie… seeing is believing – he's special,' Burke rallied. 'The punters can't get enough of him!'

'I hope you're not shitting me, Lee,' Kelly said cynically. 'Your last wunderkind looked like Miss Piggy… sounded like her too!'

'Okay, so I got that one wrong… This boy's on another level!'

'In what respect?'

'He's a gifted guitar player, writes amazing songs… and his voice could melt the hardest heart!'

'How old is he?'

'Just turned eighteen… he looks the part too,' Liam said convincingly. 'You'll be thanking me before you know it!'

Louis finally relented. 'Fax me some blurb; I'll get Stuart, my talent scout, to take a peek… and Lee darling, this'd better be good!'

*

Cunningly lured into signing a five-year agreement with Kelly's prominent London-based 'Twilight Management' stable, young JJ's propitious career soon met with a multiplicity of major stumbling blocks. It was claimed that the boy's songwriting style belonged to a bygone era, lacking the necessary belligerency and angst to win over the new generation of music fans who were turning in their droves towards Britpop.

'You're going to have to compromise, son,' Kelly laid on the line, having drawn a blank with his connections at the in-vogue labels, all of whom insisted that singer-songwriters were old hat. 'Try turning your hand to something more contemporary!'

There followed a largely inactive six-month hiatus during which Jon was left floundering, searching for a Plan B. Then a golden opportunity presented itself, in the form of a high-profile new project set to offer him a chance to jump-start his career.

'The head of A&R at Sony really likes your "Face of the Eighties" tune,' Louis gushed optimistically, going on to provide a sketchy description of the proposed ins and outs. 'This could be just the break we need!'

'A boy band…? Get real, Louis!'

'They're looking to record one of your own songs, for Christ's sake!'

'I'm a musician, Louis… not some half-assed pretty boy who gets his kicks making little girls go weak at the knees!'

'Son… word spreads like wildfire in this industry!'

'And then what? Nobody'll touch me with a bargepole,' Jon vehemently maintained. 'I don't write sugar-coated pop songs!'

The arguments raged on for weeks, stirred by a torrent of new ideas flying back and forth. Lying low in the converted cellar of his parents' Midlands home, Jon's bottled-up creative juices flowed like white-water rapids, until he felt he had something that might just satisfy all sides.

'*Guitars*, Louis!' Jon exclaimed, sliding a demo CD into the desktop player and cranking up the volume.

'Jesus, son… you're on a roll!' Kelly enthused, his mind kicking into overdrive, wowed by the driving power-pop.

'You mean you like it?'

'Like it…? I love it!' Louis gasped, instantly recognising a gaping hole in the market. 'Give me twenty-four hours to make some calls!'

*

And so JJ Gold's musical odyssey began, fronting a fresh-faced, guitar-wielding quartet known collectively as 'The Boyfriend'. Their debut single 'Wonderland', boosted by an exclusive live airing from the BBC's Shepherds Bush Television Centre, went on to reach the chart's pinnacle in a staggering thirty-seven countries.

The punishing two-year schedule that followed saw the band worked half to death. The novelty of endless touring gradually wore thin, sucking every last drop of life from the burnt-out foursome – in particular their disenchanted frontman, whose ambitions to move the music in a bolder direction finally appeared dashed to pieces.

'The formula's grown hackneyed and stale,' manager Louis remarked in a hush-hush meeting with a team of prominent tunesmiths whom he had recruited in an effort to revive the band's flagging fortunes. Heaping insult onto injury, he shipped in a group of top session musicians to lay down the backing tracks for a long overdue new album.

When Jon heard the news it was the final straw. 'You overstepped the mark, Louis!' he declared during a late-night call from Tokyo. 'Once this leg of the tour's over, I want out!'

'Take it easy son… you've enough on your plate… I'm simply trying to make things a little easier for you,' Kelly argued.

'You're suffocating me, Louis! Just let me go… I already talked it over with the guys!'

Deeply anxious not to let the 'golden goose' slip away from his grasp, Kelly cunningly changed the subject to the possibility of a solo project, hinting the time may be right for Jon to add another string to his bow.

'Finish out the last leg of the tour, and we'll talk,' he said disingenuously, advising his prodigy against acting too hastily.

'My mind's made up, Louis; I'm done. Three years, and all I've got to show for it is a stack of lipstick-coated fan mail.'

'But you're still under contract, son!'

'Huh… the contract's not worth the paper it's written on. I already sought legal advice,' came the belligerent retort.

'But we belong together, son!'

'Do away with the sweet talk, Louis. You sold me down the river!' Jon said resolutely, making to end the call.

'After all I've done for you, you jumped-up little turd!' Kelly snarled, indignantly slamming down the phone. 'Cross me at your peril, son… Let's see you take the world by storm crouched in a fucking wheelchair!'

TWO

April 2011
Leicestershire Police HQ

'THERE'S A COLD FRONT shifting in from the west... so baby snuggle up close and put your head on my chest...' Legs splayed upon the polished oak fringe of his paper-cluttered desk, music nut DS Dan Hackett (from whom the warbling was emanating) was tuned into his latest indie-band download through a pair of bright red 'Monster Beats' headphones.

'*Hackett...!*' nonplussed DI Matt Philpott bellowed, striding agitatedly from his side office, his arm malevolently sweeping the entire contents of Hackett's desktop onto the coffee-stained carpet.

'Shit, guv... go easy, or you'll give yourself a coronary!' the younger detective protested, examining the blue veins protruding from the DI's cranium.

'Enough of the wisecracks, you idle git. Just take a look at yourself – filthy feet on the table, holes in your jeans, unshaven... you're a bloody disgrace, man!' the chief said scathingly, toe-ending Hackett's right calf muscle.

'Ouch... Guv, what's got into you today?

'You!' Philpott snapped, like a wild dog. 'Sat permanently on your arse, strapped to those fucking headphones!'

'It's my coffee break, for Christ's sake!' Hackett bickered, swivelling round in his chair to meet his boss's vengeful eyes.

'Might I remind you that you're paid to solve cases... not to laze around getting a hard-on listening to some tuneless wonder!'

'Tuneless! They're an up-and-coming band called the Shrinking Violets; the girl singer's got the voice of an angel!'

'I don't give a shit if she gives a blow-job stood on her head!' the DI ranted, slamming a file down onto the desktop.

Hackett glanced at the cover page, then looked up with a frown.

'King's Meadow village?'

'An old dear's Jack Russell appears to have unearthed a severed human arm from a rubbish dump close to her rear garden!'

'And you want me to check out the area?'

'Bag up any evidence, and get forensics to run a DNA test on it. I want a report on my desk by five o'clock sharp!'

*

'And now, as promised at the beginning of the programme, we have an exclusive track from the as yet untitled "lost album" by JJ Gold, soon to be featured as the soundtrack to the new Ridley Scott movie *Angel of Death*. Here's the forthcoming single, "Endless Heartache".'

The announcement by veteran DJ Ken Bruce shook Hackett out of his bored stupor. 'Wow!' he exclaimed; and, weaving around a sluggish road sweeper, he pulled into a lay-by, bent on giving the tune his undivided attention.

A strange tingling ran the length of his spine. JJ's trademark soulful tones passionately wrung out every last ounce of emotion, above a mesmerising accompaniment of guitars, voices and lush strings.

The heavy rumble of a giant truck shook him back to his senses, and leaving the lay-by he hung the car left. Away from the sounds of the incessant daytime traffic, the stunning mini-masterpiece still rang in his ears.

'It seems our phone lines are jammed by the hundreds of calls we're receiving in response to our airing of JJ Gold's "Endless Heartache"!' Bruce again took up the reins, appealing for a modicum of patience from the listening audience. 'We hope to have details of the pending release date before the end of the show!'

A hasty scroll through his long list of contacts led Hackett to pause at a well-connected ex-schoolmate named Martin Evans. A one-time features editor for the local rag, a move to the bright lights of Fleet Street had sent Evans's journalist career spiralling upwards, his talents and insight far transcending those possessed by most of his contemporaries. Surely his position in a prominent news media group might help him lay his hands on an advance copy?

The call went straight to voicemail. 'Marty, it's Dan. I need to call in a favour… Get back to me the moment you pick up this message!' Hackett said, his thumb and forefinger poised at the volume knob to silence a previous *X Factor* winner.

Thirty minutes later

'Where the hell are you, Hackett – Cape Canaveral?' Evans bawled into the mouthpiece, his one-time playmate rendered all but inaudible amid an impenetrable concoction of static interference and blustery wind.

'Stuck in a field next to a giant manure heap... and don't ask!' the DS sputtered, the stench making his nostrils twitch.

'Shit happens, mate!' Evans said humorously. 'What can I do for you, you scrounging git?'

'Huh... harsh, but true... I'm trying to hunt down a promo copy of the new JJ Gold album; what are the chances?'

'Slim, mate... they're like rocking-horse shit!'

'I figured so... I actually need it for some research I'm doing on an unfinished case, if that makes a difference?'

'A case... involving JJ Gold?' Evans said, holding his breath.

'Don't get too excited, buddy... Listen, I have to go!' Hackett stopped him short as he eyed a chunky farmer's daughter striding purposefully in his direction, her right hand gripping a bulky Sainsbury's shopping bag.

'Is this what you're looking for?' she said brusquely. 'I dread to think what else might be lurking under all that crap!'

'Perish the thought!' he replied, thanking her for her cooperation. 'Can you direct me to Mrs Jackson's cottage?'

'Miss Jackson, you mean?'

'The old lady whose dog found the... um, piece of evidence in the dyke.'

Her hand shot to her mouth and a high-pitched giggling sound escaped from the girl's convulsing body. 'You said... dyke!' she squealed.

'No pun intended,' he said, wagging an admonishing finger in her face. 'I'm sure she's an agreeable old lady!'

'Busybody may be a fairer description... forever poking her nose in where it isn't needed,' the girl mumbled disparagingly. 'Her place is to the right of the old phone-box opposite the gates... the chocolate-box cottage, with the thatched roof.' Having pointed in the general direction of the village's main street she twisted round in the mud and began to make her way back towards the farmhouse.

'Why don't you like her?' Hackett blurted out.

''Cos she's a stuck up cow... Go and see for yourself!' the young lass shouted back, throwing up her hand in a valedictory wave.

'Guv, we need a SOCO team in King's Meadow to get an excavation under way. The aforementioned body part's been festering for an eternity in a farm dump,' Hackett relayed breathlessly as he clomped his way onto the main street, wildly slashing his coat sleeve at the roadside underbrush. 'I'm off to interview the gossip whose mutt dredged up the exhibit. I'll get back to you pronto, once I've taken her statement.'

He arrived at the quaint cottage to find a ruddy-faced senior citizen viewing him with the utmost suspicion from the adjoining front garden where he knelt, trowel in hand, by one of the borders.

'And who might you be, lad?' the oldster barked with a malicious leer, making a meal of stumbling to his feet amidst a fuss of moans, groans and cracking bones.

'Detective Sergeant Daniel Hackett of Leicestershire Police... I'm looking for a Mrs, sorry Miss Gladys Jackson?'

'*Glad...!* There's a bluebottle here to see you... you deaf old trout!' the man rudely yawped, his temper inflamed by a bossy Jack Russell snapping viciously at his ankles. Mercifully the terrier was called off by a shrill female voice.

'I've been expecting you, officer. Please come in,' she said in an affected tone. 'Can I offer you a nice cup of tea?'

'How kind... thank you!' he replied with a smile, speedily removing his boots, and stepping into the living room.

After a brief exchange of polite preliminaries, the subject matter turned to the rather gruesome discovery, randomly unearthed by her ever-faithful pooch during an afternoon ramble on the nearby public footpath. The old lady seemed, however, to be more concerned about the spate of burglaries in recent times. 'As villages go ours used to be such an idyllic place to live in. That was until the pop singer chappie moved to Granby, just up the road,' she grumbled.

'Mm, the infamous Mr JJ Gold. I visited his place the day after his father collapsed. Do I detect from your tone you weren't exactly overjoyed at having him as a near neighbour?' Hackett pried, reading her thoughts.

'Not likely... He never once attended a church service during his short spell in the village!' she whined in a holier-than-thou voice, providing him with a first-hand glimpse of the obnoxiousness responsible for her unpopularity.

He rose to his feet. 'Okay, ma'am, I've got all I need, for now… Thanks for the cuppa… and your kind cooperation.'

'But officer… you made no mention of dear Malcolm… or the dreadful Robinson family up at the farm!' she said self-importantly.

'Malcolm?' he replied, utterly confused.

'My little doggy!' she said, lightly patting the grouchy mutt's head.

'He's a hero, ma'am… and in regards to the Robinson family, the young lady I interviewed gave a full and unbiased account,' he retorted satirically, only to find himself on the end of an icy, if-looks-could-kill glare.

As if sensing her annoyance, the terrier reacted with a deep guttural growl. Teeth half-bared, eyes fixed to his tense, hunkered body, the dog observed Hackett's every move as he edged beneath the low-hanging doorframe.

'Pakistanis!' the green-fingered neighbour yelled, caught red-handed eavesdropping outside the open window.

'What was that, old buddy?' Hackett inquired, stooping down low to double-lace his mud-caked Doc Marten boots.

'Blooming Muslims, lad… right on our doorstep!'

'Here… in the area? How many?' Dan asked, his suspicion aroused.

'Too bloody many!' the nosy bigot complained, gathering up his shears and potting trowel before disappearing into the side entry.

THREE

March 2006
Lochaber District, Scottish Highlands

'PLEASE DON'T THINK me rude, but isn't that a little weird?' the windswept, thirty-something brunette asked a trifle offhandedly, somewhat taken aback by the unkempt co-passenger's decision to choose the seat opposite her.

'Sorry... what?' he answered uncertainly, offloading a backpack and guitar case onto the seat across the aisle.

She softened slightly, sizing him up with narrowed eyes. 'Forgive me... but the carriage is completely empty!'

'If I'm totally honest, I felt strangely drawn to you when you glanced my way on the platform...' With this half-mumbled response, the oddball disconsolately lifted his backside, evidently intending to relocate to the carriage's rear.

'No... no, I was way out of line... me and my big mouth... Please, stay put!' she begged, gesticulating towards the seat.

'Are you sure... I wasn't thinking straight?'

'Sure I'm sure... as eggs is eggs!'

Gracelessly he shuffled his backside into the window seat, where his eyes inadvertently closed over, arousing the woman's interest and curiosity. As she studied his hirsute, unkempt features, she felt a twisted smile cross her lips.

His head was gently bobbing to the rhythm of the train when the nasal tone of the inspector's voice caused him to come to with a start. Both travellers reached inside their coat pockets to locate their wad of tickets.

'Thank you... have a good day!' the guard snuffled, continuing on his way.

'You too!' they said in sync, inciting a short outburst of laughter, added to by the harsh croak of her hoarse, wheezy cough.

'Excuse me... you were snoring like an old sow,' she stressed in an overfamiliar tone, giggling girlishly to further lighten the mood.

'Oops, sorry… It's been one hell of a journey!'

'No apology necessary.' She extended a porcelain-like hand across the table. 'Agnes – Agnes Ryan.'

'Jonathan… or simply Jon,' he replied, omitting to mention a surname.

'Where's your final destination?'

He stifled a yawn. 'I figured I'd give the "singing sands" of Eigg a whirl, to inspire me into writing some new tunes.'

'Ugh. I can't stand the place… but that besides, it's a magnet for ageing wax-jacketed ramblers at this time of year.'

'Wielding shiny titanium walking poles?'

'You got it!'

'So where would you suggest as an alternative?'

Her answer was immediate and authoritative. 'Knoydart… with a K!'

'That's a new one on me. It must be like a pinprick in the ocean?'

'It's nothing more than a wilderness to the west of the mainland… though I should point out it's only accessible by boat!'

'Is there anything there?'

'An abundance of peace and tranquillity… oh, and a half-decent pub!'

'You're joshing me… it sounds perfect!'

The conversation between them seemed easy and natural, flowing like a stream. The journey's bumps and turns were complemented by a vivid array of undulating scenery, stretching for miles to either side of the track.

'There are no motorised vehicles to speak of… other that is than the odd tractor,' she continued engagingly. Her description painted a fascinating picture of a rugged hinterland where he could live life freely, out of sight of any prying eyes.

'How do I get there?' he asked, a half-hope in his eyes.

'By ferryboat… they depart regularly from Mallaig, at the end of the line,' she said, jumping up to gather her shoulder bag.

'Thanks for your words of wisdom… I'll be sure to check it out!'

'Should you get into any difficulties, just ask for Agnes Ryan at the post office counter in the little supermarket.'

'You live in the town… alone?'

'Yep… in a two-up, two-down fisherman's cottage, not far from the harbour.'

'Maybe I'll see you around sometime… and thanks again!'

'My pleasure… oh and be sure to try the kippers while you're in town – they're the finest on the planet!'

She stepped off the train and made her way along the platform, unaware of his admiring glance sizing up her swaggering rear.

*

September 2006
Inverie, Knoydart, Scotland

From the dormer window of his modest B & B he saw that the early-morning shower had given way to a clear blue sky. It was all the encouragement Jon needed to partake in a brisk stroll along the waterfront to blow away the cobwebs, the residue of the previous night's impromptu session in the local pub.

Spurred by a whisky-fuelled conversation with a skeletal-faced ex-army veteran, Jon wended his way towards a tumbledown shack alongside a muddy track at the end of the tarmac main street. There, gripping on to a hefty log-splitting axe, a barrel-chested man was knocking seven bells out of an elephantine tree trunk.

'Morning, fella,' Jon amiably chirped, moving smartly to avoid a flying chip.

'Morning yourself, laddie... What can I do for ye?' the guy replied, glad of the excuse to momentarily down tools.

'Your pal Big Ian suggested I pick your brains... in regards to an old crofter's cottage you might be willing to dispose of?'

'Did he now...? And you'd like to take a wee peek, is that right?'

'You got it in one!'

'There's precious little on the market just now... so it will nay come cheap... How's about this coming Friday, lad?'

'But that's three days away!'

'Ha... you're on Knoydart time now, son!' the guy cackled. 'I'll meet you in the Old Forge for a midday heart starter!'

'Friday it is!' Jon agreed, a trifle bemusedly.

*

Three days later

Balanced on the soft mattress in his modest board and lodgings, lightly plucking at the strings of his faithful Martin acoustic, an image of the brown-eyed brunette flashed inside his mind. Her long dark locks moved to and fro over her face and shoulders, partially concealing the radiant smile crossing her ruby lips.

His thumb caressing the guitar's bottom E string, a flurry of improvised notes twanged in quick succession, adeptly carved out with the fingers of his right hand clawing in sync with a progression of nifty chord shapes.

'What am I supposed to do... when I can't stop thinking 'bout you?
In a single smile something changed, and how;
And I wonder are you smiling right now?'

'Hmm... that'll do for starters,' he mumbled, suddenly alert to the bedside clock ticking ever closer towards noon.

*

The turbulent swash from a lively series of waves lashed onto the coastal road's uneven surface, slowing the beaten-up Land Rover to a crawl. It was made even worse by the mud splattering onto the windscreen.

'God, is that it?' Jon exclaimed in disbelief. As the vehicle came to a halt and he hopped out, he could make out a neglected, dew-covered stone building. It sat at the bottom of a waterlogged driveway, nestled forlornly beneath a threadbare grove of drooping Scots pines.

'Aye... Peace and tranquillity in abundance... Proper little gem!' the owner prattled, trampling into the boggy quagmire.

'And what's that awful stink?'

'Pig shit, son!' he bluntly replied. 'We polished off Victor, the sole surviving male, at last month's annual hog roast!'

'Poor Victor... and poor me. It'll take a miracle worker to fix it up!'

'Aha... I know the man – Jock Braithwaite, based on Skye. He took on a similar project at the lochside a couple of years back.'

'So what's the bottom line?' Jon asked, his heart in his mouth.

'Eighty grand lad, give or take a few brass farthings. I'll have ye know these properties are highly sought after.'

'Yeah... I can see them queuing up behind me!'

'Make me an offer!'

'Forty grand in cash, subject to planning and building costs... take it or leave it.'

'Jeez, son... you drive a hard bargain,' the guy grouchily replied, promptly snatching Jon's hand off with a knowing grin.

FOUR

February 2005

'I ASSUME YOU'RE SKINT AGAIN?' journo-cum-author Khalid Shah said cynically. His wayward younger sibling's questionable work ethic and propensity towards petty crime more often than not left him down on his uppers – that is, when he wasn't launching yet another one of his dubious money-making schemes.

'Forgive me, Mr Big Shot… I called to see how you were doing,' Rashid said disingenuously, as a prelude to laying the usual hard-luck story on his benevolent elder. 'While you're living it large in the big city, I'm squatting in a rat-infested slum!'

'Get the violins out!' Khalid shot back contemptuously. 'Unlike some, I work my butt off for every penny I earn.'

'I've changed, Khal, believe me!'

'Yeah right, so pigs can fly… What's the damage this time around?'

'Two hundred should tide me over till the weekend.'

'Listen up. This is the last time… I'll transfer a hundred into your building society tomorrow, and that's it… no more!'

'You're my hero, bro! So, what have you been up to?'

'I managed to blag an invitation to last night's BRIT Awards. You'll never guess who was sitting at the same table…'

'Dolly Parton? Bono? Puff Daddy? Go on, put me out of my misery!'

'JJ Gold… your favourite artist!'

'You're shitting me… Go on, piss on my bonfire and tell me he's right up himself!'

'Quite the reverse… But the story gets better.' Khal paused for effect. 'He's only gone and asked me to write his biography!'

'Shit bro, that's incredible!' Rash gasped incredulously.

And so the improbable tale unfurled, from rubbing shoulders with the glitterati of the world's music industry, to JJ's relocation from the bustling capital to the bucolic surroundings of the Leicestershire countryside.

'Me, just a jobbing hack!'

'You hit the jackpot this time, big bro!'

'We're planning a meet-up soon… at his country estate.'

'Where's his new gaff?'

'A tiny village out in the sticks, called Granby… and don't get any bright ideas about turning the place over – it's more secure than Fort Knox.'

'Give me a break, bro… I worship the guy… tormented genius that he is!'

'Well, let's keep it that way… and don't go shooting your mouth off to that gang of scumbags you hang out with!' Khalid said in a cautioning tone. He was already inwardly berating himself for letting the cat out of the bag.

*

'Was that your brother Khal on the phone? Did I hear JJ Gold's name mentioned?' Bengali flatmate Amir asked nosily. He was rubbing his eyes after a subliminal catnap, his filthy trainers stretched over the sofa's armrest.

'Yeah… the jammy git got to meet him at last night's BRIT Awards!' Rash said coyly, playing his cards close to his chest.

'What… he actually spoke to him?'

'They were sat at the same table. He's asked Khal to write his biography!'

'Why would some big-shot rock 'n' roll star trust a conniving Paki to pen his life story?'

'Typical… always putting everyone down… Give the guy some credit – Khal's a talented writer, he deserves a break.'

'Huh… born lucky more like,' Amir said belittlingly. He eyed his flatmate who was rooting through a rumpled stack of papers and clutter.

'Have you seen my roadmap?' Rash asked.

'I think I may be lying on it… Where are you headed?' the Hindu half-laughed, flinging the crumpled map across the floor.

'Nowhere in particular,' Rash answered circumspectly, sloping off to his bedroom for a tiny modicum of privacy.

Alone in the apartment later that same evening, Amir's curiosity was aroused by a sneaky glance through the ajar door. His eyes were drawn to the unfolded chart dumped on the duvet cover, marked with an uneven circle in blue biro.

'Granby… what's that scheming little prick up to?' he muttered. Firing up Rashid's laptop, he settled down to give the place the once-over.

FIVE

May 2011
Inverness

WITH HIS PARTNER undergoing a battery of tests assisted by an overdose of green-clad medicos, Jon killed time in a frugal waiting area kitted out with tea- and coffee-making facilities. Plonking himself onto a wooden-framed chair, his eye was caught by a three-week-old copy of the *News of the World* on a table to one side.

GOLD STAR FEARED DEAD, the front-page headline read, splashed above an antiquated shot of him performing in concert.

'What the hell's going on?' he gasped under his breath, scanning disbelievingly through the accompanying article.

'Out…! Out, *now!*' a blue-uniformed security official bawled, gripping onto the door frame to bring himself to a halt, outsmarted by a down-and-out heading in the opposite direction. 'And that goes for you too, sunshine!'

'I'm with a patient, laid up in the intensive care unit… Miss Ryan… check with one of the nurses!' Jon complained bitterly.

'And I'm Barack Obama,' the guard barked, lurching towards him. 'Now be a good lad and get your sorry butt out of here!'

'Come anywhere near me, and I'll punch your lights out!' Jon said threateningly, shoving past him into the corridor without another word.

Hidden in the shadow of a giant vending machine Jon paused to use a vacant payphone, reaching inside his jacket for his time-honoured pocketbook to locate the private number of record company exec Miles Templeton.

'Hello, you've reached the Templeton residence; Maria speaking!' an unfamiliar female voice yelped into the handset.

'Sorry, who?' Jon asked vaguely, unable to put a face to the name.

'Maria Templeton… Who's calling?'

'I need to speak with Miles please, it's urgent.'

'He's busy, I'm afraid. Might I suggest you try contacting him at a more convenient hour?' the lady said in a plummy tone.

'Tell him it's the "Golden Boy" – he'll take the call!' Jon stated presumptuously.

After a moment or two he heard the phone being picked up and prepared his eardrums for a severe tongue-lashing.

'Who the fuck is this?' the top dog's voice boomed, in typically foulmouthed fashion.

'Miles, it's me, Jon… alive, kicking, and utterly pissed off!'

'But that's impossible… you were drowned in a tragic boating accident. It was in all the papers!' Templeton softened, mopping his brow.

'Fake news, Miles. Let's just say I experienced a personal meltdown… as in the title of my posthumous album release!'

In the ensuing altercation Jon furiously gave as good as he got. He slammed Templeton's decision to kowtow to the big shots pulling his strings, avariciously seeking to cash in on their prized asset's lamentable 'demise'.

'We went through hell and high water trying to track you down after you disappeared, son… The tabloid press kicked into overdrive, running photos of you dancing butt naked around a camp fire, stalked by a tribe of face-painted cannibals!'

'I purposely locked the files in the studio vault over in Switzerland, along with strict instructions the songs should never see the light of day. You're in serious breach of our agreement, Miles!' Jon vehemently maintained.

'You vanished off the face of the earth, for Christ's sake! The whole world went crazy, clamouring to hear the "lost" tracks… so when Tinseltown came knocking it seemed the obvious thing to do. They had us over a barrel!'

Jon stood his ground. 'My original deal was for three albums, with an optional extension for a fourth. Those songs were deeply personal, until you and your cronies got your grubby mitts all over them!'

'The studio costs amounted to a small fortune. Be happy for once – the album's shifted more than two million units… and when news breaks of your survival, the sky's the limit. Everyone'll want a piece of you!'

His initial fury subsiding, and remembering where he was and why, Jon decided he needed to change tack. 'I need your help, Miles.'

'Anything, son; just say the word and it's yours!'

'I need money, and I need it fast.'

'Not a problem… Are you in some kind of trouble?'

'It's my partner, Agnes, my life's blood... She's lying comatose in a hospital bed, hooked up to an oxygen tank.'

'A woman... Jesus!'

'A soulmate... someone I connected with at last, someone beautiful both inside and out!' Jon's voice cracked with emotion.

'There's a tidy sum lying around in a client's account, gathering dust... getting on a couple of million, so I'm told.'

'*How* much...? Are you for real?'

'No shit... I'll get one of the girls to wire over fifty grand first thing... just for starters!'

The awkward silence that followed was abruptly breached by a blue-uniformed nurse scurrying along the hallway, pursued by a grim-faced, white-coated medic, skidding precariously on the soles of his polished leather brogues.

'Miles... I have to go!'

'Where's your account held, son?'

'Mallaig,' Jon said curtly.

'You're breaking up, Jon... did you say Malaysia?'

'MALLAIG, Miles... M-A-L-L-A-I-G!' Jon breathily spelt out.

'When the dust settles I need you on the first plane... Jon... Jon...? Shit!' But Jon had already left the handset dangling to swiftly give chase, leaving Miles glowering into the muted earpiece.

SIX

October 2003

NESTLED AMONG THE undulating Leicestershire countryside, and with a distinctive character that owed much to the rural ordure emanating from the surrounding arable and dairy farms, lay the village community of Granby. It housed an interesting mix of commuting lawyers, high-flying bankers and city slickers, bunking side by side with a half-dozen generations of bucolic local yokels. These disparate residents were often known to mingle in a gamut of characterful watering-holes situated hither and thither along an encompassing matrix of meandering back roads.

To the palpable excitement of the local populace, world-renowned solo artist JJ Gold had returned to the county of his upbringing. A sizeable portion of his burgeoning royalty pot had been invested into a newly reconstructed manor house, backing onto a panorama of rolling hills and valleys and concealed behind an imposing façade.

Gold waxed lyrical during an exclusive interview with *Hello!* magazine. 'I've been buttering up the local authorities with a view to converting the old stable block into a spacious annexe where my parents will feel at home during their second childhood, and where I'll have no problem keeping a discreet eye on them,' he crowed, implying that the city suburbs in which his family once resided had since gone to the dogs. 'It's also time to bid farewell to West London, and my bolthole in Leicester. The lure of the countryside proved far too strong, and living in a goldfish bowl has finally taken its toll,' the star continued, citing a need to escape from the prying eyes of a handful of fanatical followers, known to take advantage of his self-effacing nature.

'It's not that I don't appreciate the fans... where would I be without them? But give an obsessed admirer an inch, and they'll take a country mile. In a nutshell, it's probably best for me to lay low for a while!' the piece concluded.

*

Know-it-all pen-pusher Richard Turner was one such carpetbagger. Plying his trade in the finance department of the city council, he had gained notoriety in the press after foolhardily accosting a sinewy bystander lurking with intent close to his idol's luxury apartment block. He later regained consciousness in the city's Royal Infirmary, having been fortuitously spared a life-threatening beating by a passing police surveillance unit.

'JJ's eternally grateful for what I did... so much so he donated one of his Grammy awards to a charity of my choice,' he said gloatingly, speaking live on air from his hospital bed to a dispassionate BBC reporter.

Once back in the office, he was in for a shock. 'There's a three-page feature on JJ Gold's new home in the latest *Hello!* magazine!' middle-aged colleague Dorothy stated in passing. 'You didn't let on he got rid of his city-centre apartment, Richard?'

'Huh... I wouldn't go believing everything you read in the press!' Turner responded, snorting a disdainful laugh.

'According to the article he moved over a month ago, to a beautiful country estate... Here, let me show you the pictures,' she continued, sauntering over to his desk, sensing the air may be about to turn blue.

'The devious, two-faced bastard... a fine friend he turned out to be!' he seethed, eyeing the colourful fanned-out spread. 'When I last caught up with him he was preparing for a world tour, with no mention of a house move!'

'*Richard*... Calm yourself, it's not like he's relocating to Timbuktu!'

'B... but... he kept totally schtum... what an absolute arse!' he wittered on, verging on erupting into a violent paroxysm.

'An oversight, I'm sure,' Dorothy said, slightly unnerved by his behaviour, reaching to grab the magazine from under his nose.

'Where is this property? I need to know,' Turner blasted, rudely wrestling it from her hands and making off to the loo.

*

Forgoing lunch to scan the article and images into his desktop PC, Richard analysed every detail, paying particular attention to a carpet-like cricket pitch lying to the rear of the estate. A white picture-postcard pavilion sheltered beneath the giant shadow of the substantial red-brick residence, partially obscuring a rickety wooden sign on which the only letters distinguishable read: *IANS C.C.*

He slowly typed 'ians cricket club, leicestershire' into the Google search engine. A barrage of irrelevant results burst onto the screen, ranging from beauticians, obstetricians, opticians and paediatricians to a bizarre amateur dramatic society known as 'Lesbians Thespians' and a site exclusively for fruitarians, aptly named 'Playing Gooseberry'.

Blowing his stack in frustration, he tossed his computer's mouse aside. With a loud crack it smashed into pieces against the wall, much to the annoyance of head of staff Jim Bradley, who dropped everything and stepped out of his office.

'What in God's name is going on?'

'Oops, sorry Jim... I thought I was alone!'

'Giving you the right to wilfully destroy office equipment, huh?'

'No... no... I received some bad news.'

'Is that so...? Anything I can help with?' Bradley asked, eyeing him with great suspicion.

'A missing name... a village cricket club!'

'Cricket? Lord forbid... Speak to Tom Mason in the accounts department, his lad plays for one of the local sides.'

*

'I didn't know you were a sports fan, Richie?' the affable number-cruncher chirped, reaching into the centre of his piled in-tray. 'Let's start by checking the league tables in last Saturday's edition of the *Sports Mercury*.'

'Jesus... there are hundreds!' Turner exclaimed, peering over his shoulder at the multitude of stats and figures.

'Patience, dear boy... Now spell out the letters, slowly!'

'I... A... N... S!'

In a concentrated effort to disentangle the seemingly endless list of clubs and institutions, Mason put to use his trusty magnifying glass, scrolling diligently up and down the page in what appeared to be a fruitless search. 'Leicester Ivanhoe... Loughborough Carillon... hmm, we're not even close, Richie,' he said.

All at once he was struck by a brainwave. 'Hang on... I've just remembered something...'

'What is it, Tom?'

'I once knew of an Old Newtonians Cricket Club, who played at Granby, close to the Lincolnshire border... it's just a hunch...'

'And the pitch backed onto a red-brick mansion house?'

'That's right... I can just picture it now,' Bradley reminisced, releasing a soft smile. 'The views went on for miles.'

'With a large, white-painted pavilion?'

'Yes... it's all coming back to me... a beautiful, ornate wooden pavilion... I played there myself as a wide-eyed teenager.'

Without so much as a word of thanks, the overeager pen-pusher rushed off and descended the nearby staircase like a man possessed. Returning to his desk, he entered a hurried search into Wikipedia, desirous of acquainting himself with the unknown rural backwater.

'Granby is a village in the civil parish of King's Meadow and the district of South Leicestershire, England. It is about 9 miles south of the market town of Melton Mowbray and 11 miles north of Market Harborough.'

'Eureka!' he sighed triumphantly, typing a secondary search into Google to browse through a list of local letting agents.

SEVEN

Summer 1999

ONCE AGAIN JON found himself floundering on the sidelines as he awaited the outcome of a seemingly interminable locking of horns between two firms of uncompromising lawyers. Reenergised at the thought of finally breaking free from the trappings of Louis Kelly's sterile commercial regime, the maturing tunesmith used the time on his hands to good effect, pouring himself into his writing to produce some of his most inspired work ever.

'Morning, Jon; I hope you're sitting down,' caretaker manager David Bentley enthused. He was champing at the bit to deliver the glad tidings his friend had waited so long to hear, albeit at the un-rock-'n'-roll hour of nine a.m.

'Dave... I didn't hit the sack until close on five-thirty... give me a shout later when I've caught up on some shuteye!' Jon spoke through a yawn, pulling the handset away from his ear and burying his head in the pillow.

'Don't hang up, Jon... you'll want to hear this!' Bentley urged. 'Miles Templeton at Sony put a deal on the table late last night. Moreover he's willing to offer Twilight a golden handshake to sever all ties with Louis Kelly.'

A high-pitched squeal oozed into the handset, followed by a suppressed yell of 'Yes!' emerging from the back of Jon's throat.

'I knew you'd be pleased!'

'Pleased...? I'm elated! When do we sign?'

'I pencilled Friday in.'

'Cool... so now I can get down to some serious recording... wow!'

'If you have the songs. How's the writing progressing?'

'I demoed a new tune only last night!' Jon said excitedly. 'I've a feeling I may've stumbled onto something special!'

'And does it have a title?'

'Hummingbird'!

Defying the odds by winning over the world's music critics, the complexly appealing 'Hummingbird' soared to the top of pretty much every chart in existence. It was soon followed by a stunning debut solo album, aptly entitled *Let the Music Do the Talking*, which swept to the summit of the album chart in its first week of release, proving beyond doubt that Jon's spine-tingling songs made him a force to be reckoned with.

By the summer of 2003 two further albums, *Gold Record* and *Hair on a D-String*, served to cement his widespread appeal, simultaneously topping both the UK and US album charts, whereupon the hottest new property on the planet embarked on a punishing sell-out schedule of worldwide stadia and arena dates.

Midway through a string of mega-concerts spanning the southern hemisphere he was discovered by a chambermaid, flat out on the floor of his hotel room. The burnt-out artist lay anaesthetised for seventy-two hours in a Kuala Lumpur hospital, his physically overexerted body driven beyond all limits of human endurance.

'This man needs rest; if he doesn't get it he may die!' a senior psychologist sternly warned. It pointed the way towards the curtailment of the remaining dates, much to the chagrin of the tour's sponsors and organisers alike.

'Once the batteries are recharged I'll be back before you know it!' the emaciated star vowed to the massed ranks of journalists and fans gathered in the main terminal building of KL's bustling airport, anxious to pooh-pooh reports of a life-threatening illness set to bring down the curtain on a glittering career.

*

Holed up in a luxury Kensington apartment and relieved to be back on British soil, the erstwhile lure of the capital's bright lights struck Jon as artificial and overpowering. His growing conviction that he needed to give up the city and return to the quietude of his adopted county was boosted by a chance conversation with his ageing father.

'We've been considering subdividing the family home,' his old man said, blissfully unaware of Jon's best-laid plans. 'It's high time your mother slowed down; the place is far too big for just her to take care of.'

'Why not rent it out? The income could set you both up for life.'

'And live where precisely? Please don't say in a retirement home, I wouldn't be seen dead in one of those places!'

'Come and live with me, in the countryside! We could convert the adjoining outbuildings into a granny flat… The nearest town's only five minutes by car, and there's a doctor's surgery up the road in King's Meadow!'

'I'll need her ladyship's seal of approval first…'

'Mum? She'll snap your hand off!' Jon half-chortled, promising to get some plans drawn up. 'And Dad, I hope you're fond of the stench of fresh horseshit!'

*

With no distractions or interruptions the serenity of country living put him right back on track, psyching Jon into an upsurge of original ideas. His eagerly awaited fourth album was destined to be an epic tour-de-force.

Fulfilled and comforted by his parents' newfound freedom in their well-equipped, annexed home, Jon's ambitious new project soon began to take shape. His new direction was taking him somewhere he never thought he would go, galvanised by the words of encouragement offered by record company guru Miles Templeton.

'You've got all the time you need; we've got an unlimited budget… give me a masterpiece, son!'

EIGHT

Autumn 2005

'MUM, DAD... I'M OFF to the pub in King's Meadow to meet up with David,' Jon chirped, popping his head into the adjoining living quarters. 'I guess you'll both be catching flies by the time I get in. Don't leave the light on.'

'Go easy on the drink, son... I'll leave a sandwich for you on the kitchen island, just in case you succumb to an attack of the munchies,' his mother said admonishingly, wagging a chastising finger back and forth.

'Thanks a lot, Mum... there are no flies on you!' he laughed, trudging out onto the muddy lane in near gale conditions.

A curious collection of hunting memorabilia graced the walls of the characterful pub, including weapons and framed accounts of the kills, suspended either side of an ugly-looking mounted wild boar's head.

'I don't quite know how to say this, Jonathan,' Bentley muttered hesitantly, steeling himself for what was about to come.

'Spit it out, Davey boy!'

'I've been offered a prestigious position with a top TV company in Sydney, Australia... which I grabbed with both hands!'

The implication of this announcement took a moment to sink in. 'So you'll be unable to continue as my manager?'

'That's about the size of it... as of this coming December.'

'I'm speechless, Dave!' Jon mumbled, struggling to mask the sadness in his eyes.

'I only took the job on to help out... it's nothing personal.'

'I know that...'

'And it's not as if you'll have a hard time finding someone else... they'll be falling at your feet!' Bentley said unpersuasively.

'It's just... you'll be irreplaceable, Dave,' Jon said. 'Quite where I go from here I don't know!'

As he polished off the dregs of his pint, a mischievous glint crept into his eyes. Seeing Jon's doleful expression replaced by a look of playful defiance, his glassy-eyed pal rose from his stool and placed a hand on his shoulder.

'Are you thinking what I'm thinking?'

'Something along the lines of getting absolutely hammered?'

'Exactly my thoughts, dear boy!'

Suiting the action to the word, David ordered up two pints of the guest beer, along with a pair of whisky chasers.

*

A few minutes shy of the witching hour, the worse-for-wear twosome tottered onto the street arm in arm and staggered towards a pre-booked minicab. Having helped bundle David into the back seat, the driver sped off into the darkness.

'Piss off and don't come back,' Jon hollered in jest.

He swiftly found himself questioning his decision to brave the elements and leg it homewards. His face and ears were stinging from the cold, biting wind sweeping over the surrounding hills.

'*My heart's all aflutter like the wings of a hummingbird,*' he blasted out, paying scant heed to his own tune's melodic opening line, as he careened his way through an assault course of potholes, mud puddles and roadside debris.

Finally, he picked out the house's distinctive features silhouetted in the murky moonlight. The rustle of a badger in the bushes triggered the motion-sensor light; its yellow glow revealed an old banger dumped at the roadside, most likely belonging to an amorous couple huddled beneath the shadows of the overhanging trees.

'Dirty bastards!' Jon cackled, sidestepping around the vehicle and punching in the alarm code to enter via the main gates.

As he clumsily peeled back the cling film from a chunky ham sandwich, a peculiar babbling sound from the abutting annexe attracted his attention. Taking it to be the barely audible cooing given off by his sleeping parents, he perched himself precariously on a stool at the breakfast bar and took a bite. But the sporadic, high-pitched whimpering continued to ring in his ears and, his curiosity roused, he slunk through the passageway to take a peek into the granny flat.

A glance into the living area caused him to freeze with horror. His terror-stricken mother was crouched over his father's stock-still body, their hands and mouths bound with a multi-layered wad of silver duct tape.

'Is he still breathing, Mum?' Jon asked wheezily, slowly removing her binding and catching sight of her bruised face.

'I think he may have suffered a stroke... He tried to protect me,' she groaned, placing her head on his chest.

'Protect you... from who?'

'The hoodie who assaulted me!'

Jon's heart skipped a beat, quickening in an instant as the horror rose up in his throat, augmented by the alcohol's effects.

'Nod your head if he made his way into the main house.'

She nodded, whispering, 'Be careful Jon – he's carrying a crowbar!'

'Call the emergency services on the house phone,' he murmured, before veering quiet as a mouse into the adjoining games room where he grabbed the baseball bat gifted to him by a World-Series-winning slugger.

Impelled by a surge of adrenaline coursing through his veins, his shoeless feet tiptoed out into the hall. His catlike eyes pinned instantly on a moving shadow, cast onto the ceiling by an eerie shaft of pallid moonlight.

THW... ACK! the blow echoed, resonating like the crack of a gun. He had struck with such force as to send the intruder crashing to the floor, where the body came to rest in the scary silence and lay completely paralysed.

As Jon sank to his knees to check for a pulse, the youth's passive eyes stared up at him through the dimness, unmoved by the sound of raised voices emanating from a blue-flashing vehicle parked by the front gates.

His biceps bulging, Jon grabbed at the filcher's armpits, adeptly sliding the cadaver into the concealed passageway and out through the back door. By and by he lugged the dead weight towards the woodshed through a squelching morass of slimy leaves.

'God forgive me,' he snivelled, forcing the door open and propping the torso upright against a stack of sawn firewood. His stomach was gripped by a crushing wave of nausea, and he trudged back to the house in a state utterly disconsolate and despairing.

*

His father was pronounced dead on arrival at the city's bustling Royal Infirmary. A ubiquitous Japanese doctor broke off briefly to diagnose the probable cause of death as an acute ischaemic stroke, before darting off like a madman into the adjoining bay to at least allow the family members a quiet moment to reflect on their loss.

'My dear, sweet husband,' Jon's Mum sniffled, placing a tender kiss onto Eddie's porcelain-like brow. Pain was etched in every crevice of her face. The tears finally began to flow upon meeting her son's troubled expression.

'You still have me, Mum… and Kirsty!' he said ruefully, uncertain about his long-lost sister's current whereabouts.

'She's in Dubai,' she said, and urged him to pass on the sad tidings.

'I will, Mum,' he vowed.

He ambled aimlessly into the hallway only to find his path blocked by a leather-jacketed stranger.

'It's Jonathan, isn't it?' the man asked quizzically, instantly setting his nerves on edge. 'Hackett's the name… Detective Sergeant Dan Hackett. I was wondering if you could spare me a few minutes of your time?'

'Okay,' Jon said laconically, sauntering heavy-legged towards a table full of empty tea-stained mugs. 'How can I help?'

'Pardon me if I'm speaking out of turn, but I'm a huge admirer of your music,' the cop stated somewhat embarrassingly.

'Not at all… thanks.'

Hackett offered his condolences and then said: 'If you feel up to it I'd very much like to ask you a few questions.'

'Let's get started… I'm as anxious to find this scumbag as anyone else.'

'Scum*bags* may be a more accurate description, sir.'

'There were two of them?'

'Undoubtedly… we have an eyewitness report.'

'Which specifies what?'

'That in addition to a short stocky individual sighted entering via the main entrance gates, a taller, hooded man was seen scaling the property's rear boundary wall around an hour before the ambulance crew arrived.'

'But that's not possible… I saw him with my own eyes… He must've doubled back through the shrubbery!' Jon said, a touch unconvincingly.

'From the property's driveway?'

'Without a doubt… the son of a bitch who attacked my Mum!'

His mouth dropping open with surprise, the bewildered detective paused to collect his thoughts, scribbling vigorously into his pocket notebook, all too painfully aware of the grieving son's fragile emotional state.

'You witnessed an assault… on your mother?'

'I saw the marks on her face!' Jon cried out, his elbows slumping onto the tabletop to cup his face in his hands.

'Look, I'm sorry for putting you through this, especially at such a sad time... Perhaps we should call it a day and reconvene at some point tomorrow,' Hackett reflected, jotting down his name and number on a page in his notebook.

'Maybe you're right... it's been a long night.'

'Thanks for your time,' the DS said, zipping up his jacket and patting Jon affectionately on the shoulder. 'It might be scant consolation, but *Hair on a D-String* is probably my favourite album of all time.'

'Huh, I spent half my career writing about other people's misfortunes, but it seems the boot is now on the other foot.'

'Chin up... Take your mother home, and try to get some sleep,' Hackett advised, and scuttled off down the corridor to find his vehicle.

*

A disorganised muddle of CD cases lay strewn across the car's back seat. Hackett rummaged into the pile and, having found what he wanted, shoved the black and gold disc into the car's Hitachi stereo system, pumping up the volume to its maximum:

'*Fare thee well my old trusted friend*
All good things must come to an end
It's back to the road, of no fixed abode
To a world of strange faces and exotic places
But wherever I go I'm never far from the truth
Just a tragic hero, maybe a little uncouth
I am a vagabond, driftwood, no good
I am a vagabond and no one knows me.'

'You're a rare talent, Mr JJ Gold, of that there's no denying... Call it a copper's intuition, but I've a hunch you're keeping something from me!' Hackett mumbled contemplatively, hoping that his instincts may, for once, have failed him.

NINE

April 2004
County Hall, Glenfield, Leicester

'I'D LIKE TO PUT in for a transfer to Melton Mowbray, Jim, if possible,' Richard Turner appealed to his boss Jim Bradley, citing personal reasons as cause for his departure. 'Ha, I'm the only Englishman left on the street!'

'Excellent pork pies, the very best… although as I recall there's isn't much else there to crow about. Are you certain, Richard?' Bradley asked in a doubting tone, questioning the wisdom of such a rash decision.

'Ha-ha… I won't be settling down in the town; there's a quaint little cottage I've got my eye on, nestled in a sought-after village on the edge of a picturesque valley,' Turner over-elaborated. 'What are the chances, Jim?'

'I'll ping an email to an ex-colleague of mine, and should there be any vacancies I'll be happy to recommend you. That said, we'll be sorry to lose you Richard,' the councillor said, half-choking on his hypocritical choice of words.

*

One day later

The office's giant photocopiers were grinding a constant rhythmic pattern adjacent to Turner's cluttered desk as they churned out the day's first paper run. He reluctantly fired up his computer and typed in the characters of his password. Bang on the dot of nine a.m., the boss made a detour to the junior's desk.

'Good morning, Richard… I've fixed up an interview for you at eleven o'clock this morning, with a lady called Marianne in the housing department at Melton Borough Council,' Bradley said enthusiastically. 'So chop-chop, you'd better get your skates on!'

'Ha… it's almost as if you can't wait to get rid of me. I'll just finish entering these figures into the ledger, then I'll get my backside in gear... Oh, and Jim, thanks a million!' he said, unaware of the irony of his statement.

*

May 2004
Granby, Leicestershire

Kitted out with a pair of high-visibility binoculars, the new tenant wasted no time in exploring his new surroundings, zipping two steps at a time up to the cottage's crow's nest, before gazing gleefully over the boundless landscape.

'Perfect... absolutely perfect,' he said exultantly, tingling with excitement at the sweeping, bird's-eye view across his illustrious neighbour's estate, with its vibrant fusion of flowering cherry, Vulcan magnolia and lilac trees elegantly swaying in the cool breeze amid a verdant haven of well-tended gardens.

'You've done well for yourself, JJ, and understandably everybody wants a piece of you... but don't fret – I'm here to watch over you!' he cooed psychotically, unpacking a telescope and tripod from a rigid cardboard case.

TEN

November 2005

A BURNT ORANGE SUNRISE greeted the inconsolable couple's arrival back at the house, carving out a carpet of light leading up to the front porch, while fashioning an array of glistening shapes over the encircling meadows.

'I'll let myself into the flat,' Jon's crestfallen mother said dolorously, pausing briefly by the door to peck him on the cheek. 'Go and grab a few hours' sleep, if you can. And Jonny, thanks for being such a wonderful son!'

'Be strong, Mum... I'll catch you later,' he croaked. He stood for a moment, watching her round-shouldered body shamble into the alleyway, before twisting the key in the lock.

A harrowing sight awaited him, enough to send him crumbling to his knees. His sapped body shook feverishly as he eyed the shiny wooden object lying in the hall, and a piercing, howling scream resonated upwardly to the exposed beams, lowering to a heart-wrenching, agonised sob.

'What've you gone and done?' he wailed, paralysed with fear and loathing at the hideous task that lay ahead.

*

A candle flickering through the annexe window shed a golden glow over the sleeping widow's wizened features as Jon, seeking desperately to cover his tracks, crept quietly into the adjacent games room.

Carefully, he rubbed his forefinger along the wooden barrel and uttered a whistle of relief. 'Whew... there isn't a scratch on it,' he said, cautiously replacing the bat into a vacant slot amid the impressive display of sporting paraphernalia hung from the walls. The nerves mercifully settling in his stomach, he fumbled his way to the passage door.

A shower of dewdrops sprinkled upon him from the overhanging trees. His evasive dive to one side caused him to lose his footing on a patch of sodden leaves, toppling him backwards onto the seat of his pants.

Swallowed up in despair, Jon dejectedly rolled onto his hands and knees, malevolently cursing the damp autumnal weather. His squinty eyes were fixed directly in front of him on the ghostly woodshed's lurking shadow. Somewhere in the near distance a solitary canine mimicked a wolf howling at the veiled moon, briefly accompanied by the muffled hoot of an owl. They seemed to be mocking his efforts to heave his body into an upright position.

Gripping the shed's sliding handle, he gave a frantic tug which gradually worked the bar loose. As the door creaked open, his numb body backed away in sick horror and hopelessness, totally unprepared for the shock of his life.

The body had gone.

*

Two hours later

Buried in a deep-seated armchair, Jon's uneasy slumber was abruptly cut short by a sharp rat-tat-tatting at the front door. Squinting in the bright sunlight flooding the hallway, he slapped barefoot across the marble floor and unlocked the door.

'Hello again… Uh, your gardener kindly buzzed me onto the drive,' the half-startled DS Hackett hemmed and hawed.

'Hi… yeah, no worries.'

'I hope I haven't called at an inconvenient time?'

'No, no, I was half expecting you,' Jon drowsily replied.

'How are you holding up?'

'Bloody awful if I'm honest,' he voiced weakly, resting a hand against the doorframe in an effort to steady himself. 'What happened last night seems more and more like a bad dream… Sorry, please come in.'

'Are you sure you're okay?'

'As well as can be expected. Perhaps the reality of it all hasn't hit me yet.'

'And your mother, sir… how's she coping?'

'I haven't looked in on her yet… and call me Jon, please,' he replied affably, keen to get off on the right foot.

'I'm no fan of formalities myself!' the detective concurred, slipping off his boots and placing them on the mat, before Jon led the way into the kitchen.

The spacious entrance opened onto a sprawling multi-level lounge area replete with plush leather sofas and chairs set before an enormous wall-mounted television. 'Wow, what an amazing place!' Hackett gasped, gazing out over the gardens stretching endlessly into the distance.

'Make yourself at home,' Jon said, slouching onto a barstool. 'After all, you're likely to be in this for the long haul.'

'And why would that be, sir... sorry, Jon?'

'Because of my father's death, not to mention my Mum's brutal beating... why else?' Jon replied with a stinging tone.

'You have every right to feel aggrieved; but, for the record, I've been asked to conduct a thorough investigation on these premises, based on information provided by a member of the local neighbourhood watch.'

'W–what information?' Jon asked waveringly.

'*Two* men were reported as seen parking a dark blue Ford Mondeo on the grass verge outside the property shortly after midnight. One of them scaled the garden wall by jumping from the car's roof, while his accomplice breezed nonchalantly through the main gates after tampering with the security mechanism.'

'I noticed a car parked askew at the roadside on my way home from the pub... I figured it must be two young lovers.'

'And did you notice, or hear anything suspicious when you re-entered the property?' Hackett pressed inquisitively.

'Not a dickie bird. Surely you're not suggesting... oh my God, the intruder was still inside the house!' Jon gasped melodramatically. 'The man who attacked my mother was in my house, as my father lay dying on the floor?'

'A dark-brown-skinned man was observed fleeing the scene in the same vehicle mere seconds before the emergency services arrived... presumably leaving the accomplice high and dry somewhere inside the building.'

'Lurking in a dark corner, waiting to cosh me over the head...'

'So you're saying the intruder was armed?'

'He struck my father with a crowbar, before he laid into my Mum!'

Hackett's brain spun into overdrive. The investigation could well be leaning towards a murder enquiry; and yet he questioned the motivation behind an act of violence against an elderly couple readying themselves for bed.

'I'm still uncertain as to who buzzed the gates open when the paramedics arrived on the scene. Could it have been you, sir?'

'I must've done... Everything was a complete blur – I'd had a hell of a lot to drink. Who else could it have been?'

'The intruder himself? It's just a hunch.'

Could it be the detective knew more than he was letting on? Had the village snoop spotted something that could prove to be his undoing? As Jon pondered he fell silent, mindful that one small slip of the tongue could prove fatal.

'Based upon a gut feeling?' he said dismissively, making towards a door on the far side to look in on his mother.

'A copper's nose... an educated guess, that he gained access to the estate by inserting the correct PIN code!'

'Hmm... I could murder a cuppa,' Jon said, trundling out to the passage, inwardly kicking himself for his crass choice of words.

*

'Mum,' Jon purred, stretching up onto his toes to peek through a crack in the annexe door blind. He was palpably relieved to see her dressing-gowned figure flopped out on the sofa, getting some much-needed sleep.

'Is everything okay?' the guileful Hackett asked. He was crouched down low in the middle of the alleyway, to all intents and purposed checking out the drying remains of a muddy footprint.

'She's fast off... I'll wake her later.'

'I followed your lead and put the kettle on, sir. If you could spare me a few more moments of your precious time, I promise I'll get out of your hair,' the DS vowed, scrambling up to follow Jon back to the main house.

'You've got all the time you need, detective.'

'Oops!' Hackett had stalled dangerously close to the woodshed, his curiosity aroused by a patch of dislodged pebbles.

'Derp... Blame Harry, the gardener!' Jon hesitated, feeling his heart begin to pound like a jackhammer in his chest.

'He was here this morning?'

'Just pottering around... I suggested he take the day off.'

'Understandable, given the circumstances,' the cop half-muttered, disoriented by Jon's eagerness to hurry on ahead.

*

A mind-bending hour-long grilling ensued, examining every aspect of the previous night's turn of events. Eventually the conversation strayed somewhat from the subject and shifted, perhaps inevitably, to rock 'n' roll.

'The song "Vagabond" strikes a unique chord with me,' the likeable detective acknowledged, homing in on his pet subject. 'I've listened to it time and again, but can't help thinking the lyrics conceal a hidden meaning.'

'You're reading too much into it... In simple terms it's just a song about how lonely life out on the road can be.'

'Do you have a significant other in your life?'

'Not right now. Affairs of the heart scare me shitless... I'm too darned selfish!'

'Hmm, given half a chance I'm sure they'd be queuing up,' Hackett said amiably. 'Anyway, I've taken up enough of your time.' He was suddenly interrupted by a cacophonous buzzing sound issuing forth from the main gate.

'Okay, thanks... By the way, it's good to know someone's listening to my lyrics!'

'Ha-ha... Oops, sorry, just one more thing, but how many people other than yourself have access to the gate code?'

'As far as I'm aware just the gardener and my Mum, oh and Mrs Bacon the cleaning lady who pops round twice a week,' Jon responded, punching a hand-held gadget to zap a multi-coloured florist's van onto the drive.

'If there's anything else you think I should know – or you simply need someone to spill your guts to – just pick up the phone... and the name's Dan!' the DS helpfully advised as, playing the middle man, he accepted a fragrant bouquet of red and yellow roses passed on to him by the speechless, star-struck delivery man.

*

Jon's fingers reached inside a sash draped at an angle across the scented spray and ripped open the attached golden envelope. As he pored over his big sister's heartfelt tribute, belatedly the waterworks began to flow.

'My mentor, my one true rock... God I'll miss you,' he reflected, gazing at a caricature of his father on the wall with tears coursing down his cheeks.

A hailstorm of conflicting thoughts swirled in his head:

a) Presumably Perp 1, the ringleader, broke into the granny flat for speed of access to the main house, while Perp 2 most likely acted as a lookout?

b) Why would a common criminal put all his energy into a frantic, reckless assault on a defenceless elderly woman?

c) Where was Perp 2 when the bully-boy bit the dust? Did he see, hear or get a whiff of the fate that befell his sidekick?

d) If Perp 2 was lurking in the darkness close to the woodshed, could he have been an eyewitness to the body's disposal?

e) If Perp 2 was sighted making a bolt for it shortly before the ambulance arrived, why then would he risk his neck and circle back, unnoticed, to retrieve his partner in crime's dead body?

f) Or… did the fall guy miraculously survive the blow, before somehow alerting his right-hand man?

Momentarily sidetracked by the dull thud of a wayward pigeon dive-bombing the windowpane, he felt the fog of confusion at last begin to subside, and turned his focus once again to his inconsolable mother, hoping against hope that sister Kirsty's touching floral tribute may provide her with a meagre shred of comfort.

He crept cautiously back along the passageway. A lone shaft of sunlight filtering through the granny-flat's roof light picked out her wan features. She was slumped against the sofa's arm in the self-same position as previously.

'Mum… wake up,' he softly whispered, taking hold of her icy, upturned hand.

The realisation hit him like an emotional sledgehammer. His body reeled backwards against the wall, sliding down despairingly onto his backside.

The light peal of the mantel clock jarred him back to the moment, his eyes transfixing on his mother's lifeless corpse, too sad to be depressed, too afraid to let the bottled-up tears flow, fearful they might never stop.

At a loss as to how to pull himself together, Jon fumbled inside his jeans pockets, retrieving the scrap of paper handed to him by the helpful detective, before reaching his arm up to dislodge the wall-mounted phone and ham-fistedly punching in the digits. The continuous ringtone set his nerves on edge, eventually halted by a loud electronic click.

'Hackett,' the DS's voice barked authoritatively. He had recklessly swerved into a lay-by, sensing that all was not well.

'It's Jonathan Gold. I couldn't think of anyone else to call. It's my mother… she passed away, in her sleep… I felt for a pulse but there was nothing. Tell me this isn't happening!' he wailed, his knuckles white from clenching the handset.

'Take a deep breath and count from one to four, then exhale slowly… I'll be there before you know it… And Jon – hold it together… please!'

Hackett rammed the gearstick into reverse and spun away on two wheels.

ELEVEN

AN INCOMING CALL from an 'unavailable' number caught Khalid temporarily off guard. His wrist throbbed from the repetitive tapping motion on his computer keyboard while responding to a stack of recent emails.

'I need a massive favour,' Rashid asked grovellingly, setting the tone for the conversation in his usual unsubtle way.

'Sorry, but I don't accept cold calls from people looking for handouts. Go out and get a job, for Christ's sake!'

'For your information, I'm stuck in the middle of two weeks' community service, freezing my tits off weeding in the park gardens!' Rash complained, alluding to his wrongful conviction for a crime he didn't commit.

'The fresh air will do you good. How much this time around?'

'Don't be like that, bro… I was hoping you could help me out by laying your hands on a couple of items to auction off for a charity bash I'm helping to organise… as in a signed CD or T-shirt donated by your new mate JJ?'

'What? You haven't got a charitable bone in your body. They'd be on eBay in seconds flat!' Khalid said cynically.

'Spare me the sarcasm… We're trying to raise funds for kids with a muscular disorder. Anything would be amazing!'

A small pang of guilt tugged at Khalid's stomach. His sibling's odd softness of tone reminded him of the honest-hearted, runny-nosed kid hanging on his every word during the summers of their childhood.

'Are you for real?'

'Darned right I am. I've been sailing close to the wind for too long.'

'Way to go, bro… I'll be driving up to Jon's place at the weekend, to make a start on the book. I'll try and twist his arm.'

'Shit, fam – you're staying over at his mansion? Wow!'

'I mentioned you were an avid fan.'

'My big bro, hanging out with the great and the good... whew!'

'I'll introduce you, when the opportunity arises.'

'The guy's voice sends shivers down my spine... especially on his song "Hummingbird",' Rash said breathlessly. 'What a top tune!'

'I'll tell him!' Khalid said preparing to sign off. 'And Rash... keep up the good work, and stay out of trouble?'

'Huh... I will. See you Sunday!'

*

Friday evening

'*Five-seven-o-five... but there's no reply!*' Jon's phone trilled startlingly. The ring tone was the hooky opening line to one of his all-time favourite seventies chartbusters, recorded by little-known British band City Boy.

Jon, who had been whiling away the time waiting on his house guest's imminent arrival, answered the call. 'Now let me guess, the traffic on the A1's nose to tail, as per usual on a manic Friday evening... so you're running late?' he uttered presumptuously.

'Try looking directly outside your main gates... I'm stuck in my car, awaiting the appropriate security clearance!'

'Please enter the quarantined zone,' Jon jested in a shrill robotic voice, zapping the flash BMW onto the forecourt.

Khal clambered out of the car and stretched his muscles. 'Nice gaff,' he cooed. 'The kid's done good... very good!'

'A pretty swanky set of wheels too... Come on in – you've been allocated the bridal suite,' Jon chuckled, leading the way.

*

Later that evening

A bottle of vintage Pol Roger rammed into an ice bucket stood tantalisingly on the patio table alongside two slim champagne flutes. Wrapped in blankets by a glowing fire-pit, the two men sat chewing the fat.

'But... my religion!' Khal whined, smirking behind his hand.

'A teetotal British Muslim...? Shut up, and drink up!'

'Despite your best assumptions, I'm a good Catholic boy!'

'Glory be, so you're partial to a drop of the hard stuff?' Jon said, sighing with relief.

'A full-bodied red often hits the spot...'

'Check out the wine cellar under the stairs. It's pretty well stocked.'

'Aha... so you're an oenophile?'

'I take everyone at face value... you included!'

'An oenophile – a wine connoisseur, you bloody ignoramus, not a sodding xenophile!' Khal guffawed, pushing his glass forward for a refill.

'What say I dig out a bottle of Mouton Rothschild to accompany Sunday lunch?' Jon said proudly.

All of a sudden he reeled back in his chair, half-startled by his cell phone's piercing call alert: '*Five-seven-o-five...*'.

'Back in a sec,' Khal whispered, before slipping indoors to answer the call of nature, his body quivering from a cold nip in the air.

Perched on the throne examining his notes, his eye fell upon a framed Double Platinum plaque taking pride of place on the wall, its lustrous outer case reflecting shapes onto his notepad. The award was adorned with the stars and stripes emblem, certifying that the song 'Hummingbird' had achieved sales in excess of two million copies in the US alone.

'Good news?' Khal inquired, returning to the kitchen area to find Jon reclined in a wicker chair looking pleased as punch.

'You bet... BMW want to use my song "Vagabond" in a worldwide TV campaign to launch their new Three Series!'

'Whew... any freebies up for grabs?'

'I asked if they'd throw in an M-Six coupe – my record chief almost had a coronary... What are you smiling at?'

'Two million copies, in a single territory... that's some going, Jon!' Khal gasped, referring to the plaque hung in the loo.

'Ha, for "Hummingbird"... they're just numbers.'

'My brother's favourite tune... Which reminds me, he got involved with a bunch of tin-rattlers, who've asked for a signed item to auction?'

'There's a cupboard full of stuff in the store on the landing... help yourself before you turn in,' Jon said, yawning widely.

'I'm seeing him on Sunday... he'll be thrilled!'

'Sunday... but I thought...?'

'Sadly I'll have to forgo lunch... and besides, I'm driving.'

'Ne'er mind... It's way past midnight, let's hit the sack.' Jon hugged his pal and lumbered wearily up the staircase.

*

Sunday evening

'I wouldn't leave a posey car like that parked there!' Rash's surly flatmate shrieked from the upstairs window, enviously peering down at Khalid squeezing into an empty space. 'It'll be on bricks before you know it!'

'In which case would you be kind enough to inform my brother that his chauffeur is waiting?' Khal yelled back.

'Hey, big bro… How's it going, where are we headed?' a strangely upbeat Rashid bade a moment later, leaping into the passenger seat.

'I thought we'd check out a little country pub where I used to hang out,' Khal replied. Glancing across at his brother he instantly noted his stubble-free, clean-cut appearance, complemented by a blouson and slacks rounded off with a pair of polished brogues.

'Are you okay?'

'I'm fine. How 'bout you?'

'Good… Take a peek underneath my overcoat on the back seat.'

Rash's mouth fell agape at what he found. Tightly crammed into a bulky shopping bag was a veritable treasure trove of goodies, made up of signed CDs and T-shirts further supplemented by a valuable assortment of rare tour memorabilia.

'Amazing… incredible, what a top bloke!' Rash whooped with delight, his face lighting up like a kid's on Christmas morning.

The tight harmonies of a familiar refrain suddenly blasted out of the car radio's speakers. *'Hey operator, five-seven-o-five… but there's no reply…'*

'How weird… speak of the devil!' Khal gulped, leaning forward to adjust the volume control.

'You dumbass… that isn't JJ!'

'Duh, I know… I must've heard that chorus a dozen times or more over the past couple of days. It's Jon's mobile call alert.'

'Really?' Rash grunted perplexedly.

As the car sped on, he studiously tapped into his cell phone's settings in an effort to change the ringtone.

TWELVE

May 2007
Mallaig, Scotland

THE SHABBY GROUND-FLOOR BANK had seen better days. The air of fetid dampness it exuded was further exacerbated by the disobliging, hard-of-hearing old hag tasked with overseeing the daily comings and goings of the branch's small number of regular clients.

'Good morning!' Jon said amicably, his nose pressed against the service window. 'I'm new to the area, and I'd like to open a current account, if it's not too much trouble? I have my passport, for identification purposes.'

'Perhaps you'd care to make an appointment...? We're a wee bit short-staffed at the moment,' the assistant said priggishly.

Jon was momentarily flummoxed at this, given the dearth of customers near at hand, but pressed on.

'I was rather hoping to get it sorted today... Could I perhaps speak to a senior member of staff?'

'I'm the acting manager,' she stressed self-importantly. 'The senior manager will be halfway to Fort William by now.'

'How thoughtless of him... particularly when you're rushed off your feet!' Jon said facetiously.

Giving it up as a lost cause, he had turned on his heels and was making for the exit when she suddenly experienced a change of heart.

'One moment, sir... Silly me... I have a gap at twelve-fifteen!' she trilled. 'If that's of any help?'

'Indeed it is... I'll nip and grab a coffee... ta very much!' Jon replied, before bounding across the street to the railway-station café.

*

Forty-five minutes later

The piercing clack of the door's high-security lock echoed within the stark reception area as Jon made his grand re-entrance five minutes ahead of his appointment and parked his backside on a vacant chair.

'Take a seat at the desk in the corner... I'll be with you shortly,' the assistant snapped in an ill-mannered tone.

'There's no particular rush!' he dourly replied.

After a moment or two he observed her handing the reins to an apprehensive bespectacled underling before strolling over, nose in the air, to complete the necessary paperwork.

'How much do you plan to deposit today?' she inquired.

'Five hundred thousand I guess... for starters,' Jon vaguely acknowledged, plucking the figure out of thin air.

'H-half a million pounds, d-did you say?' she half-sputtered, her eyes piercing through him above the rim of her bifocals.

'That's correct... from my Coutts account in London.'

Her frosty manner was mollified in a heartbeat. As he briefly outlined the complexities involved with his ambitious renovation project, the harsh brusqueness of her voice rapidly softened to a helpful, almost obsequious, tone.

'Goodness me, so you're planning on moving to the Highlands... Where precisely?' she inquired, far less haughtily.

'The Knoydart peninsula.'

'Are you a renowned painter... or a famous author perhaps?'

'Nope... I just got tired of the rat race!'

'I just need a couple of signatures and that's the formalities out of the way,' she said, sliding the forms across the table together with her Parker fountain pen. 'Oh, and could I have a daytime contact number, please?'

'I don't have one.'

'You don't possess a mobile telephone?'

'No... I'm incommunicado!'

'One moment, please,' she begged. She lumbered her way into a side office, where before long a muffled conversation ensued.

Jon sat staring at the ceiling, patiently drumming his fingers on the table. A distant roll of thunder hinted that a shower might be in the offing. The sensation was compounded by the fluctuating current playing havoc with the in-house security system.

'Seems there's a storm brewing,' Jon remarked, acknowledging her pudgy figure waddling back to the desk.

'It's Mr Macfarlane, our area manager; he'd like a wee word!' she bleated, thrusting a cordless handset into his mitt.

A brief confab with the silver-tongued big cheese more or less dispelled any misgivings about the hefty sum's legitimacy. This was confirmed without delay by Jon's big-city bankers, much to the relief of the jittery subordinate.

'Is there anything else I can help you with?' she queried, slipping on her raincoat and pulling the hood over her head.

'Um… yeah… Could you point me in the direction of Agnes Ryan's place?' he asked, buoyed by a quickening of his pulse.

'Huh… be on your way now,' she said scornfully, as she grabbed an umbrella, thankful for the opportunity to make herself scarce.

*

His only other choice was to try his hand in the nearby post office.

'Excuse me, ladies,' Jon asked, squeezing past a small group of tittle-tattling females who were clogging up the gangway, sounding like a brood of clucking hens as they engaged in a stream of meaningless gossip.

The mere mention of Agnes's name stunned everyone into silence.

'A book of first-class stamps… that'll be two pounds and four pence,' the server snorted, curtly handing over his change.

'She lives in her late uncle's cottage, not far from here,' a kindly man of the cloth intervened, glowering disapprovingly at the grim-faced gathering. 'Contrary to local opinion, I rather like Agnes. Have you known her long?'

'We met fleetingly on the train from Fort William… I've got an hour or two to kill and figured I'd look her up!'

'She's a bright, god-fearing lassie… Take a right off Station Road, and look out for the pebble-dashed cottage at the end of the row,' the cleric said animatedly. 'It's the one with the shabby-chic blue door.'

'It'd be good to see her… before she's burned at the stake!'

'Ha-ha… quite. Be sure to tell her Duncan said hello,' he said, laughingly, pinning a colourful flyer onto the noticeboard.

*

Aimlessly wandering beside the lapping waters of the east bay, Jon felt a briny blast of air ripping into his lungs. His latterly found hermetic lifestyle had brought him some calm; and yet a range of emotions flickered behind his eyes, aroused by the memory of the metamorphic events of little more than eighteen months before: the consequences of a vengeful rush of blood.

Away across the choppy loch, the jutting peaks of his chosen refuge lurked uncompromisingly in the distance, trapped beneath a weighty bank of menacing clouds, barely unaltered by the recent changing of the seasons.

Up ahead in the filmy haze a scattering of whitewashed cottages twisted downwards into a small cul-de-sac. They fitted the priest's description sufficiently for him to quicken his pace, alert to a flock of seagulls swooping overhead.

A sharp knock-knock at the bizarrely painted door drew no response at all, save for an unwanted souvenir spattering onto the tiny porch's supporting posts, just a little too close for comfort to his cowering head.

Flittingly coming to rest on the bespattered wall, the potbellied critter unleashed a perforating caw. It grated inside Jon's mind like a discordant tune, accentuated by a strong wind shriek diminishing to an eerie whistle.

Yet again the gull admonishingly squawked, its beady red-rimmed eyes sizing him up with a look of sheer belligerence.

'Don't fret, buddy,' Jon whispered. The bird's pink webbed feet inched boldly towards him, its bill repeatedly pecking at an imaginary titbit before, with a whoosh of its wings, it relocated to the eaves of a nearby boathouse.

His head bowed low as he surveyed a hash of pavement cracks, Jon's quiet solitude gave way to a searing loneliness. It crawled all over his body like a contagious rash, brought about by his inability to feel a sense of belonging. A series of horn blasts from the harbourside heralded the arrival of a heavily laden ferryboat, labouring towards its berth beset by an unruly herd of 'white horses', its queasy passengers clinging on for grim death.

A chipper, puffer-jacketed passer-by carrying a bulky shopping bag paused mid-step to converse with a ruddy-faced local man, who set down a cumbersome LPG tank onto his drive, glad of a chance to catch his breath. Through his open front door the melodious chimes of a grandfather clock tolled the quarter hour. Roused from his uneasy torpor, Jon's hazy eyes brought into focus the head-scarfed woman skipping across the road.

'Oi... Mr Ragamuffin man, you sure took your time!' she cried out, meeting his glance with a glimmer of recognition.

'Hello... it's Agnes, isn't it?' he said hesitantly, at once captivated by her piercing brown eyes. 'I hammered on your front door, around ten minutes ago... I thought perhaps you'd care to join me, for a plate of kippers?'

'Kippers… you sure know how to sweet-talk a woman,' she said half-mockingly, shooting him an impudent grin.

'Sorry… I can see you're busy,' he said coyly.

'Busy? Not at all… Step inside, make yourself at home!'

'I would, but I promised faithfully I'd pop back to the bank… to make the big white chief's acquaintance.'

'The Bank of Scotland?'

'Yeah… next to the railway station.'

'Ugh… time waits for everyone in this neck of the woods… especially a self-righteous slime-ball like Finlay Macfarlane!' she bristled, tearing the self-styled pillar of the community's dubious reputation to shreds.

In the cosy, dimly lit living room Jon burrowed his backside deep into the sofa and took in his surroundings. The numerous knick-knacks on the walls were scattered amongst a quirky collection of tastefully arranged photographs and paintings.

'Permission to speak, Miss,' Jon lightened, before bringing up the subject of his return trip to Knoydart on the day's final ferry.

'Hush your mouth,' she shot back, pulling him up with a reproachful finger.

'Forgive me for asking… oh, never mind,' he responded half-smilingly, well aware he may be fighting a losing battle.

'I couldn't help but notice how much weight you've shed… you're all skin and bones man, like a frigging prisoner of war!' she fussed, pointing towards a seat at the dining table. 'You need fattening up a bit!'

'Stop mothering me, woman!' he reciprocated, accidentally placing his stockinged feet onto the arm of the sofa.

'Feet off…*now!*' she yelped. 'Make yourself useful and uncork the bottle of Chianti next to the stack of cans in the larder.'

An hour or more fairly flew by. The banter between them brimmed over into boisterous fits of laughter, aided in no little way by the effects of the Italian plonk, flowing thick and fast from the unwieldy double magnum.

'Say hello to Mr Armitage!' Jon muttered comically, staggering to his feet to enact his favourite drunken-sailor routine.

'Hah… who's he when he's at home?'

'It's just a figure of speech… a metaphor, for getting pissed!'

'You mean s-p-l-e-e-c-h?' she responded, performing her very own sozzled impression.

'What are you like?' he chuckled, glancing fleetingly at his watch. 'Just a thought… where will I bed down tonight?'

'On the sofa you've become so attached to. Up your kilt!' she cried, raising her wineglass, highly amused by the puzzled look on his face.

*

The kitchen-cum-parlour window grew black with night, lightened only by the dull glow of the hidden moon poking its nose through a bank of slow moving cloud, cast in half-shadow on the beaming faces of the chattering couple.

'I can't get my head around what satisfaction a coven of meddlesome old witches could derive from dragging someone's name through the mud. It really gets my goat,' Jon said irately, broaching the subject of the spiteful rumblings from the small community's scandalmongers.

Agnes responded with a simple shrug of the shoulders. She stretched her arm forward to load a disc into the CD player and dreamily rose to her feet, batting her eyelashes at the house guest to entice him into joining her for a twirl. 'Hey There Lonely Girl', Eddie Holman's seventies classic, oozed into the room, persuading Jon to take the bait. He swept the lady into a warm embrace, and the couple breezed from side to side, blissfully content to hold one another near.

In the exposed side alley the wind squalled aloud, dumping the plastic wheelie-bin noisily on its side. It made scant difference to the twinkle-toed twosome smooching barefoot across the terracotta tiles.

'Oh there lonely girl, lonely girl, don't you know this lonely boy loves you… ooh-a-ooh-ooh,' Jon cut loose, soaring spellbindingly into a full-voiced falsetto, crowned by a superhuman top G to nail the heart-rending climax.

'Wow! You're good!' she gasped, experiencing a freak hot flush.

'Singing used to be my passion,' he sheepishly admitted, withstanding a potent urge to squeeze her even closer to him. He was smitten by her sensual smile and long wavy locks flickering seductively in the soft ochre candle-light.

' *'Cos I've been too long in the wind… too long in the rain… taking any comfort that I can…'* Millie Jackson's 'Loving Arms' bled out of the speakers, motivating a moment of unbridled affection, as their lips met for the very first time.

'This song could've been written especially for me,' Agnes sighed in reply, tuning in to the moving heartfelt lyrics.

53

'The one who said she'd rather be alone,' Jon's dulcet tones purred into her ear. 'Someone like you deserves to never be alone.'

'And if I didn't know any differently I'd say you were coming on to me.'

'What if I am?'

'Have you seen the weather out there?'

'You wouldn't!'

'Don't test me… Tell me about yourself.'

'How long have you got?'

'All night!' she exclaimed bang on the stroke of midnight, cuddling up close as their extraordinary tales unravelled.

*

Born within spitting distance of the Emerald Isle's Wild Atlantic Way, Agnes Ryan's post-adolescent years sank into a sad decline, skidding off the rails in the cruellest way possible by virtue of her beloved mother's premature death.

Welcomed into her ailing grandmother's modest home on the outskirts of Galway's select Taylor's Hill area, the plucky teenager slowly came to grips with her tragic loss. She spent much of her time in the stable block of school governor Charles Aitken's palatial residence, mucking out between learning the ropes.

Forewarned of the landowner's penchant for young girls by the stable's protective head groom, the dewy-eyed Agnes kept her head down low, ably going about her duties while taking care not to arouse any unwanted attention.

'Let me help you with that, I can still hear him saying. Eyeing me from the far side of the quadrangle struggling with an unmanageable hay bale, midway through his Sunday morning rounds,' she unfurled apprehensively.

'He took advantage of you… is that right?' Jon said, hanging on her every word.

'He invited me for afternoon tea, in the main house.'

'And you accepted?'

'I'd not long turned sixteen.'

'Please don't go on if it's too painful,' Jon whispered caringly, putting his arm around her in an effort to comfort her.

'No… no… it needs to be said!' she murmured, pecking him on the cheek before continuing with her story.

She was prettily decked out in her best pink linen dress. The dazzled host's eyes lit up like jewels, his fingers snapping rudely to summon an unwomanly aide. In response she began wheeling a silver drinks trolley into a side reception room, loaded with a variety of spirits alongside a tempting array of canapes.

Young Agnes was ushered first into the library, from where a lingering trail of cigar smoke floated round into an oak-panelled sitting room. Relaxed in an arrangement of leather lounge chairs, a trio of tweed-clad toffs broke off mid-conversation.

'I was as high as a kite and powerless to stop it. They passed me round like a piece of meat... Aitken's hidden camera filmed everything!' Agnes poured her heart out, blaming no one but herself for her foolish naivety.

UK CABINET MINISTER IN "LOLITA" SEX TAPE SCANDAL, a popular tabloid's front page announced a few days later, leading with a snapshot of the disgraced politician, side by side with a still of the pouting sex kitten.

'I'd never even heard of Geoffrey Bowman!' she said, sniffing into a hankie. 'I rue the day I ever laid eyes on him!'

'The name definitely rings a bell... Go on.'

'Within a week or so I'd dropped out of school, and made the mistake of my life by taking off to Dublin, where, as if things could have got any worse, my fortunes hit rock bottom... but we'll leave that for another time!'

'And some fruitcake in the Scottish Highlands got wind of the tape... years later? It's difficult to get your head around.'

'A perverted computer geek, who lives with his equally twisted uncle in Marine Place, barely a stone's throw from here.'

'Call the cops!'

'And reopen all those painful wounds? I don't think so.'

'But you're being stalked!' Jon said, gritting his teeth. 'Perhaps I should turn up unannounced on their doorstep!'

'What's the point...? I'm planning on selling the place.'

'B–but... where will you go?'

'Somewhere far away from prying eyes and venomous tongues... where I can smell the dew on the morning grass and wander free with the wind in my hair,' she said longingly, leaving the room to grab some sheets and a blanket.

Through the room's ill-fitting window seals came an intermittent high-pitched whistling noise. It screeched inside his brain like fingernails on a blackboard, his mind wandering, unable to dislodge the words playing through his head.

Never before had he felt such a connection to any woman, save for his mother. Everything about her stirred his senses and made his body come alive, from her rich hazel eyes, dark and gentle in their expression, to her chocolate-brown hair cascading loose onto her shoulders, glowing silken in the dim lamplight.

His nose twitched, drawn to the savoury smell of bacon sizzling in a frying pan. Watching over it was the pyjama-clad lady of the house, in between busily toing and froing to the tiny dining table, wielding a spatula in her right hand.

'Tea or coffee?' she asked, tapping him lightly on his upright knee. 'The clock's just ticking round to eight-thirty.'

'Uh... oh, tea with milk please... just a spoonful of sugar!'

'Helps the medicine go down,' she chirped semi-tunefully, skilfully cracking two eggs directly into a smaller second pan.

'Medicine?' he grunted questioningly.

'The song... from *Mary Poppins*...? Never mind, sit yourself down at the table.'

'You're amazing! I wasn't expecting this.'

'Slide it down your gullet,' she half-joked.

All at once, her face became serious. 'I've been thinking about what you said last night.'

'Ditto... I barely slept a wink!'

'To lose one parent is devastating, let alone both, in the space of twelve hours.'

'Amen to that!'

'But something's been bothering me...'

'Spit it out.'

'Why the sudden exile? I don't get it... you don't just go from being a world superstar one day to a recluse the next.'

'It seemed the right thing to do... Knoydart ticked all the right boxes. But what about you... what does the future hold?'

'We all have to move on at some point,' she sadly reflected, chasing a morsel of fried bread around her plate.

'Come and live with me!' he impetuously suggested. 'You can come and go as you please… with no strings attached!'

'Easy, tiger… you're getting way ahead of yourself… Sharing the same roof with a man I barely know… whew!'

'Sleep on it,' he said, hopefully, carrying both empty plates from the table. 'You wash and I'll dry!'

*

Two hours later

His body bobbing in rhythm with the ferryboat's hypnotic sway, a swarm of butterflies fluttered in his stomach, filling him with a deep sense of dread. Would he ever see her again? Or had his reckless tongue scuppered his chances of forming some kind of meaningful relationship? Either way, his world was spiralling out of control.

THIRTEEN

October 2005
Granby

'GOOD MORNING, MR GOLD... Our paths have actually crossed before, though with your hectic lifestyle I doubt you'll remember!' Nosy mega-fan Richard Turner was oozing smarm, having waylaid his idol at the village postbox.

Jon instinctively smelt a rat. 'Mm, yeah, help me out here... Where is it I know you from?' he guardedly responded.

Eager to ingratiate himself with his renowned neighbour, Turner took the opportunity to bang on about his plucky attempt to intercept a strong-arm hatchet-man found loitering close to JJ's previous address. 'My apartment overlooked your penthouse in the city centre,' he added cringingly. 'We met on a couple of occasions!'

'Wait a minute... I visited you in hospital; it made the evening news!' Jon exclaimed, all of a sudden recalling Turner's horrifying injuries. 'The guy roughed you up pretty badly. I'm relieved to see you made a full recovery!'

'I knew it wouldn't have slipped your mind!'

'Mm, indeed... So what brings you to Granby... family, friends, or perhaps just the open countryside?' Jon inquired.

'I was headhunted for a new position in Melton Mowbray, and happened upon a cottage in the village up for rent!'

'On Main Street?' Jon asked distrustfully.

'Yes, number two to be precise!'

'In the renovated farm buildings opposite my driveway?'

'Yep... it's a startling coincidence, don't you think?' the creep laughed, falsely, dogging Jon's footsteps to the imposing main gates.

'Um, quite... Maybe I'll see you around,' Jon muttered with undisguised contempt, jabbing in the PIN code under Turner's watchful gaze.

The whine of the vacuum cleaner blotted out his short sharp rap at the granny flat's door, where his house-proud mother was busily going about her daily chores. She suddenly felt an uncomfortable presence elsewhere in the room.

'Jonathan, darling... you gave me a start!' she said, before observing the troubled look on his face. 'What on earth's the matter?'

'Mum, I need a contact number for the lady who fixed up your blinds... urgently!'

'Barbara Fitch,' she responded, with an admonishing glare towards his mud-crusted boots. 'Why the sudden rush?'

'Oops, sorry Mum... To black out my bedroom windows. I've a nagging suspicion the guy opposite's spying on me.'

'Jonathan... you're becoming paranoid!'

'Take it from me, Mum... I'm a dab hand when it comes to weeding out weirdos, and this guy's a twenty-four-carat nut job!'

'I'll give her a call. It's high time we caught up anyway,' she said, rooting in the under-sink cupboard for a floor cloth.

*

Much revived and invigorated from an afternoon shower, Jon was getting dressed when a mystifying shaft of light cut through a tiny gap in the bedroom's net curtains, colliding blindingly into a piercing sunbeam reflected onto the dressing-table mirror.

'Whoa,' he yelped, squinting through the fingers of his shielding hand, his curious eyes drawn to the laser-like incursion. As his gaze focused on a pair of glimmering circular lenses trained on him from an elevated lookout in one of the cottages opposite, he freaked out. 'Fuck... this is outrageous. He's eyeballing me through a set of binoculars!'

Incensed by this invasion of his privacy, his right foot savagely connected with a nearby waste bin. Its messy contents spilled out onto the carpet as the trill of the in-house intercom system warbled in his ear.

'Barbara's dropping by tomorrow, for a cup of tea and a natter!'

'I think I'll forgo the blinds Mum, and plump for some traditional wooden shutters... similar to those in a stately home.'

'Isn't that a little drastic?'

'He's observing my every move, Mum!'

'Call the police, Jonathan!'

'To what end? A cosy little chat… a light rap on the knuckles?'

*

Three hours later

A prolonged Google search threw up a surfeit of choices, from a variety of Victorian, Georgian and Edwardian shutters, through a whole range of modern and stylish options reading like a never-ending who's who.

Having relocated to the secondary master suite on the far side of the house, Jon took a moment to compose himself, breaking off from reorganising his clothes and effects to gaze down admiringly over the lush gardens.

'So much for living a peaceful life!' he mumbled, his blood still boiling, cursing his newly discovered neighbour from hell.

FOURTEEN

November 2005
Three weeks after the break-in

OVERWHELMINGLY UNDERWHELMED FOLLOWING a heated parley with a burglarised landlord at an upmarket rural gastropub, a rather testy Dan Hackett sought consolation in a concealed woodland clearing. He was puffing without thought on a mentholated cancer stick when an urgent radio dispatch yowled into his left lughole.

'*Control to all mobiles in the Melton Mowbray area,*' the message conveyed, requesting patrol officers in the locality to attend the scene of a domestic violence incident, said to involve a young married couple.

Hackett semi-reluctantly stubbed out the butt end on the protruding wing mirror and executed a speedy U-turn, leading him onto a manure-strewn back road, well clear of the flow of heavy traffic building up on the nearby main drag.

A stroke of luck brought him to a development of purpose-built dwellings, assembled side by side into a featureless cul-de-sac, each tiny plot backing onto a stretch of open land presumably acquired for an ongoing project.

'Uh-oh,' he said warily, fearing the worst upon bending an ear to a high-pitched whining sound. It seemed to be carrying through the window of a white stuccoed bungalow erected in the shadow of a tall red-brick house.

Five minutes later, the car safely parked at the roadside, Hackett prowled stealthily along a fenced-off gravel pathway. Halting momentarily in his tracks, he heard the constant moaning turn into a painful cry.

With every growing second his heart beat faster, quickening in sync with the stream of images flashing through his head, as he pictured a maniacal bully inhumanly knocking lumps out of his defenceless spouse.

He couldn't have been more wrong. Through the lounge window, an erotically clad, fat-bottomed female strutted up and down, menacingly wielding a long leather riding crop a little too close for comfort to her partner's erect manhood, his upright torso securely strapped to a high-backed solid oak dining chair.

'I'll show you who's boss!' the temptress bellowed, straddling him like a small horse, to send waves of fat rippling all over his body.

'False alarm, Maureen!' Hackett radioed back to base, laughing convulsively between filling her in on the sordid details.

'She did what…? Good grief, the poor guy!' she half giggled, half screamed. 'Too much information, Danny boy!'

'A full-blooded re-enactment of the Kama Sutra, Mo!' he continued. 'Oh well, enough excitement for one day!'

*

'If you're delivering a package would you mind leaving it outside the gates?' Jon's voice crackled out of the security system's loudspeaker, mistakenly confusing the visitor with the notoriously loose-tongued postman.

'It's Detective Sergeant Dan Hackett, sir. I just happened to be in the neighbourhood,' the officer stated, stepping back to allow the gates to slowly part. 'I just thought I'd drop by to see how you're holding up?'

With a friendly pat on the shoulder, Jon led the way into a spacious spare room kitted out with an upright Yamaha piano, surrounded by an array of rare and precious instruments suspended proudly on all four walls.

'Please ignore the facial hair – I've been hard at it all night, demoing a couple of new tunes in the basement studio.'

'Wow, I can't wait to get an earful!'

'How about a sneak preview?' Jon said, clearing his throat prior to bursting into a spontaneous acapella rendering:

'Time to take flight into the night got to run… my business here is done.

Time for me to go, an invisible foe…leave without a trace to vanish into space.'

'Whew,' Hackett half-whistled, struggling for a moment to find the right words.

'It's depressing, don't you agree?'

'I wouldn't have put it quite that way.'

'Come on… give me your honest, unbiased opinion.'

'You want it, you got it… The snippet I heard made the hair stand up on the back of my neck. Stop doing yourself down!'

'Slap on the cuffs, and do me a favour!'

'And why would I want to do that?' Hackett asked bluntly, ignoring his attempt at humour with a blank stare.

'Check out the song's lyrics,' Jon said, reaching up onto the piano lid to retrieve a handwritten sheet of A4.

Something didn't add up. Hackett's instincts told him Jon knew more than he was letting on. Written somewhere between the lines of the self-damning tirade was something almost akin to a mind-boggling admission of guilt.

'I'm confused… This song is about you… and not some AWOL hoodie who disappeared off the face of the earth?'

'You got it in one. I feel like a prisoner, confined in my own home. I need to break free… to rid myself of the shackles.'

'But, you're free to come and go as you please!'

Jon fell silent. No words could describe the feelings rushing through him. The deceit. The utter loneliness. The anguish and fear which wracked his brain. He threw up his hands and mumbled a laconic reply.

'I'm tired… knackered!'

'Get some sleep… some proper rest. Buzz the gate, and I'll let myself out.'

*

Leicestershire Police HQ
Three days later

The scraping noise of chairs on the wooden floor presaged the opening of the emergency morning meeting. Surrounded by an indifferent group of fellow officers, Detective Sergeant Dan Hackett rose to his feet.

'In regards to the Gold case, the dots don't quite connect, guv. I get this feeling he's either hiding something, or lying about something.'

'Be that as it may, the case has finally run its course,' DI Philpott barked. 'We're no closer to our suspect than we were the first night.'

'Please, just one more week, guv!'

'The kid could easily have fled to Pakistan by now!' spotty-faced DC Phil Cass chipped in, not helping matters at all.

'No ifs, no buts, that's final!' the chief snapped.

'Jeff Wade and a team of PCSOs are out asking questions as we speak. Plus, there's something perhaps even more significant which I urgently need to check out,' Hackett contended, not about to take no for an answer.

'And what might that be?'

'Not what – but who.'

'Jesus, Hackett, get on with it!'

'Rashid Shah... the Karachi Kid, as Wade nicknamed him?' he said, provoking a rumble of laughter in the room.

'Simmer down, boys. Hear him out!'

'I caught sight of him at a glitzy charity bash in the city... hobnobbing with the dignitaries in the roped-off VIP section.'

'Go on... what's the significance?'

'I clocked him chatting to the guest of honour, as if they were bosom buddies.'

'Who, for Christ's sake?'

'Who else but Mr JJ Gold? Something stinks to high heaven, guv!'

'You've got forty-eight hours... and not a minute more!' Philpott finally yielded, abruptly winding up the meeting.

Time was of the essence, and the race was on.

FIFTEEN

Autumn 2006

TRADING THE ROLLING Leicestershire countryside for the foothills of the Alps in close proximity to the lakeside town of Montreux, Switzerland, Jon immersed himself into an intensive bout of recording. For a three-month period he worked twenty-four-seven, manically pushing himself beyond all reasonable limits.

'Play like you mean it!' Jon yelped angrily into the talkback, putting sax player Martin Jameson through the wringer.

'I'm blowing my nuts off, man!' the musician shot back, petulantly removing his headphones and setting his sax down on a stand. 'Much more of this shit and I'll be on the next plane out of here. I'm not your slave!'

'Be my guest... I'll do the fucking solo myself!' Jon said belittlingly, hastening Jameson's departure into the common room.

It was several days into the recording, and tensions were running particularly high: fuelled not only by Jon's fanatical attention to detail, but rather more his frequent uncharacteristic mood swings which set everyone on edge.

'Something's eating away at him, that's for sure,' drummer and long-standing friend Harry underlined, doing his best to placate the bevy of top-drawer musicians drafted in to lend weight to the project.

'All the same, I can't take much more!' percussionist Luis groaned exasperatedly, languishing over his umpteenth mug of coffee.

Abruptly, and to everyone's surprise, Jon emerged from the adjoining kitchenette. He had evidently caught the drift of the conversation.

'We all know that this isn't working... for which I can only apologise. Ultimately, other than Harry, you're all free to go!' he said staggeringly, before moving towards the console room door as if nothing had happened.

'So that's it? Just like that, we're done?' trumpet-player Andy grumbled in disbelief. Head shaking, he wandered off towards the accommodation block, quickly followed by all but one of the equally disgruntled musos.

*

One hour later

'Klaus, set up the grand piano,' Jon barked to the engineer, re-entering the studio with a renewed sense of purpose, buoyed by a productive stint of lyric-writing while hidden away in the peaceful solitude of his producer's suite.

'The boys… they came to bid me goodbye!'

'Que sera, sera… such is life!'

A worried look crossed the Swiss man's face. 'There was a telephone call from Mr Templeton in your absence.'

Not wasting any time, Jon punched in the big boss's number, holding the receiver away from his ear in anticipation of one of Miles's inimitable tongue-lashings. Much to his surprise, it was expressed in an oddly subdued tone.

'Speak to me, son… tell me what's going on.'

'I'm starting over from scratch, Miles, using a totally new concept.'

'Without a frigging band?'

'I want lush strings, French horns, tubas, bassoons… a thirty-strong gospel choir… the works. I want it to sound huge!'

'I only hope you know what you're doing, son!'

'I can see it now, Miles… a grand tour of the world's great opera houses, accompanied by a sixty-piece orchestra!' Jon rambled excitedly. 'The Bolshoi in Moscow, the Metropolitan in New York City, not forgetting London's Royal Opera House!'

'What about Sydney… and Milan's La Scala? And then there's the Colón in Buenos Aires… Keep me posted on your progress, son!' Templeton signed off, resolved for the time being to keep his prize asset sweet.

*

Three months later

His heartbeat roaring like a runaway train, a notably edgy Miles Templeton summoned PA Jenny into his airless top-floor office and demanded to know Jon's whereabouts a few weeks after the Montreux session's curtailment.

'Both of his phones appear to be out of service,' Jenny said.

'We have a potential number-one album on our hands, and the artist's gone AWOL! Find him, hire a PI... whatever it takes!'

'You could try talking to Khalid Shah, the author penning his biography? Rumour has it they've become pretty close.'

'Well, don't just stand there!' Templeton urged, lustfully eyeing her curvy rear disappearing through the door.

*

Fifteen minutes later

'Mr Templeton, what a pleasant surprise!' Khalid said cordially, sliding the office window shut to block out the traffic noise. 'Doubtless you've feasted your ears on the rough mixes from the Montreux sessions?'

'I haven't heard jack shit. Let's stop the idle chatter and cut to the chase. When was the last time you spoke with Jon?'

'When I flew out to Montreux last month, to sit in on the session.'

'And you haven't heard hide nor hair of him since?'

'Nothing to speak of,' Khalid said, a touch furtively. 'But, if the truth be told, he's a physical and emotional wreck.'

'Have you, or haven't you?'

'I'm sworn to secrecy, I'm afraid.'

'Shit... That's the last thing I wanted to hear. I'm drowning over here! For Christ's sake man, throw me a lifeline!'

'There was something...'

'Tell me... I have his best interests at heart!' Miles yelled frantically.

'He does have a new lady in his life!'

Without another word, the line went dead.

SIXTEEN

Late November 2005
Leicester

CAUGHT UNAWARES OUTSIDE the Meadow's Court care facility by a casually dressed young detective, Rashid Shah stubbed his cigarette butt into a patch of bare earth.

'Don't I know you from somewhere?'

'Detective Constable Mike Warren; we've crossed paths on a couple of occasions. I've been asked to bring you in for questioning!'

'By who?'

'DS Dan Hackett.'

'Am I being arrested?

'Not unless you refuse to cooperate.'

'But… my morning shift begins in ten minutes!'

'Huh, is this a wind-up? What morning shift?' the gobsmacked DC asked.

'I work here, as a care assistant.'

'In an old people's home? Pull the other one!'

'Give me a break; my position's soon to be made permanent, once the authorities sign off on my community service.'

'Congratulations!' the cop said, sarcastically.

'I could spare an hour at one o'clock… if I forgo my lunch break?'

'Good enough… Make your way to the satellite station in Spinney Hill Park. I'll let DS Hackett know…'

*

12.55p.m.

The whiff of stale body odour permeated the air in the stuffy, enclosed interview room. It was made slightly more bearable by the half mug of black coffee kindly offered to him from the thermos flask of the anaemic-looking duty constable.

'I must be hearing things, Rashid!' a coarse voice echoed from out in the hall, growing firmer as the DS entered the room.

'Mr Hackett… it's so nice to see you again,' he answered cuttingly. 'I presume you know sarcasm is the lowest form of wit?'

'Blah, blah, blah… same old crap. Always whingeing and complaining!'

'I have every right to be bitter, Mr Hackett!'

'Change the record. So you took the rap for your pal Mistry… which begs the question, where is that slimy reptile?'

'Hell… if I knew I'd tell you!'

Menacingly pacing the floor like a caged lion, the DS took stock of Rashid's snappy appearance, from his neatly coiffured locks and trimmed facial hair, to his designer-label blouson over his matching shirt and slacks.

'You cleaned up your act, Rashid!'

'Bought with my own hard-earned cash, Mr Hackett.'

'Working nights?'

'Pretty much round the clock, Mr Hackett.'

'Excluding the night of October the sixth… when you were sighted sucking up to JJ Gold at a swanky charity wingding in the city!'

'My brother Khalid cried off at the last minute and offered me his VIP passes… why would I pass up such an opportunity?'

'Why indeed… What makes your brother so special?'

'JJ recently commissioned him to write his biography. They've been spending a lot of time hanging out together.'

'Biography! When you have difficulty stringing a sentence together…? I want the truth Rashid, and I want it now!'

'It *is* true, Mr Hackett… They shared a table together at the Brit Awards in February and hit it off like a house on fire!'

'But how do *you* know JJ?'

'He donated a stack of items to a spina bifida charity I was helping raise funds for… I just wanted to thank him personally.'

'Spare me the sentimental crap… as they say, charity begins at home, not turning over some famous rock star's home!'

With mouth agape, a wounded look spread across Rashid's face. '*Me*, steal from JJ? I worship the ground the guy walks on!'

'Where were you on the night of the eleventh of November?'

'I was working the late shift at Meadow's Court, I swear! Until five in the morning. Speak to my boss – he'll vouch for me!'

Hackett hesitated, feeling compelled to say something, but finding himself at a loss for words. His hard-hitting approach was getting him nowhere fast, evident in Rashid's coolness in tackling his barrage of questions.

'You're free to go... and thanks for your cooperation!'

'What... that's it?'

'Maybe I was wrong about you... now get your scrawny arse out of here!' Hackett said, tongue in cheek, making rapidly into the corridor.

*

Leicestershire Police HQ

'So what've we got, Sherlock?' DI Philpott asked wryly, his patience wearing thin midway through the morning meeting.

'In a word, nothing, guv. By my reckoning Shah's as clean as a whistle,' Hackett mumbled, awaiting the final hammer blow.

'No further leads as to Mistry's whereabouts?'

'Not a jot... though I'd give anything to lay my hands on him!'

'And do what precisely?

'Pin the wrongful deaths of two elderly citizens on a cruel, demented criminal!'

'Courtesy of a stroke and a heart attack...? Wake up Dan, the show's over!' Philpott said, nodding his head resignedly. 'Gentlemen, let's move on... please!'

SEVENTEEN

June 2007
Knoydart

THE MELLIFLUOUS TONES of a lone song thrush peeping and chirruping in the surrounding shrub land provided Jon with an early-morning wake-up call, his naked torso stretched across the bed like an ancient Olympian.

Hastily throwing on a sweater and jeans before scuttling down the wooden staircase, a light breakfast of tea, toast and jam prepared him for the arduous walk ahead, risking life and limb to make the mid-morning ferry.

Unperturbed by the bracing un-summer-like weather, the clean salt air refreshed his senses. His thoughts were mainly preoccupied with a woman on the far side of the loch, with whom he felt some kind of connection.

A sudden rustle in the undergrowth revealed a playful mud-soaked otter scrambling towards the nearby burn, its smooth-coated body slithering down the inclined bank prior to twisting into an ungainly somersault.

'Midge,' he whispered, likening the creature to the lovable main character of his favourite childhood movie *Ring of Bright Water*. His eyes observed its fun-loving antics through a glittering cascade of silvery spray.

Further along, a welcome trail of downtrodden earth made the going easier, snaking through the craggy terrain beneath the day's first beam of sunlight, drawing him ever nearer to the flat, gravelly coastal track.

'Bright Water… Brightwater Croft… that's it, perfect!' he said jubilantly, pausing to gloat over his flash of inspiration.

A distant cluster of heads peeped through the drifting mist, dilly-dallying on the pier ahead of the eleven o'clock ferry. It could be viewed from afar slicing through the white-capped waves, hampered by the notorious undertow.

'The boat's running twenty minutes late, darling,' a wax-jacketed toff bellyached within earshot. 'The bearded chappie over there made mention of an incoming passenger taking an eternity to load her luggage on board!'

'Lord knows why; three days in this godforsaken place is more than enough!' his better half said haughtily, warranting a cutting look from the hirsute stranger strutting purposefully along the L-shaped jetty.

Slowly but surely the vessel emerged out of the misty gloom, steering a wide arc out to the right to gun the throttle into reverse and puttering alongside the concrete sea wall adjacent to the sloping metallic gangplank.

'I could use a couple of able-bodied men!' the skipper's voice bellowed from the underdeck. His call fell largely on deaf ears, save for a sole passenger rudely weaving his way through to the front of the queue.

'*Agnes!*' he yelled out in amazement, galloping down the aluminium slope, his eyes fairly popping out of their sockets.

'Jon...? But... I don't understand!'

'I was just on my way to see you... I thought I'd surprise you!'

'Ditto,' she gasped, struggling with an assortment of bags. 'Well, don't just stand there, you dodo. Give the guys a hand!'

Without further encouragement Jon vaulted over the side rail, his weight supported by a muscular crew-hand, who thumbed towards the mini-mountain of assorted cargo which Jon promptly set about the task of unloading.

'Heck, you shipped a ton of stuff... where's it headed?' he asked optimistically, his body resembling a human packhorse.

'To the muddy green Land Rover parked at the end of the pier.'

'Oh!' he said curtly, lurching forward.

'And then out into the back of beyond... to inspect my new living quarters!'

Her voice carried like a song on the whistling wind.

*

The same evening

Their stomachs fairly bursting following a helping of fresh salmon plucked from the loch just the previous day, Jon sprang from his chair to gather up the dirty dishes. He was alive to an odd look flashing across Agnes's face.

'I'll wash... you dry!' he said warily, squeezing a splash of Fairy Liquid into the bowl, content to let the matter lie.

'Walked into a door in the dark, eh?' Agnes spoke up, mildly perturbed by the discolouration still evident on his cheekbones.

'I knew something was bothering you.'

'Not nearly as much as the wily gossipmongers across the loch... News spreads like wildfire in this neck of the woods!'

'Chinese whispers, I don't doubt.'

'From the lips of the local bobby? There's a warrant out for your arrest!'

'It's simply a case of mistaken identity.'

'Really... a bearded white male, sporting a blackening eye and a bloodied nose, seen leaping onto a departing ferryboat!'

'By whom?'

'The harbourmaster, for crying out loud!'

'It seems he neglected to mention the drunken mob at my heels baying for my blood!' he laughed, sinking back into the sofa and patting a hand lightly on the cushion beside him. 'Perhaps I'd better do some explaining!'

*

One month earlier

The latch on the tiny cottage door slowly clicked into place, her gentle goodbye bringing a lump to his throat. Once again his heart began to race. Could this be the beginning of a meaningful relationship? For sure no woman had affected him the way she had, or stirred his passion quite so fiercely with a single smile.

His backpack loaded to the brim with home-baked goodies and essentials, Jon strutted jauntily to the portside, swaying in rhythm with a wet-fish trawler chug-chugging into the harbour through the oil-flecked water.

'Oi... Grizzly Adams!' a raspy, quarrelsome voice from behind him hollered.

Jon gave a dismissive glance over his shoulder and brushed the hail aside, his better instincts urging him to resist the temptation to exact some form of revenge.

'Hey, Hagrid,' a reedy, higher-pitched voice chipped in, emanating from a pale-complexioned, anorak-clad youth.

'Jesus... no!' Jon said in breathy amazement as he cottoned on. Agnes's description of her gutless tormentors had been near-perfect.

'Ignore me at your peril, son,' the older guy persisted, before launching into a relentless, profanity-laced verbal assault. Perhaps mercifully, his accent was largely unintelligible; but the words 'filthy whore,' 'porn queen' and 'Jezebel' cut through.

Jon's muscles began to quiver with suppressed rage. The taunts rankled in his heart like tiny daggers digging into his flesh. Whatever it took he vowed to get even, somehow, some way, as and when the opportunity arose.

He upped his pace, half-jogging towards a grassy embankment, where a snaking, well-trodden footpath caught his eye. He figured it would offer an alternative route to the harbour by way of a redundant dry dock.

Somewhere within earshot the needless mud-slinging continued, coming thick and fast in bilious, malevolent waves. The incessant small-mindedness only served to intensify his anger. Simply put, enough was enough.

Atop a semi-steep incline close to the revamped police station, Jon hopped agilely onto a grassy knoll from where he could see without being seen. His newfound arch-enemy was swaggering like a conquering hero towards the doors of a roadside pub.

In seconds he scampered to the rear exit doors. A withered old-stager was leaning against a pyramid of used beer-kegs, puffing fitfully at a foul-smelling reefer in between swatting at the growing number of flies.

'Are there many customers inside?'

'Only my dominoes partner and his interfering hag of a wife!'

'And no one else?'

'Not a soul. Just a wee word of warning, laddie…'

'Sure… go on!'

'Steer well away from the watered-down piss they serve up in there!' the man half-croaked, half-laughed. He barely noticed Jon's rapid disappearing act, made good using a side alley to the lounge's main entrance.

'What can I get you?' the thick-set bartender inquired.

'Just a Diet Pepsi please… I'm looking for a couple of local guys who I believe slunk in here all of five minutes ago?'

'You mean Jimmy Logan, and his creepy nephew?'

'Yeah, that'd be them!'

'I'd choose my company more carefully, if I were you,' the host advised. 'I banned the pair of them six or seven months ago!'

Jon took off without another word, scampering up towards the high road with the door rocking on its hinges. A rare burst of sunshine cast a far-flung shaft of light over an idling mob of ruddy-faced rowdies.

An abandoned garage provided a concealed vantage point from which, squatting down behind a heavily loaded skip, he could hear a familiar voice. The wearisome yammer grated inside his head like a timeworn pneumatic drill.

The bartender's words echoed back to him. The short, sharp intake of breath at the mere mention of Logan's name. His reputation as a rabble-rouser preceded him. In short, he needed knocking down a peg or two.

Egged on by his group of flunkies making merry in a boisterous tone, a cacophony of catcalls further inflamed Jon's wrath, seemingly set in motion by a buxom teenager making her way out of the nearby convenience store.

'Mark my words, old man, your day of reckoning will come sooner than you think,' Jon half-silently fumed. He shifted his position and made the mistake of straying too close to an adjoining wire fence, behind which the fierce yap of a guard dog sent him whirling backwards.

'Speak of the devil, lads… it's none other than the village whore's shagging partner!' Logan snarled hatefully, beckoning to his deaf-eared henchmen, who, throats parched, continued legging it to the next port-of-call.

Jon backtracked to the hidden shortcut whence he came, getting a glimpse of the ferryboat making towards the harbour. He was torn between a lust to wreak some form of revenge, or to simply shrug his shoulders and head back across the loch. He froze, again sighting the mob strutting towards a shabby hotel with the gabbling Logan bringing up the rear.

His mind was made up. He had all the time in the world.

*

A seedy, inhospitable air permeated the bar room, its clientele made up of a posse of seafarers fresh in from an early morning jaunt, perched alongside a handful of waifs and strays seeking shelter from the elements.

'He should fuck right off out of here, and take that stuck-up hussy with him,' Logan ranted, too wrapped up in his own petty concerns to spot the hooded stranger slinking across the bar to an exit marked 'Residents Only'.

A lissom vault up the staircase brought him to a handful of guest rooms located down a narrow hallway. On the badly frayed carpet, a housekeeper's trolley stood idly to one side.

Scarcely able to believe his luck, Jon gleefully helped himself to a king-size roll of cling film before cantering towards a precarious metal fire escape spiralling down to a cluster of latrines on the ground floor.

'You!' the pimply nephew gasped, spinning round from the stinky urinal, nervously fumbling at his unbuttoned flies.

'Aren't you going to wash your hands?' Jon growled, baring his teeth, at once driving a sweet sucker punch into the pit of his stomach. It was executed with a force sufficient to send him hurtling towards a vacant cubicle.

Dazed from the blow, the youth's whimpering cry threatened to blow Jon's cover. Stifling it with a thick wad of tissue wedged into his mouth, an evil glint came into his eye as he set his quirky master plan in motion.

He stepped back to admire his handiwork, checking the binding's tightness to ensure the kid could breathe, his chest, armpits and shoulders coiled with multiple layers of viscid wrap to effectively form a makeshift harness.

The coast seemed to be clear, so he lugged the finished article out into the empty hallway, using all his brute strength to loop the thick outer layer over the uppermost portion of the staircase's vertical support column.

He snuck behind the broom-cupboard door to lie in wait, delighting over the dangling showpiece, legs and feet lolling helplessly in mid-air. He momentarily held his breath while a sozzled patron lurched out of the bar.

His neck twisting upwards, the old sot uttered a single grunt, pausing for a moment to bring his eyes into focus, confusedly forgetting the purpose of his exit from the bar, and subsequently heading back the way he came.

Jon quietly sniggered; but the smile was immediately wiped from his face by the sharp nasal timbre of Jimmy Logan's voice.

'Duncan… son? Where are ye, lad?' the uncle yelped, to no avail. 'Puking your guts in the yard I don't doubt!'

A solid right uppercut slammed into his chiselled jaw, sending him thudding to the deck like a sack of potatoes. It was swiftly followed with a wild kick to his lower stomach, much to the horror of the suspended audience of one.

Again the bar door bobbed to and fro, signalling the arrival of reinforcements in the shape of a trio of half-cut ruffians.

'Jimmy, man… what the fuck's going on?' a tattoo-headed man inquired, clasping Logan around the chest and yanking him to his knees. His bitterness overflowed on his colleagues, who were glaring up open-mouthed at the boy.

'Unhitch him, you fucking idiots!'

After a minute or two of slowly burning through the multi-layered cling film using the naked flame of a cigarette lighter, Duncan's tailbone abruptly crash-landed onto the stairway's bottom rung, his arms and legs flailing in all directions.

'He legged it up the stairs!' he howled.

'Who?' a dim-witted clod uttered.

'The Sassenach, you moron!' the half-stunned Logan blasted. 'Get your arses up that stairway while we check the bar!'

A frenetic chase ensued, the ranks soon swelled by a half-dozen reinforcements. Feet thundered over the upstairs landing while bodies scurried towards the fire exits to cut off every possible avenue of escape.

The game was up. Jon had little choice but to re-enter the bar, his head bowed and shoulder muscles tensed to shape his upper body into a human battering-ram. He went for broke, charging into the room like a raging bull.

In no time at all a flurry of blows rained pitilessly down onto his unprotected skull, the sheer weight of numbers rendering him half breathless. His right leg kicked out, instantly poleaxing a ginger-topped man whose wobbly frame backpedalled into the scattered tables and chairs, clutching in agony at his private parts.

Eventually pinned to the floor beneath an ever-increasing mound of assailants, amid the dull thud of knuckles striking against flesh he was thrown an unexpected lifeline. Agonised grunts and screams of pain intermingled with the high-pitched jangle of shattering glass, in a scene reminiscent of a Wild West saloon brawl.

'Get your arse out of here... *move* yourself!' the white knight's voice bellowed, his lightning quick reflexes dodging the ponderous swipes of two incensed ruffians, their heads meeting face to face with a crunching splat.

'But... you're badly outnumbered!'

'Grab my wrist,' the vigilante called out, extending his arm forward to tug Jon from under the melee. 'I've got this sorted... *Go!*'

'I owe you one!' Jon vowed, making straight for the exit.

'You owe me nothing!' the man said, spinning agilely around to continue where he left off.

*

'So there you have it... Put simply, I got slightly waylaid on my way to the terminal, and chose to take a later crossing instead.'

'Pursued by a gang of bloodthirsty psychos!'

'Yep... in all likelihood I'd still be recovering on a hospital ward were it not for my guardian angel's timely intervention.'

'Your very own shadow warrior... You got lucky... very lucky!' Agnes said softly, sneaking discreetly behind the sofa.

'Yeah, I did... I only hope I get a chance to show my gratitude someday,' Jon replied, unmindful of Agnes slipping out of her bathrobe.

'But then, some people are born lucky!' she reflected, creeping unashamedly on tiptoe into his line of vision.

For one fleeting moment his knees went weak, his stare fixed on the vision silhouetted against the fire's flickering flames. Her hand reached out to touch his, sending shivers and shockwaves through his body. He swept her up into his arms, feeling the softness of her breasts against his chest. He carried her to the bedroom.

EIGHTEEN

November 2005, three days after the incident

STILL HALF-ASLEEP FOLLOWING a late-night session surfing the internet, an irritable Richard Turner donned a grey sleeveless sweater over an ineptly knotted tie, shabbily finished off with a pair of ill-matching corduroy slacks.

A tedious eight hours of number-crunching lay ahead. First of all, though, would be his regular morning ritual of checking up on his celebrated neighbour's tree-lined estate, his digital binoculars trained upon the now familiar sweeping forecourt and grounds from a high-backed vantage point in his seedy crow's-nest lookout.

His position allowed him to see over the top of the tall wrought-iron gates to where a lone, bowed figure pounded his fists against the block-paved driveway, weeping inconsolably in the midst of an emotional breakdown, his mournful voice crying to the heavens.

'I know exactly how you feel, my friend… It's been a difficult week for the both of us,' Turner mumbled to himself. As he closely observed JJ's body language, his uncanny, over-curious fascination bordered on the disturbing.

He pored over the extraordinary pictures saved into the device's memory, basking in the warmth of a self-satisfied glow. His vow to maintain a constant vigil over his needy hero suddenly took on a new importance.

*

Nineteen days later

The Venetian blinds to the front of Turner's cottage blocked out the morning sun's glare. The only smidgen of light came from the screen of his Toshiba laptop, fired up in advance of some time alone indulging his fantasies.

His narrow lips curved into a leering smile, his right index finger sliding the mouse onto a cryptic icon to lay bare a sordid patchwork of risqué images, shared online with a cadre of similarly depraved internet chums.

He cooed lasciviously, slipping his free hand into his half-open bathrobe, transfixed in a low, dirty world of deprived innocence.

His concentration was abruptly broken by a sharp rat-tat-tat hammering at the front door, the awkward moment at once triggering his notoriously short fuse. Slamming the lid of his computer shut, he bolted to the window to peep through a crack in the blinds, preparing to vent his anger on some busybody neighbour. By contrast he made out a raven-haired man, smartly decked out in a navy cashmere overcoat.

'Morning, sir; my name's Detective Constable Wade. We're in the process of conducting a few enquiries in the area, in an effort to shed some light on an incident which occurred close by some three weeks ago.'

'I'm afraid I'm in the middle of something right now... Perhaps you might try calling again at a more convenient hour?'

'You've obviously got company, sir,' the DC said, making reference to a young girl's voice overheard as he approached the door.

'No... um, it must've been the TV, officer!'

'I'll be in and out in a jiffy... It's purely precautionary.'

'But I'm improperly dressed!'

'I spend my off-duty Saturdays playing rugby sir, so I've grown used to the sights, and smells, of exposed male flesh!'

'Oh well, if you insist,' Turner finally relented, apprehensively unhooking the security chain from its mounted bracket.

A stale, heavy odour permeated the airless room, made gloomier still by the absence of daylight. Wade looked around uncomfortably, backing dubiously towards the TV set. He placed his hand on top. It was stone cold.

'What were you watching, sir?' he asked, a trifle perturbed by the tiny balls of sweat clinging to the young man's upper lip.

'Watching... I'm sorry?' Turner half-panicked, before quickly latching on. 'Ah... one of those awful, chaotic kids' shows, officer!'

'Hmm... I used to love *Tiswas* when I was a lad!'

'Really... Now, if you don't mind?'

'Forgive me, sir... I digress,' Wade grunted, curtailing the niceties. 'I'd be much obliged if you could try and cast your mind back to the night of Friday the eleventh of November, between the hours of eleven and midnight.'

'That would be the night of the Jonathan Gold robbery?'

'Bang on, sir!'

'What an unimaginable tragedy, to lose both loved ones in such awful circumstances.'

'Shocking indeed, sir… Do you recall seeing any unusual activity in the immediate vicinity on the night in question?'

'Not a thing, officer.'

'The most minor details can often be critical to solving a case.'

'I was fast off at the time… It came as a complete shock when I switched on the BBC breakfast news the following morning.'

'Do you often sleep with the bedroom light on, sir?' Wade asked intrusively, acting on a lead provided by a co-villager.

Caught completely off guard by the question, every muscle in Turner's body tensed. He hesitated momentarily. He glared at the detective, his cold eyes brimming with fury, evident in the defensive tone to his response.

'I'm not sure where you're driving at, officer!'

'Rest assured, sir, it's not a loaded question… I'm merely looking to eliminate you from my enquiries, that's all.'

'I spend hour upon hour at my desk upstairs taking care of all my paperwork, and most probably left the light on.'

'Fine… and at what time did you turn in for the night… roughly?'

'Eleven… eleven-thirty perhaps.'

'Just one more thing, and then I'm out of your hair.'

'Very well, fire away.'

'Did you happen to see a vehicle parked on the grass verge opposite?'

'Like I said, I was out for the count… It would've taken a bomb to wake me!'

'Around the time you were preparing to hit the sack… I'm simply attempting to determine the make and model.'

'Not that I recall,' Turner lied.

'In which case that'll be all. I'll see myself out, thank you!' the DC acknowledged, ducking under the low-hanging doorframe.

*

Monday morning

'Dan… it's Jeff Wade. I hear Philpott pulled the plug on the Gold case? It may be a little late in the day, but in retrospect I should've spoken up sooner… The nosy neighbour I interviewed really spooked me out.'

'You must be referring to the infamous Richard Turner,' Hackett responded.

'How did you guess? He made my skin crawl. And the stench in his cottage – it was as though something had died in there!'

'Huh… just like the case Jeffrey, dead and buried!'

Wade gave an account of his vexing head-to-head, including Turner's bizarre body language, coupled with the girlish squeals that had supposedly been emitting from a Saturday-morning kid's show, though more likely via an illegal website.

'I don't even want to go there!'

'Gold likened his collection of surveillance gear to the observatory at Jodrell Bank, trained at all hours on the windows of his home.'

'A peeping Tom I can handle… but kids, Dan! If my hunch is right the bastard should be strung up by his balls!'

'I get it… you want a Section 19 to seize his computer? Philpott was adamant, Jeff – the investigation's closed.'

'I figured you'd say that,' Wade sniffled, preparing to sign off.

'He'll get his due, Jeff… These things have a nasty habit of coming back to bite you on the arse… often when least expected!'

*

Slightly before nine a.m. a rather jittery Richard Turner phoned his office and left a message on the answerphone feigning illness, before jumping into the car and speeding off in haste towards the town of Market Harborough.

His head was in a spin following the DC's off-the-cuff house call; and he was eager to check out an IT outlet which purported, by way of a local newspaper ad, to offer free guidance and advice to every first-time customer entering through its doors. A tediously long exchange with an acne-ridden technophile culminated in the purchase of a high-capacity external hard drive, essentially to eliminate any potentially incriminating data stored on his laptop.

The return journey saw his spirits lighten, the butterflies in his stomach settling. He meticulously heeded the IT wizard's instructions, leaving the transfer in progress prior to slipping on a jumble of shabby work clothes.

He set about scouring the cottage from bottom to top, going all out to pile a hash of damning evidence into a wad of black polythene refuse sacks, bent on covering his tracks should any more unwelcome visitors stop by.

The murky night sky allowed him an opportunity to load up his vehicle unseen. The dull glow of the half-moon cast an eerie shadow over the mini-mountain of waste compressed into the minuscule rear passenger seat.

Winding down the window to help fight back the bile rising up in his throat, he rashly hung the car right onto a badly rutted bridle road, well-trodden by the horsey set usually found frequenting the village on a weekend.

Midway along the track he sloppily reversed onto a patch of raised earth, slithering to a halt in a secluded woodland clearing alongside an avenue of trees which ran parallel to an expanse of open farmland.

Again the foetid smell invaded his nostrils, not helped by the molten quagmire of decaying debris squelching under his feet, separating piece by piece with every full-blooded thrust of his splintering trench shovel.

He repeatedly jumped up and down to force the bulging bags in amongst the morass, cursing JJ under every panting breath. The actions of a madman taking the law into his own hands had brought him here; yet a man so consumed with himself he refused to give him the time of day.

Physically and mentally exhausted from the ordeal, he removed his mud-caked boots in favour of a pair of tattered trainers and slid his backside onto the driver's seat. He uttered a weary sigh. His dirty work was almost complete.

*

Back up in the crow's nest of the freshly sanitised cottage only one last chore remained. It was quickly set in motion by means of a USB cable extended from the rear of his 'scope into a socket on the side of his cleaned-up laptop.

One after another the downloading images came into focus on the screen, depicting a man clearly battling his demons. Before he knew it the eyes of those who idolised him would see JJ for who he really was.

'It's high time you got your comeuppance, Mr Jonathan "Big Shot" Gold!' Turner snarled, viciously ripping down a poster Blu-Tacked to the bedroom wall. The church clock chimed three a.m. He smugly crept beneath the duvet.

NINETEEN

Late November 2005
Leicester

ARGUABLY ONE OF the most multi-cultural inner-city areas of the UK, the once prosperous Highfields district plays host to a diverse mix of Asian, Eastern European and Caribbean communities. Most of its inhabitants ply their trades in a variety of family-run businesses, among a low-life fraternity of pimps, hustlers and drug dealers.

Charles 'Chukka' Allen, a half-Jamaican, half-Indian weedhead, spent much of his time holed up in a Highfields slum, hanging out with a crowd of like-minded punks looking to make a fast buck by whatever means possible.

His sleep interrupted by a persistent thumping on the outside door, Chukka found himself confronted by a brace of glorified errand boys, sent to hunt down and put the frighteners on the oddly elusive Amir Mistry.

'I haven't seen him in three weeks!'

'Stop fuckin' with us… Word's out he crashed here just the other week.'

'For one night, man… that's the truth!'

'Bullshit!'

'The dude's a fuckin' psycho… I don't want nothing more to do with him!'

'What the fuck are you talking about?'

'He beat up on some old biddy… I watched him with my own eyes!'

'What the fuck?'

'He seen her through the window of this out-of-the-way crib we was sussing out… and it was like he just flipped!'

'So you pulled a ghost on the motherfucker… cool!' the younger man laughed, earning a black look from his sour-faced sidekick.

Chukka's story somehow rang true, backed up by the aggrieved expression crossing his dark, pockmarked face. Amir's brutal antics had clearly freaked him out, so much so he stood nothing to gain by lying.

'I got my arse out of there and laid low for a while… but when I went back there was all kinds of lights flashing and shit!'

'And he hasn't been seen since?'

'Neither hide nor hair… I could use a draw, man,' Chukka said edgily, fumbling in the pockets of his tracksuit bottoms.

'Here… this one's on the house!' the main peddler half-grunted, his stance softening.

'Cheers dude… much appreciated!'

'Hey… just one more thing.'

'Spill it, man!'

'If you happen to see, or hear from that piece of shit… tell him Uncle Frank would like a quiet word in his ear.'

'Consider it done!' Chukka said, tapping the side of his nose with his forefinger. 'He could be dead for all we know!'

'Huh… by the time Frank's finished with him, he'll wish he *was* dead!' the young flunky spat, slamming the door on his way out.

*

Chukka sank back into the flea-bitten armchair and stuck his feet up on the bamboo coffee table. He lit up the joint, drawing at it several times to inhale the hash into his lungs, punching at the remote control to switch on the pilfered plasma-screen TV. A quintet of mouthy females were wilfully putting the world to rights, laying into a former soap star with a seemingly incurable coke habit.

Chukka's attention was suddenly caught by a rather more interesting newsflash scrolling horizontally across the bottom of the screen. The Gold investigation had run its course, reportedly due to a total lack of concrete evidence.

Chukka sighed deeply, taking it in with a self-satisfied nod of the head. The heat was off, at least for the foreseeable future.

TWENTY

April 2008
Knoydart

JON WAS GRADUALLY coming to grips with his sequestered lifestyle. Cooped in an unforgiving hinterland, enriched by a cornucopia of solitude and serenity, the erstwhile fatalist metamorphosed into a blithesome, zestful backwoodsman, content to share each living moment with the soulmate who had captured his heart.

Each and every day he put his back into a series of menial tasks, ranging from lopping hefty branches from the encroaching trees, to constructing a wooden waterwheel to assist in providing a reliable electricity supply.

At last the highland winter's numbing coldness began to subside. The rush of sprouting greenery was augmented by a joyous chorus of the new season's first songbird's carolling in the glistening first light.

'Jon, I'd like a quick word.'

'Go for it... I'm all ears!'

'While I appreciate the time and effort you've put in to make the place liveable, I reckon it's time we took a crack at reconnecting with the outside world,' Agnes said, shoving a plateful of kippers under his nose.

'Come again? You can't be serious... This is our very own piece of paradise! You love it here, every bit as much as I do!'

'Oh, my poor shaggy monster... I'm not suggesting we uproot from the croft. I'd just like us to take a few days out to do some shopping and other stuff... you know, like normal everyday people!' she put ultra-persuasively.

He almost choked on a mouthful of coffee. 'Shopping? Are you for real? I have everything I need right here!'

'Take a long hard look at yourself in the mirror, Jonathan. You resemble a caveman,' she said, tugging her fingers at his wild growth. 'It's no joke, Jon. Sometimes I wake up startled to find Ben Gunn sleeping next to me.'

'What exactly do you have in mind?'

'You need to clean up your image… courtesy of an extreme makeover.'

'Shit… you want me hung, shorn and quartered, is that it?'

'That's one way of putting it.'

He responded in the only way he knew how, achingly wrapping his dulcet tones around the lyrics of a much cherished early recording:

'Take me… take me for what I am.

If ever I'm wrong-wrong-wrong… just you be strong enough.

To love me… love me for all my faults.

I can only be me. Not perfect… nor will I ever be.'

'Your imperfections make me love you more,' Aggie said tenderly, reaching out and stroking her fingers through his beardy growth, weakened by a faint, painful smile etching its way nervously onto his lips.

'I don't deserve you, Aggie. Never have. Never will!'

'And so you sing like a caged bird from a hidden part of yourself that I can't find, and you won't share. Whatever it is that's tearing you apart, I beg you – let it go. I'm not going anywhere. And I'm not going to stop loving you!'

'What would you say if I told you I killed a man?'

She pulled him to her, cradling his head against her chest. When the time was right he would share the dark secret which so haunted him. She would find a way to understand him, to empathise, to forgive him.

*

Holborn, London

Khalid Shah was in the midst of a conference call with a quondam best-selling novelist, ostensibly looking to reinvent himself by way of a collaboration with a highly touted Johnny-come-lately, when he heard the beep of his 'call waiting' alert and put the outmoded scribe on hold.

'Shah,' he snapped into the handset.

'Khal… I don't know quite what to say… other, that is, than I'm truly sorry,' Jon's voice croaked in a hoarse, uncertain tone.

'Jon…? Holy moly!' Khalid answered all aquiver, astonished to hear from the missing wunderkind after a prolonged hiatus of more than thirteen months. 'Bear with me for half a second… and don't you dare hang up!' He indelicately excused himself from the existing call and returned to his absentee friend.

'Where the hell have you been?'

'I shut myself off... from everyone.'

'Tell me about it... I'd almost given you up for dead!'

'It's a long and crazy story, Khal.'

'Let's get started... I've got all the time you need.'

'I'll keep it short, Khal... The thing is, I'm in a better place now,' Jon said, and went on to touch on the reasons for his newly discovered zest for life.

'You met someone, and severed all communication with the outside world? I missed you... I was worried about you!'

'She rocks my world, Khal... She's smart... and beautiful!'

Khalid's reply faded beneath an abrupt onrush of white noise, hissing and crackling in Jon's earpiece like a deep-fat fryer. As he held the handset away from his ear, a dull clunk terminated the call.

'No, no... shit,' he cussed, ramming the phone back into its cradle. He was at once shaken by its loud, chirruping ring.

'Inverness, of all places. I did a one-four-seven-one... It's a relief to know they have communications up there.'

'Oh Khal. I was broken beyond repair... beyond healing... and then I found myself in a place where I could start over on a fresh slate, picking up the pieces of a shattered life, where nobody gives a shit who I am!'

'But why the hell didn't you keep in touch? And what about the book I poured myself into, for two toilsome years of my life?'

There was an embarrassed silence. Jon knew first-hand of Khalid's endless passion and dedication in piecing together a hoard of material, scrutinising every word, line and paragraph with meticulous attention to detail.

'We can always pick up where we left off.'

'From a prison cell, when the cops finally catch up with you?'

'What are you saying?'

'That the police hounded me for months... not to mention the press. You're in a whole heap of trouble, my friend!'

Jon was stunned. 'I had no idea!'

'Don't you ever read the papers or watch TV?'

'Not if I can help it... I don't possess a TV... no telephones, or internet!'

'So you know nothing about anything? Whew!' Khal gasped, bringing to hand an old tabloid shoved into a document tray.

'Gold diggers: hunt for killer rock icon intensifies. Police search team unearth gruesome evidence linked to missing murder suspect,' he narrated, staring at the accompanying mugshot splattered across the page.

'Khal… Khal… I'll call you later from the hotel,' Jon panicked, curtailing the call, in need of some time alone to collect his thoughts.

Khalid castigated himself for his insensitivity, calling to mind a drunken conversation with Jon just days before his disappearing act. His mention of the girl on the train, the rugged, spectacular coastline, and the multi-coloured boats bobbing to and fro in the tiny harbour. He rooted inside the drawer of a filing cabinet to retrieve a tattered AA road atlas, promptly spreading it out into a space in the middle of his desk.

He narrowed down the smaller seaports within close proximity to the city of Inverness, carefully scrawling a circle around each of the likely candidates. Oban… Ullapool… Kennacraig… or perhaps even Mallaig.

*

5.15p.m.
Inverness

'Glory be… it seems I have a new man in my life,' Agnes said as Jon entered the lounge bar of their designated early-evening rendezvous point. 'You look almost human beneath the shaggy mane and facial hair… handsome even!' she added flatteringly, eyeing his neatly trimmed designer stubble and freshly coiffured locks.

'The cheeky git charged me double,' Jon moaned, greedily gulping down a large mouthful of ale from his pint pot.

'How so?' she impishly responded.

'He said my hair was unkempt, tousled and out of control.'

'And he wasn't far wrong!'

'I swear he used a pair of pruning shears!'

'As long as he didn't chop anything else off,' Aggie giggled, sidling up to him to plant a light peck on his cheek.

A nine-strong party of snappily clad office workers swept in off the street, evidently itching to celebrate the end of an arduous week's work, their braying chitchat sending the decibel level up a notch or two.

'What's your poison, Hamish?' an English-sounding voice yelped, fighting above the strains of Kylie's latest chartbuster.

'Grey Goose and tonic, Roger. Make it a double.'

'Did you say double…? Jesus, that guy in the corner, he's an absolute ringer!'

'What guy?' Hamish inquired.

'Sat next to the ravishing brunette… Surely not, it can't be!'

'Bugger me blind, Rog… you're bang on, it's what's-his-face… bloody JJ Gold!'

In one swift movement he swivelled round, lining up his phone's camera to capture a priceless off-the-cuff snapshot, but was inadvertently stopped in his tracks by a broad-bottomed glass-collector stepping into his path.

'Uh-oh… drink up, Jonathan!'

'What's up, Aggie… why the mad dash?'

'Let's just say that I'm camera shy… on your feet, man!' she urged, hurriedly ushering him out onto the street.

She bulldozed him round to the building's rear loading-bay, where they hunkered down behind a pair of giant rubbish receptacles. In the near distance the thud of multiple feet pounded the pavement.

His cover was finally blown.

TWENTY-ONE

Mid-October 2006
Granby

A THICK MASS OF COBWEBS clung to the ceiling joists of the old village hall. Silhouetted under the glow of a single lightbulb, Parish Councillor Evelyn Priestly held court before a sparse gathering of half-interested residents.

'I apologise for the interruption, but surely you must be mistaken!' Richard Turner butted in, responding to her opening announcement. 'Jonathan would never consider selling up without keeping me informed!'

'I'm awfully sorry, but your name escapes me...?'

'Richard Turner, ma'am, of Inglenook Cottage. I'm a long-standing friend of Jonathan's!' he self-importantly replied.

'Nevertheless, young man, I am in receipt of a letter passed on to me by Jean Bacon, Mr Gold's housekeeper, which grants us permission to hold a fund-raising bonfire party in the grounds of the Old Manor House on Sunday November the fifth. Essentially as a parting gesture before the property changes hands.'

Turner's blood instantly boiled within him. Spit bubbles formed on his lips, stretching into the corners of his mouth. To say more would merely add to his humiliation; the best plan of action was to make himself scarce.

*

'I've watched over that place like a hawk, and this is how you repay me!' he smouldered, pausing for a second outside of the mansion's iron gates. His thoughts were suddenly put on hold by the deep tones of a man's voice.

'You seem upset, young fella!'

'Whew... Mr Brownlow. You gave me a start!' Turner said jumpily, making out Jon's gardener beneath the streetlight.

'I decided to leave the meeting early myself... The wife's laid low with an attack of pleurisy.'

'I'm sorry to hear that.'

'The poor old gal's struggling like hell for breath; still, not to worry, eh… I didn't realise you were a friend of Jon's?'

'Huh… he seems to have difficulty in keeping friends!' Turner said, ramming his key into the cottage door's mortice lock.

'I'd become quite fond of him… I had a tear in my eyes when he rang to say goodbye.'

'He won't be coming back… is that what you're insinuating?'

'No, sadly he won't. The place holds too many painful memories.'

The door abruptly slammed shut, without as much as a polite goodnight.

*

Shortly after eight a.m. the guttural thrum of a mammoth HGV manoeuvring into position provided him with an unforeseen wake-up call. His eyes peered through a gap in the blind to focus on the flurry of activity below.

A revitalising flutter of hope lifted his spirits tenfold. A large removal truck was edging cautiously onto the Gold estate's driveway, under the diligent supervision of a tweed-clad estate agent.

Within moments of dressing he appeared on the doorstep, eager to attract the fop's attention with a wave of his hand.

'Good morning… I'm glad I caught you!'

'Greetings… is there anything I can help you with?'

'Indeed there is… The name's Richard Turner. I have a number of personal items belonging to Mr Gold stored out of harm's way inside my cottage. It appears to have skipped his mind to pass on a forwarding address.'

'Ha-ha, the celerity of the sale caught everyone on the hop. I'm merely acting under instructions from the vendor's firm of solicitors to transport an inventory of movable furniture and equipment to an alternative location.'

'And where might that be?'

'Sorry old chum, but for security reasons mum's the word; I'm sure you understand. Try contacting the legal eagles handling the sale – I'll scrawl down the name and number once I've unlocked the property's doors.'

'That would be most helpful… please don't let me keep you any longer,' Turner said smarmily, content to bide his time.

*

Three hours later

He cautiously tailed the first of two removal wagons, wending through a matrix of uneven B-roads towards a maze of industrial warehousing units, finally grinding to a halt in the very centre of a sprawling courtyard.

From a distance he observed the movements of the thickset driver, busy barking orders at a pair of youthful lackeys. Somewhat begrudgingly heeding his call, they responded by lowering a ramp from the van's rear doors.

Driven by a motorised pulley, an influx of bubble-wrapped and boxed items slowly worked their way beneath a high-reaching roller shutter, to be stacked neatly on top of one another by the super-efficient four-man crew.

'Hello, is that Knight, Hunt and Ripley?' Turner enquired on his Bluetooth car kit. 'Could I speak to Mr Franklin Hunt please?'

'Mr Hunt is currently tied up with a client,' the PA replied affectedly. 'I can check to see if his assistant, Mr Barnes, is free?'

'I'm sure you're more than capable of handling this!' he soft-soaped, setting out to explain his rather odd predicament.

Piece by piece he watched as the first consignment was offloaded, the vehicle swiftly replaced by the second van reversing into position, accompanied by an irritating beep-beeping sound echoing across the quadrangle.

'Gould, you say...? I'm afraid we don't have any clients going under that name,' the girl said, coming back on the line.

'No... Gold... G-O-L-D... as in JJ Gold, the famous singer!'

'If he was a client, I'm sure we'd know about it!'

'I took a number of his possessions in for safe keeping while he was away on tour, which I need to forward on to him!'

Reliably informed that the firm's senior partner was in the throes of conducting a 'hush-hush' private sale, Richard yet again found the call put on hold. His patience typically snapped. Gold was leading him on a merry dance. He toed the accelerator out of the yard like a demon, vowing somehow, some way to make him pay.

TWENTY-TWO

August 2009
Scottish Highlands

AWARD-WINNING JOURNALIST Duncan Bertrand had spent the bulk of his professional life working in London's hectic Fleet Street, before opting to call time on his illustrious career after thirty-odd years to retire to the Isle of Skye, his heart set on whiling away the days fishing and composing poetry. One look at a picturesque harbourside retreat had proved too great a temptation to resist and, dipping deeply into his tidy nest egg, he made his home perched by the sheltered bay overlooking a much-photographed row of colourful cottages.

'It never dawned on me there's little more than a pond between the pair of you,' Khalid half-yelled, responding enthusiastically to Jon's call amidst the hustle and bustle of Luton Airport's congested departure lounge.

'Had I known he was your mentor, I would've looked him up long ago!'

'So you know Skye?'

'I visited a couple of times to go over the plans for the croft's renovation. I can see it across the loch on a clear day.'

'Lucky you... all I get to see from my office window is a patch of wasteland which more resembles a bomb site.'

'My boat docks into Armadale at three-forty-five... Agnes, alas, won't be making the trip,' Jon said a mite forlornly.

'What a shame... I hope she's okay?'

'She's good... it's just there's a young couple hankering for a second viewing of the cottage her uncle bequeathed her.'

'It must be a wrench for her to part with it?'

'Not a bit of it... she truly can't wait to see the back of the old place... along with her unneighbourly fan club.'

A tannoy announcement in the background brought the chitchat to a momentary halt, drawing Khalid's attention to the illuminated flight information board. A flashing orange light depicted: *Inverness Gate B14.*

'They called my flight… I'll catch up with you in a few hours.'

'Over a couple of flagons of ale, I hope!'

'Duncan's a real wine buff. He's also a grumpy old man… you'll get on like a house on fire!' Khalid chuckled, and he was gone.

*

Three hours later
Skye

'How about some music?' the cabbie enquired, toeing it out of the ferry terminal towards the island's main settlement, Portree.

'Must we? I came here hoping for a bit of peace and quiet!'

'Don't be a killjoy… when this guy sings, even the birds sit up and listen!' the cabbie said, sliding a CD into the stereo system.

The all-too-familiar strains of his own mini-masterpiece 'Vagabond' pulsated through the small oval speakers. The driver gave a positive nod of the head and glanced sideways at his passenger, though remarkably with no hint of recognition.

'Whatever rocks your boat, pal,' Jon said, looking incredulously out of the window.

'Don't you think it's sad? Tragic, even?'

'You completely lost me.'

'The papers… they're saying he popped his clogs!'

'Who did?' Jon asked.

'JJ Gold, who else? Other than the bloody *Star*, that is.'

'And what's their take on it?'

'The bastards plastered a blurry image of him on the front page, dancing around a campfire… in the altogether!'

'Are you kidding me…? Where?'

'Papua New Guinea… the report said he'd been crowned king of some native tribe!'

'Ha… I once spent a night in Port Moresby, when my flight to Melbourne made an emergency landing in a freak storm,' Jon reflected. Through the cab window he could make out a dusky-skinned figure gesticulating from the tiny town's main street.

'Twenty-five, please… Sorry the music wasn't to your taste!'

'You have no idea!' Jon sniggered, handing him a twenty and a ten. 'Keep the change buddy, and keep listening!'

*

Three days later

The remains of a hangover lingered stubbornly, not helped by the unhealthy full Scottish fry-up provided by a surprisingly sprightly Duncan, who jumped into his trusty Land Rover and promptly turned the ignition key.

'It's been an absolute pleasure having you both… and thank you for allowing me to sit in on your sessions, Jon,' he said, swerving alarmingly around a mammoth combine harvester blocking up the narrow carriageway.

'What say we do it all again real soon, across the waves at Brightwater… that is, if we make it out of here in one piece?'

'Sounds good to me!' Duncan chuckled, ignoring the latter remark.

'Hell… give me enough time to dry out and sober up,' Khal chipped in, busily sifting through the contents of his briefcase on the rear seat. 'I've got reams of stuff. Lord only knows how I'm going to piece it all together!'

'When your ideas come unstuck, stick with it. Write badly… but don't stop writing!' Duncan softly advised, speaking from his own experience.

All of a sudden he gripped the wheel to yank the vehicle to one side.

'Wow… just look at him go!' Jon gasped, clocking the hindquarters of a huge red deer majestically clearing the hedgerow.

'They're pretty common on Skye, especially in the summer months.'

'The "Monarch of the Glen"… We see them too, along with our fair share of otters… including my little pal Tariq.'

'Tariq… how come?'

'Ha… it's just a name!'

'I get it!' Khal abruptly pitched in, spotting the Armadale pier perched high at the water's edge in the not too far distance.

'Tariq… as in a play on terracotta?'

'No, you retard… the solitude. It's like another world up here!'

'Come visit Brightwater, and knock your head into shape. Stay for as long as you like. The same goes for you, Duncan.'

The jeep came to a sudden juddering halt, a little too close for comfort to a party of dithering ramblers ambling slowly towards the terminal entrance, acknowledged by Duncan with a contrite wave through the open window.

'I'm sorry I ever doubted you!' Khal said, drawing Jon into a bear hug. 'With a bit of luck I'll see you next month.'

'Fingers crossed... must skedaddle... Safe flight!' Jon responded, slipping a scrap of paper torn from his writing pad into the palm of Khal's hand. With a rueful grin he skipped nimbly through parting double doors.

Khalid hopped back inside the Land Rover, semi-interestedly unfolding the note to take a peep, then looking immediately again.

Jon Ryan, Brightwater Croft, Knoydart, PH41 4PL, the scrawled handwriting read.

His sudden startled reaction did not go unnoticed by the man at the wheel. 'Dear fellow, is everything okay?'

'Jon Ryan, eh? The crafty so-and-so,' Khal muttered inaudibly, not letting on. 'Er... yes thanks... nothing to get excited about!'

*

Mallaig

He stared out over the waves from the ferryboat's bow, his hands shielding his eyes to block off the blinding glare of the sun, futilely attempting to pinpoint the jetty where Agnes would be awaiting his arrival.

She'd been right all along: he needed to break free from his cocooned existence, to interact now and then with normal everyday people, unbothered by the odd glance of recognition cast questioningly in his direction.

The vessel drew alongside the wharf's steps, creating a flurry of excitement among the babbling trekking party. Animated by the example of their intrepid leader, they clambered impetuously up onto the gangplank.

He strode towards the ticket office, ignoring the gesticulating arms of a shiny-headed stranger vying for his attention from up high on the jetty. Where was she? He found himself rattled by her odd non-appearance almost to the point of feeling sick.

'Over here, mate,' a half-familiar London twang hollered. It was the stranger, again motioning to him to make haste up the slope. With a peculiar lurch in the pit of his stomach, Jon realised he had seen this man before.

'What going on... is it Agnes?' he cried out, kicking his legs into a frantic sprint. 'What happened? Tell me, please!'

'She collapsed at the side of the road...'

'Where? When?'

'A couple of hours ago… I took it upon myself to rush her to the nearest hospital.'

'In Fort William?'

'Yeah… the Belford, A & E.'

'You took her there… and came back for me… why?'

'It seemed the decent thing to do. Get in the car, for Christ's sake!'

Jon dragged the door open and ducked inside, instantly feeling the force of the acceleration pinning him back against the seat. Speechlessly he clung on for dear life in anticipation of an impromptu white-knuckle ride.

'Holy mother of God!' he uttered in fright, darting an anxious glance towards the stranger. He was completely mystified by this man's uncanny knack of being in the right place at the right time whenever he found himself in a tight spot.

'Hold on tight!'

They continued in stony silence, tearing away from the small town at breakneck pace. Very soon his guardian angel manoeuvred the car onto the main drag and stepped even harder on the gas. The souped-up Clio fairly ate up the miles.

'First the bar-room brawl, and now this!' Jon said hoarsely, finally breaking the silence. 'I guess I owe you one!'

'You owe me nothing,' the altruist said matter-of-factly, guiding the car skilfully around yet another tortuous bend. His hands firmly gripped onto the wheel, and his eyes were steadfastly fixed upon the road's grainy surface.

'Do you have a name?'

'Just call me CJ… We're roughly half way.'

'Jonathan… I'm forever in your debt,' Jon mumbled appreciatively, offering a smile and a nod in preference to a handshake.

'I know exactly who you are!' CJ responded with a sly wink.

*

Belford Hospital, Fort William

The mid-thirties, white-coated pulmonologist looked up from checking the clipboard containing Agnes's notes and flashed her a warm, reassuring smile, sufficient to suggest there was nothing too out of the ordinary.

'How are you feeling, Miss Ryan?'

'I'm fine, thanks Doctor,' Aggie said groggily, shuffling upright onto a stack of pillows. 'I don't know what came over me!'

'The scan we did this morning revealed traces of a slight scarring of the lungs, but your breathing patterns are back to normal.'

'Thank goodness!'

'We're eager to determine if there's a family history of respiratory-related illnesses, such as asthma, bronchitis or cystic fibrosis... I was hoping you might be able to shed some light, and help me resolve this question?'

'My Mum died of pulmonary fibrosis in her early forties,' she said tentatively, reaching to the bedside for a tissue.

'Rest easy, Miss Ryan – most cases are not genetic.'

'So I'm not ready to punch my ticket to the pearly gates quite yet?'

'Absolutely not... although I'd like to run some tests on you at some point to explain your shortness of breath, over at the SPVU* in Glasgow,' he indicated, passing her his card. 'Give my secretary a call when it's convenient.'

He scurried off, handing over the reins to a friendly blue-uniformed ward manager. Assiduously wheeling an overbed table against Aggie's midriff, she proceeded to fan out an assortment of printed forms for her to sign.

'These are your discharge papers, lovey,' she said. 'Can I offer you a cup of tea while we wait for your hubby to arrive?'

'My hubby...? Jonathan... he-he, he's not the marrying kind!' she tittered, scribbling her illegible squiggle on the papers.

'He's a man of few words, that's for sure!'

'Who... Jonathan?'

'Your partner, the muscle man... He took off in a flash once he knew you were in good hands, mumbling something about the Skye ferry!'

Agnes frowned deeply. Jon could hardly be called muscular, or ripped. She opened her mouth to speak, but the matron had gone, speedily hotfooting it through the swing doors clutching a pile of empty clipboards.

*

Fort William

The jagged coastline gave way to a broad rolling glen. Shimmering in the sunlight, a mazy tributary carved its way into a distant loch, enveloped by an awe-inspiring backdrop of tree-flanked serrated mountains.

'So... what brought a cockney geyser up to the Scottish Highlands?'

---

* Scottish Pulmonary Vascular Unit, based in the Golden Jubilee Hospital in Clydebank, Glasgow

'Harry Potter,' was the laconic reply.

'What, he just waved his magic wand and, hey presto, here you were?'

'Ha-ha, not exactly!'

'Talk to me!'

'I worked up here as a rigger on a film crew, shooting the Hogwarts Express crossing the Glenfinnan Viaduct on the West Highland line from Fort William… you'll see it over on the right-hand side in a mile or so.'

'And you decided to set down roots?'

'Yep, that's about the size of it… I plied my trade in the music business for a good many years, calling in clients' debts and minding the rich and famous… Does the name Louis Kelly ring any bells?' he said, glancing Jon's way.

'I was signed to his company, Twilight, in the early days of my career… So he used you to carry out his dirty work?'

'He employed me to beat the living shit out of you… and, let's just say things didn't exactly go according to plan!'

Jon winced, screwing his face into a distasteful scowl. His mind instantly pictured Richard Turner's crushing multiple injuries, witnessed first-hand at his hospital bedside years before, sustained by virtue of a foolhardy attempt to intercept a professional hatchet-man preparing to inflict harm on his unsuspecting hero.

'Kelly thought he owned me.'

'He specified that I break both your legs.'

'Ouch… I guess Lady Luck smiled on me that night!'

'Me too. The guy came charging at me wielding an evil-looking spiked cudgel.'

'Turner… the bane of my life?'

'That's him. I saw him later spilling his guts in a TV documentary.'

'He stalked me for years!'

They chatted on as the car raced through an area of open farmland, dotted with shaggy Highland cattle peering above the hedgerows from behind their long ginger fringes, their wide-spreading horns gleaming in the bright sun.

'Kelly threatened to turn me in to the cops.'

'For doing the job he paid you to do?'

'We managed to square things up… after I showed up unexpectedly on his doorstep!'

'Hmm… I can only imagine!'

A series of right- and left-hand manoeuvres through a deserted housing estate sent the car practically tipping onto two wheels. Eventually it brought them onto a busier A-road, where within seconds they reached the A & E's main doors.

'I don't know what to say,' Jon said pensively.

'Jenkinson... on Cameron Avenue... Look me up some time,' CJ acknowledged, before again putting his foot to the floor.

TWENTY-THREE

September 2009

HIS DAY'S WORK almost complete, the yawning Khalid prepared to turn in for the night. All at once a distinctive ping alerted him to yet another incoming email. Upon inspection it proved to be from a North Leicester signature care facility.

```
Hey big brother, good news. Give me a shout on my
direct line at the foot of the page. I'll be in the
office until around two a.m. Best regards, Rashid.
```

The email's positive tone immediately roused his curiosity. Reclining in his chair with his legs stretched out over the paper-strewn desktop, he picked up the phone to ascertain what all the fuss was about.

'So, what's the story bro?'

'I'm buzzing, Khal… Guess what dropped through my letterbox yesterday?'

'Rash… it's late… spit it out!'

'The top brass promoted me – to manager, no less!'

'That's amazing, little bro!'

'With a substantial pay increase!'

'Let's celebrate over a curry, on you… I need a break from the book.'

'Shit bro, you must be gutted!'

'Gutted! Why?'

'The Channel Four documentary screened last night?'

An awkward silence prevailed. The public's obsession with Jon's disappearance simply refused to go away, encouraged in no small measure by the spate of bogus sightings frequently reported in the tabloid press.

'So where is he now? Chopping down trees in the Brazilian rain forest? Or maybe hunting down orphans for Madonna to adopt?'

'This one's legit, Khal!'

'How so?'

'The guy spilling the beans purported to be JJ's ex-manager!'

'David... David Bentley?'

'You know him? Jesus... I hate to be the bearer of bad news, but he's written a book; it's called *FINDING JJ*!'

'Shit... he emigrated Down Under. Three or four years ago, if I remember rightly,' Khalid mumbled incredulously, swiping his arm across the books and papers littering up his desk in a petulant outburst of temper.

'This probably isn't the best time... but I need your help...'

'Okay. Shoot... what's on your mind?' Khal said, trying to calm himself.

'I'm appealing my case.'

'Let it go, little bro. What's done is done.'

Rash had taken on his managerial responsibilities with relish and aplomb, already nurturing ambitions to step even further up the ladder; but to date his progress had been hampered by the stigma of his criminal conviction hanging over him.

'I need a lawyer, to help me clear my name!'

'I know the very man,' Khal said, springing back to life in a flash of inspiration.

'Don't keep me in suspense... who?'

'Dipak Mistry!'

'Amir's father? Have you lost your mind?'

'Trust me... I know exactly what I'm doing,' Khalid said self-assuredly. 'I'll call you back after I've chewed his ear off!'

*

King Richard's Chambers, Leicester

'There's an incoming call on line one, Mr Mistry,' long-standing PA Mary said through the intercom, interrupting the ageing criminal lawyer in the midst of running the rule over a comprehensive and detailed testimony.

'I'm rather busy, Mary... who is it?'

'Khalid Shah. He's anxious to talk to you.'

'Good gracious... Very well, put him through, Mary!'

He stalled for a moment, placing the papers he'd been perusing into the relevant folder. An apprehensive, queasy feeling began gnawing at his stomach, caused by his doubts about the exact nature of the call.

'Khalid... how are you? To what do I owe this pleasure?'

'I'm good, thanks Dipak… I heard a whisper you're considering closing up shop and riding off into the retirement sunset?'

'Nonsense… there's life in the old dog yet!'

'Glad to hear it. Allow me to cut to the chase, Dipak. I'm seeking a judicial review on my brother's case dating back zero-one.'

'On what grounds?'

'It would appear the defence failed to raise the issue of key evidence having been withheld during the original trial.'

'Bunkum! What evidence?'

'Information which exonerates Rashid from any involvement in the assault.'

'On the elderly shopper?'

'Yes… unequivocally!'

'Doubtless this new evidence arose from the lips of a somewhat unreliable individual, popularly known as Chukka?'

'I can't reveal my sources.'

Dipak recalled their heated altercation in the trial's aftermath; how he'd boxed clever to clear his son Amir of any wrongdoing, almost coming to blows with Khalid in the judge's chambers shortly after the verdict's announcement.

'And where exactly do I come in?'

'Sir Malcolm Grossman, the Director of Public Prosecutions… and more to the point your respected and esteemed friend…'

'The penny drops… and you'd like me to drop a discreet word in his ear?'

'Rashid was sentenced for a crime he didn't commit!'

'Be that as is it may, it's highly improbable the courts would even consider rehearing the case after all this time.'

Khalid bit his tongue, sipping at his water glass to compose himself. The natural thing to do was to go for the jugular, but to alienate Dipak may blow the whole thing. He thought again and adopted a more tactful approach.

'I'm asking you as a friend!'

'And I will, purely as a gesture of friendship, broach the matter with Sir Malcolm over supper this coming Saturday evening,' Dipak reciprocated in kind. 'But you'll need much more than mere argumentative proof.'

'I have more than enough evidence to seek an expungement.'

'Concrete proof?'

'In all its gory horror,' Khalid said with utter distaste, his mind forming a picture of the elderly victim's bruised and battered face.

'Photographic evidence?'

'Together with a written statement... from the lady's son.'

'You've been busy, Khalid!'

'Forgive me for opening up old wounds.'

'Literally, from the sound of things. Would you email me copies, to satisfy my curiosity?'

'They don't make for pleasant viewing...'

The dialogue turned to reflect upon his wayward son's disappearance, Dipak's concerns further deepened by the long list of various criminal misdemeanours for which Amir was alleged to be responsible.

'Rumour has it that he returned to India.'

'Amir's whereabouts remain a complete mystery. I don't know who or what to believe, though if the truth be told I'm long past caring.'

'How incredibly sad...'

'Hmm... I'll be in touch Monday, or Tuesday at the latest.'

'Just one more thing...'

'Spit it out!'

'Knock me down with a feather... let me sleep on it!'

TWENTY-FOUR

January 2007

THE COLD, DANK WINTER weather only served to fan the flames of Richard Turner's jittery temper. Index finger hovering over the phone's keypad, he shaped up to turn informer and rat on the star who'd been his world.

'Wade!' the policeman's voice echoed from an isolated location.

'Uh...oh... yes, detective... I'm not sure if you remember me... You stopped by at my cottage some considerable time ago to investigate a robbery at the singer JJ Gold's property, in the out-of-the-way village of Granby?'

'And that would be Mr Turner, if I'm not mistaken,' Wade replied in a facetious tone. 'What can I do for you, sir?'

'You specified I should contact you if any further information sprang to mind... Perhaps I should try your senior officer instead?' Turner said snootily, instantly put off his stride by the officer's hostilely brusque manner.

'Forgive me, sir, but I'm surrounded by a herd of huge dinosaur trucks; the noise is absolutely deafening!' the officer bawled, finding his wagon boxed in by a queue of vehicles pulling onto the service station forecourt.

'Officer... are you still there?'

'It's a really bad line. Shout out your number and I'll arrange for a fellow officer to get back to you before the end of the day!'

The loud rumble of a mammoth freighter thundering past on the abutting dual carriageway further marred the conversation, compounded by the smack of heavy raindrops lashing down onto the roof and windscreen.

'I'd appreciate a few moments of your time, if it's not too much trouble?'

'Bear with me,' Wade shrieked, skidding into a U-turn. 'Give me five minutes, and I'll call you back on this number.'

The line went dead. Turner flew into an angry, out-of-control rage, the blood flushing his skin with a mask of red fury. He glanced down at the latest bout of mud-slinging splashed in the centre pages of a daily tabloid sprawled on the kitchen table, described in all its damning detail by an attention-grabbing ex-supermodel.

POSSESSIVE SEX MONSTER JJ WRECKED MY CAREER, the caption spelt out, omitting to mention the well-documented addiction-related issues which had been largely responsible for the former girlfriend's fall from grace.

By Percy Tatchell 17:01, 10 Jan 2007, the accompanying credit read, confirming the 'poison pen' article came courtesy of an investigative journalist who thrived on digging up dirt about celebrities and public figures.

Turner brought up Google and typed briskly in the search box, soon finding himself confronted with a high number of hits headed by an official website. Clicking the mouse onto the highlighted text revealed a 'Call us' helpline.

'You've reached the offices of the Tatchell Media Group. Please leave your name and contact number, together with the reason for your call,' an impassive answerphone message specified.

'Er, yes, the name's Turner. I'm calling in regards to the incident at JJ Gold's home back in zero-five... I was an eyewitness!' he nervously jabbered, reciting his details in the manner of a Stephen Hawking soundalike.

He rose to stick the kettle on, his lips twisting in a leering half-smile. Within a matter of seconds the return call came in.

*

Leicestershire Police HQ

His mangy trainers perched on top of a three-drawer filing cabinet, the dulcet tones of Alicia Keyes poured through Hackett's in-ear headphones, shutting out the incessant chatter permeating every corner of the room.

A smartly attired colleague stepped into his eyeline in an effort to snap him out of his dreamlike stupor, frantically pointing to the trilling cordless phone obscured in part by his outstretched right foot.

'Hackett,' he announced, finally coming up for air.

'Dan... can you hear me?' DC Wade bawled semi-incoherently.

'Just about, JW. Where the hell are you?'

'In deepest darkest Herefordshire… stuck out in a place called Hay-on-Wye!'

'I can barely hear you, Jeffrey…'

'Cast your mind back to the sicko I interviewed in Granby.'

'The kiddie porn freak?'

'Got him in one,' Wade squawked, briefing him with the details of the call.

'Leave it with me… I haven't yet had the pleasure!'

'Be on your mettle, Dan; he's argumentative… and calculating!'

'The kid gloves are off, Jeff. Text me his number.'

*

Midday

Mentally drained from spending the entire morning catching up on paperwork, Hackett was sipping at his third black coffee inside the space of an hour when he clapped eyes on the to-do list scrawled on his notepad. The name Richard Turner instantly leapt out from the page, sufficient to direct his attention to the task at hand.

He was abruptly interrupted by the familiar bark of DI Philpott's voice battering as ever against his eardrums.

'Danny boy… I need a favour!'

'Fire away, guv.'

'Drop everything, and get your arse over to Melton Mowbray.'

'Don't tell me, guv… there's a phantom pork pie pilferer on the loose?'

'Very droll, I don't think,' the chief said peevishly, going on to fill him in on the latest in a string of armed robberies in the town.

'I have one more call to make,' Hackett said, quickly alert to the possibility of killing two birds with one stone.

*

Granby

Ably furnished with a sworn statement imparted by a beleaguered Asian sub-postmaster, the DS weaved the car through an obstacle course of winding country lanes, hampered only by the fading light of dusk.

The tall wrought-iron gates of the unoccupied Gold residence stood solemnly over to the lane's right-hand side, overshadowing a picturesque cluster of ivy-clad cottages which fitted Wade's description to a tee.

Oddly intrigued to meet the man who'd given his workmate the creeps, Hackett parked up and strode to the front door, alive to a slight movement in the curtain seconds before the unlatched lock pulled back on its chain.

'Who's there?' Turner's tremulous voice inquired.

'Detective Sergeant Hackett from the Leicestershire CID, sir. I left a voicemail on your phone to say I'd be dropping by?'

'I didn't receive any messages!'

'Timed at twelve-sixteen precisely, sir.'

'Concerning what exactly?'

'An incident which took place in the vicinity in 2005.'

'The JJ Gold break-in?'

'Spot on, sir... I understand you contacted my colleague DC Wade?'

'Who was too busy to take my call!'

'That's not strictly correct, sir... you caught him in the middle of an undercover operation.'

'You don't say... I feel I must warn you I already set the wheels in motion to ensure Jonathan Gold is brought to justice!'

'For what reason, sir?' Hackett gasped disbelievingly.

'The man's a killer... a brutal murderer!'

Hackett was dumbfounded by the boldness of Turner's statement. 'Whew, that's quite an assumption to make... May I step inside, sir?'

He entered the cheerless living area. Something about its occupant made his skin crawl, further exacerbated by the cottage's oppressive, clammy atmosphere.

'Perhaps I should've come forward sooner.'

'That would be an understatement, sir... particularly as the case is now closed.'

'But officer, there's a killer on the loose!'

'Perhaps you'd care to elaborate?'

'I watched the whole episode unfold right before my eyes from the observatory window upstairs... It was just awful!'

'DC Wade's brief clearly stated you were sound asleep at the time of the break-in... so why the startling about-face?'

'Put simply, I withheld the truth!'

Stumped for words in a state of perplexity and confusion, Hackett gestured towards the flight of stairs spiralling up to the building's top floor, desirous of checking out the bird's-eye view overlooking the Gold estate. Turner led the way.

'Take your time and tell me exactly what you saw,' Hackett said, straining his eyes to catch a glimpse of the sprawling grounds.

'A dead body, officer... dragged along the side path from the main house!'

'But sir, no reference was made to a dead body, either at the crime scene or in the aftermath of the break-in?'

Turner bowed his head in mock embarrassment, quickly laying the blame for his prolonged silence on a mawkish wave of sympathy for Gold, evoked by the distressing double loss of his beloved mother and father.

'I can only apologise,' he said insincerely.

'May I take a peep through the 'scope?' Hackett asked, stooping to the eyepiece.

He twisted the knurled dial to bring the forecourt into focus, watchfully homing in on the path running to the side of the property. With the lens trained on the self-same area, Turner must have witnessed every single detail.

'Powerful, isn't it?' Turner chuckled, stating the obvious. 'The pebbles are the size of golf balls!'

'Imagine fixing the zoom lens on the bloodied head of a human cadaver!'

'You seem to be implying it was a blow to the head that killed the deceased... These are very serious allegations you're making.'

'A deep gash, officer... on his upper forehead, which must've penetrated to his brain!'

'And you're certain the victim was dead?'

'Beyond a shadow of a doubt, officer... the body was still as stone!'

'It's not often that I'm speechless, sir,' Hackett sighed, bewildered beyond words with a mass of questions unasked and unanswered. 'We'll need you to come into the station to make an official statement.'

'But of course, officer,' Turner smirked unctuously, offering a limp handshake prior to showing him to the door.

*

7.00p.m.
Leicestershire Police HQ

'Maureen, can you ask one of the control room operators to run a PNC* check on a Richard Leslie Turner of number two, the Grange Cottages in

---

* Police National Computer

Granby,' Hackett barked, entering the main office in something of a hurry.

'You left it late, sonny boy; I was halfway out the door!' she snapped in a motherly tone. 'You sound a tad flustered?'

'A crazy day, Reenie... sorry, I clean forgot the time!'

He sat in front of his computer, still reeling from Turner's revelations, casting a casual glance at the evening paper dumped on his desk. A prominent local MP finally answered to sleaze allegations dating back to 1994, flatly denying any wrongdoing on his own part in a widely publicised 'cash for questions' affair.

He paused briefly to collect his thoughts. A sudden notion crossed his mind, succeeded by an online search via a digital archive brimming with the paper's back issues, extending way back to the late nineteenth century.

His mouth dropped open in amazement. He stared at Turner's pained mugshot dominating the front page, colourfully revealing the horrific extent of his wounds, complete with an exaggerated, attention-grabbing headline:

ACCIDENTAL HERO HOSPITALISED BY JJ HITMAN

Hackett chose to ignore the accompanying text, describing every detail of his gutsy intervention. Instead, he harked back to a previous conversation with Wade: *He's full of shit... I wouldn't trust a word he says...*

He cast doubts over the credibility of Turner's story, questioning his motives for stalking Gold from one home to the next. Perhaps he'd been party to the psychotic ramblings of a deranged fan upset over a perceived injustice, driven for whatever reason to humiliate him publicly. Either way he'd probably never know for sure.

TWENTY-FIVE

September 2009
Knoydart

'YOU ARE SO BEAUTIFUL... to me...' Jon warbled, hands akimbo. His passable imitation of the gravelly-voiced Joe Cocker had been stimulated by the goddess-like figure frolicking half-naked in the bay's shallow waters at low tide, captured entrancingly as the day's last rays of sunlight danced on the rippling surface.

'Come and join me, you scaredy-cat; it's invigorating!' Agnes shouted back, brazenly removing the top half of her bikini.

'I think not, exquisite though you are!' he replied, leaning back on his hands in the sand, feet pointed towards the water.

She crept quietly up on him with water cupped in her hands, soaking his chest through and darting back into the ocean whooping girlishly with delight, at long last enticing him to rip off his T-shirt and give chase.

'Pussy!' she yelled impudently, mercilessly taunting him for shrinking back as his feet touched the bone-chilling water.

He stumbled awkwardly towards her, grimacing at every step. From lying comatose in a hospital bed just two weeks earlier her near-miraculous recovery filled him with awe, acknowledged with a knowing smile to the heavens.

She dodged sideways to evade his grasp, sending him hurtling into a clumsy belly-flop, complemented by a full-throated roar.

'It's bloody freezing!' he hollered, reaching up to take her hand, only to again lose his footing and topple onto his backside.

'Did I ever tell you, you bungling, red-bellied fool, that I love you more than every single "I love you" ever voiced?' she said, pinning his shoulders to the sand, followed up with an affectionate kiss pressed to his salty brow.

He remained silent, and gazed lovingly into her deep brown eyes, pulling her closer to his wet and tingly skin. Their bodies entwined, rolling as one into the gently lapping surf, caught in the soft glow of the rising moon.

They paddled hand in hand through the swishing wavelets before crashing out on the dry sand, their eyes fixing skywards on a white-tailed eagle hovering above the water's surface ready to swoop down on his prey.

'A penny for your thoughts,' he casually remarked.

'If this were to be my last day on earth, there'd be no better place for me to be right now,' she responded with a flicker of emotion, playfully wresting his skull into the cleft of her softly cushioning bosom.

'I can hear your heart speaking to me,' he whispered.

'What's it saying?'

'It's telling me everything will be just fine.'

She worked her fingers through his tousled locks, feeling her heartbeat quicken. Her thoughts turned towards her impending MRI scan, primarily to diagnose the severity and true extent of the scarring on her lungs.

'The butterflies in my stomach are the size of bats!'

'Be positive and stay strong, Ag.'

'If only I could!'

'Heed the doc's advice – the tests are purely precautionary,' he said reassuringly, trying hard to conceal his own uneasiness.

'Learn to live in the moment, my Mum used to say.'

'Wise words, indeed!'

'Only the moments we cherished proved too few and far between.'

They towelled themselves down in the darkening twilight before meandering slowly through a trail of autumn leaves, their once bright colours fading to a yucky brown. In the distance the croft lurked in the shadows under the trees, urging them to up the pace to a light jog.

She gazed back; her frown had changed to a broadening smile.

*

8.15p.m.

His wet hair plastered to his head following a piping hot shower, Jon moseyed into the kitchen-diner clutching his trusty old Martin acoustic guitar. He sank down into the sofa's cushions and picked at the strings, eager to serenade his sweetheart.

'If only you believed in you, the way that I believe in you
You'd smile at me and say that everything will be okay.

And brush aside the nagging qualms then melt into my loving arms
And as we gently sway, the clouds of doubt will wilt and fade away.
I gaze into the moonlit sky and wish upon a star
And all I ask is you'll believe in all that you are.
So walk with me and talk to me and be just who you want to be
And hold on to my hand and let's retrace our footprints in the sand.'

'Jon, that's beautiful!' Agnes exclaimed, rendered agog midway through deboning a jumbo rainbow trout. 'Is it an old song?'

'No, I just wrote it... for you. It'll need some work to knock it into shape.'

'So it doesn't have a title yet?'

'Huh, that's the easy part!'

'Well go on then... tell me what it is?'

'Must you know all and everything?' he teased.

'Jon... you'll be wearing this bloody fish in a moment!' she said, glowering at him back over her shoulder.

'Okay, okay... what else but "Song for Agnes"!'

TWENTY-SIX

King Richard's Chambers, Leicester

THE CLOCK ON THE office wall ticked towards six p.m., at last convincing Dipak Mistry to knock off for the day. His severe fatigue was made worse by the slow pangs of hunger gnawing at his innards like a half-starved rat.

He was on the point of shutting down his computer when the distracting ping of an incoming email caught his attention. The sender's address was curiously unfamiliar:

```
From: KShah@KSMedia.com
Subject: Photos/Letter
```

Clicking the mouse on the accompanying attachment, he forced his mind towards full alertness, impatiently drumming his fingers on the base of the keyboard while the pixelating images merged into shape.

Tears began to form at the corners of his eyes, fostered by a feeling of intense shame and regret. He backed giddily away from the screen, his face contorting into a mask of pure loathing. His worst fears had been realised.

The true horror of his son Amir's evil handiwork hit him like a sledgehammer blow, depicted in a montage of gory headshots of a sadly disfigured aged female gazing heart-rendingly into the photographer's lens.

He stared long and hard at the enlarged images, studying every contour of her severely swollen face. The heavy bruising around her half-closed eyes faded to yellowing purple smears, turning his stomach like ground glass.

The piercing warble of his phone provided a welcome distraction, his hand grabbing at the receiver in a flash.

'You're working rather late, sweetheart… is everything okay?' his wife Zara asked, her voice soft, brimming with concern.

'I've had better days, my dear.'

'Dipak, my darling… what's the matter?' she asked, sensing all was not well.

'Zara… where did we go wrong?'

*

8.30p.m.

Zara frowned at him pushing his food around the plate. Unnerved by his continued silence, broken only by the clink of cutlery on the plates, she could no longer bear it and spoke through the uncomfortable quiet.

'It has something to do with Amir… doesn't it?'

'Forgive me, Zara darling… it has been just an awful day!' he responded, promptly excusing himself from the table.

He poured his third large scotch and sipped noisily from his tumbler. All of a sudden he caught a glimpse of a fox dashing across the adjoining meadow, its reddish-brown fur rapidly disappearing into a thicket of spruce saplings.

He unlatched the sliding doors leading out onto the patio and stepped outside. Slowly treading the dirt path surrounding the large rectangular lawn, he paused to brush away a stray tear from his cheek, shed for the son who'd broken his heart.

The cold clean autumnal air partially raised his sagging spirits, before being replaced in the blink of an eye by the monstrous images implanted in his head. What could possibly have spurred Amir into committing such a heinous act?

Khalid's words resounded in his ears, penetrating through his skull and into his pounding guilt-wracked brain. 'You deserved to be disbarred,' his one-time protégé had forewarned, pulling no punches in his stinging verbal attack.

A helpless feeling nestled in the pit of his stomach. His past had come back to haunt him, forcing him into the tightest of corners. He'd lied at trial, he could not deny it, and the only way out was to set the record straight.

He sauntered back inside. He would take Rashid's case, and fight tooth and nail to overturn his conviction, in what would prove to be the closing arguments of a long and, for the most part, distinguished career.

TWENTY-SEVEN

A DEAFENING JACKHAMMER shook the office building's foundations to the core, its sporadic judder interspersed with a constant volley of effing and blinding spewing from the lips of a sizeable gang of industrious road-workers.

A light ringing barely audible above the racket prompted him to shut the open window and rush to the phone. His expression turned to one of confused surprise, sparked by the unfamiliar number flashing on the display.

'Khal... it's me, Jon!'

'Glory be... Aren't you taking this incommunicado crap a little too far? I left messages all over the place begging you to call me!'

'The pub phone's been temporarily out of order.'

'Try pulling the other one!'

'It's true... though you'll be pleased to know I solved the problem.'

'You bought a mobile?' Khal gasped.

'Don't be stupid... Add this name and number to your list of contacts,' Jon shot back, 'before my phone card runs out of credit.'

Khalid tutted in exasperation, fumbling around with his free hand to search for a writing pad and pen. His clumsy efforts sent a stack of loose files tumbling to the floor as he endeavoured to scribble down the number.

'What was the name again?'

'Carl Jenkinson... affectionately known as CJ.'

'Who's he when he's at home?'

'A friend... a handyman... very handy indeed!'

'Jon... I don't quite know how to put this, but we've run into a bit of a problem.'

'Uh-oh... what's wrong?'

'It's the book. It seems someone else has beaten me to it... and get this, they're shooting a TV documentary to go out alongside its release!'

'You're kidding me… who?'

'Your ex-manager.'

'Louis Kelly? He can't string a sentence together!'

'David Bentley, to be exact.'

'David! We were best pals… childhood friends!'

'He claims to have your blessing.'

'What are you insinuating? He emigrated Down Under four years ago. I haven't heard anything from him since!'

The phone cut off abruptly, leaving Khalid to think in silence. He knew he'd hit a sensitive spot, made doubly clear by Jon's uncharacteristic petulance. But something indicated he wasn't being entirely honest with him.

*

Two hours later

Khalid had typed the name David Bentley into Google and was poring over a half-page resumé of the media man's rise to prominence as head of the research and strategy department of Australian TV giants Network Ten.

He relocated to the channel's easily navigable website, scrolling through a whole mishmash of information and ads, busily clicking at a selection of *Find out more* tabs, until he happened upon a page of *Upcoming documentaries.*

A highlighted news-ticker caught his eye, crawling from right to left across the foot of the screen, its content focused on the up-to-the-minute pop-culture gossip. It was tailed by a scoop which made him look again.

Hunt for eccentric star put on back burner due to accidental death of film-crew cameraman… click here to read more… the report spelt out, prompting him into hitting the page to peruse the full story:

> Filming on a prospective documentary believed to include recent footage of missing rock icon JJ Gold was yesterday suspended until further notice following the tragic death of highly respected cinematographer Nigel Evans. Reports confirm Mr Evans suffered a harrowing fall from an overhead gantry erected close to a lofty escarpment in a remote region of the Papua New Guinean highlands. The directors and staff of Network Ten wish to extend our deepest sympathies to Nigel's family and loved ones.

Khalid let out a long, astonished sigh, speedily lowering in pitch to a relieved horse-laugh. A colourful collage of snapshots lay directly beneath the feature article, ranging from the merely humorous to the outright absurd.

'Would you credit it,' he said breathily, pulling on his reading specs to take a closer look. A shaggy-haired JJ lookalike continued to lead the world's media a merry war-dance, culminating in the death of a production crew member. He seethed at the senselessness of it all, well aware he owed Jon the very humblest of apologies.

He scurried upstairs to pack for an overnight flight to Kuala Lumpur, vowing to bury the hatchet immediately upon his return.

TWENTY-EIGHT

Late September 2009
Mallaig

A DISOBLIGING EX-SEAFARER led the way across a sodden stretch of wasteland, looping round to the rear of a decrepit fisherman's cottage. A neglected albeit sturdy-looking vessel sat idle among a hoard of assorted junk.

'Is that it?' Carl Jenkinson muttered. 'It's an eyesore!'

'Fifty quid and she's all yours.'

'Come off it! That thing hasn't set sail since Frank Sinatra was a boy!'

'I'll have you know she's still seaworthy!'

'And I'm a Dutchman… I'll give you a tenner to take it off your hands.'

The wily old codger winced and sucked air through the gaps in his teeth, briskly stepping to one side to avoid a small-dog-sized rat scurrying perilously close to his boots from beneath the boat's rotten bottom boards.

'Oops, where did that come from?'

'Shit… there's hundreds of them…! The only thing I'm likely to catch in that crate is a dose of the plague!' CJ laughed incredulously, catching a glance of a gaping hole amid a patched-up section of ruptured planks.

'All right then, thirty!' the old scallywag grunted.

'Twenty… and not a penny more!'

'You tight-fisted young bugger… Ah, go on then,' he begrudgingly agreed, ignoring CJ's attempted handshake.

*

The next day

'A birthday present… for Jonathan? Come off it, CJ, you're having a laugh. It's nothing but a beaten-up old rust-bucket!' Agnes said mock-despairingly, casting a disbelieving eye over the splinter-damaged wreckage.

'She's completely watertight!'

'Hallelujah…! He'll think we're both stark raving bonkers.'

CJ coughed, concealing his mouth behind his hand to stifle a loud guffaw gushing from his lips. He kicked out carelessly at a badly misshapen slat, wedging his size-ten Doc Marten in amongst a tangle of splitting plywood.

'Well, don't just stand there!'

Aggie's appalled expression turned to unbridled glee, causing her nearly to split her sides laughing. Her body collapsed forward onto the boat's gunwale, her watery, half-closed eyes looking up to meet his gaze.

'Billy Macpherson,' she said randomly.

'You mean Merlin… the Falklands war veteran with the long silver beard?'

'Got him in one!'

'Where does he fit in all this?'

'He's forgotten more about boats than you'll ever know.'

'And you reckon I should seek a second opinion?'

'My thoughts exactly!'

*

Two days later

The promise of an early heart-starter in his favourite watering hole proved sufficient for Billy to break up his everyday routine. It was retrieved by the landlord from the bar's top shelf in the liquid form of a Glenmorangie single malt.

The silky smooth liquor slid blissfully down their throats, putting fresh colour in both men's cheeks in preparation for the upcoming task. They strolled slowly towards the patch of land where the abandoned skiff came into view. It was keenly observed by the Merlin lookalike, whose wild eyebrows raised in evident surprise.

'How much did she set ye back?'

'Twenty smackers.'

'It seems ye have yourself a wee bargain, laddie.'

'What? That's fantastic!'

'I reckon she's between forty and fifty years old… which in the overall scheme of things is nay age for a durable timber vessel.'

He ran his hand along the thick sheer strake, casting an eye over the planks running from stem to stern to check for signs of dry rot. His fingers dug vigorously into the wood to seek out any crumbling spots.

'So she can be made seaworthy?'

'I see no reason why not. Pretty much all of the hull is the original wood, though a few of the seams look to have dried out.'

'Brilliant... What do I do next?'

'You'll be needing three or four new planks... teak would be preferable... and then there's the matter of a half-decent outboard.'

'What'll the damage be... off the top of your head?'

'Hmm, it won't come cheap... roughly three hundred I'd say.'

A sudden and unexpected downpour, made all the more unusual by the placid blue sky overhead, cut short their little tête-a-tête. Left with no other choice they dashed for cover beneath a nearby corrugated canopy.

'Another wee dram perhaps?'

'Now you're talking my language, laddie!' Billy cackled through his whiskers, purposefully striding back into the rain.

*

October 8th 2009

'Happy birthday to you, happy birthday to you, happy birthday dear Jonathan... happy birthday to you!' Agnes and CJ wailed in near unison, after which they counted from one to three before casting aside the canvas tarpaulin.

Jon started back in sudden surprise, his jaw dropping in sheer astonishment. He stared at them both, his face giving nothing away, trying in vain to articulate what he was thinking. But the words just wouldn't come.

Aggie shot an 'I-told-you-so' look in CJ's direction, before averting her glance to Jon, striving with some difficulty to read his expression.

'Please say something!'

'Ugh... b–but, I don't know w–what to say,' he stammered, unable to tear his eyes away from the unexpected gift.

'Sorry, pal,' CJ cut in, attempting to clear the air.

'I love her!' Jon said softly.

'Jon...? What are you saying?' Aggie warily responded.

'Almost as much as I love you!'

He threw his arms around her, dragging her into a spontaneous jig a trifle close to CJ's toes. Not wishing to be left out, CJ reached into his cold box to grab a bottle of champers which he duly cracked open in a cascade of fizz.

Loud outbursts of laughter echoed across the workshop, their relief palpable at Jon's unexpected reaction. More hugs and kisses followed as the bubbly began to flow, culminating in the ring of glasses chinking together.

'Cheers!' Aggie yelped.

'Wait… shouldn't we be smashing the bottle over her bow?' Jon intimated, momentarily putting the toast on hold.

'At sixty-odd quid a throw? Not likely!' CJ shot back.

'*Spee–ee–eech!*' Aggie bellowed, half in jest.

'Okay, okay… I name this vessel *Hummingbird*!'

All at once Jon's expression changed. 'But this is not about me…'

He set his glass down and withdrew a half-folded buff envelope from inside his coat pocket, the originating address clearly marked in the top corner: *SPVU, Golden Jubilee Hospital, Clydebank, Glasgow G81 4DY*.

'My test results… dammit!'

'I took the liberty of opening it…'

'And?'

'You got the all clear!'

For one stunned second she stood frozen, glancing at him as if seeking reassurance. She'd feared the worst would happen, but his words of comfort lifted her spirits tenfold. Overjoyed she clambered up onto the boat's rear seat, raising up her glass in tomboyish fashion. The day was young, and a joyous double celebration had begun.

TWENTY-NINE

August 2009

EARLY RISER RICHARD TURNER awoke to a fine sunny morning, drawing open the curtains before squeezing into a pair of royal blue Speedos. However, adjudging them to be far too skimpy in view of his noticeably bulging waistline, he quickly changed his mind and slipped instead into a lightweight towelling bathrobe, pilfered some years before from the laundry basket of a five-star London hotel where he'd been attending a three-day seminar.

After habitually logging into his computer, a Huffington Post headline grabbed his attention:

In Pursuit Of Gold: Hunt For JJ Hots Up
New footage emerges of reclusive rock star

He ran his mouse over the link, noting JJ was indeed alive and well, holed up with an ancient tribe known as the Korowai in a mountainous region of the state of Papua New Guinea, far away in the south-western Pacific.

Turner snarled like a rabid dog, examining the article with hate-filled eyes. 'They'll hang you out to dry the minute you set foot back on British soil,' he growled maliciously, slamming down the PC's lid in a small fit of anger.

Through a haze of condensation clinging to the downstairs windows he spotted a police patrol vehicle crawling slowly by. It instantly reminded him of the incompetent CID double-act whose investigations had led to his doorstep.

He scrolled through the list of contacts stored on his Nokia handset, searching out the entry marked 'DC Jeffrey Wade'. A slip of his forefinger led him to tap instead onto the name 'Deirdre Turner', the chirpy reply catching him unawares.

'Dickie, darling! What a nice surprise!'

'Mum... is that you?'

'Of course it is, sweetie!'

'It didn't sound like you, that's all,' he lied. 'I wondered how you were keeping?'

'I'm good, darling… You're not in any trouble are you?'

'No–no–no Mum… there's just something I've been meaning to tell you…'

A melodramatic fairy tale spouted glibly from his lips, pertaining to his crucial cloak-and-dagger role in assisting a crack task force unit assigned to hunt down a vicious killer. It was taken by the lady with her usual pinch of salt.

'Goodness, Richard, it sounds awfully risky!'

'I've been asked to go on television, as part of a Channel Four documentary.'

'Wow… how exciting!'

'I'll keep you in the loop pending the programme's scheduled airtime.'

'Please do, darling… Oh, by the way, your Aunt Phoebe was asking after you. She Skypes me from time to time.'

'You're online… on Skype?' he said incredulously.

'Since February.'

'So you finally took my advice?'

'No Richard, I did it completely off my own bat… Must dash, sweetie!' she subtly hinted, giving up on the son she gave up on long before.

*

The afternoon of the same day

A short and to-the-point message on DC Wade's cell phone persuaded Turner to call in to the main police switchboard. His overbearing, self-important tone proved sufficient to rub the operator up the wrong way.

'DS Hackett is an extremely busy man.'

'Huh, you don't say… In which case, perhaps you'd do me the courtesy of putting me through to someone in authority!'

The girl put him on hold, not taking kindly to his over-the-top ear-bashing, expressed in an ill-mannered tone more befitting a spoilt teenage brat.

'Maureen, have you seen Dan Hackett…? I've got a hot-headed ignoramus holding on line three, who's insisting he talks to him!' she stressed, calling through to the desk constable for some much-needed support.

'I'm looking at him now, through the glass panels of DI Philpott's office… Wait a sec, they're wrapping up as we speak.'

The DS sauntered back to his desk grim-faced and plonked disconsolately down in his chair. The boss's brutal tongue-lashing reverberated inside his head, not eased by the cacophony of chatter prevalent in the room.

'Dan… there's a call for you… irate by the sound of things!'

'Okay, Reenie… did you get a name?'

'Turner… Richard Turner.'

'Bloody marvellous… the self-same jumped-up nobody who filed a complaint against myself and Jeff Wade earlier today!'

'Uh-oh… good luck with that!'

A disdainful leer flitted across his face. The mere mention of the guy's name made his skin crawl, soon underlined by his obnoxious manner.

'About time too… huh!'

'And a very good afternoon to you, sir… What can I do for you on this bright sunshiny day?' Hackett led off, facetiously.

'Don't humour me, detective!' Turner insolently answered back, launching into a bitter and vitriolic verbal assault. 'Your wanton disregard for public safety is utterly scandalous; there's a cold-blooded killer on the loose!'

'Whoa, whoa, let me stop you right there. I took no pleasure in my superior's decision to prematurely close the case!'

Turner became uncharacteristically tongue-tied. Things were not going the way he'd planned. Someone somewhere had to carry the can, but Hackett's response caught him totally off guard. His voice reduced to a low murmur.

'Three long years!'

'Come again?'

'Free to come and go as he pleases!'

'Could it be you bear some form of grudge against JJ Gold?' the DS speculated. 'I seem to recall a disfigured Grammy award concealed in that observatory of yours. And what about the defaced poster dangling on the back of the door?'

'It was j–just a copy, a fake… the Grammy!'

'And in a fit of pique you smashed it to smithereens?'

'We all have our moments!'

'And my hands are tied, Mr Turner.'

'After sitting on them for far too long, officer!'

Hackett ignored the snide remark, choosing instead to continue grilling him about his relationship with the missing star.

'He upset you somehow... didn't he?'

'He may've done, but I fail to see the relevance...'

'Are you seeking your pound of flesh, Mr Turner?'

'What? I called as a matter of courtesy!'

'To rub my nose in it?'

'H–how ridiculous... w–what on earth are you implying?'

Turner's tremulous response indicated that Hackett had struck a raw nerve, prompting him to chance his arm and go straight for the throat.

'You're becoming a pest, Mr Turner.'

'This is outrageous!'

'And once your ridiculous complaint is filed under "waste paper" I don't want to hear another peep out of you!'

'But... I'm not done yet!'

'Do I make myself clear?'

'Um. Uh... I suppose so!' Turner at long last succumbed, snivelling like a schoolboy chastened by his headmaster.

'Now... is there anything else I can do for you?'

'Nothing... nothing at all!' he feebly replied, his voice disappearing in the wake of a short sharp clunk in the earpiece.

*

Six days later

'Can't a man get five minutes' peace?' Hackett lamented, fumbling for his phone midway into a Sunday-evening power nap.

'Switch on your TV right now, Danny boy... and punch in Channel Four on the remote,' DI Philpott's voice urged.

'Half a sec, guv... what's happening?'

'It's your new best pal... it seems he's taken it upon himself to blow the whistle on JJ Gold. Call me back in half an hour!'

Hackett activated his brand-spanking-new HDTV, promptly feeling the blood rise to his cheeks. Turner's head filled the screen, his heavily made-up features contributing to give him the appearance of a waxwork dummy.

'And as for the police... well! It was like talking to a brick wall...' he rabbited on, as Hackett switched off.

THIRTY

November 2009
Mallaig

'I'M LOOKING FOR A Mr Carl Jenkinson,' the trilby-clad, overcoated stranger put firmly, sneaking stealthily into the lock-up. Caught in the thick of it, CJ and Jon were taking it in turns to smooth down a pile of bowing slats.

'Who shall I say wants him?' CJ said, setting down the hefty jack plane, glad of the excuse to take a short breather.

'Detective Inspector Raymond Menzies of the Metropolitan Police in Scotland Yard, London, sir,' the giant of a man proclaimed, carefully checking Carl's features against a mugshot image displayed on his swish new iPhone.

CJ gazed sullenly towards the floor, his face wearing a defeated expression. He'd known all along that this day would eventually come, but that it should be at what was perhaps the happiest period of his life cut into his heart like a knife.

'I guess my luck finally ran out.'

'I am required to read you your rights...'

'Go ahead,' he said sadly.

'You are now under arrest for the brutal assault of one Dennis Arthur Hickling in the London Borough of Islington on May the sixth 2007. You do not have to say anything but it may harm your defence if you do not mention when questioned something which you later rely on in court.'

A flurry of movement in the doorway revealed a stockily built blue-uniformed figure, his shovel-like right hand clutching a pair of glinting handcuffs. Step by step he drew closer, eyed with suspicion by the unfazed CJ.

'Chill out, big boy!' he said, standing his ground.

He was spared any bother by an unlikely ally in the shape of the senior officer. 'Back off Docherty, there's a good lad!'

The titan paused mid-step, acknowledging his superior with a nod of assent. He teetered backward slightly, slyly attempting to remove a bead of sweat on his brow, complemented with a giveaway smile of relief.

'Take a look at this,' the chief murmured, unearthing a frayed-edged photograph from his overcoat pocket. It was a heart-rending depiction of a battle-scarred, wheelchair-bound man staring pitiably into the camera-man's lens.

'A far cry from the animal that terrorised the East End back in the day,' CJ said, swallowing hard and exhaling sharply.

Behind the boat's stern on the opposite side of the room Jon's heart began to race like a runaway train. He shielded his face in the hood of his tracksuit top, determined to avoid making any kind of eye contact.

'The *Hummingbird*... what'll I do?' he said to CJ, sniffing.

'She's all yours, Columbus!' CJ responded, squeezing his sinewy body between the gunwale and the lockup's wall.

They clasped one another in an emotional embrace, disrupted by the rumble of the police wagon reversing onto the drive. A moment later Jon watched through a haze of restrained tears, as in a surge of acceleration his friend was gone.

*

Fifteen miles east of Mallaig

'So where are we headed?' the prisoner tentatively inquired, shifting uncomfortably in the vehicle's upright back seat.

'Burnett Road clink,' the big man said.

'Mongo's rarely the most talkative of souls... He's referring to our main headquarters up in Inverness,' the chief pitched in. 'You'll be placed in a holding cell overnight, pending a flight tomorrow to London Luton airport.'

'First class I hope,' CJ joked.

'Very funny!' the DI coughed, pausing to clear his throat. 'Your friend back there... how long have you known him?'

'Let me think a moment... seven years, at a guess... Why?'

'There was something familiar about him... beneath the whiskers and shaggy locks... Does he have a name?'

'Tommy... Tommy Ryan,' CJ lied, making light of the question. 'He's a long-lost descendant of Long John Silver's pal, Ben Gunn!'

His taut muscles tensed, sending a quiver of fear shooting down his spine. Solving the riddle of Jon's whereabouts had become a national obsession, ramped up on a daily basis across the media. Could it be the web of fate was closing in around him, or was the detective's naturally suspicious mind simply working overtime?

He stared pensively out of the vehicle's side window, for once blind to the ruggedly undulating landscape. Through every twist and turn the hues of autumn stretched vividly to the horizon and beyond, enriched by the outreaching rainbow-coloured trees trembling in the gentleness of the light, wispy breeze.

The DI's gruff voice pulled him back to the present, at once fading beneath a horribly distorted call alert. He snorted a short, cynical laugh, tuning his ears to a celebrated Rolling Stones classic: *'Da-dah, da-da-dah… da-da-dah,'* the opening riff to 'Satisfaction' rang out, sparing him the aggravation of yet another grilling.

He leaned back against the headrest to feign sleep, fiercely determined to repulse all efforts at conversation. Should the subject threaten to rear its ugly head again, he would bite his tongue and simply play dumb.

*

Eventide
Brightwater Croft

'And that was that… the Chuckle Brothers led him out to the meat wagon and he just disappeared into the sunset… gone… out of our lives in a New York minute!' Jon reflected, breaking the news to the stunned Agnes.

She glimpsed the anguish etched on his face, shaping her body into the curve of his back to somehow take away his pain.

'As of this moment, it's back to plain old me!'

'Huh… I guess things could be a whole lot worse,' he whispered back.

They sank down together into the softness of the sofa, their bodies separated by his Martin guitar. Within moments he grabbed it by the neck and began to play, his lithe fingers plucking at the strings to carve out a melancholy tune.

'Sing to me,' she interjected, her head reclining in amongst the high-piled cushions. She closed her eyes and slipped into a serene state of semi-consciousness, instantly captivated by his off-the-cuff rendering:

'Imagine a world of me without you
Doomed to a joyless existence, under a sky of featureless blue

Where the icy stillness of winter makes way for a flowerless spring
In a barren lifeless woodland where the birds no longer sing
And teardrops fall in rivulets, disguised as morning dew
It's a melancholy unimaginable world of me without you.'
'Such poignant words,' she sighed.

She perceived a worrisome shift in the contours of his face, as his thoughtful, dreamy eyes gave way to a strained, bulging, hollow look.

'What's wrong?' she shrieked, wheezing spasmodically.

'I'm a wanted man, Aggie... and guilty as hell. They hunted CJ down... relentlessly! And now they're coming for me!'

THIRTY-ONE

December 2009
Granby

'DADDY, I SPOTTED A MAN from one of the cottages over the road spying on me from his upstairs window,' fourteen-year-old Rebecca Watson disclosed at the breakfast table, preparing herself for a full-on week of private education at a prestigious independent school located in the abutting county of Rutland.

'That's disgusting! William, we must do something!' mother Beatrice snapped, twisting round to meet her spouse's gaze head on, wary of displacing the Prada sunglasses perched on her perfectly coiffed blonde hair.

'Are you one hundred per cent certain, darling?' wealthy banking magnate Bill asked, peering sternly above his *Financial Times*.

'I saw something glinting in the sunlight while I was dressing… then the second I moved to the window he ducked to one side!'

'We must call the police, Billy!' Beatrice said agitatedly.

'Let's not be too hasty,' he replied, his voice sinking to a growl of restrained anger. 'Explain it to me slowly, sweetheart.'

Despite the tiny worry lines creasing her ivory-coloured skin, she spoke in a manner far beyond her tender years, painting a picture of the circular shapes reflecting into the room from the lens of a form of magnifying device.

'A telescopic lens… it has to be!' Bill roared, condemning the man's conduct, and vowing to take swift, decisive action.

Beatrice rose from her chair to gather up the dirty tableware, slinking across the gleaming tiled floor to load the dishwasher.

'You used to be friends with Douglas Jennings… didn't you, darling?'

'We were golfing buddies… why?'

'I heard a whisper he was promoted to Chief Constable,' she said, dropping a subtle hint.

'Indeed he was... Wait a sec – who's a clever girl?' he whooped, scampering off to his study to renew his auld acquaintance.

*

Two days later – 9.30a.m.

One too many large vodka and Cokes the night before had left Richard Turner nursing a whale of hangover. It was further compounded by the rustle of paper on the doormat, soon followed by the sharp rap of the letterbox.

He casually ripped the corner from the official-looking envelope, and placed the two-page missive in front of him on the table. Beneath the printed heading the words EVICTION NOTICE hit him right between the eyes: '*You are hereby notified that you are required to vacate the premises of the undersigned within seven days...* '.

The order sent him into a disturbingly hysterical screaming fit. A criss-cross of blue ugly veins began protruding from his forehead. '*Unneighbourly and lurid conduct*,' the text cited, supported by a lengthy list of residents' complaints condemning his lewd and inappropriate behaviour.

Just then, the landline phone rang, almost instantly switching on to his impersonal recorded message:

'*This is Richard A. Turner. I'm busy right now. Please speak clearly and leave a message after the tone.*'

'Richard. It's Bob Fisher. Perhaps you'd be good enough to call me at your first opportunity?' the head of staff's message squawked through the tiny loudspeaker, its impassive tone serving only to arouse his suspicion.

He gathered his wits by means of a sluice at the kitchen sink, feeling his anger begin to wane amidst his crazed confusion. He scrolled down his list of contacts to locate Fisher's direct line. Surely the day couldn't get any worse.

'Bob... good morning. You asked me to call?'

'Er, yes. And a good morning to you, Richard. I'll keep this short... I'm directed to inform you on behalf of the chief executive of your instant suspension from duty, pending a further decision expected later today.'

'Fucking hypocrites!' Turner growled scathingly. 'You all hated my guts from the very moment I set foot in that office!'

'Nonsense... A member of the IT maintenance team located a folder full of disturbing images stored on your office computer... Need I say more?'

Turner clammed up, his hand shooting over his mouth in shock. He'd finally been exposed for the sham he was, shunned by the co-workers who, if nothing else, admired his keenness to work beyond the stipulated hours.

'They must've been planted on my PC by a member of staff!'

'You're being absurd, Richard!'

'Am I really? This is nothing short of a witch-hunt... I'll drag you and you cronies through every tribunal in the land!'

Fisher pluckily held his ground, unswayed by Turner's fiery temper tantrum. The courts would surely take a dim view of his depraved shenanigans. 'Why delay the inevitable?' he thought, opting to wield the axe at once.

'Your indefensible behaviour amounts to a serious breach of professional and moral conduct, punishable with a penalty of instant dismissal.'

'You can't do this to me!' Turner cried frantically.

'Sure I can. I just did!' Fisher retaliated, abruptly hanging up.

*

3.00p.m.

The day had turned to an ugly grey, its cold drabness streaked by the first signs of dusk creeping in from the east. He walked on, still on edge, his ears pricking to the yap of a barking dog, succeeded by the rumble of men's voices.

The moss-covered trunk of a cedar provided the perfect camouflage, from where crouching low he suspiciously eyed a yellow-jacketed policeman engaged in a conversation with a Barbour-clad member of the public.

'Excuse me sir, but I'm looking for the principal occupant of cottage number two. You wouldn't happen to have seen him... would you?'

'If I never laid eyes on that degenerate again it'd be too soon!' the man said, continuing on his way shaking his head in disgust.

He shrank back behind the tree, taking the utmost care not to move a muscle. His head throbbed from the PC's incessant rapping at his front door, wracking him with a feeling as though the world had turned against him.

A nettle-infested thicket mercifully offered him an escape route, skirting round via a covert stile to a sweep of adjoining pastureland at the property's rear. He doubled back furtively, an evil plan brewing in his twisted mind.

He located the spare key hidden under a plant pot, picking up on a lively chitchat emanating from the cottage next door. 'I haven't seen hide nor hair of him, officer,' the elderly resident babbled, winding up the conversation.

The throaty roar of the departing patrol vehicle at last signalled that the coast was clear. His audacious two-fingered salute was complemented through a gap in the blind by the cry of 'Bastards... good riddance!'

With a rush he gathered up his essentials and stuffed them into a giant duffle-bag retrieved from the loft, tripping lightly up the staircase to disassemble his collection of surveillance gear that had been repeatedly focused on the Old Manor House.

Rustic village life had never much suited him. The cliquey wax-jacketed locals didn't take kindly to outsiders, snubbing him at every opportunity despite his efforts to fit in. He devilishly plotted one momentous last hurrah, to go out in a blaze of glory and heap yet more misery on Granby's sleepy community.

*

Hessle Road, Hull (the red-light district)

Phoebe Russo had always been the black sheep of the family, worlds apart from sisters Meg and Deirdre owing largely to her outgoing personality, not to mention the hourglass curves which could render a man speechless.

By her mid-to-late forties she'd established a prosperous, moneymaking enterprise, fulfilling the needs of a who's who of upper-crust clients, firmly resolved to live out a wide variety of weird and wonderful fantasies.

Slowly squeezing her body out of a raunchy black leather number, she immersed herself in a corner bath full of foaming bubbles, relaxing back onto a padded headrest, and sipped indulgently at a flute of Pol Roger champagne.

The ornate porcelain telephone broke her silent reverie, lightly trilling a tad too close to her ear. She hesitantly picked up.

'Hello?' she answered tersely.

'Aunt Phoebe... it's Richard!' he said, disoriented by the slosh of lapping water. 'Have I caught you at a bad time?'

'Richard?' she asked questioningly.

'Your nephew!'

'Darling boy... forgive me, it's been so long!'

'Indeed it has... Mum tells me your finances are in something of a mess,' he uttered, quickly cutting to the chase.

Again she rested her back, feeling the water's soothing warmth on her tired body. She continued with a light sniffle.

'Dear, dear Derek!' she sadly muttered.

'Derek…? I'm not with you?'

'My bookkeeper and close personal friend… He silently popped his clogs, during a strenuous Thai body massage!'

A lascivious smile crossed Turner's face. He'd harboured a special fondness for her that stretched back to his early teens. She'd caught him peeping through the door of the guest bedroom where she posed naked before a full-length mirror. She giggled and made no effort to cover herself. It was a moment forever etched in his memory.

'Good lord… I'm sorry to hear that.'

'And you're offering to step into his shoes… is that right?'

'I need a fresh challenge, Aunt Phoebe… a change of scene. I'm sick of kowtowing to people less qualified than myself!'

'How absolutely awful… When can you start?'

He exhaled heavily through rounded lips. His devious masterplan was coming together, driven solely by a need to lay low for a while. They continued chatting amiably, essentially to outline the task that lay ahead.

'Five parlours, you say… It sounds like I'll have my work cut out for me. I can leave right away if you so wish!'

'So soon… I'll check the guest room's made up.'

'You always were my favourite aunt!'

'How sweet… although I am, after all, your one and only remaining aunt!' she giggled, missing the next few words as his signal faltered. 'Richard… Richard…? Oops!' she said, stepping gingerly from the bathtub and fumbling for a towel.

*

'Hasta la vista, baby,' Turner hissed with a triumphant snarl, guiding the overloaded Smart Car along the winding country lane. In the distance a blurry smoke cloud billowed upward into the murky evening sky, accentuated by a series of flashing red and blue lights moving one after the other from the opposite direction.

THIRTY-TWO

Four days later
Granby

THE SULPHUROUS SMELL of burning soot permeated the air inside the cremated cottage. A jumpsuited crack forensics team foraged through the hash of charred remains littering up every nook and cranny.

DS Dan Hackett entered through the back door, his eyes watering from the smoky malodour.

'What've you got, Jim?'

'Not a lot, Dan… but the likely cause is arson,' the main man surmised. 'It's most likely the guy torched the place, before doing a runner.'

Hackett shuddered and froze still, calling to mind the collection of bloodcurdling whips and artefacts suspended from the walls of the renovated attic room, intermingled with a bizarre array of sex toys and music memorabilia.

'How about the upstairs observatory?'

'The top floor bore the brunt of the damage,' the dab hand chuckled, drawing his attention to a bagful of half-scorched items.

'What in fuck's name is that?'

'A hooded spandex body-binder… There's a pair of pink fluffy handcuffs too!'

'Whatever gets you through the night,' Hackett said amusedly. 'John Lennon… from his *Walls and Bridges* album?'

'Oh my god!' a womanly voice suddenly cried out. Its owner emerged from beneath the crumbling staircase, where sifting through a pile of blackened debris the horrified operative had uncovered a gigantic antique Bakelite dildo.

'Finders keepers!' a male colleague mocked girlishly to a coarse uproar of laughter, responded to in kind with a middle-finger salute.

Hackett kicked at the remains of a wooden dining chair, sprawled among the wreckage of its one-time matching table, and ducked circumspectly beneath the smouldering embers of a ceiling joist to toe-poke at the remnants.

'Did you happen upon a gruesome-looking wooden cudgel with three countersunk screws jutting out at the top?'

'I don't recall anything like that, Dan,' Jim vacantly replied. He flashed a look towards a fresh-complexioned female tapping at a shiny Apple MacBook perched, a touch precariously, on her lap. 'Try having a word with Cissy!'

Hackett introduced himself, stunned by the speed of her fingers zipping across the keyboard. She threw her head back and gave him a wide, gleaming smile. 'Cissy Hiaasen,' she announced, extending her petite right hand.

An engrossing inventory of information appeared on the screen, dismissed here and there at the click of a mouse. She narrowed down the cumulative list to a single page of burnt implements, none of which fitted the mace's description.

'I'll wait for your report, Jim!' he hollered across the room, bidding the team a polite if somewhat rueful goodbye.

*

He took a short stroll in an effort to clear his head, rehydrating his parched throat with a gulp of water from a plastic Evian bottle. An upward glance revealed a lone buzzard soaring majestically beneath a bank of low drifting cloud cover, its wingspan gloriously carved out by a welcome, albeit rare burst of radiant sunshine.

He paused awhile to admire the bird's gracefulness, studying its rich brown markings under a moving shadow. In one gravity-defying moment it swept down before him, eventually coming to rest on an isolated tree stump. He gazed fascinatedly into its yellow dappled eyes, smiling and tilting his head to mimic its inquisitive movements

His pleasant diversion was quickly brought to a halt by a maniacal pick-up driver screeching off-road into a hidden bridleway.

Curiosity got the better of him, goading him into a light jog towards the mud-churned track. He stopped to observe, taking cover behind a row of tall cypress trees, from where his prying eyes fixed on the idling pick-up.

He edged closer to get a clearer view, squatting down behind an aged dung heap overlooking an expanse of shallow swampland. Through a gap in the undergrowth he observed an eco-destructive moron scampering to and from his truck to offload a vast accumulation of household rubbish and worthless junk.

Hackett blinked in disbelief, barely able to contain the fury raging inside of him. He scribbled the vehicle's plate number on the back of his hand, somehow resisting the urge to reveal himself and feel the man's collar.

Totally oblivious to anyone around him, the driver of the wagon reversed and sped off, kicking up a volley of mud and gravel, much to the ducking Hackett's displeasure. 'You mindless bastard!' he shouted out, wasting his breath.

One plucky step forward almost sent him sprawling, his fall fortuitously checked by the upright of a bedstead protruding out of the oozing mire. Sinking deeper, he felt his ankle catch on a gunge-covered spike, close to where a shiny gramophone-shaped accolade bobbed to the surface. Hackett recognised it at once: it could only be Turner's fake Grammy award.

In a second, his mind clicked. Somewhere within his grasp lay the scary missing bludgeon, buried in the deep morass just like the missing piece of an unsolved puzzle. All of a sudden the toe of his boot latched on to a protruding screw-end, and a thrust of his foot sent the cudgel soaring towards the solid upper ground.

*

Back at the car he peeled off his sodden jeans, buoyed by his unexpected stroke of good fortune. He slipped into a spare pair of cargo pants to protect his modesty, diligently draping the mildewed weapon in a moth-eaten picnic blanket. His eyes were drawn towards a quaint red-brick cottage lodged captivatingly to the fore of the picturesque backdrop, displaying an advertising placard in the front window:

Grainger's Bed & Breakfast
Winter Rates Available Until Easter
~~~
Vacancies

</div>

'Maybe some other time,' he mumbled, reflecting on an upcoming dinner date with the new lady in his life.

THIRTY-THREE

February 2010

'I HAD DINNER LAST NIGHT with Teddy Goldsmith,' tubby record-chief Miles Templeton said boastfully, initiating a hush-hush behind-closed-doors meeting with his Harrow-educated head of A&R, Marcus Hubbard-Brock.

'Sounds interesting, boss. Where do I come in?'

'He's been commissioned to provide the score for an upcoming Ridley Scott blockbuster called *Angel of Death*. The budget is colossal, and we're in with a shout of getting our mitts on the soundtrack lock, stock and barrel!'

'Excellent! Judging from the title we'll need something dark and macabre... I hear Leonard's busy writing again?'

'No, no, Marky; the esteemed Sir Ridley's a huge JJ fan... They're begging for the exclusive music rights to his unreleased fourth album!'

Hubbard-Brock whistled cautiously through his teeth, briefly weighing up the pros and cons. He'd moved mountains to track down Gold's Montreux recordings, only to come up against a whole host of obstacles.

'But Miles, no one knows of the masters' whereabouts!'

'Bullshit... I know exactly where they are!'

'And when, and if, JJ gets wind?'

'He's missing, for Christ's sake. For all we know he could be dead... buried in a ditch on the far side of the planet!'

Brock paused to think again for a moment. Notwithstanding his best efforts, he'd been unable to determine the rights holders for the so-called 'lost' recordings. Maybe the boss was right, so why not take a leap in the dark?

'So what's the plan?'

'I need you to get your ass over to Montreux... to hunt down every last damn thing Jon recorded on those sessions,' Templeton ordered. 'We could be sitting on a goldmine, and whether he likes it or not he's still under contract!'

Twenty-four hours later
Montreux, Switzerland

In-house producer and technical wizard Max Schelling stood, hands on hips, his ears ringing from Hubbard-Brock's carefully prepared speech, aided by a fanned-out copy of the seventy-two-page JJ Gold agreement.

'Despite the long-winded legal jargon, clause eighteen states that we have total freedom to exploit the recordings in any way we see fit!'

'I gave Mr Jonathan my word that under no circumstances would I allow anyone else access to the files,' Schelling articulated in perfect English. 'Which I intend to keep until I hear otherwise from the man himself!'

'Clause twenty-seven states that the masters were due for delivery in excess of twelve months ago; JJ's clearly in breach of contract!'

'But no finished masters actually exist... only an archive of unmixed computer files stored on an external hard drive.'

Hubbard-Brock groaned in utter frustration, knowing his powers of persuasion may for once have failed him. Schelling's loyalty to Jon stemmed from a long-standing relationship based on mutual respect, established in the course of their years of working together, striving creatively to reach an epic common goal.

'And you're friends... right?' he said, taking a new tack.

'I guess so... we became pretty close.'

'Where is he, Max?'

'Somewhere in in the Papua New Guinean jungle... dancing naked around a campfire with a tribe of crazy head-hunters!'

'A hoax report... Help me find him, Max!'

Schelling slid open a filing cabinet situated beneath the studio console, eventually bringing to hand a wad of dog-eared track sheets. A nifty flick of his finger uncovered a set of lyrics scrawled in biro on a scrap of loose paper:

Somewhere out in the wild sylvan yonder, where a lone sparrow-hawk glides. But he doesn't hear me... Nobody hears me.

'This is all I have from the last session we did.'

'Is there some kind of significance?'

'The song is unfinished... under the working title of 'God's Own Country'.

'But what does it mean?'

'Scotland.'

'You're shitting me!'

'He bought a house… in the sylvan yonder… these words I don't understand.'

'In the backwoods… where we have no hope of finding him!'

Hubbard-Brock sank forward, head in hands, contemplating throwing in the towel. He saw Templeton's apoplectic features in his mind, and thought to mention the soundtrack to the major new Hollywood blockbuster.

'Did you say Ridley Scott? Schelling asked inquisitively.

'The very man.'

'Wow… the director of *Gladiator*… Jonathan's favourite movie!'

'My career's on the line here, Max. There's absolutely no way I can return to London without that hard drive!'

'The files are stored downstairs in the studio vault… I want no part of this!' Schelling grudgingly relented, throwing him a key and slipping away.

*

London
Thirty-six hours later

The Thames's muddy-brown waters snaked below the congested urban skyline, the river unhurriedly weaving its way between the thronged pavements and unstoppable buzz of the post-lunchtime traffic.

A self-satisfied Miles Templeton peered down from his high-rise office, eagerly awaiting the arrival of head of A&R Marcus Hubbard-Brock, fresh from his supreme efforts to hunt down the invaluable JJ Gold recordings.

'Come in,' he said, a touch overexcitedly. He was unable to hide his disappointment at seeing duteous PA Jenny enter the room.

'You summoned me, Miles?'

'I did…? Oh yeah… what happened to Marky?' he said, his eyes at once straying towards her low-cut V-neck top.

'His plane touched down an hour late. He's due any minute now.'

He snarled in annoyance, before his attention was suddenly diverted to the clunk of the private lift grinding to a halt. He scurried onto the landing in anticipation, rushing through the parting doors to embrace the returning hero.

'We need to work fast, Marky… sit your ass down!' Miles said abruptly, wasting no time getting down to business.

'Don't stress, boss… I'm on it!'

'I want the hottest producer on the planet working his magic on those mixes!'

'Already done... I contacted Max Martin's agent first thing, plus I'm waiting on a call from Japan from Dude Kennedy.'

'You're aiming high, son!'

'The very top, boss. The buzz around the office is incredible... even more so than when I worked on the second Winehouse album!'

Templeton sat back, clutching the hard drive to his chest like a small child hugging its favourite Teddy bear, blind to the canoodling couple in the corner. Something special was in the air, and nothing was going to spoil his day.

*

Dean Street, London W1

High-flying businessman Teddy Goldsmith sat poring over a selection of photos of a stunningly luxurious Majorcan retreat, once favoured during the early years of their marriage by British royals Charles and Diana.

'Teddy, brace yourself for the best news ever!' an overexcited voice roared through his hands-free speakerphone. It was Templeton, manically singing the praises of JJ Gold's extraordinary collection of modern day mini-masterpieces.

'That's music to my ears, Miles. Who's in the hot seat?'

'The crème de la crème, Teddy!'

'Will-I-Am perhaps?'

'Not even close, Teddy. Dude Kennedy... he dropped everything to work on the project!'

'Good call... though you're sure to be talking megabucks!'

'He's winging his way above the Sea of Japan on a flight from Tokyo as we speak. Make ready for something mind-blowing!'

'Way to go, Miles... I'll set up a preliminary meeting with Ridley and his entourage. Doubtless they'll be champing at the bit!'

With that Goldsmith shiftily signed off, rather more concerned with his forthcoming sunshine sabbatical.

THIRTY-FOUR

Mallaig
March 2010

'WHATEVER HAPPENED TO your pal, Carl Thingamajig?' the old seafarer rasped, wending his way through an Aladdin's cave of scattered engine parts before stooping down to uncover a filthy, rusted old outboard motor.

'He's Down Under, taking a well-earned sabbatical,' Jon fibbed, eyeing the contraption with a modicum of suspicion.

'He was nay a bad lad for a Sassenach.'

'CJ's a one-off… a real gem.'

The old salt stooped downwards to grip the handle of a plastic five-gallon jerry can, and cautiously dribbled a paltry amount of marine fuel into a rusting metal funnel loosely wedged into the turbine's crankshaft.

'My back's killing me, lad!'

'Here… let me,' Jon offered, promptly removing his jacket.

He pulled fiercely at the starter cord, leaning his head to one side in anticipation of a lungful of fumes and acrid smoke.

'Put your back into it, laddie!'

'I am doing. The sodding thing's on its last legs!'

'She ran sweet as a nut when I turned her over first thing,' the old timer argued, spraying a squirt of WD40 onto the spark plugs.

'One last shot, and I'm out of here,' Jon said pessimistically, yanking at the cord as if his life depended on it.

The old bag of bolts' guttural honk resembled a giant bull elephant seal locked chest to chest in combat with a rival dominant male. It spluttered out a succession of heaving breaths, until miraculously it somehow burst into life.

'See, I told you so,' the old codger croaked.

'How much?' Jon tentatively asked.

'Two hundred,' he fired back, striving desperately to keep a straight face.

'Fifty... not a brass farthing more!'

'You bloody skinflint!'

'Attached to the craft... including transportation to the harbour!'

The trace of a wry smirk formed on the grease monkey's pursed lips, supervened by an indifferent albeit courteous handshake. The unforeseen deal would help line his pockets, and keep him in beer for the weekend ahead.

*

Four days later

'Whoa... steady as she goes... Okay son, hop in and let's go for broke,' the old boy recommended, urging a quartet of brawny smokehouse hands to spare no effort in hauling the vessel down the steep launching ramp.

'The waves are getting angrier by the minute!' Jon bleated, finding himself stricken by an attack of the jitters.

'Keep calm, and take your time laddie. She'll feel a wee bit wobbly at first, but you'll soon get the hang of her.'

'What should I do in the event of an emergency?'

'Call the harbour master's office.'

'But I don't possess a mobile phone!' Jon screeched upwind, his words partially lost in the blustering ocean breeze.

He drew no response, save for a half-hearted wave from the top of the ramp, where hands in pockets the motley crew ambled up to the pier, making towards the more favourable surrounds of the closest watering hole.

*

Slowly but surely Jon came to terms with the seesawing motion, his head tilting and bobbing like a marionette doll. An invigorating breeze wafted through his matted locks, added to by a burst of spring sunlight streaking through the shifting clouds. He smiled a contented smile. Life didn't get much better than this.

A swirling gust of wind coming from the starboard side prompted a necessary course adjustment to port, cleverly compensated by the frequent dispersal of his weight to keep the *Hummingbird* on an even keel.

He laughed exultantly, catching sight of the arcing 'Bay of the Alder Trees' through a blur of shimmering light. The salty air intoxicated him, sparking him into a spontaneous rendition of the vessel's eponymous tune:

'And why would I need wings to fly when I'm floating on air
Carried by the weightlessness of knowing you are there
Buzzing in flight, etched bright with sunlight
Beating, hovering on wings of song
Like a hum-hum-hum-hum-hummingbird...'

His maiden voyage almost complete, he adroitly altered course in the midst of an unexpected shower, bearing away slightly downwind to make for the turquoise waters calmly lapping towards the shingly white beach.

He gently ran aground on a mudbank, ripping off his protective upper layers to feel the rainfall caressing his skin. With a mighty heave he dragged the ketch ashore, where his attention was caught by a pebble clattering into the bow.

'Halt... who goes there?' he called out playfully in the direction of a mound of giant boulders flanking the shore. She stepped out to reveal herself, careening ankle-high down the sandy hillock into his manly embrace.

'How long have you been waiting?'

'All my life, Jonathan... all my life,' she lovingly replied, sending him toppling backwards onto the mottled sand.

THIRTY-FIVE

March 2010

'The Criminal Cases Review Commission agreed to look into your case,' Khalid said via a Skype call, passing on the panel's recommendations following a brief, albeit productive, closed hearing with solicitor Dipak Mistry.

Rashid heaved a huge, whimpering sigh of relief, his drawn features awash in a surge of weariness and mixed emotions.

'It seems I owe you one, bro!'

'Not me... but we both owe Dipak a special debt of gratitude.'

'I guess so... Let's celebrate – there's a cracking new Italian in the centre of town... or we could do a Tikka Rogan Josh at Ali's place?'

'Cool it, little bro... The law can be a cruel mistress!'

'I'll pick up the tab.'

'Jeez... I must be hearing things!'

'So we're on, yeah?'

Khalid stalled, quickly checking his diary. Something in his tone reminded him of the snotty-nosed, mischievous kid permanently treading on his heels, vowing faithfully: 'Someday I'll make you proud, big bro!'

'I wouldn't miss it for the world!'

'Ha-ha, very droll. Bring an overnight bag... you can bed down at my new gaff,' Rashid proudly threw in. 'Oh, and before you hang up, rumour has it Amir fled to Iraq to join up with some extremist Islamic group!'

'Hmm... good riddance, I say!' Khalid responded with a grunt, mindful of keeping his true thoughts to himself.

*

Leicester
Three days later

A walkabout tour of the Meadows Court care home provided Khalid with an interesting insight into the workings of a facility for the elderly. His nose twitched from the prevalent 2-nonenal odour, intermixed with the scent of wintergreen.

'And this is our in-house Casanova, Mr Barresi,' Rashid said teasingly, leading the way into the semi-crowded day room.

'It's his Latino roots!' well-groomed inmate Dorothy commented, swatting away the hand reaching for the hem of her skirt.

Sloping craftily away through a tangle of legs and walking frames, they were halted by a knotted stick thrust into their path by a slobbering Alzheimer's sufferer, his left fist raised threateningly.

'Am I seeing double?' he said cantankerously, proceeding to rattle on about the Burma campaign up against the Indian army.

'This is my brother, Khalid,' Rash said, striving to pacify him.

Once again they moved on, passing a separate TV lounge where a party-hatted woman made merry with a pyjama-clad old boy. Spotting Rashid, she called out.

'Ramesh… aren't you going to wish me a happy birthday?'

'Oh yeah… have a good one, Evelyn!' Rash said abruptly, eager to press forward.

'Have a heart, bro!'

'Huh… best not to encourage her, eh?'

'What? How old is she?'

'Three hundred and eleven at the last count… she's been a serial birthday girl for getting on nine months now!'

Khalid forced back an embarrassed chuckle, not knowing whether to laugh or cry. He stood transfixed, unable to tear his eyes away from the cavorting couple, their unbridled joy mixed with a deeply touching sadness.

'It would seem you have your hands full, Rash,' he shouted ahead, scurrying along the corridor into a newly renovated wing. It was approached via a set of automatic swing-doors beneath a sign marked 'Day Care Centre'.

'*Five-seven-o-five… but there's no reply,*' Rashid's mobile erupted, echoing down the hallway like a megaphone blast.

'Your ringtone?' Khal said questioningly, watching him wrap up the call.

'It's just an app I downloaded.'

'A nod to Jon perhaps?'

'I suppose you could say that… It's time for you and him to kiss and make up, bro!' Rash advised, giving vent to their recent fall-out.

A vibration inside Khal's trouser pocket signalled an incoming message alert, responded to with a sly glance into his hand. Speak of the devil, he thought, eyeing the text:

> Message for Khalid – Jon Gold will call at 7pm this evening.

'Everything okay?' Rash asked, as if sensing his unease.

'Duty calls… I need to make the earlier train.'

'Something's eating at you, bro… anything you'd like to share?'

'You're right… I should make an effort to patch things up!' Khalid said, sauntering back to the main office to pick up his overcoat.

*

'Tickets please,' the inspector sharply announced, putting paid to Khal's fitful catnap in a weary blur of disorientation.

He grabbed at his Crombie from the adjoining seat, clumsily spilling a pocketful of odds and ends out onto the carriage floor. Stooping beneath the table he located his railcard, duly handing it to the po-faced ticket collector.

'I believe this also belongs to you, sir,' the man said, knees cracking as he crouched down to retrieve a mislaid envelope.

'Oops, sorry… I'm not sure how that got there!'

Their little tête-a-tête was broken up by the clattering wheels of the refreshment trolley, piloted in slovenly fashion by a pudgy, down-in-the-mouth attendant, morosely bawling, 'Tea, coffee, hot chocolate… assorted snacks…'

He ordered a black coffee, reacting with a blunt 'Whoa, be careful!' to a slipshod spillage on the tabletop. His admonition was greeted with no more than a disdainful nod as, buttocks wobbling, she continued on into the next carriage.

Khalid sighed exhaustedly, again tilting his head back onto the bolster before slowly drifting into a stupor-like slumber. A jumble of thoughts began to dance wildly in his head, flitting to and fro like dark shadows.

'The ringtone… the security code to Jon's gated driveway… no–no–no… You've come so far, little bro… This could blow everything out of the water!'

He shuddered back to alertness, resting his elbows on the table by his pile of belongings. His forefinger tore at the flap of the mystifying white envelope, curiously revealing a wad of goodies tucked inside a handwritten note:

Dear Khalid

Here's a small token of my gratitude for being there when I needed you. I've heard this band are the mutt's nuts, so if we can't get to see the real JJ in concert this will have to do for now.

Incidentally the second ticket is for Tanya Roberts who I bumped into a few weeks ago. Guess what, she'll be travelling down with yours truly. She's looking amazing and can't wait to see you!

Yours

Rashid

And then he read the letter through again, thinking back to the balmy summer of 2003. Tanya Roberts, the only girl to ever make his heart flutter, visualised in a hazy dream beyond the carriage window.

He unfastened his shirt's top button to relieve a sudden hot flush, roused by a flood of memories seesawing back and forth in his mind. The secret rendezvous curled closely together on the banks of the rippling reservoir, whiling away the post-sunset hours petting and canoodling in the throes of a tropical heatwave.

The train lumbered into its first port of call, juddering to a halt with an almighty bump. *Whoosh...* a further disruption roared, coming by way of an oncoming express train bulleting at full tilt in the opposite direction.

He glanced downwards at a pair of buff tickets poking out from beneath the discarded envelope, bearing the details of an upcoming event:

```
                     STA GAO 229
    STALLS SEATED
    PMT CONCERTS PRESENTS

    AUSTRALIAN GOLD
    THE MUSIC OF JJ GOLD

    27.00 CARLING APOLLO HAMMERSMITH
    QUEEN CAROLINE STREET W6
    WED 24-MAR-10 19.30

              2275
```

He pushed any negative thoughts to the back of his mind, touched at the kind gesture, not to mention Rash's role as the guileful matchmaker. A gentle smile passed over his face, soon wiped away by a piercing announcement:

'*Due to a signal failure between Bedford and Luton Parkway, the train's arrival time into London St Pancras is now estimated at seventeen forty hours...*'

He imagined the noise and frustration of the rush-hour traffic, the busy pavements teeming with commuters rushing hither and thither, to all appearances a million miles away from a little-known hideaway north of the border.

After six months of silence they would finally talk again, to settle the differences triggered due to a regrettable misunderstanding. He'd take the tube, squashed up together in a crush of sardine-like strangers, each ignoring one another in their own little world. Whatever rift that had occurred could and would be healed.

*

7.05p.m.
Putney, London SW15

'Jon, is that you?' he asked, grabbing the phone to his ear.

'No. It's Pope Benedict the sixteenth!' JJ joked in a far-off tone, partially lost in a hubbub of squeals and static.

'It's good to hear your voice, Jon... I'm lost for words.'

'You don't have to say anything... The Aussies had it all wrong!'

'And so it would seem did I!'

They exchanged pleasantries, broaching the subject of a misinformed TV crew immersed in a wild-goose chase, hunting down a drug-crazed imposter somewhere out in the rainforests of the southwestern Pacific.

'What would they think if they knew the truth?'

'But what's to know?'

'You don't know the half of it, Khal...'

'Try me!' he said, pulling the handset a mite closer.

But Jon's voice was rudely interrupted by an announcement in Khal's ear: '*The person you are calling is temporarily unavailable. Please try later.*'

He frantically redialled the number, only to meet with a silent deadness. Perhaps his battery had died, or there was a fault on the line; but, whichever, the long-awaited conversation had reached its conclusion.

A thousand or more thoughts began to swim in his head. What really happened that night in November 2005?

THIRTY-SIX

February 2011
Knoydart

A BITTER NORTH-EASTERLY WIND swooped down upon the bleak headland. It howled menacingly through the Scots pines that drooped dejectedly over the croft's slanting slate roof, beneath which, by a roaring log fire, Jon squatted, guitar in hand.

'Does the date March the twelfth mean anything to you?' Agnes asked, cutting in on his inspired burst of creativity.

'Hmm… could it be the Running of the Bulls in Pamplona… or even the day of the "Baby Tossing" ritual in Western India?'

'Be serious, Jon… just once!'

'March the twelfth… nope, I'm drawing a blank.'

'It'll mark five years since our chance encounter on the train from Fort William.'

He clawed at the Martin's strings, cleverly shaping his digits into a thumb-and-three-finger, all the time working his left hand up and down the fretboard to magically carve out the opening bars of an old blues classic.

'You played hard to get,' he said, pausing awhile.

'I was just a little shy, that's all.'

'You looked radiant!'

'And you nonchalantly bid me goodbye on the platform… I thought I'd never see you again,' she said with a soft smile.

She knelt at his side to snuggle up beside him, rapt with admiration at his effortless style of playing. He played on, as if stuck in a trance.

After a moment or two, his eyes deviated towards a stiff-backed envelope placed in front of him on the rug.

'An anniversary card… so soon?'

'Take a look, Jon!'

He rested his guitar up against the sofa, and peeled out a multi-coloured glossy brochure. Flicking through the pages he eyed an idyllic retreat, perched among a stand of giant weeping willows at the foot of Loch Lomond.

'Very posh… especially for a couple of muddy-booted dropouts, don't you think?'

'Let's spoil ourselves, and celebrate!'

He sniffled apathetically, again grabbing the Martin and plucking ponderously at the strings. Right alongside him he could feel her anger burning into his skin, meeting with a response in the only way he knew how:

A pocketful of secrets no one knows
Hidden beneath the underbrush where the deep forest grows
Where lies fall like dead leaves onto the woodland floor
And in a rumble of distant thunder, peace is no more.'

'Anything for you,' he half-spoke, half-sang, watching her wrathful glare turn into an expression of joyous disbelief.

She leant forward, casting aside his guitar and smothering his face with kisses. 'You'd—you'd really do it… for me?'

He toppled blunderingly onto his back, rendered helpless by the weight of her body bearing down on his chest.

'So, what's the damage?'

'Small potatoes to a man of your means.'

'And what the hell will I wear?'

'Your best bib and tucker.'

'But I don't have one… In any case, I wouldn't be seen dead in a suit!'

'*You* will do as you're told, Jonathan!' she said, poking him in the ribcage, unaware that her carefully laid masterplan was about to unravel.

*

March 2011
On the bonnie, bonnie banks of Loch Lomond

From a prime position on the hotel terrace Jon and Agnes gazed above a lichen-coated stone balustrade and nuzzled closely together, feasting their eyes on the sweeping panorama stretched out before them.

'The location is something else!' Jon observed.

'Stunning!' she agreed.

They skipped merrily up a timeworn set of flagstone steps and wandered aimlessly into an ornately furnished reception room. Suddenly halting in his tracks, Jon cast an eye over a full-size concert grand piano.

'It's a Steinway, no less!' he gasped.

'Give it a go. There's not a soul around,' Agnes said, egging him on.

He gleefully pulled up the stool and flexed his fingers above the keyboard, scarcely able to believe his good fortune. In no time at all his left hand began carving out a bassline on the reverberant lower staff, thunderously resonating through the room's rafters like the sound of a freight train rumbling along a railway track.

'*Both hands hammering at the eighty-eight*
'*Spanning all the octaves trying to rise above the waves*
As the music drags me under.'

His inimitable, gravelly voice soared above the pulsating rhythm, augmented by his sprightly right hand rolling and twisting up and down the treble clef's upper keys in a blur of manic triplets and demisemiquavers.

'Take a listen to that!' a lunching delegate said breathlessly, shooting up from the table in the adjacent restaurant, his ears straining to overhear the mind-blowing sound spilling forth from the abutting room.

Amid a clatter of plates and cutlery the diners scattered every which way, very soon joined by a gathering of similarly curious hotel guests, all climbing over one another to catch a glimpse of the off-the-cuff performance.

'Wow, that boy can play!' an American tourist bleated.

'OMG… strike me down dead… It's JJ Gold!' a young executive suddenly realised.

'The missing rock star?' the Yank gasped.

'The very same guy!'

'Yikes… he's a goddam wizard!'

Jon seemed oblivious to all the fuss, continuing in blissful ignorance into a tumultuous, *1812*-esque grand finale, its booming, thunderous bassline threatening to dislodge the overhanging crystal chandeliers.

He fleetingly lifted his head, looking aghast at the superfluity of eyes observing his every move. A brief flash of panic gripped him. Shutting down the piano lid, he grabbed Aggie's hand to make good a swift exit.

They backed away through the double doors onto the terrace whence they came and made a crafty about-face through the labyrinthine gardens. Somewhere behind an ornate archway they heard the sound of excited voices. Their eyes were drawn towards a giant candelabrum-shaped cedar, where they could lie low for a while.

'Do you think we threw them off the scent?' Aggie sighed. Her voice grew concerned as she studied his crimson features. 'Jon... are you okay?'

'I feel alive, Aggie... almost as if the shackles have been removed!' he said, straddling a stout out-jutting branch.

'Be careful, Jonathan!'

Ignoring her warning, he climbed agilely among the drooping boughs, reaching his arm down to tug her up alongside him. Before he could take hold of her hand, Agnes cried out, feigning a fall into the undergrowth, obscured by the tree's hefty lower trunk.

'*Aggie!*' Jon hollered, dangling by his arms into an ape-like position, and crashing painfully to the ground.

He looked to his left, then to his right, craning his neck above the bordering shrubbery to somehow try to find her.

Then he heard a rustling in the bushes, at once aware of something moving slowly towards him. Soon cottoning on to her little game he tiptoed back to the mammoth cedar, almost jumping out of his skin as he twisted round.

She stood like a vision before him, silhouetted against a backdrop of the loch's silvery-topped waters. They sank down onto their knees and flopped onto their backs, looking up through the leaves at the dusking sky.

*

Private banker Jenny Driscoll strutted through the reception area gabbing into her iPhone. Her thin, reedy voice echoed high up into the stairwell, loud enough for the gathered hotel guests to tune into her conversation.

'Mary, honey, have I got a scoop for you!' she blabbed.

Friend and confidante Mary Scott was part way through a sub rosa editorial meeting, discussing the paper's strategy for blowing the lid off a seedy MP's questionable private life.

'Jen babe, I'm up to my eyes,' she muttered distractedly, put out by the untimely interruption.

Driscoll persisted. 'Don't hang up on me, babe!'

'Go grab a coffee, everyone,' Scott said snappily, dismissing the youthful gathering. 'We'll reconvene in ten.' Once they were all out of the room she returned to the call. 'I'm here, Jen... and this'd better be good!'

'As good as it gets, hon!'

Scott moved to the window of the high-rise Canary Wharf office suite, her jaw dropping between pacing hither and yon. The story would doubtless go global, and hit the front pages of every newspaper on the planet.

'What makes you so certain it was him?'

'The unmistakeable gruff voice… the frenzied piano playing…'

'Did you get a snapshot?'

'Great minds, angel… I captured an amazing headshot, together with a sneaky image of his panic-stricken lady friend.'

'Ping them over to me… like now!'

'I already did!'

'I owe you big time, Jen!' Scott signed off, strutting out onto the landing to make straight for the senior editor's office.

*

Six hours later

Satiated from an excess of vintage Burgundy and champagne consumed in the privacy of the hotel's spacious honeymoon suite, they clinked glasses for the umpteenth time, staring lovingly into each other's eyes.

'All I know is, the privileged few present were completely spellbound,' Aggie said half-tipsily, her face becoming oddly pallid.

'They need to get out more… Hey, are you okay?'

'I just need to spend a penny, that's all,' she slurred, promptly leaving the table to zigzag off towards the bathroom.

Once more replenishing his glass, Jon shifted onto the deep-cushioned sofa. His head leant back against the soft damask covering as he tuned in with a smile to Agnes's passable imitation of Adele's current chart-topper.

'*Never mind I'll find someone like you,*' her echoing voice carried, silenced abruptly by the shrill sound of breaking glass.

He thought little of it at first, figuring it to be nothing more than a minor mishap as a result of her half-drunken condition, and for a moment his mind wandered.

Suddenly he was spooked by a sixth sense warning him that all was not well.

'*Aggie!*' he yawped, scampering across the bedroom to find her lying prostrate on the cold, porcelain-tiled floor.

He carefully lifted her body into an upright position, gently supporting her head against a heaped pile of towels. Above his head he grabbed at the phone on the wall, urging the receptionist to call an ambulance pronto.

His knees almost buckling, he hoisted her dead weight up into his arms, eventually lowering her down onto the unmade bed, where he listened intently for her every sporadic breath.

A rumble of footsteps jolted him out of his stupor.

Boom-boom-boom the room door resounded, heralding the arrival of a team of breathless paramedics. They were pursued by a high-handed, cell-phone wielding member of staff, seemingly intent on poking in her nose.

The obtrusive flash of her phone camera surprisingly stirred Agnes back into consciousness, her outstretched hand tugging Jon down towards her to fortuitously shield his face from another uncalled-for snapshot.

'Madam… please!' a quick-acting orderly intervened, ushering the woman to the door in a no-nonsense manner. His firm-handed approach sparked a tirade of expletives, echoing out into the nearby stairwell.

As though roused by the raised voices, Agnes shot bolt upright on the bed. Her left hand ripped away the mask to the emergency oxygen container, and by and by her heavy eyes brought Jon's features into focus.

'I had a not-so-funny turn,' she murmured.

'I was worried sick!' Jon said, clinging onto her hand.

He was oblivious to the flustered orderly re-entering the room. 'A missing rock star… ha, whatever next!'

'Krakatoa erupting, perhaps!' his sidekick joshed. He stooped over to check Agnes's pulse. 'All clear, I'm pleased to say.'

Jon offered a heartfelt apology for the uncalled-for false alarm, discreetly hiding his face beneath his bushy locks.

'All in a night's work, sir!' the guy said chirpily, tootling off behind his colleagues humming the chorus to Jon's song 'Vagabond'.

Like it or lump it, his cover was blown.

THIRTY-SEVEN

March 2011
London

IDEAS FLEW THICK and fast at the extraordinary morning meeting ahead of the company's most anticipated release in years. The atmosphere was ramped up by the arrival of a pumped-up Miles Templeton, kitted out in a gaudy satin tracksuit.

'The wheels are greased and ready to roll in the run-up to the Easter period!' he roared to the production team. 'I got the green light from Scott Free and Miramax, though I gather the movie's premiere has been put back again.'

Buxom PA Carrie quickly took up the reins. 'The advance sales have gone through the roof, boss, on download and CD... Brad in New York Skyped at two a.m. to say the US orders already topped the million mark!'

'I've got the *Mail* and the *Sun* lined up for a simultaneous exclusive on the three-track sampler,' press secretary Dawn chimed in. 'Plus Paul at *Q Magazine* has guaranteed us a five-star review should he get first bite ahead of the release date!'

'Did you hear back from the BBC, Carrie?' Miles asked.

'Yes, boss... they're looking at running a one-hour special featuring a who's who of A-listers who've worked with JJ in the past, essentially to discuss the merits of each new track... I'm also waiting on Channel Four.'

'Make sure you keep the movie-makers in the loop. I don't want their noses put out of joint... at any cost!' Templeton said domineeringly.

His attention was distracted by the raised hand of his deputy PR officer, Stanley.

'You're not going to believe this,' the lad mumbled uncertainly, looking up from his iPad wearing a puzzled expression.

'Spit it out, son!'

Amidst an astonished chorus of howls and gasps he placed the device in the middle of the table. Its screen displayed an image of a smartly attired, bushy-bearded character caught in full flow performing on a grand piano.

'The shot's far from conclusive,' Carrie quickly surmised.

'Jon-boy sporting a winged collar and tie... in Scotland?' Templeton added doubtfully, squinting to scan the accompanying text.

'According to his CV he was born in Edinburgh,' Dawn cut in. 'Perhaps he'd been hankering to revisit his roots?'

'Who broke the story... and when?'

'News Corp, ten minutes ago... Wait... there's more!' Stanley gasped, right after typing a new search into his cell phone.

'Read it, son, for Christ's sake!'

He paused to clear his throat, aware that every eye in the room was upon him, each ear hanging upon his every word:

'Filmed on a hotel guest's phone-camera serenading a small gathering of dumbfounded onlookers, the eremitic superstar showcased a previously unheard-of new song, rumoured to be taken from his eagerly awaited fourth album *Angel of Death*.'

Templeton began to hyperventilate, uneasily sweeping his arm across his forehead to wipe away the beads of sweat. His mind filled with a jumble of thoughts, soon put into words in the resulting torrent of orders.

'Caz, get on to our contact at News Corp right away... Stan, contact the area reps for Edinburgh and Glasgow... Dawn, concoct a piece to keep the daily rags off our backs... As for everyone else, find JJ, wherever the fuck he is!'

*

Three and a half miles away in the less salubrious surrounds of his stark Scotland Yard office, Detective Inspector Ray Menzies studied a detailed coroner's report pertaining to one Louis Patrick Kelly. The cause of death was determined to be asphyxiation during a perverse sex game gone awry, although the coroner refused to rule out foul play given the excessive quantity of cling film applied to the body by one or more co-conspirators.

He carefully scrutinised the attached photographs, his face squirming with distaste at the rope burns on the corpse's wrists, ankles and neck. He was further perturbed by the large initials tattooed on the side of the man's penis: '*JJ*'.

THERE'S GOLD IN THEM THERE HILLS the morning paper's headline splashed, above an ill-defined likeness of the runaway star montaged onto a backdrop of rolling Scottish slopes and mirror-like lochs.

He imagined the world's media gearing up for a feeding frenzy; the blood-hungry reporters and TV satellite trucks flocking northward in droves, bent on exploring every nook and cranny for the paltriest scraps of information.

A gut feeling convinced him to remain on familiar ground, well away from the vultures descending on their prey. A wry smile crossed his lips; he'd bide his time and leave the dirty work to his confederates north of the wall.

THIRTY-EIGHT

Early April 2011
Knoydart

THE POSTMAN'S MUD-SPATTERED quad bike slid to a halt on the sodden drive. His squelchy footsteps were followed by the springy thud of the letterbox's flap and the pitter-patter of mail dropping onto the mat.

'Thanks a million, Tommy!' Jon hollered through the window, skipping into the hallway to pick up the scattered envelopes.

'Anything for me?' Aggie asked.

'Yep… there's a letter bearing an Irish postmark… and another one for yours truly addressed to a Mr Jon Ryan!'

He slid his finger under the tab to prise open the envelope, feeling a tinge of satisfaction as he scanned the letter's contents.

JENKINSON 12410
HOUSE BLOCK 2
HM BELMARSH PRISON
WESTERN WAY
LONDON
SE28 0EB

Dear Jon Boy

First of all you'll have to forgive me for the dodgy handwriting and broken English, but this is the first time I've put pen to paper since I was a snotty-nosed schoolkid, so perhaps understandably my grammar's on the rusty side.

A little dickie-bird informs me that all the mail is screened, so much as I'd like to give you all the sordid details I guess I should watch my P's and Q's.

My days are largely spent cooped up in my cell, which allows me plenty of time to think, often drooling over my time up in the Highlands hanging out with you guys.

The burly copper who felt my collar while we were fixing up the Hummingbird paid me a surprise visit last week to bend my ear in regard to a geyser I once worked for named Louis Kelly, who it seems was found bound and gagged at his home with an item of fruit jammed into his mouth. He tried to make out you were the missing rock singer JJ Gold, who Kelly 'handled' at the beginning of his career. I almost choked on my cuppa, and told him to try widening his search to Poppa New Delhi, or wherever it was the newspapers said he'd gone into hiding.

I need a massive favour Jon. I rather hoped you'd stick my house on the market and oversee the sale. I know it's a lot to ask but I've hardly got a pot to piss in and could do with freeing up some funds ahead of my release in eighteen months, which may have been sooner had I not assaulted an inmate who tried his luck at feeling me up in the shower.

Well I guess that's all for now, I look forward to hearing from you. Please give my best to Agnes.

Your friend

CJ

'Louis Kelly dead,' Jon thought out loud, looking briefly upward to heed a stray teardrop streaming across Agnes's cheek. 'Bad news?'

'My granny passed away,' she choked, struggling for words.

'I'm so sorry, Aggie!'

'The funeral's taking place on Thursday... I have to go, Jon, to pay her my respects!'

Her body shook with sobs as she fell into his arms, his hands caressing her hair to help soothe her grief. She lifted her head to flash him the saddest of smiles, opening her mouth to speak, but the words wouldn't come.

'I won't let you go alone.'

'But I must... Don't make it difficult, Jon.'

They donned their coats and walking boots to prepare for the arduous path ahead and took off at a brisk pace towards the village. On the way they endlessly hearkened back to Aggie's adolescent years, spent in the guardian-ship of her beloved gran. In his efforts to raise her spirits Jon literally fell over himself, his ankle crashing into a jutting out rock while ducking from a dive-bombing seagull, its white head swooping down threateningly enough for him to lose his foothold.

She laughed irrepressibly, his antics serving to subdue the feelings of emptiness in her stomach. They marched on arm-in-arm to her friend Cara's guesthouse, where in moments she got online to book her air ticket.

'Let's do lunch on the way back?'

'Fresh lobster?'

'Washed down with a bottle of bubbly… to offer a toast to the memory of your gran!' Jon said, hurriedly relacing his boots.

*

The morning after

And so Agnes's marathon journey began. Although the *Hummingbird* rocked this way and that, jolted by the loch's choppy waves, it was ably piloted by the remarkably assured rookie seaman, whose nautical adroitness had come on in leaps and bounds.

Jon slowly cut the boat's revs to begin manoeuvring into an available quayside berth. He was more than a little perturbed by the ongoing issues with the misfiring outboard, which he put down to the fact that the boat had been idle for some time.

'I'll continue on round the bluff to get her checked over,' he vowed, looping the rope over a rusted horn cleat.

She clocked the lines of concern etched across his forehead as she stooped down to thread her arms through the straps of her bulky backpack. He forcefully grasped her arms to hoist her body up onto the jetty steps.

'Call me this evening… on the pub phone?'

'I will… I promise!' he said, stretching up to peck her one last time on the cheek.

Striding off in search of the taxi rank, she was almost immediately accosted by a youngish photographer racing frantically along the pier, his outstretched arms blocking her path.

'That guy… the guy in the boat!' he gasped, his shoulders sagging from the weight of the camera dangling around his neck.

'What about him?' she said, abruptly.

'Is it who I think it is?'

'And who might that be?' she replied, sidestepping him to continue on her way.

'Just a minute of your time… please!'

Her whole body tensed as she spun round to face him, her irritation more than evident in the curtness of her response.

'He's a local fisherman!'

'Pull the other one!' he laughed derisively, shuffling forward to train his zoom lens on the departing skiff. 'Where's he heading?'

'Out to sea, you dodo… like most fishermen!'

'But I received a tip-off from a trustworthy source at the *Mirror*…'

'The *Mirror*… trustworthy…? I love a good oxymoron!' she scoffed, finally turning on her heels to beat a hasty retreat.

*

Thirty minutes later

At the mercy of a ferocious tailwind, the *Hummingbird* catapulted forward off the tip of the tiny isle of Eilean Ighe as Jon gamely circumnavigated towards the bay of Arisaig, summoning up all his brute strength to hold her flat.

Seemingly out of nowhere a monstrous wave smashed heavily into the port side, instantly flipping the vessel over in a spiralling skyward arc, the unmerciful ocean's fierce current sucking him down into its hungry maw.

Beaten half senseless, a renewed burst of energy helped thrust his body upwards to the surface, where he was able to raise his head above the surging whitecaps and breathe in a lungful of life-giving air.

Still more the rush of backdraught drew him down deeper, a little too close for comfort to a gargantuan basking shark. With a swish of its tail, he was magically propelled into a placid stretch of water.

He cried out to the heavens, writhing to toss aside his stymieing outer layers of clothing. His legs pumped wildly, arms flailing like windmills, driving him ever closer to the white sands shimmering in the distance.

*

'Ye look like a drowned rat, laddie!' retired boatswain Ted said dryly, scuttling across the yard with the briskness of a man half his age, eager to offer a helping hand to the drenched visitor zigzagging up the pathway.

'My boat capsized… in a freak squall!'

'Good lord, son!' the old salt croaked, hurriedly draping a gunk-smeared tarpaulin over Jon's trembling upper body.

'I'm lucky to be alive!'

'The ocean can be a cruel mistress, lad.' Ted's experience spoke, as he ushered him round towards the rear of the workshop.

Five minutes later Jon found himself perched by a roaring wood stove, cloaked in a thick blanket while his wet things aired on a rickety clothes-horse, sipping fitfully at the mug of hot tea cradled in the palms of his hands.

'Hey Da… I'm off to Fort William,' a voice boomed. It came from a young strapping figure shadowed in the door frame.

Jon's ears pricked up immediately, his legs scrambling unsteadily out of his chair to clasp the lad's proffered hand.

'Did you say Fort William?'

'Aye… are you heading that way?'

Ted cast a wary glance Jon's way, his questioning look eclipsed by a shaft of dazzling sunlight streaming in through the skylight.

'Are ye sure you're up to it, laddie?'

'I'm okay – really. I have to see a man about a generator!'

'Ha, that'd be Ollie Randall!' son Bobby chimed in, with a suspicious chuckle.

Jon looked up, seeking some sort of reassurance, his doubtful gaze flickering back and forth from Bobby to Ted.

'If ye Jenny's on the blink, Ollie's your man,' Ted said comfortingly. 'Just be careful he does nay have your pants down!'

The persistent jangle of Bobby's keys pulled Jon from his brown study. 'You've been more than kind!' he said, grabbing at his freshly aired clothes and traipsing outside to the pick-up, where he was ably assisted with a leg-up onto the raised seat.

'Go easy now!' Ted's voice echoed over the nearby cliff edge.

Beneath it, from a raised vantage point, a paparazzi cameraman captured on film a jumble of sodden belongings drifting beside the upturned *Hummingbird*.

*

The cocksure photographer scurried back to his parked rental car, frenetically scrolling down his list of contacts to locate press guru Harry Swan, hoping against hope this was the big break he'd been waiting for.

'Harry, it's Chris Lindsay… Harry!' he squawked, one hand on the wheel, weaving recklessly from side to side.

'Where on Google Earth are you…? Jesus, Chrissy, the connection's fucking awful!' Swan responded impatiently.

'In Mall...*click...click...* the sun's blinding... *click...* JJ Gold...*click...* dead... *click...* accident at sea,' Lindsay's voice hemmed and hawed.

'In Malaysia?'

'What...? *click...* on... *click...* the airport!'

'Wire whatever you've got to me... before you board that plane!'

The phone went dead, the static noise reduced to the constant rhythm of the tyres, rolling towards a small roadside hotel on the left. Tilting up unsafely on the two outside wheels, the car screeched to an abrupt halt.

He strode across the shale forecourt, dipping beneath the *NO VACANCY* sign suspended above the entrance doors.

'We're fully booked, I'm afraid!' a timid female voice announced, resounding from halfway up the creaking staircase.

'Do you have an internet connection in this neck of the woods?'

'Fibre optic, no less!' she said boastfully, gently tiptoeing down into the lobby.

'I urgently need to get online!'

'You're welcome to make use of the facilities... should you be kind enough to make a donation to our WI charity fund?'

'Ah, okay... but of course!'

He extracted a solitary fiver from a wad of notes pulled from his jeans pocket and squeezed through a gap in the reception desk into an office to the rear. In moments he had connected to the lightning-fast broadband.

He waited uneasily, his eyes glued to the laptop's screen while the images uploaded. A click of the mouse attached the file to a hastily worded email, the flashing 'Sent' icon duly greeted with a jubilant fist-pump.

Back behind the wheel he hammered down on the accelerator, hell bent on making the late flight south out of Inverness airport.

He hummed a joyful tune as an exhilarating rush of adrenaline travelled through every inch of his veins. Making light work of the hazardous twists and turns, he casually upped the revs on a stretch of newly laid tarmac flanked by a row of giant pines, their shadows painting shapes on the surface of an ovular loch.

An austere-looking hamlet loomed up in the near distance. Disregarding its unpronounceable name, he tapped out a one-fingered message on his mobile's keypad and restlessly awaited Harry's response.

He focused straight ahead, gripping the wheel with just the wrist of his left hand. '*Beep-beep*' the message alert sounded. His wide eyes wandered distractedly to the iPhone positioned precariously on his lap.

'You hit the jackpot this time, Chrissy. Call me the moment you land – Harry.'

As he inwardly rejoiced, he felt the car veering wildly to his right. He looked up from the screen just as everything went black.

*

Kinlocheil, Lochaber

As if struck motionless, a headscarfed rambler stood riveted to the spot. Surveying the crash scene through a watery haze of tears, she dazedly attempted to comprehend the sheer horror of what she'd just witnessed.

She crossed herself and recited an inaudible Hail Mary. At last she was able to pull her gaze away from the mangled wreckage; but nothing could banish the endless flurry of images replaying over and over in her mind's eye.

She glanced up at the driver climbing down from the truck's cab, the world around him spinning as he collapsed into a heap. With effort he rolled into a crouched position, his eyes shielded behind a veil of inconsolable grief.

The woman rushed to his side to try to comfort him, stooping down to offer him a white hankie to dab at his eyes. His shoulders convulsed as he sobbed his very heart out, ultimately summoning the strength to speak.

'He swerved in front of me!'

'I know,' she whispered sincerely.

Suddenly alert to the whine of a distant ambulance's siren, their eye was caught by a roving onlooker beside the crumpled wreck. His morbid curiosity evidently satisfied, he made a sickening gesture, drawing a finger across his throat.

About to close in on the crowning achievement of his all-too-brief career, a fatal error of judgement had cost Chris Lindsay his life.

THIRTY-NINE

THROUGH A SMALL CRACK in the bedroom door Richard Turner watched his aunt's every move. He was unable to tear his gaze away from her full-figured semi-naked body, the sight of which awakened a potent stirring in his loins.

'Richard... have I caught you peeping?' she asked, sauntering to the door, her forearms folded across her breasts.

'N–no... I wanted to have a little chat!'

She unabashedly pulled back the door. Slipping into a flimsy, see-through housecoat to preserve her modesty, she semi-amusedly noted his bulging eyes coupled with a thick layer of sweat formed on his upper lip.

'Is something bothering you?'

'I was rather hoping I could take a few days off... to visit a terminally ill friend of mine up in the north of Scotland.'

'But of course... A terminal illness, you say?'

'Lung cancer, to be exact... I'd so like to see him one last time.'

'You're such a sweet, caring boy, Richard... How long will you be away?' she asked, fluttering her false eyelashes at him.

'Until Monday... at the latest.'

She nodded her consent, stepping back to the door, deliberately rotating her hips to offer him a glimpse of her upper thigh.

'Safe trip, darling. Give my regards to Ben!' she said, giggling playfully.

'Ben...? Ben who?'

'Ben Nevis, you silly boy... Godspeed!'

He dashed to his room to gather some clothes and essentials, quickly logging into Facebook and Twitter to pick up the latest gossip. His destination was at last confirmed through the words of a couple of recent Tweets.

Neil
@WesternCelt106

JJ Gold sighted 'off his face' in one of Fort William's downmarket watering holes

---

Ronald
@BigBoyCrudup

Rock legend Gold seen hanging out in Fort William pub The Grog & Gruel

The corners of his mouth pulled back in a wicked leer. Gold's cover was blown, and the net seemed to be closing in around him. In a blur his fingers bore down on the keyboard. He desperately needed to stay ahead of the pack.

*

The outskirts of Fort William

He thumbed through a newspaper in the hotel's half-empty breakfast room, still jaded after the never-ending journey north. At a nearby table a trio of Scots sat chewing the fat, their conversation instantly grabbing his attention.

'The place is crawling with reporters and smart-arsed media people,' a full-throated guy bleated to his companion.

'In hiding… on Knoydart of all places!' a second man said, emptying an excess of ketchup onto his morning fry-up.

'Excuse me,' Turner interrupted. 'I couldn't help but overhear you… were you referring to the missing rock star, JJ Gold?'

'Aye, laddie… the hairy bastard whose mugshot was splashed across the *Mirror*'s front page a day or so ago!'

'Where did you say he was…? New Dart?'

'K-N-O-Y-dart laddie, a wee ferry boat ride across Loch Nevis!'

He tapped the Google Maps app on the screen of his phone, futilely putting in a search to locate his journey's end.

'Damn it… there's no Wi-Fi signal!'

'Just keep going laddie, right to the arse-end of the A830… you can book a ferry at the Pier Office in the port.'

'Is there anywhere to bed down… for a night or two?'

'Huh, you'll be lucky son. There's pretty much bugger all there… other, that is, than an outlandishly pricey pub!'

'I'm much obliged, guys!' he said gratefully, scurrying frantically up to his room to throw his things into his rucksack.

*

Ten minutes later

'I have you down as staying for three nights. I'm afraid the full payment is due, sir!' the flustered receptionist stated, not taking kindly at all to Turner's cock-and-bull story, supported by a lengthy list of complaints.

'Consider yourselves lucky I'm willing to settle up for one night!'

'This is most extraordinary… you received a substantial discount for booking a non-refundable room online… sir!'

He whined about the musty smell and general aura of uncleanliness, throwing in the foul odour of stale chip fat prevalent in his room. She tried to calm him but to no avail, instead turning her back on him to call security.

All of a sudden the lobby filled with a group of Japanese tourists, providing him an opportunity to slip away unnoticed. Ducking behind the loose circle he seized his chance, racing like the wind through the automatic sliding doors.

'Where did he go?' the girl shrieked, peering above the throng, deaf to the Smart Car squealing on two wheels out of the car park.

*

Pier Office, Mallaig Harbour

'Fully booked…? What kind of service are you running here?' Turner growled, testing the stoical ferryman's patience.

'An extraordinarily busy one, young fella,' the man unflappably responded. 'Particularly for this time of year!'

He glanced studiously down at his schedule, doing his utmost to juggle things around by dint of a secondary headcount.

'Pardon my tetchiness… it's been one hell of a journey!' Turner squirmed, acknowledging the man's willingness to help.

'Nay bother; ye can go up front with my lad Davie… are ye planning to stop over?'

'A little birdie told me it's totally desolate?'

'You'd be wise to book a B & B.'

'Really?'

Turner fumbled in his coat pocket for his mobile phone, briefly stepping away from the desk into the light of the open doorway. His more restrained demeanour was quickly put to the test by the total lack of a signal.

'If you're on O2 I would nay bother!' the ferryman called over, gesticulating to him with his raised right hand.

'Is there anywhere in particular you'd recommend?'

'Aye, there's a couple of places… I'll gladly phone ahead, if ye like?'

For the briefest of moments he couldn't find his tongue. His disbelieving response was expressed with an uncharacteristic smile.

'Brilliant… I'd be eternally grateful!'

*

One hour later he zealously alighted from the ferryboat. His focus was immediately drawn to the desolate terrain. All around him the gaggle of passengers made off along the jetty, leaving him lagging behind to ponder his next move.

The moist sea air mingled with a stiff cool breeze, sweeping down the mountain slopes forming the backdrop to the tiny village. Its line of unprepossessing buildings lay subdued under the immovable grey cloud cover.

He looked up to the sky, thinking a higher power had led him here, a driving force pushing him into the unknown. The search had begun.

FORTY

Isle of Skye

A LATE-EVENING CALL from his erstwhile protégé Khalid provided Duncan with a much-needed pick-me-up. His wiry frame lay sprawled out across the couch, not for the first time afflicted with a debilitating sciatic condition.

'What are you doing this coming Thursday?'

'Let me check my diary!' he joked.

'I'm scheduled to hook up with the ex-Lib Dem leader Charles Kennedy at his constituency office in Fort William.'

'Good heavens… so, are you flying up?'

'Yes, to Inverness.'

'Wonderful; I'll make sure the honeymoon suite's made up!'

They engaged in a friendly chitchat, the conversation mainly centred upon Khalid's newly found penchant for digging up political dirt, interspersed with a full-blown account of Duncan's niggling aches and pains.

'I couldn't pass by without saying hello!'

'Indeed, dear boy… So what's the deal with Charlie?'

'It's a human interest story I've been commissioned to write. Nothing sordid, he's as clean as a whistle.'

'A damn fine parliamentarian, in my view.'

A fleeting mention of Jon's biography met with an almost indifferent reaction. It was swiftly passed off as low on Khal's priority list, mainly as a consequence of Jon's peculiar unwillingness to maintain close and regular contact.

'I put it on the back burner.' The inflection in his voice suggested he was holding something back. This impression was made all the more evident by his attempts to lay blame on an increasingly heavy workload, further complicated by a reignited affair of the heart.

'The penny drops… Anyone I know?'

'Tanya Roberts!' he replied, feeling his heart skip a beat.

'Dear Tanya... I remember her well.'

'We've been dating for over a month.'

'Speak of the angels and you can hear their wings!' Duncan quoted out of nowhere, clearing his throat with a nervous cough.

An awkward silence prevailed, broken only by a whistling wheeze emanating in fits and starts from deep in Duncan's chest.

'Dunc... are you okay?'

'Hmm... I was just thinking... that's all.'

'Anything you'd care to share?'

'A rather sensitive subject, perhaps,' he said, prudently stopping himself. 'Hmm, it's really not my place to interfere...'

Khal urged him to speak, listening intently, hanging on to every word. Duncan begged him to think twice before embarking on his marathon journey, pressurising him into stopping off to make peace with his closest friend.

'Jon's got issues,' Khal said, gulping guiltily.

'Which need to be resolved.'

'Now isn't the time.'

'Think again, Khal... I'll tag along with you.'

'You'll need a pair of walking boots!'

'Timberlands – size twelves to be precise. They're pretty much standard issue in this part of the world... Thursday it is!'

*

Five days later
Knoydart

Khalid's mouth dropped open. All along the pier a mob of pressmen threaded their way through a milling horde of tourists, lugging a variety of camera equipment in the direction of a convoy of pick-up trucks.

A sixth sense told him that something awry was afoot, borne out by the hot topic on the lips of every man jack.

'The guy's a recluse, there's no way he'd live on the main street!'

'It's not exactly a metropolis; we can ask around, someone's sure to know!'

'We're running up a blind alley... the bloody postcode's the same for the entire peninsula!'

'These guys are hunting Jon down like a wild animal!' Khal commented, slyly eavesdropping on the ensuing conversation.

'We'd best keep a low profile,' Duncan advised. He felt the weight of a tripod striking him on the back of his left thigh.

'Pardon me, chap!' the man said cockily.

'Apology accepted,' Duncan grudgingly answered, sidestepping around him.

'Where do you hail from, fella?'

'The Isle of Skye.'

'Not too far from here, huh?'

'Little more than a stone's throw away.'

'Do you know Jonathan Gold?'

The very mention of Jon's name rendered him almost speechless, his features freezing like ice into a mask of stunned surprise. He dallied awhile, placing a hand over his mouth to hide any obvious tell-tale signs.

'That's a new one on me.'

'As in JJ Gold... the rock singer?'

'I haven't the foggiest idea who or what you're talking about!'

The guy's head tilted despairingly towards the cloudy sky. Shoulders slumped, he aborted the mission and made off instead towards the idling ferryboat, his crew trudging behind him like a defeated army.

Midway along the pier a pouting female reporter performed a short piece to camera. Her striking blonde locks wafting in the breeze over her lips and cheeks were in stark contrast to the bleak background of colourless, rocky hills.

More than a little preoccupied, a blundering figure lurched backwards onto Duncan's left foot, the man's heavyset frame stomping onto his big toe to send him hopping on one leg towards the safety of the side barrier.

'Forgive me... I got a little distracted!'

'Understandably so!'

'Superintendent James Wilson, of the Inverness Police.'

'Duncan Bertrand... from Skye.'

'What brings you here today... if you don't mind me asking?'

'My penchant for seafood, officer,' Duncan fibbed, keeping his cards close to his chest. 'I'm a regular visitor to the Old Forge.'

'Do you know this man?' the cop asked, promptly thrusting the front page of a well-known tabloid under his nose.

Duncan snatched it from his hand to examine the half-blurred image, his granite-like expression giving nothing away. With a negative shake of his head he readjusted his rucksack, offering no more than a polite smile.

He continued onwards to join Khalid, who lingering by the pier entrance found himself surrounded by an ITN camera crew in the throes of assembling a stack of equipment in preparation for a further on-the-spot report.

'I see you made a new friend!'

'A senior police officer, no less… Is Jon in some kind of trouble?'

'How senior?'

'A superintendent, from Inverness.'

'Dammit… We have to find Jon, before anyone else does!'

*

One hour later

They came to a densely wooded area to the rear of a network of dykes. In the distance a sooty chimney-pot jutted into view, its stack perched atop a black slated roof sheltered by a group of tall Douglas firs.

'Almost there,' Khalid said encouragingly.

'You could hear the proverbial pin drop!' Duncan said, approaching the driveway. 'The place looks completely deserted.'

Khalid forcibly unbolted the greening five-bar gate, raising his nose in the air to sniff for the faintest whiff of smoke.

'Take a peek through the living-room window, Dunc, while I nip round the back to search for the spare key.'

He snuck down a small side path to check out the lean-to at the rear, besieged by a thicket of thorny bushes grabbing at his clothes and hands. Diligently he dropped to his knees to slide his fingers beneath a giant wicker basket, mindful not to unsettle the wood pile stacked precariously against the wall.

'Any luck, Khal?' Duncan's voice called out, followed by the pounding of footsteps. 'I'm guessing they jumped ship!'

Almost as if entering from the wings in a comedy sketch, Duncan sloped into view, his comical-looking figure covered from head to toe in dust, complemented by a thick layer of cobwebs clinging to his thinning grey hair.

'What happened?'

'I took a peek in the cellar!'

Khal doubled over with laughter. His minor fit was subdued by a sudden movement in the underbrush. Something was out there lurking in the bushes, made even more evident by the sharp crack of a breaking branch.

'Duncan... freeze!'

Duncan heeded the call, taking care not to move a muscle nor to make a sound. His mind began working overtime, imagining the snooping eyes of the press tracking their every move from a secret vantage point.

'Talk to me,' he softly whispered.

'Turn around... very slowly...'

He gently twisted his head around, staring in awe and wonderment at a giant-antlered, limpid-eyed stag camouflaged among the trees, its rusty-red markings caught in a shaft of light streaking through the branches.

'Bambi reincarnate!' he whispered half-kiddingly, backing away at a snail's pace into the shadows of the doorway.

Amazed glances were exchanged, the stag's head tilting slightly to one side in curiosity. Duncan looked to Khalid, his shoulders lightly convulsing trying to hold back a sneeze. It came nonetheless, with the force of a thunderbolt.

In the ensuing confusion Duncan fortuitously took evasive action, ducking down behind the hedgerow to dodge a salvo of mud and rocks launched like missiles from the buck's powerfully splayed hooves.

He dusted away the debris stuck to his clothing and clambered back upright with the help of Khalid's offered hand. Again silence prevailed, but for the sweet trill of a song thrush flitting between the overhanging boughs.

They removed their boots and stepped inside, at once carrying out a recce of the downstairs living areas. From the neatly arranged tables and chairs to the spotless worktops everything seemed to be spick and span, save only for a heavily chipped, tea-stained mug carelessly dumped in the middle of the sink.

Khalid flicked on the light switch to no effect. Agilely sliding in his stockinged feet to check out the built-in appliances on the opposite wall, his suspicions were confirmed with a tug at the door of the upright fridge-freezer.

'There's no power!'

'That explains it!' Duncan stated, snapping his fingers.

'How so?'

'The generator... it's knackered!'

'So they just upped and left?'

'That's about the size of it.'

'But why?'

'Welcome to the inhospitable Highlands, Khal!'

A brief visit to the upper floor revealed little more in the way of clues, other than Jon's cherished Martin acoustic leant against a mixed bag of pillows and cushions, together with a set of lyrics left on the bedside table.

Duncan shot a glance at his pocket watch, mentally calculating how long it would take them to reach home. Before dark they could be filling their bellies ensconced in front of a cosy fire. The decision was a no-brainer.

*

Three hours later
Portree, Skye

The caw of an airborne seagull filtered in through the open kitchen window. Keeping one eye on a bubbling vat of fish stew, Duncan transferred the contents of a Grand Cru claret into a wide-based crystal decanter.

'Mouton Rothschild? A little extravagant, don't you think?' Khalid whistled inwardly, taking stock of the dusty label.

'I like to indulge friends, as I love to be indulged myself!'

'As the old saying goes… you can't take it with you!'

Duncan leaned across the table to ladle a large helping onto Khalid's plate, before gently setting down the tureen to fill their empty wineglasses. As he raised his glass to propose a toast, a rueful smile crossed his lips.

'So… I'm living on borrowed time, eh?'

'Simply a turn of phrase!' said Khal, his voice faltering slightly. He feared that time may be running out for Jon.

FORTY-ONE

Fort William

THE BLUE-BOILER-SUITED grease-monkey slapped down a hastily scribbled invoice onto the service hatch's flap, complete with a black oil stain and a grimy thumbprint. He looked Jon up and down with a puzzled expression.

'You look a wee bit dishevelled, lad!' he said.

'I took an unforeseen dip in the ocean earlier today,' Jon said wearily, trying to muffle a yawn. 'My boat capsized.'

'Mm… the currents can be a wee bit unpredictable!'

The thunderous roar of an engine of some description caught both men by surprise, reverberating in a deafening shockwave from the adjoining workshop. Its sudden blast caused them to clap their hands over their ears.

'What the heck is that?'

'One of those quad bike contraptions… sodding racket!'

'Mind if I take a peep?' Jon asked.

'Be my guest!'

He led the way to the adjoining workshop, where from a supine position a strapping, bright-eyed lad sprang to his feet in a single movement, his grimy right hand precariously wielding a giant monkey-wrench.

'All right mate?' he said.

'What a beauty!' Jon gasped, tingling from a rush of ideas running wild in his head. 'How much did she set you back?'

'Two hundred smackers.'

'I'll give you five hundred for her!' Jon said, impetuously.

'Whoa… she's no exactly roadworthy as yet!'

'How long… to fix her up?'

The lad blinded him with science, rattling on without taking a breath. The fuel pump and air filter needed to be replaced… the breather hose was failing… on top of which, there was some leakage from the exhaust.

'Tomorrow lunchtime?'

'You're on!' Jon responded gleefully.

They shook hands to seal the deal, and made towards a back room in the corner of the building. It was equipped with an ill-matching assortment of moth-eaten furniture crammed in alongside a pool table and small kitchenette.

'Do ye live locally?

'Knoydart... eight or nine miles, overland?'

'On a quad... awesome!'

The elder man's head turned quickly round, his brow contorting in a dubious frown. He shambled towards them carrying a tea tray full of steaming mugs and goodies, setting it down with a sigh of relief.

'By land, did I hear ye say?'

'You sound sceptical.'

'Aye... it can be a treacherous route, even on foot.'

'So it's a definite no-no?'

'Not necessarily... though you'd need to keep your wits about you!'

A minute later, his mind already made up, Jon inquired after a place to bed down for the night. An address was promptly scribbled down on a yellow Post-it note, sending him happily on his way to a small, family-run B & B.

'See you tomorrow... and thanks for the cuppa.'

'One o'clock... on the dot!' the lad shouted, raising his hand aloft. 'Check out the Grog and Gruel on High Street!'

'Maybe I will!' Jon said, rapidly upping the pace.

*

2.15p.m.
Canary Wharf, London

News editor Harry Maguire gazed intently at his laptop, his eyes focused on a mixed bag of images ghosting across the display screen, sent by way of a zipped attachment from his new blue-eyed boy Chris Lindsay.

'Doug, are you there?' he barked into the adjacent office.

'Sure thing, boss.'

'Get your ass in here a sec!' he urged. 'I need this shot in the early editions!'

'Holy shit!' Doug exclaimed, scrutinising the shot over Harry's shoulder. 'Is that a shark's fin jutting out of the water?'

'A great white, at a guess.'

'The poor bastard!' Doug gulped, his eyes pinning to the discarded clothing drifting in a circle around the upturned vessel.

'I'm guessing he got caught up in a freak storm,' Harry said lugubriously. 'Tossed like a rag doll on the ocean's raging waves!'

'Jesus H. Christ!' Doug exclaimed with bated breath. 'Boss… zoom in on the tiny black object up at the top of the screen…'

With each click of the mouse the image pixelated into an ovular blob, little by little revealing the rounded peak of a baseball cap poking above the water's surface, astonishingly emblazoned with the initials 'JJ'.

'It's all we need, and more… Get to it, Dougie!' Harry snorted excitedly. 'Before we have a feeding frenzy on our hands!'

'I'm on it,' he retorted, rushing to the door and pausing. 'Hey, wait a sec… I need a name, for the picture credit?'

'Chris Lindsay,' Harry murmured, incredulously. 'And before you say a word, I thought exactly the same thing!'

*

2.35p.m.

Harry sat marvelling at the awesome, cleaned-up shot, wracking his brain to concoct an eye-catching leader. His concentration was broken by the relentless pitter-patter of Doug's fingers zipping over his computer keyboard.

'Almost there boss,' he shouted out, halting briefly. 'Rizzo… Lindsay… where was he, when the shots were taken?'

'In some Far Eastern beach resort,' Harry yelled back.

'Boss… help me out here!'

'Malaysia… or Mali, at a guess.'

'Langkawi… or Penang?'

'There was way too much static on the line… Malaya… or something close!'

'Malé… in the Maldives?'

'You hit the jackpot, Dougie… run with it!'

*

Lochaber District, Scotland

His knuckles white from clinging onto the quad's handle grips, Jon finally slipped off-road, guiding her along the shale-surfaced foreshore of the serpentine Loch Arkaig. The sound of the wind filled his ears with joy.

'Fly like an eagle, let my spirit carry me, I want to fly like an eagle 'til I'm free,'* he bellowed out, his husky tones wavering up and down between zigzagging playfully to shy away from a minefield of ruts and potholes.

Directly in front of him a burnished amber glow swept across the stark headland, ebbing and flowing on the near horizon, gilded by a vertical shaft of sunlight that cascaded like a waterfall over the daunting descent below.

He eased back on the throttle to take stock, rubbing an arm across his brow to fend off a surge of fatigue. At an incline to his left he sighted a decaying bulldozer, its rusted cab poking out from a sheltered hollow.

Moments later he dismounted, eager to seek a brief rest well away from the biting wind. With his back propped up against the digger's tilted blade, his eyes shut to, and in no time at all he drifted off into a blissful slumber.

A whip-like crack all of a sudden awakened him with a start, thrust with unerring force from the tail of a shaggy-coated bovine creature, its wet, bulbous nose seemingly put out of joint by the stranger's unwelcome presence.

Slowly, but not so surely, he turned to rest on his forearms, speaking in a soft, calm tone. As though listening, the heifer's head tilted bewitchingly to one side, its elongated horns in part disguising its weepy eyes.

A curious buzzard overhead swooped down to check out the situation. Its far-reaching shadow served to unnerve the mammal, which launched its hindquarters high into the air and fearfully relocated to the higher ground.

Jon leapfrogged onto the bike from a tuft of solid earth. The faint beginnings of a crescent moon hung on top of the skyline ridge, softened by a web of clouds veering westwards to reveal a first glimpse of nightfall.

The engine roared at the turn of the ignition key, the chunky tyres making light work of the pebbly upward gradient. Pretty soon the route flattened into a smooth plateau, from where a sheer wall of rock stood before him.

He breathed in deeply to steel himself for the task ahead, his mind pondering his brush with disaster barely twenty-four hours before. Thoughts of Agnes filled his mind to somehow soothe his overwrought nerves, as though hastening him rapidly in a homeward direction. He smiled, and twisted his hand on the throttle.

*

---

* 'Fly Like an Eagle' – Steve Miller Band, 1976

The stocky superintendent called over to his youthful lackey, urging him in no uncertain terms to take a peek at the property's rear doors, unaware that his movements were being observed by a figure lurking in the bordering shrubs.

Turner strained his ears to catch a hint of the conversation, picking up instead on the DC's footsteps clomping along the abutting path. Like a shot he ducked behind a giant fir, thankful not to give the game away.

The lad halted a short distance from his hideout, his interest aroused by the trail of muck and sludge on the slabs, quickly figured to be from a creature of the night returning to the safety and warmth of its lair.

'Nothing doing, boss!' he muttered, continuing in a circle to find the chief snooping in a decrepit open-fronted outbuilding.

'Ah, Perkins!' the super sighed.

'What is it, boss?'

He pointed through a narrow gap to a cobweb-ridden contraption mounted on a pile of bricks in the far corner, urging him to squeeze his lean body between a mishmash of tools and oddments blocking the way.

'Reach your arm through son, and place a hand on the Jenny.'

'On the what?'

'The generator, you knucklehead!'

Using the flashlight on his phone to check for any hidden obstructions, he all at once stopped dead in his tracks.

'Footmarks… somebody was here!' he exclaimed.

The super's knees cracked as he sank down to the balls of his feet, his forefinger instantly shooting over his lips.

'We've got company, Perkins!'

Something rustled in the bushes, succeeded by a dull thud and a muted howl. The cell phone's beam retraced the muddy tracks back onto the drive, oddly snaking in the opposite direction towards the front door.

'Wildlife, boss?'

'Hmm, perhaps,' the super grunted, unconvinced.

Just metres away, Turner whinnied in shocked horror, as his right boot somehow hooked underneath an exposed root clump and the resulting loss of balance sent him hurtling into a patch of soft marsh grass. He irritably pulled the boot back on, cupping a hand over an ear to once again catch wind of the continuing parley.

'I saw him on the Jonathan Ross show, boss.'

'Who?' the super asked, frowning.

'JJ Gold!' the lad mumbled, still very in the dark as to the true purpose of their mission.

'And?'

'It's just… he came across as a top bloke.'

'As opposed to what, Perkins?'

'A criminal… possibly a murderer!'

'A murdering scumbag, Perkins!' the chief chuckled disparagingly. 'I simply want to ask him some questions in connection with the death of a notable gay socialite… who just so happened to be his ex-manager!'

'Uh oh… How did the guy die?'

'He was found suspended from a rope secured to a ceiling joist.'

'Hung out to dry, boss!'

'Spot on, Perkins… A hooded man matching Gold's description was sighted leaving the same West London apartment block.'

From his concealed vantage point, Turner huffed an exhalation of utter disbelief. There were so many conflicting stories, but none came close to the truth. 'You don't know jack shit,' he snarled inaudibly, buoyed by the sound of the gate swinging closed.

He tarried a while longer until they lumbered out of earshot, quietly sneaking out of his hidey-hole to finally make towards the croft. The way was hampered by a row of recently planted saplings lining the boundary fence, but a narrow gap allowed him just enough space to squeeze his lower body over the top rung. His feet hit the ground with a thud, throwing him against the side of the building, where luckily he managed to remain upright.

He peered through the kitchen window. Energised by a lust to uncover the merest scrap of evidence, his balled fists thumped fiercely at the sturdy frames in a determined effort to force open the metal crossbar lock.

How stupid, he thought, squatting down to grab a shard of broken slate wedged between the slabs. Ramming it against the quarter-pane with an explosive crack enabled him to slide his right mitt inside.

A further abortive yank left him no other choice but to stretch his arm along the tiled sill. Gripping his finger onto a small ovular picture frame, he carefully dragged it through the opening into the daylight.

His smug expression confusedly transformed into a frown, his icy glare focusing on a glossy keepsake of a smiley, loved-up couple posing before a camera. He'd never laid eyes on either of them in his entire life.

'Shit… shit… shit!' he ranted, hot-headedly despatching the memento into the brush behind him, unaware that the cheesy grins belonged to Gold's devoted partner Agnes, locked arm-in-arm with their close friend CJ.

Resigned to throw in the towel he double-checked in his mobile's saved messages, rapidly deleting the plethora of texts littering up the memory, pausing for a moment to dwell on a recently forwarded email:

THE KNOYDART PENINSULA, 2.2 MILES TO THE WEST OF INVERIE VILLAGE. POSTCODE: PH41 4PL.

So precise and to the point, but so badly misinformed, he figured confusedly, finally deciding to give up the ghost.

*

Sgùrr na Ciche, Lochaber

Jon's vibrating lips trumpeted the brass parts of the Paul Simon pièce de résistance 'Late in the Evening', his backside bouncing up and down on the quad's padded seat as it ascended towards the summit of a green grassy hillock.

He stamped on the brakes to gaze out into the unknown. An unyielding formation of aged igneous rocks jutted from the sunken gorge as though sculpted into the shape of an impenetrable stronghold. The changing shadows cast by a flickering ray of sunlight skipped in and out of a slender column slicing through the rocks. The light's trickery bizarrely enticed him forward, urging him to take courage in both hands.

Forearms trembling from the sheer strain on the handle grips, he dauntlessly ascended the precipitous hillside, manoeuvring the bike at an oblique angle before killing the engine dead at the curving ridge crest.

Partially concealed in the shadow of the lower escarpment, a tapering cleft offered a further glimmer of hope. It was accessed via a vitreous angular rock face scarcely broad enough to accommodate both man and machine.

With the bike almost defying gravity at a forty-five-degree angle, he guided the front wheels up into the slanted ingress. The hard suspension sent an agonising darting pain shooting along his spinal nerves.

Aslant to his right the bike dipped into a channelled recess. His biceps and shoulders collided with the cragged walls, made all the more disheartening as the bulkier rear tyres snagged against the narrowing lower ledge.

He breathed hard to summon up every ounce of strength he possessed, heaving this way and that until incredibly the wheels unlocked, finally freeing up the back end enough for him to skid out onto a smooth plateau.

The wide expanse of grassland spread in front of him caused his heart to leap. It was approached through a steep declivity of fragmenting bedrock, opening up onto a mountain-fringed valley stretching as far as the eye could see.

Tiredness started setting in as the light grew dim. His blurry vision made out an old sawmill situated a stone's throw away in a sunken hollow, its mildewing roof timbers captured under a flicker of the fading evening sun.

The notion of sleeping rough reminded him of his college days, camped out under the stars with a guitar in his hand, warbling the latest hit tunes with his muckers, under the influence of strong cider and marijuana.

Still more the twilight edged towards darkness, prodding him into finding a way through the more hazardous terrain. Luckily it was navigated without the slightest hitch as the bike chuntered in the direction of the ramshackle lean-to.

*

6.20a.m.

A melodious dawn chorus awakened him, rudely interrupted by the distant caw of an ill-mannered crow. Rubbing at his eyes, he thrust out his chest to sniff in the chilled, early-morning air. There had been a distinct change in the weather, he warily noted, owing to a bank of grey clouds encircling the billowing mountain peaks.

He crawled from in between the manky tarpaulin sandwiching his body and sluiced himself down with the remaining contents of an Evian water bottle picked up at the journey's outset. His growing hunger pangs were at least partly chased away by a flavourless Peperami snack retrieved from the front pocket of his gaberdine sailing jacket.

A further twist of the ignition key primed him for the final assault, the gentle gradient expanding through a sweep of mossy hills and hollows at last leading him to the familiar surroundings of the village outskirts.

He swung through a belt of patchy tarmac, chugging innocently past the oddly bustling ferry terminal, somewhat mystified as to the disquieting horde of would-be passengers killing time waiting for the early-morning departure.

The invigorating scent of the sea breeze snapped at his senses, and a playful thrust of the accelerator propelled him forward into the home stretch, totally oblivious to the comings and goings of the previous forty-eight hours.

FORTY-TWO

Canary Wharf, Isle of Dogs

THE CORK ON AN ice-cold bottle of Pol Roger popped and bounced against the ceiling, and moments later half a dozen glasses were raised in celebration. The toast was led at a crucial late-night soirée by a beaming Harry Maguire.

'Way to go, guys,' he said smugly, instantly replenishing his glass. 'Let's just sit back and watch the shit hit the fan!'

'Charlie Payne's already been sniffing around,' deputy Doug chipped in. 'He's convinced something big is about to break.'

'Payne by name, pain by nature,' Maguire sniggered, looking forward with relish to getting one over on his old adversary.

Fact-checker Babs's face turned livid with anger at the sound of her former employer's name, bringing to mind a turbulent two-year spell working ostensibly under the guidance of the notoriously self-centred big shot.

'He's nothing but a fat, arrogant, male chauvinist pig!'

'Don't mince your words, babe!' Doug laughed, one eye on the clock, counting the minutes until all hell broke loose.

His complexion beginning to redden, Harry set aside his champagne flute, opting instead to go for a drop of the hard stuff, pretty soon gushing from a bottle of fine Islay malt extracted from the boardroom drinks cabinet.

'Dougie, put in a call to Chris Lindsay; surely he'll be back by now.'

'No dice, boss; his phone's completely dead.'

'Probably still in flight mode,' Harry said, moving to the middle of the room to take centre stage. 'Okay everyone, let battle commence. All together now: *five... four... three... two... ONE!* It's all or nothing, gang!'

*

Hull, England

Phoebe slipped from beneath the sheets and snuck out onto the landing, thrown nervously off guard by the sound of an unexpected intrusion in the predawn hours. In the dim night light she stood motionless by the ornate balustrade at the head of the stairs.

'Hello... who's there?' her timid voice sounded.

'Only me,' Turner mumbled, freezing on the staircase, stupefied by the sight of her stark naked body. 'Oh my god!'

'Richard!' she half-squealed, making no effort to cover herself. 'I wasn't expecting you until tomorrow morning!'

'I... I... op–opted t–to drive through the night,' he stammered, struggling to avert his eyes from her curvaceous body.

She giggled unabashedly, evidently relishing the attention, and reached inside the adjacent bathroom to grab a towel from the handrail, more to spare his blushes than to preserve her own modesty.

'How was your trip, darling?'

'Huh, much ado about nothing, in Shakespearean terms!'

'Oh no... what was the problem?'

'The man's a certifiable hypochondriac, if I'm honest!'

'Let me make you a drink,' she offered, at last slipping into a satin housecoat. 'Did you hear the tragic news... on the radio?'

'News... what news?' he replied, somewhat intrigued, scurrying in her wake back down towards the kitchen.

She turned the radio on and put a saucepan of milk on the boil to prepare two mugfuls of cocoa. At the sound of the back-to-back recordings pouring out through the speaker, her face took on a sad expression.

'He's dead!' she muttered, a touch insensitively.

'Who?' he said, utterly confused.

'JJ Gold... the singer you idolised for so long... He was found washed up on a paradise island, somewhere in the Pacific!' she sniffled. 'I heard it on the late bulletin, before I turned in... The report was so moving!'

'Dead, you say? Well I declare!'

His stoic glare perturbed her, made worse by a flicker of a smile forming across his face. Without a trace of sympathy he gulped down the remains of his drink and sprang to his feet good and ready to hit the sack.

'But... I thought you worshipped the ground he walked on!'

'Just a passing phase, Phoebe... Nighty night!'

*

South Leicester

Shuffling along the corridor armed with a miscellany of Sunday newspapers, Rashid was suddenly afflicted by the beginnings of an asthma attack owing to the headline splashed across the tabloid at the top of the pile.

He took a sharp turn towards his office, only to find himself waylaid by an elderly couple teetering towards the empty day-room, both eager to stake an early claim to the armchairs directly facing the TV screen.

'Good morning, Saeed,' the hard-of-hearing hubby loudly greeted him, customarily mispronouncing his name.

'*Rashid*, Mr Barker... oh never mind!' he said exasperatedly, snapping down the handle on the electronic office door.

He scrolled through his contacts straight to Khalid's number, working himself into a mini-frenzy as it immediately switched to voicemail. His underlying panic was evident in the curtness of his half-garbled message.

'Khal, call me urgently... and check out this morning's *Screws of the World!*'

As he made to leave the room his ear-splitting call alert erupted, almost catching him off guard. '*Five-seven-o-five!*'

His brother's voice was barely audible. 'I'm about to board a plane... a small crop-sprayer out of the Isle of Skye. I'll give you a buzz when I reach Inverness.'

'Don't hang up, bro... It's JJ!'

'What about him?' Khal screeched, fighting to make himself heard above the whirring noise of the aircraft propeller.

'They're saying he didn't make it... in a freak boating accident!'

'Who's "they"? Where? When...? How?'

'The gutter press... In Thailand... or Malaysia!'

'But that's impossible!'

'How so?

'I was in Knoydart... barely forty-eight hours ago. The place was crawling with media people, acting on a tip-off as to his whereabouts.'

'But all the reports say he was swept under... off the coast of some exotic island!'

'They're talking crap! My guess is they got the hell out o' Dodge when they realised the vultures had begun to gather.'

'Then how do you explain the baseball cap with the initials "JJ" floating alongside the pectoral fin of an enormous shark?'

'Take a long, close look, and tell me if the boat's markings are red, white and blue,' Khal suggested, a tad overconfidently.

'How the hell would you know that?'

'You heard of the house that Jack built?'

'Spit it out, Khal!'

'You're looking at the boat that Jon built... At a guess, some happy-snapping local got very lucky, and sold the shot on.'

Rash again deliberated over the picture.

'But there's an incredible white sandy beach in the foreground,' he argued. 'And the sea's a glorious turquoise-blue colour!'

'Get yourself online, and search out the Scottish Highlands... the whole coastline is awash with deserted sandy beaches.'

'Khal... he's dead, it's all over *Daybreak* as we speak!' Rash said, catching a glimpse of the TV from the office's front window.

'My gut feeling tells me otherwise,' Khal replied, pulling back in his seat as the plane juddered along the runway. 'Must go!'

*

Shannon Airport, Republic of Ireland

Agnes stepped in line with boarding pass in hand, failing to spot the headline running across the front page of the *Sunday World*, conspicuously bulging from the racks of the terminal building's disorderly news stand.

END OF THE RAINBOW FOR GOLD

She moved her hips in a gentle swaying motion, soothed by the husky heartfelt tones of Gladys Knight pouring through her iPod's earbuds, completely oblivious to the chitchat going on among the other queuing passengers.

'I saw him live in concert at the Waterfront in Belfast back in '05,' a stocky Ulsterman yammered to a sceptical-looking youth, in the act of opening his passport for inspection. 'It's tragic; the boy was a rare talent!'

'Call me cynical, mate, but I reckon it's a massive publicity stunt... What, with a brand new album on the horizon!'

'Poppycock, son!' the verbal spat continued.

The forty-eight-hour mournful gathering had left her emotionally drained, not helped one bit by the announcement of a minor delay, to potentially create an issue with her connecting flight via Dublin's fair city.

'How long... the delay?' she called out to a passing air steward, briskly removing her headphones to halt his gallop.

'Ten minutes, max, miss!' he helpfully advised, forking left through the check-in counter to make off down the ramp.

She retuned in to the more mellow tones of her 'Classic Soul Ballads' compilation, at long last finding herself summoned forward to show her ID and passport, deaf to the earth-shaking topic of conversation.

*

Oadby, Leicester

Happily ensconced at his new lady friend Sheila's antique dining table, the off-duty Dan Hackett chewed on a charred Sunday roast, his befuddled brain striving to make some sense of the hot-off-the-press revelations.

'First he's in Papua New Guinea, dancing around a campfire exposing his dangly bits. Then he's spotted in a swish hotel on the banks of Loch Lomond serenading a roomful of guests... And now, worst of all, this!'

'This report says he relocated to a derelict homestead up in the Scottish Highlands, supposedly with a one-time call-girl,' Sheila added, shoving an abandoned broadsheet dumped on a vacant chair under his nose.

Singer-songwriter Gold feared drowned as boat capsizes
Continued on Page 3

'It seems Murdoch's rag is the only paper carrying the picture,' Dan said, flipping the page to peruse the text. 'Just look at his career record; five multi-platinum albums, on top of countless million-selling hit singles... wow!'

'Doubtless his record company will be rubbing their hands together,' Sheila voiced, suitably topping up his wine glass.

'For sure there'll be something in the pipeline... against his better wishes!'

'What do you mean?'

Hackett recounted his brief coming together with the star at his country estate some years before, by coincidence under similarly tragic circumstances. The lump in his throat was mollified by a large swig of Cotes du Rhone.

'It's the whole tortured genius thing,' Sheila sadly reflected. 'Angst-ridden, soul searching lyrics, sung with such heartrending emotion.'

'What a tragedy.'

Dabbing lightly at her lips with a starched napkin, she noticed the wounded look washing over his normally impassive features, and used it to wipe away a tear escaping onto her cheek.

'He cut a sad and sorry figure, that's for sure.'

'He wasn't at all like that!' Hackett said, jumping to his defence. 'I found him to be intelligent and sharp-witted.'

She softly recited a line from the track 'Soldier of Misfortune' as though drifting off into a little world of her own.

'That song stayed with me for days.'

'I must give it another listen.'

'Promise me you will... during a quiet moment.'

'Consider it done, sweetheart... And so – to JJ!' he said, raising his glass. 'May his soul, tortured or otherwise, rest in peace.'

*

Belmarsh Prison, south east London

The veins on CJ's face threatened to explode, his blood pressure escalating to dangerous levels. For the umpteenth time he examined the photo of the *Hummingbird*, encircled by Jon's discarded articles of clothing.

'Fuck... this can't be for real!' he cursed, pacing to and fro.

'What's up, Jenks?' cellmate Benny croaked, his mid-morning catnap interrupted by CJ's untypical fit of anger.

'Take a gander at this, Ben!'

'Hmm... Malaysia... I once went to Singapore,' he said dozily.

'Malaysia...? I'd know that beach anywhere! It's Camusdarach, five minutes from the gaff where I used to live!' CJ said, not knowing whether to laugh or cry.

'So what's the big deal?'

'The beach in the photo... how could the press get it so badly wrong? The headline says he drowned... my old mate Jon!' CJ whined with a heavy heart, suppressing the urge to smash anything within his grasp.

'Wait a minute... you knew JJ Gold?' Benny snorted apprehensively, squinting down his bulbous nose at him.

'The skiff in the photo... we built it almost from scratch with our bare hands,' CJ snivelled. 'And what about Aggie...? She'll be devastated!'

'I haven't a clue what you're talking about... but JJ, a tasty snack for a great white? It don't bear thinking about!'

They both slumped heavily onto their bunks, the springs creaking from Benny's excess body weight. He made to crack a joke, but thought better of it, knowing only too well CJ was not in a chatty frame of mind.

*

Ascot, Berkshire

A particularly crotchety Miles Templeton slurped noisily at a glassful of freshly squeezed orange juice, his head throbbing from an excess of red wine and port consumed during the previous evening's lavish dinner party.

He grabbed the cordless phone from its cradle, squinting through a blurry haze to make out the numbers on the handset's face, finally focusing sufficiently to punch in the area code for the office dogsbody, Stan.

'Pick up, you fucking idiot,' he muttered, tapping impatiently on the table.

'Boss… is that you?'

'No, it's Osama bin Laden!' Miles raged. 'I need you to organise for a glass master to be dropped at the pressing plant in Mitcham.'

'No problem, I'll be on it first thing tomorrow.'

'*Now*, you bonehead!'

'Shit, boss… I'm in the middle of something!' he said above a girlish giggle in the background. 'Why the sudden urgency?'

'Switch on the news, Stanley son. I want every individual JJ track available for download within forty-eight hours.'

'But I've got plans… for the day!'

'And I'm a genie in a bottle, here to grant you three wishes. First, wish your lecherous arse out of that crib right away; and second, aspire to get back to me pronto, before you piss me off and ruin my day completely!'

'And the third wish?' Stan asked with trepidation.

'Thank your lucky stars it's a Sunday, son… or you'd be wishing your pathetic little life away searching for a new job!'

He rudely hung up and slid across the marble floor towards the atrium. Waiting expectantly, a petite Japanese masseuse greeted him with an extended hand to nimbly lead him into the swimming-pool complex.

'Be gentle with me, Manaka,' he kidded.

His eye was drawn towards a portrait of JJ suspended from the wall. 'I'll miss you son, more than you could ever know. But trust me – you're about to go out with a bang… of seismic proportions!'

FORTY-THREE

Brightwater Croft

With the quad bike parked out of harm's way in the cluttered outbuilding, Jon slothfully made his way to the front porch. His curiosity was more than a little aroused by a trail of downtrodden earth cutting across the driveway.

His frown tightened and his hackles rose. An unwelcome visitor had been poking their nose where they were not welcome, a fact made even more evident by the sight of a broken windowpane close to the rear entrance.

'What the hell's been going on?' he mumbled, utterly confused. 'A break-in, here on Knoydart...? Surely not!'

He crept through the living area and unlocked the lean-to. A scattering of jagged shards lay spread across the tiles. Perhaps the window was hit by a stray bullet, he thought, fired by a myopic member of a shooting party?

A familiar voice rang out from the direction of the half-open front door. 'Hello, is anybody there? Mr Ryan?'

'Hey, Tommy, how's it going?' Jon said, acknowledging the off-duty postman. 'What are you doing working on a Sunday?'

'Your other half sent word to say she'll be arriving on the late ferry,' he divulged, adding: 'You look a wee bit hot and bothered!'

'Nothing I can't handle, Tommy... though it does seem someone's been snooping around the place during my absence.'

'Morag at the Lodge did mention how busy they'd been for the time of year... like bees around a honeypot, she claimed!'

'Ah well, thanks for the info, matey,' Jon said. He caught the postman's eyes veering towards the mean machine standing in the outhouse.

'What a smashing piece of kit!'

'Not bad, eh? She sailed through her maiden voyage with flying colours... across the rough bounds, can you believe?'

'I'm green with envy! Anyway, must fly,' Tommy replied, before halting on the drive. 'I swear there was something else...'

'I'm all ears, buddy!'

He scurried back to his tiny Subaru pick-up ticking over by the gate, pausing mid-step to shout back in an 'aha' moment.

'Your boat... it's all fixed up!'

Jon flashed a cheerful thumbs-up and stepped back inside, cursing himself for his dumb forgetfulness. He needed to shower and make himself presentable in advance of Agnes's much-anticipated homecoming; first though, he deftly set out two wine glasses and a bottle of her favourite tipple in the centre of the dining table.

*

The Old Forge, Inverie

'I was simply tucking into a... *hic*... plateful of prawns and... *hic*... got talking to a couple of locals... and... *hic*... what do you know – the ferry-boat... *hic*... puttered out to sea without me!' the worse-for-wear wanderer spluttered into the pub payphone. 'So you could say... *hic*... I'm up a creek without a paddle!'

He turned towards the lengthening queue, teetering to one side before passing the phone to the next woman in line.

'The last ferry departs at six-thirty!' she said.

'It's chock full... *hic*... so I'm told!'

'You could go on foot,' Jon chipped in, trying to hide his amusement. 'But then again, you're hardly in a fit state!'

'How far... approximately?'

'Twenty miles... as the crow flies!'

The guy's hands reached up to cover his temples, his face bearing the giveaway signs of deep disappointment. He stared at Jon and mumbled incoherently, instead making back towards the bar to drown his sorrows.

'I could get you halfway in just shy of an hour.'

'How?' the guy asked.

'On the back of my quad bike.'

'You'd do that?'

'Why not? But I must be back at the pier by six-thirty sharp.'

The guy laughed, as if sobering up instantly, and athletically skipped up to his room. Seconds later he reappeared laden with a bulky backpack,

196

promptly strapped onto his back so they could get the show on the road.

'I desperately need to be in Manchester by the crack of dawn!' he said, arms dangling like a puppet's on broken strings.

'Brace yourself – and hold on tight!'

The bike raced away pretty much at full tilt, pretty soon veering off into an area of rougher, bumpier terrain. His knuckles whitening, the passenger hung on for grim death, gripping his hands on the rear wheel arches.

'What brings a scholarly Englishman to a backwater like Knoydart?' the guy shouted out from his pillion position.

'I found love!' came Jon's laconic reply.

'How wonderful… and what do you do to make ends meet?'

'Boatbuilding… and you?'

'I'm an investigative journalist… currently employed by the BBC.'

'Doing what exactly?'

'Working on a documentary… which it appears has gone completely tits up.'

'What kind of documentary?' Jon asked cagily.

He became quieter, mumbling something about the ill-fated central character who'd gone and got himself killed, before he was rendered speechless by the sight of the endless terrain stretching for miles ahead of him.

'Shit happens, doesn't it?'

'I guess so,' Jon grunted, jerking back on the throttle. 'Wrap your arms around my waist, and don't let go until I say!'

Following Jon's instructions, and anxiously taking stock of the granite outcrop shimmering up ahead like a mighty fortress, he closed his eyes, willing the bike up the near-vertical slope as it edged ever closer to the dizzying summit.

At the top Jon killed the engine, and they stood gazing out admiringly across the desolate valley pointing in a straight line to the western tip of the loch. The stranger glanced at him, smiling a half-sad smile.

'So rugged, yet so beautiful!'

'Enjoy it… you're on your own from here on in.'

'How far do you reckon?'

'Seven, possibly eight miles.'

'The name's Neil – Neil McClelland.'

'Jon… er, Jon Ryan.'

'I really can't thank you enough, Jon!'

Jon clasped his hand. 'It was the least I could do… Good luck!' he said warmly, and remounted the bike. With a mischievous spin of the rear wheels, he spun it around in a semicircle and hastened off into the untamed wilderness.

*

Knoydart

His heart skipped a beat when at last he clapped eyes on her alighting from the ferryboat, his feet quickening to a brisk pace on the jetty. Within moments, her mouth pressed hard on his in a passionate kiss.

'I have something to show you,' he said, grabbing her rucksack with a spring in his step. 'I bought a set of wheels!'

He strode purposefully to the mud-spattered quad, strapped the luggage on the rack and proudly fired her up.

'Boys and their toys,' Aggie muttered with little enthusiasm. 'Knoydart used to be such a peaceful place, Jonathan!'

'She'll be worth her weight in gold, Aggie!'

She straddled the seat a trifle reluctantly, pulling her hat's earflaps over her ears to blot out the annoying racket. Her disgruntlement was patently obvious from the scowl etched upon her face.

'What about the fuel?'

'Jerrycans… I'll stock up, and keep them in the outhouse, like I do with the two-stroke for the *Hummingbird*'s outboard!'

'The dear sweet *Hummingbird*… where is she now?' she asked pensively, glancing away.

'Convalescing, in a nearby boatyard.'

'But she capsized… and sank!'

'She's all fixed up, like new… we're just waiting for the motor to dry out.'

Agnes looked aghast, biting her tongue to stop herself giving him a piece of her mind. Lady luck had been kind to him, yet in no time his flirtation with death only seemed somehow to have strengthened his resolve.

'What are you like?' she snapped at him, finally warming to the idea of his new mode of transport. 'Take me home!'

*

Glasgow, Scotland

'*The train will shortly be arriving at Glasgow's Queen Street station, where it will terminate.*' The automated announcement caused the exhausted Neil McClelland to wake suddenly from a mind-numbing slumber.

'Phooey... I was out for the count!' he said, stretching his arms into the air and forcing himself into an upright position.

A young Scot acknowledged him from the seat opposite. 'Alright, pal?'

'I'm all aches and pains, to be honest,' he puffed.

The lad sniggered behind his hand and pulled his headphones around his neck, ready to engage him in light chitchat.

'You were snoring like an old sow!'

'Was I? Oops, sorry... What are you listening to?'

'Something I downloaded illegally... do you promise not to tell?'

'I swear to God.'

'The new JJ Gold album!'

'Really? I didn't realise it was available yet... What's it like?'

'Extraordinary!'

'*Jesus H. Christ*!' McClelland shrieked, jumping to his feet.

'What the hell's wrong, man?'

'It was him!'

'Who, what, where, when, how?'

'JJ frigging Gold!' he exclaimed, stunned with the sudden realisation.

The train came to a juddering halt, stalling the youth's gobsmacked reply. Bag in hand, McClelland was gone in a flash.

FORTY-FOUR

Television Centre, Shepherd's Bush

'GOOD MORNING, YOU'RE WATCHING BBC's *Breakfast* on a wet and windy start to the day here in London... Firstly some breaking news which looks set to end the speculation regarding the death by drowning of the missing superstar JJ Gold. The BBC's very own Neil McClelland is here exclusively, live from our Manchester studios. Neil, we're hearing the reports may be inaccurate – please tell us more.'

The sleep-filled eyes of the public looked on in disbelief. The memory of Gold's recent death was still fresh in their minds. Yet just a few days later they braced themselves for news of a remarkable Lazarus-like comeback.

'I'd been researching a docuseries up in the Highlands of Scotland and, how should I put it, got into a tight spot... whereupon I was approached by a total stranger, who out of the goodness of his heart offered me a lift.'

'Across some pretty unforgiving terrain, or so I gather?'

'Bumpy as hell... riding pillion on the back of a souped-up quad bike.'

'And to the best of your belief, the man to whom you're indebted was none other than the missing rock icon JJ Gold?'

'Indisputably... in spite of his hirsute, unkempt appearance!'

'So at first you weren't sure?'

'I had the strangest feeling that I knew him from somewhere... but it took a while before the penny finally dropped.'

'How would you describe his general wellbeing?'

'He appeared in fine health... and in exceptionally good spirits!'

A cynical smirk laced the anchorman's twitching lips, his silky-smooth voice taking on a sceptical, almost detached tone. This was sharp-wittedly heeded by his female co-host, who waded in to pick up the slack.

'Unlike someone struggling with a mental health disorder?'

'I'm under no illusions that the man I met was the real McCoy. I have, after all, been sifting through a heap of stock footage to piece together the career-spanning, warts-and-all retrospective I previously referred to.'

'A rather revealing docuseries, you say; pray tell us more… such as when it's likely to be aired on our TV screens?'

'I haven't a clue… and following yesterday's events there's a possibility the piece may never see the light of day.'

'Not even in response to the public's growing interest?'

'He should be hailed as a national treasure,' McClelland spoke out, 'rather than hunted down like a wanted criminal!'

A long, pregnant pause was filled only by the sound of nervous laughter from the host. Her male counterpart reacted quickly to rescue the situation, reading from a clipboard on his lap.

'Despite the fact his new album *Angel of Death* has rocketed straight to number one within minutes of its release?'

'Is that so? I wasn't aware.'

'With sales already topping the million mark!'

'I very much doubt he knows.'

'Really? Could you expand on that?'

'It's crystal clear he no longer craves the limelight… and in my view we should respect his wishes and leave him alone.'

'Thank you, Neil McClelland. Here's Carol with the weather!' the host said exhaustedly, his hand grasping at his tumbler of water.

*

Kingston upon Hull

Richard Turner sat transfixed in front of the TV screen. His immediate reaction was to doubt the veracity of the unheard-of hack's tale, delivered with the smug confidence of someone eager to make a name for himself.

'The devious bastard!' he cried out, too immersed in McClelland's ramblings to spot Phoebe entering the room.

'Richard… what's got into you?'

'Huh, there's a complete nutter on TV, spouting a pack of lies!'

'He sounded pretty convincing to me,' Phoebe said, shooting him a curious glance. 'He'd been visiting the Scottish Highlands.'

Turner's face flushed, his fingers tugging embarrassedly at the hem of his dressing gown riding up his bare legs. Sometimes he felt she could see right through him, and decided just this once to give it to her straight.

'I know a thing or two about Mr Jonathan Gold,' he said scathingly. 'Things that would cause ructions at the BBC!'

She snuck up behind the sofa and proceeded to manipulate her thumbs into the middle of his neck, her healing fingers massaging the muscles between his shoulder blade and spine with a deliberate slowness.

'Anything you'd care to share, darling?'

'Gold is a vicious criminal!'

'He is?' she asked, showing keen interest.

'I could tell you things that would make you hair curl!'

Her eyes lingered just a moment on the tell-tale bulge under his bathrobe, before his ardour was swiftly nipped in the bud as she increased the pressure on a painful knot, banishing any further lewd thoughts from his mind.

He whimpered, quickly realising the error of his ways. His lustful smile was soon replaced by a dreamy-eyed expression as, relaxing into the gentle swaying motion, his head again fell back, her calming voice smooth like velvet.

'Just lie back… and tell me all about it!'

FORTY-FIVE

Late April 2011

HIS HOUSEHOLD CHORES COMPLETED, DS Dan Hackett chillaxed. Slouched in his favourite chair, he used the remote control to pump up the stereo, content to while away an indolent hour poring over the new JJ Gold masterpiece.

The continuing rain splattered loudly against the windows, very soon quelled by the sweet tones of a solitary cello echoing poignantly through the speakers, trailed by a fervid ensemble of soaring violas and violins.

He stiffened against the pile of upright cushions, his lips rounding in amazement at the opening bars of the title 'Luckless', as its wondrous orchestral overture rose almost to fever pitch in a fusion of woodwind and booming timpani.

Then his throat tightened, as from beneath the prelude came the inimitable voice, choking over the track's delicate beauty, rendered with a gut-wrenching honesty and vulnerability to melt the hardest of hearts:

'*Lost in a place I once knew so well*
Endlessly spiralling downward into hell
Choked, bereft, not coming up for air
Hopelessly drowning in a river of despair
Loveless, lifeless, luckless.'

He hit the rewind button to delve more deeply into the tune's lyrics, racked with the feeling a hidden meaning lurked between the lines. The man was messed up, but he'd never shown any suicidal tendencies; yet the inconsolable and anguished timbre in his voice suggested his world had come crashing down.

The birdlike trill of his cell phone moved him to mute the volume, inopportunely spelling the end to his all-too-brief Saturday respite. The familiar rasping tones of his chief, DI Philpott, barked in his ear.

'Danny boy… we finally got the lab report back on the severed limb found at King's Meadow. It appears we have a match!' the gaffer unveiled. 'I suggest you get your arse down here post-haste, if not sooner!'

Hackett dashed up to the bedroom and pulled on the work clothes strewn on the floor. His inquisitive mind was still very much focused on the impact of the jaw-dropping masterpiece continually ringing in his ears.

'Why in the world did you just take off?' he mumbled to himself, zapping the car from inside the house and heading out.

*

Leicestershire Police HQ

'The deceased's DNA shows him to be of Asian origin,' Philpott revealed, sliding a copy of the report to the DS. 'Jim Frobisher, the forensics top dog, estimated the time of death to be in excess of three years ago. Get a load of the mugshot attached to the page. It's none other than your old adversary, Mean Mr Mistry!'

Hackett shot bolt upright, immediately picturing the scar-faced slimeball with a long history of run-ins with the law, not to mention a psychopathic obsession for beating up on a handful of elderly ladies.

'Amir Mistry?' Hackett said, finding his tongue.

'Sidekick of Rashid whatsisname.'

'The Karachi kid!'

Philpott laughed coarsely. He proceeded to remind Hackett of a notorious corner-shop robbery some years before, when, fleeing from the premises at the arrival of the police, the slippery Mistry left his supposed best friend in the lurch.

'… And Shah took the rap!' the DI recalled.

'He only entered the store to ensure the old dear was okay,' the DS sighed. 'He saw everything from the getaway car.'

Hackett went on to explain how Rashid Shah had turned his life around working in a care facility for the elderly and infirm. Moreover, the court had reversed his conviction, as all the allegations made against him deemed false.

'On appeal, if I'm not mistaken,' Philpott interjected. 'Wasn't it Mistry's namesake Dipak who finally got him off?'

'His father, to be exact.'

'A cunning old fox if ever there was one!'

They quit talking to turn their attentions to the comprehensive report. Its findings were set forth in a thick wad of documents, accompanied by an inner layer of stark, glossy images unearthed from the extra-size A4 folder.

'Ugh!' Hackett said, wincing with disgust. 'I understand the old boy disowned Amir soon after he walked free.'

'I never did like bullies!'

'Me neither,' the DS concurred, his complexion whitening over as his head swam with a jumble of conflicting thoughts.

'What's up, Danny boy? You look like you saw a ghost!'

'The ghost of a vanished rock star, perhaps.'

'Get a grip!'

'Think about it, Matt... King's Meadow, a proverbial stone's throw from Granby!'

'Shit, here we go again!'

Hackett pulled up a chair and rolled up his shirt sleeves, an outbreak of goosebumps covering his bare forearms.

'Guv... trust me!'

'Okay, Sherlock... what is it?'

'We urgently need to reopen the Gold case,' he said, with a sinister tone. 'Only this time around as a murder investigation.'

FORTY-SIX

AGNES'S BLOOD BEGAN to boil. She fixed her narrowed eyes upon the spoor of muddy footprints encircling the croft, unable to fathom why anyone of sound mind would seek to encroach on their own little piece of heaven.

'I'm not happy, Jon. Not happy at all!'

'A posse of hip-flask-carrying deer hunters, I'd imagine,' Jon shot back. 'In all likelihood completely off their faces.'

"More akin to a herd of wild elephants!' she continued. 'Running amok in very our own back yard. It beggars belief!'

A shaft of moonlight poured through the kitchen window, silhouetting the row of objects lining the shelf. Her compounded feelings of anger towards the intrusion were all too evident in her infuriated expression.

'Aggie... what's wrong?'

'The framed photograph of CJ and me cuddled up beside the boat... it's missing!'

'There must be some rational explanation,' he responded, as though trying to convince himself as much as her.

She looked daggers at the empty space on the ledge, before unleashing her fury on the numerous cupboards and drawers, turning the contents from top to bottom in a wild, frantic search for the missing item.

'Go back to the pub and call the police, Jon!'

'Uh-uh... no cops, Aggie!' he retorted.

Feeling an urgent need to quell an attack of the munchies, he grabbed a frying pan from the shelf.

'No Jon, put it back!'

'What's got into you, woman?'

'It's high time you started looking after yourself,' she urged him, finally calming herself. 'Take a quick look outside.'

He gazed out of the window at the star-studded sky, then tilted his head slowly back towards her. The moon's feeble rays illuminated her pale, glowing features, somehow making her look more beautiful than ever.

Jon felt his mood lightening. 'Let's take a moonlight dip!' he said, his forceful grip tugging at her arms to entice her towards the door.

*

Sandaig Bay

They splashed waist high in the biting albeit invigorating water, in turn plunging with barely a ripple beneath the glassy-topped surface. The near perfect silence was all at once broken by the husky strains of Jon's voice:

'I forgot my shirt at the water's edge.

The moon is low tonight.

Nightswimming deserves a quiet night.

I'm not sure all these people understand.'*

'What an amazing song!' Jon hollered, happily splashing in the rippling tributary. 'I played that album over and over.'

'Me too... I loved that band!'

'We worked together at a couple of major festivals... across the pond.'

'You worked alongside R.E.M.? Wow!'

He turned his attention to the song 'Everybody Hurts', lustily belting out the lyrics in his own inimitable style before flipping over in the water like the Man from Atlantis to backstroke effortlessly to her side.

'Don't, Jonathan... When I hear that song, my heart melts!'

'I didn't yet ask... how was your trip?'

Her wet skin glistened yellowish in the paling light, the contours of her upper body emanating a silky reflection. It made her look more beautiful than ever, only serving as a reminder of how much she meant to him.

'Just about bearable,' she said, frowning.

'Tell me – don't bottle it all up!'

She ducked beneath the surface to try to hide the tears welling in her eyes. Before long she had bobbed up behind him, her arms playfully enveloping his waist in an unsuccessful attempt to tug him backwards into the water.

'I spent most of the time crying.'

'Ah, Aggie!' he said sympathetically.

'On my childhood sweetheart's shoulder,' she let on, sighing deeply. 'I hadn't seen him in more than twenty years.'

'You sure kept that one quiet!'

---

* 'Nightswimming' by R.E.M. (Warner Bros 1992)

He drew a long breath and dived under out of arm's reach, half-jestingly turning a deaf ear to her light patter. He felt safe in the knowledge he could always trust her implicitly, despite any obstacles that were placed in their way.

'We were like sister and brother.'

'You don't have to explain anything,' he said, coming up for air and breast-stroking through the surf towards her.

'But, I thought you should know!'

She squealed in surprise as he mischievously lunged forward to sweep her off her feet. In an instant she was sucking the breath from his lips while backpedalling a mite unsteadily through the shallows towards the shore.

'So tell me... if you must!'

She cheekily urged him to put some clothes on, laughing and gesticulating towards his shrivelled, shrunken manhood, as playfully escaping his clutches she scampered, brassiere in hand, up onto a sandy hillock.

'He headed off Down Under... I'd not long turned fourteen.'

'With his family?'

'Just his mum... his father did a runner before he reached his teens.'

'And he was related to your gran?'

'No, she took him in, while his ma slaved day and night to make ends meet.'

They trudged up to the gateway to the croft, Agnes's teeth once again gritting at the tracks very much evident on the drive. In truth though it was good to be home, safe in the embrace of the only man she'd ever truly loved.

FORTY-SEVEN

Leicestershire

DS Dan Hackett's imagination ran wilder than he ever thought possible. His head, clutched in his hands in blinding despair, was filled with the same inconceivable images replaying over and over as if locked on permanent rewind.

The thought that Turner had been telling the truth, and the nightmarish vision of Jonathan Gold hacking at a freshly dead corpse before ditching the body parts into a festering quagmire, filled him with a sense of dread.

He prayed he was wrong but guessed he wasn't, acknowledging that his first impression of Gold had been way off base – his judgement perhaps clouded by a desire to interact with a man he held in such high regard.

*

Head down and seizing a rare moment of peace and quiet at his desk, DI Philpott was leafing through a *Telegraph* article spotlighting a 'journey through the clouds' on board Canada's spectacular Rocky Mountaineer train. He ground his teeth in frustration at the sound of his cell phone vibrating on his melamine desktop.

'Matt, it's Dan,' the DS said, receiving no response. 'Matt... *Matt!*'

'Sorry, Dan... I was miles away,' he at last answered. 'Somewhere between Vancouver and Calgary, to be exact.'

'Eh...? You're kidding me!'

'If only... So, what's eating you today?'

'My arch-nemesis Mr Turner mentioned something about an industrial unit over in Market Harborough, where a heap of Gold's possessions were put in storage,' Hackett said eagerly. 'I'd like to take a root around ASAP, guv!'

'I'm on it... Any clues as to the address?'

Hackett flipped speedily through his pocketbook to ferret out the name of the removal company previously noted down by an alert young PC responding to a needless call-out from a resident in the Granby vicinity.

'Try E. C. Thomas and Sons on Charles Street in Leicester... they provided two separate crews to shift his stuff.'

'Got it... I'll organise a warrant, and a couple of uniforms to lend a hand.'

'Bang on, guv!'

'And Danny...' The chief's tone softened uncharacteristically. 'I'm not too proud to admit I may've got this one wrong.'

'Forget it, Matt... every rose has its thorn!'

'I also neglected to mention a call which came in from the BBC's legal department.'

'About what, exactly?'

'In reference to a nut job who contacted their news team.'

'Don't tell me... Richard Turner?'

'*Panorama* pre-recorded an interview with him,' Philpott said startlingly. 'Scheduled to air at eight-thirty tomorrow night.'

Hackett's face turned red, a deep shade of pink spreading across his cheeks. He felt the urge to cry out and smash something, anything within his reach. Thankfully he was able to gather his senses and somehow hold his temper in check.

'That's crazy... he could blow the whole gaff!'

'He claims to have been an eyewitness, back in '05.'

'And subsequently withheld key evidence...? Slap a charge on him, guv!'

'Let's keep schtum and see what he has to say,' Philpott said circumspectly. 'I don't want him running scared again.'

Hackett saw the wisdom of this. 'KEEP CALM AND CARRY ON' was the motif on the chief's coffee mug, perchance in keeping with his oddly laissez-faire approach; yet somehow it prodded him into seeing things from a slightly more relaxed perspective.

'Rashid Shah... the Karachi Kid?'

'What about him?'

'What say we bring him in for questioning? My instincts tell me he may be a little more cooperative now Mistry's breathed his last!'

'Stay put, Dan... I'll get DS Wade on it,' the chief said sympathetically. 'This is just the beginning of the calm before the storm.'

'Cheers, guv... Wait... did you say *DS* Wade?'

'Yep… he sailed through his interview!' Philpott said, to Dan's astonishment. 'Now put your feet up and get some rest, son!'

*

Two days later
Market Harborough, Leicestershire

Turner's exaggerated revelations during the previous night's broadcast had done nothing to lighten Hackett's demeanour. It was not helped by the arrival of a pair of ill-equipped PCs deployed to the outlying warehouse unit.

'No torches? You pair of muppets!' he hollered in exasperation. 'You can't see the back of your hand in there!'

'Er… um… sorry, sir!'

In almost comical fashion their heads nodded back and forth, bizarrely reminiscent of a bumbling double act. The detective's response was scathingly caustic.

'This is a murder investigation, not a fucking chimps' tea-party!'

'M–murder?' the younger PC gasped in horror, glancing back at his colleague to search for some kind of reassurance.

'That's what I said. Now get your arses back to base and don't come back until you're both properly kitted out!'

An eerie wind pulsated through the roll-up doors of the capacious metal-walled unit, flapping at the polythene dustsheets spread out over an agglomeration of furniture and personal effects piled haphazardly within, captured in the penetrating beam of Hackett's prized special ops flashlight.

He pluckily worked his way deeper amongst a stack of rack-mounted electronic gear, his eyes drawn to a silver-handled object glinting in the torch's beam. On closer inspection it proved to be a pristine baseball bat bearing a signature in felt-tip pen, presumably scrawled by a US slugger previously unknown to the sports-mad DS.

Smoothing his hand along the barrel, Hackett dug his fingernail into a groove located in the bat's curved end-cap. In the flashlight's beam, he pored over a sliver of chipped lacquer lodged precariously between his forefinger and thumb, before easing it with the utmost care into a plastic contact-lens case retrieved from his jacket pocket. Something inside him told him this could blow the case wide open.

He was making his way back outside to his vehicle to bag and tag the spoils when the returning cop car skidded to within a metre of his boots.

Hackett resolutely stood his ground, keenly clutching his prized possessions to his chest. He glowered through the car's open window, catching the driver's dumb expression while trying not to crack his face.

'What's your name, boy?'

'R–Rogers, sir!' the PC said, blinking uncertainly.

'Not Hamilton…? As in Lewis?'

'N–no sir!'

'Well Roy… or is it Ginger…? You missed the boat by a long chalk, so get out of my face and take your pal Trigger with you!'

The hapless lad quickly took the hint and dropped the gearstick into reverse, much to the relief of his equally bemused partner. Glancing back across the dark courtyard he gormlessly put in his own twopenn'orth.

'Trigger? The tall guy, from *Only Fools and Horses*?' he said, looking hurt and indignant. 'I look fuck all like him!'

FORTY-EIGHT

Leicestershire Police HQ

'*THE PERSON YOU ARE CALLING is temporarily unavailable; please try later,*' Khalid's recorded message squawked at the second time of asking. Spiralling towards a panic attack, Rashid once more hung up.

He motioned despondently to the female PC in attendance, somehow heartened by her tolerant and calming attitude. Her soft voice offered him her seal of approval to leave a message or try an alternative number.

Yet again the phone went directly to voicemail. He opened his mouth, but the words came out no better than gibberish.

'Khal... Khal, I need your help!' he cried in desperation. 'I've been detained in connection with the murder of Amir!'

'Do you have a solicitor you wish to appoint?' the girl asked. 'Or do you wish one to be appointed on your behalf?'

'I honestly don't know,' Rashid glumly replied.

'Think it over,' she said, rising from her seat and advancing towards the door. 'Can I get you a cup of something, tea maybe?'

'Coffee, please!'

'How do you take it?'

'White with one sugar, brown preferably.'

She casually ambled along the corridor to a nearby vending machine, momentarily put off her stride by a hissing sibilant sound filling her ears like the penetrating whirr of a dentist's drill: '*Five-seven-o-five...*'

'Khal... I'm in deep shit, bro!' Rashid answered irately.

'Hey, little bro... what's going on?'

'I'm caught in the middle of a living nightmare, Khal!'

'Whoa, take it easy... and fill me in on exactly what's been going on...'

*

Rashid's factual albeit garbled explanation seemed to shake Khalid to the core. The numerous questions burning within him were stemmed by a feeling of tension in his forehead, causing him to bite his lip and stay silent.

His stomach retched at the mention of the human remains discovered so close to the Gold estate, compounded by a nightmarish vision replaying in his mind; but his brother was no killer, let alone an unmerciful butcher.

'Are you serious…? They're trying to pin the murder on you?'

'My name's on a short list of suspects!'

'Be vigilant, Rash… and whatever you do, stay cool,' Khalid advised. 'I'll be on the first available train out of St Pancras.'

'It's not quite so easy!'

'Simply tell them the truth. You have nothing to hide!'

Close to where the stairs entered the main hallway a minor kerfuffle appeared to be taking place, at first glance initiated by a tall, gangling figure kitted out in a multi-coloured tracksuit and a reverse baseball cap.

Rashid turned towards the disturbance just as Chukka's elbow connected with the chin of a yellow-jacketed officer, who though partially dazed from the blow somehow gathered himself sufficiently to slap a cuff around his wrist.

Gently, the WPC nudged Rash's arm, motioning for him to move along to a significantly quieter part of the building. She ushered him into a sparsely furnished side room and beckoned to him to take a seat at the table.

'DS Wade will be with you shortly.'

'Uh… whatever happened to Mr Hackett?'

'He's up to his eyes,' she said, as if amused. 'I'm sure it hasn't escaped your attention, but things are a little manic around here!'

They waited in silence.

*

Custody suite

'Interview commencing at 1150 hours. Detective Sergeant Jeffrey Wade and Police Constable Monica Burke in attendance,' the WPC ceremoniously announced, acknowledging the DS's arrival.

'Morning!' Wade greeted him briefly.

'Hi!' Rash similarly replied.

'I want you, if possible, to cast your mind back to the night of November the eleventh, 2005.'

'How can I be sure?'

'A dark blue Ford Mondeo registered in the name of Rashid Mohammed Shah was seen fleeing the Leicestershire village of Granby between the hours of one and two o'clock in the morning… Perhaps you'd care to explain?'

'It was my car, but I wasn't behind the wheel.'

'Which begs the question: where were you between the hours of midnight and three a.m. on the night in question?'

'I went over this with Mr Hackett just a few days after the incident!'

He returned Wade's gaze as though engaging in an infantile contest to stare one another down. He was scarcely able to make head or tail of the detective's good-humoured air, expressed in the wry smile twisting his lips.

'Think back. Try to remember!'

'Amir's bags were packed, and dumped outside the door.'

'Mistry… the deceased?'

'Absolutely!'

'So you booted him out… why?'

'Simples… he stopped contributing to the rent.'

'So you changed the locks?'

'No… I swiped his keys, while he was sleeping.'

'And you fell out… presumably?'

'We had words!'

'As in a disagreement? An altercation?'

'Something like that,' he said, becoming hot under the collar. 'It was five and a half years ago, for Christ's sake!'

Despairingly he rose to his feet, his teeth clenched, about to spit blood. Not quite knowing what to do with himself he cursed angrily under his breath, the words 'streak of piss' and 'Chukka' audible to the DS's ears.

'Sit back down!' Wade barked authoritatively. 'I take it you're referring to our regular jack-the-lad, Mr Allen?'

'You bet I am!'

'Who, it may interest you to know, is being detained under the UK Misuse of Drugs Act for supplying Class A substances.'

'He conned me into lending him my Mondeo!' Rash startlingly revealed. 'Just a couple of days before the Gold robbery!'

Wade said nothing, save for a few inaudible mumblings between scribbling his observations in his notebook. He jumped up to make for the door, pausing midway to snap his fingers and turning back towards Rashid.

'Just one more question…'

'Go ahead.'

'By what lucky chance did you stumble across the security code used to access the Granby property's main gates?'

'Security code? Gates? I'm at a loss here!'

'Five-seven-o-five!'

'My call alert?'

'Got it in one... the seventies tune!' Wade said purposefully. 'The self-same code used to access the Gold estate!'

'But I downloaded it!' Rash panicked. 'Out of respect for JJ!'

'But it isn't one of his songs!'

Rashid felt all the energy drain out of him. His head tilted back until he hung there, helplessly staring up at the ceiling. Patiently, Wade hovered above him awaiting his answer, which came in a tremulous, defeated tone.

'I wish to remain silent, until my brother arrives!'

FORTY-NINE

May 2011
Leicestershire

HACKETT LEFT OFF FROM sifting through a stack of mostly unwanted paper-work, in need of a quiet moment perched on the loo with the daily rag's sports supplement, catching up on the ins and outs of the weekend's football.

'Dan… my office!' DI Philpott snapped, inconveniently waylaying him. 'Something's come up on the Gold case!'

Hackett instantly doubled back, discreetly placing the paper out of sight before putting on a spurt to catch him up.

'What've you got, boss?'

'Do you know of a place called Knoydart up in the Western Highlands?'

'It rings a bell…'

'I just received a call from a Superintendent James Wilson up in Inverness. It would appear Gold owns a property there.'

'So it was true?' Hackett gasped. 'The journo's story?'

'What fucking story?'

'The tale of the hairy quad biker, on the early news!'

The pieces of the superintendent's story began to fall into place. His puzzling visit; the gaggles of media people swarming all over the place, each vying for their own slice of the cake, no matter whose toes they stepped on.

'The Beeb! It all adds up… Wilson contacted them!'

'And?' Hackett said, in a fog.

'Journalists, huh?'

'A law unto themselves, guv!'

'The guy on the box… what was the purpose of his visit?'

'Research… for a documentary.'

'Any wonder they won't hear a word against Gold!'

'A word in his ear might not go amiss?'

'No, we wait, Dan.'

'Until the fuss dies down?'

'You got it in one.'

The chief twisted his torso towards a giant map pinned to the wall, slowly tracing his finger up over the Scottish Highlands, drawn to a bulbous kidney-shaped area where finally the letters KNOYDART came into focus.

'Uh-oh… I can feel a recce coming on,' Hackett said, smelling a rat.

'Bear with me… and stay put at your desk!'

*

Thirty minutes later

Sheila's solemn tone urged him to seek out a quiet spot.

'I'm going to have to cry off tonight.' Her words were partially drowned out by the unearthly hullabaloo emanating from the sliding doors of the Infirmary's overcrowded Accident and Emergency department.

'We can reschedule,' he said graciously. 'And besides, I've a feeling something's about to break on the Gold case.'

'Speak of the devil!'

'What now?'

'No–no… he's playing on someone's car stereo.'

'Shit, the lyrics… I clean forgot!'

'Track three, "Soldier of Misfortune" stayed with me for days.'

'Must go – Philpott's on the warpath!'

'Good luck!' she chuckled.

The DI's ungainly figure came charging out of his office like a greyhound out of a trap, careering through the aisles in the direction of the DS's desk with no regard for anything or anyone that got in his way.

'What is it, boss?'

'The SOCO boys… they unearthed a package,' he panted wheezily.

'Containing what?'

'Human body parts! Hidden amongst a pile of rotting animal carcasses, not far from where the arm was found.'

'Which once belonged to Mistry?'

'It gets worse… The sick bastard used a power saw to dismember the corpse before dissecting the torso into four!'

'Who… what sick bastard?'

'Jonathan Gold… The man's a butcher, Dan!'

Hackett's four-day growth of beard failed to hide the look of horror on his face. He'd always considered himself a pretty good judge of character, but the DI's gruesome ramblings rendered him almost unable to articulate.

'This defies all logic, guv!'

'All of the remains matched the original exhibit.'

'But still no sign of the head?'

'Not as yet, although a tiny clump of hair was found embedded in the baseball bat's tip… containing an intact follicle.'

'And the source individual is of Asian origin?'

'You got it!'

Hackett shot the chief an expectant look, as if he was reading his mind. His worst fears came to fruition moments later as a detailed itinerary was quietly slipped into the centre of his desk right under his nose.

'So I'm off to Bonnie Scotland?'

'How did you guess?' the DI said, with an audacious smirk. 'I'm just waiting on Inverness to give us the green light.'

'How long for?'

'Just a couple of days, that's all.'

'For what purpose?'

'To arrest him!' Philpott exclaimed. 'Throw some things together and catch up on some beauty sleep – it's a long haul.'

*

A couple of minutes later the sound of heavy footsteps caused Hackett to leave off from tidying his desktop, his gaze wandering along the aisle to make out the robust figure of his friend and colleague DS Wade.

'Jeffrey, dear boy!' he acknowledged, enfolding him in a bear-like man-hug. 'I gather congratulations are in order!'

'Cheers Dan, onwards and upwards!' Wade reflected, turning an inquisitive face towards him. 'You around tomorrow?'

'No mate, I'm headed north.'

'On a case?'

'Prospecting for Gold!'

'Eh?' Wade said, perplexedly.

'As in JJ Gold!'

He sucked in his breath sharply through his teeth, his interest instantly aroused as to the true nature of the mission. Discreetly, Hackett leant his head to one side and whispered into a hand cupped against his ear.

'Whew… I guess I drew the short straw.'

'How so?'

'Your old pal… Richard Turner!'

'You tracked him down?' Hackett asked, excitedly.

'He came forward of his own volition,' Wade said, pacifying him. 'He's due in tomorrow to attend an ID parade.'

'The guy's not for real!'

'Pop in to say hello before you set off,' Wade joked.

'No way, Jose!' Hackett said, slapping him a parting high-five. 'And Jeffrey… I'd sooner stick pins in my testicles!'

FIFTY

May 2011
Brightwater Croft

DISORIENTED, JON LAY MOTIONLESS, flat on his back, his mind frazzled following a fitful night's sleep. It had been mostly spent gazing up into the dim, musty nothingness, as if he were confined within the bedroom's stony walls.

Up above him in the sloping triangle of the wood-framed ceiling, a lone insect darted hither and thither. Its buzzing was out of sync with the oscillating wheeze emerging from the very depths of the inert Agnes's lungs.

He carefully leaned across to take hold of her wrist, noticing her pulse pumping steadily, albeit at a quicker rate than normal; then he pressed his body against the soft contours of her skin, his head rested on the back of her neck.

On the bedside table the luminous hands of the alarm clock ticked silently round to five o'clock. The first glimmer of daybreak was greeted by a light twittering in the trees, pacifying him sufficiently to again close his eyes.

*

8.30a.m.

'Jon... I hate to wake you,' Agnes softly murmured. 'You mentioned something about a grand reunion with the *Hummingbird*?'

'God... what time is it?' he said with a start. 'Aggie, are you okay? Your heart was pounding during the night!'

She nonchalantly laughed, placing a tray of tea, toast and jam on the chest of drawers under the window. Her arms reached out to vigorously yank back the curtains and reveal a glorious, brilliant sunny morning.

'The weather's fine. So am I!' she said chirpily. 'If a trifle heavy-headed!'

He worked his way upright and threw back the sheets, stretching his arms and shoulders whilst letting out a Tarzan-like roar, before hopping on one foot across the floor in a comical effort to slip into his jeans.

'Wait… something isn't right.'

'Jon… what is it? Don't look at me that way!'

'Breathe, Aggie… slowly!'

She stood completely still, her figure silhouetted in the door frame like a supermodel posing for a shoot. The silence was near-deafening but for a strange wheezing sound rising from deep inside her throat.

'I'll take a rain check.'

'I'm fine!' she said emphatically.

'I'm worried about you!'

'No ifs, no buts Jon. Go off and enjoy a bit of male bonding!'

The lively chitchat continued downstairs at the kitchen table. Their voices battled against the electric buzz of the coffee machine, its gurgling pot removed from the hotplate as Agnes stooped above him to play mother.

'The boat can wait; my main concern is you.'

'Jonathan… it's a speck of dust trapped in my windpipe!'

'Okay, okay!'

His chair scraped across the tiles. Sauntering to the sink, he rinsed out his mug before setting it on the draining board.

'And Jon, watch your back,' she said, almost randomly.

'Eh… Why?'

'Jimmy Logan's back on the scene.'

'You saw him?'

'Staggering out of the Marine Hotel, on my way back from the station,' she unveiled. 'Held upright by his perverted nephew.'

'Beavis and Butthead, back in town,' Jon huffed disparagingly.

'Be careful… that's all!'

'I will!' he promised, scooping her up into his arms in one smooth motion. 'Besides, Bobby's built like a silverback gorilla!'

'Really?' she said derisively, utterly unimpressed. 'Now for heaven's sake put me down, and get the hell out of here!'

*

Mallaig, Lochaber

A thick line of foam from his Guinness hung over Bobby's top lip, a tiny fleck of which rested on Jon's polo-shirt collar, spat out inadvertently from

Bobby's jabbering mouth in the midst of a sprightly conversation.

'The outboard's well on the blink!'

'Is it fixable?'

'I very much doubt it,' he said, a touch mockingly. 'It was farting like my grandad when I fired it up this morning.'

They chewed the fat between guzzling down another pint, animatedly discussing this, that and the other. Grabbing a copy of the local weekly rag dumped on a table, Bobby took a gander at the classified ads.

'It's your lucky day, Jonny!'

'How come?'

'There's a reconditioned Yamaha for sale, in Glenfinnan,' he said excitedly. 'Do ye want me to check it out?'

'If you could… though with the quad and a brand new generator I've been pushing the boat a bit too far of late!'

'Hah… capsizing more like!'

'Don't remind me!'

He ambled to the bar to replenish their empty pint pots, only half alert to a raspy-voiced man taking issue with a nose-pierced bachelorette seated on a stool.

The hothead grunted a further string of inaudible remarks, his offensive tone clearly upsetting the girl. Shoving past him as she attempted to leave, she sent him staggering backwards and crashing heavily into Jon.

'*You!*' Logan roared, slowly regaining his balance.

'I might've known it!' Jon responded.

With a swift movement Logan twisted round to grasp an empty pint glass, promptly smashed it against the bar top's rim and thrust it dangerously in Jon's direction. He backed away, hands reached up to shield his eyes.

'*Jimmy… put the glass down!*' the bartender screeched, helped out in the nick of time by Bobby's hulking figure. With a sudden show of strength he hooked his arm around Logan's neck, his left hand gripping the slack in his pants to drag him head first to the exit, where as if dumping the trash he duly dispatched him onto the street.

'Why would he want to stick a glass in your face?' the returning Bobby asked. 'The guy should be behind bars!'

'He's a sad case… a raging Anglophobe.'

'A raging what?'

'In short… a people-hating prick!'

They wound up the session in style, downing a brace of whisky chasers which barely hit the sides, before both stumbling outside into the half-blinding daylight. As if on autopilot Jon veered towards the ferry terminal.

'This way, pal!' Bobby yelled, chuckling wryly.

'There's a crossing in five minutes,' Jon absentmindedly replied.

'But, what about the boat?'

'Shit!' he exclaimed. 'I knew there was something!'

*

Two hours later

The grainy remnants of the ocean's salt clung to Jon's skin, sprinkled over his forehead, cheeks and arms by the forceful sea breeze which partially deadened the effects of the eventful lunchtime drinking session.

Blithely he wandered up to the five-bar gate, scaling the top slat as opposed to tugging at the spring catch, his cheerfulness put into words through a spontaneous rendition of an age-old Tom Jones sixties hit song.

'I am coming home to you... ooh

'Cos I am nothing without you!'*

After fumbling in his pocket for his keys, he stepped inside and called out Aggie's name, but there was no response. Distracted by an attack of the munchies, he raided the cupboard to grab a loaf and a giant wedge of Cheddar cheese, avidly shoving it between two slices of buttered bread, all the time chattering away.

'Guess who I bumped into today!'

The stony silence continued; but he thought little of it, teetering in his stockinged feet into the adjacent living room.

To his horror, Agnes's motionless body lay face down in front of the dormant fireplace.

Her utter stillness set his nerves on edge, as sinking down to his knees he softly caressed her cheek. He was immediately buoyed by a faint but perceptible expiration of moist breath coursing between her blueing lips.

Painstakingly, he manoeuvred her into a seated position, straining every sinew to heave her leaden weight up onto his right shoulder, then trundling awkwardly over the kitchen floor and out into the adjoining porch.

After setting her body in a comfortable position against the glass partition wall, he raised his hands upward and muttered a prayer to the

---

* 'I'm Coming Home' by Tom Jones, Decca Records 1967

cloudy heavens, before sprinting athletically across the yard to fire up the quad bike.

In the overhanging treetops a gust of chill wind swept through the rustling branches, spurring him to race back inside to gather up a wad of bedclothes, promptly swathed with loving care around her shivering shoulders.

Guilefully, he pulled a sailing harness over her upper torso, looping a safety tether back through her legs and up onto the D-rings attached to the buckle of his waistband. With Aggie held in place on his back like a giant haversack, he stumbled outside towards the bike, somehow managing to cock both their left legs over the long bench seat, his back muscles screaming out for mercy as he bent sideways to secure her feet onto the rear foot pedals.

Now faced with the task of boarding the *Hummingbird*, he sped through the mud to the water's edge, awkwardly paddling through the shallows to the hull's upper edge to gently lower her down against the stern.

Up above their heads an amber moon emerged from behind the shifting clouds, its beam shedding a burst of light upon the boat. Tilting the engine forward to start up the motor, he gently nursed her out to sea.

Putter, putter, putter, putter, she chugged on.

All of a sudden, the outboard jerked back with a fit of the hiccups before hesitantly decelerating to an agonising halt.

Jon and his precious cargo were left literally up a creek without a paddle, stranded midway across the loch.

FIFTY-ONE

Leicestershire Police HQ

A UNIFORMED OFFICER told Khalid he would not be allowed access to the interview room, where his sibling Rashid was undergoing a rigorous grilling in the company of Dipak Mistry's partner, Vihaan Bhatt.

'We'll be detaining your brother overnight without charge,' the PC informed him, pointing him to a nearby waiting area.

'Why?' he asked, becoming more and more fidgety.

'To stand in an identity parade scheduled for tomorrow morning.'

'An ID parade…? I thought they died out with the bubonic plague,' Khal said acerbically. 'Who's the eyewitness?'

'I'm not at liberty to say, sir.'

Pulling a disparaging face, Khal shifted back into the corridor to supposedly head for the restroom, pausing for a moment to overhear the conversation spilling from the room. He was relieved not to catch any raised voices.

Again he took a seat, arms folded across his chest and his face stern. He was beginning to doze off when the hum of voices brought him back to his senses, echoing in the adjacent hallway along with the clomp of heavy feet.

'Khal… you made it!' Rashid said, rushing towards him, his body language reflecting that things may have gone far worse.

'I've been here for an hour or more. How did it go?'

'I'm free to go, Khal.'

'Eh? But I thought… Forget it!'

'Vihaan was awesome!'

Just then the door swung back to reveal a distinguished-looking man clutching a leather Montblanc briefcase, his highly polished shoes gleaming under the ceiling lamps as he courteously extended his free right hand.

'Mr Shah senior, I presume?'

'Vihaan… I'm truly in your debt!'

'Not in the least,' he replied in a likeable, self-effacing manner. 'Your brother put on quite a performance in there.'

Khalid forced a laugh and stepped to one side to summon him into the relative privacy of the waiting area, eager to hear Vihaan's account of the afternoon's events away from any wagging ears.

'How's Dipak holding up?'

'He said to pass on his regards,' he replied, in a measured tone. 'Suffice to say, he's a shadow of his former self.'

'How remiss of me… not keeping in touch.'

'I wouldn't worry; he's been in India,' he sadly reflected. 'Primarily to deal with his son's funeral arrangements.'

'How tragic… and so, in regards to my brother's situation?'

'I requested the police authorities for permission to interview an individual named Charles Allen, whom I understand is currently detained in a police cell awaiting a hearing before magistrates scheduled for tomorrow morning.'

'On what charge?'

'A catalogue of drug-related offences.'

At the mere mention of his name Khalid felt a rage begin to boil up inside of him. His memory flashed back a decade to a distressing court hearing when, blatantly perjuring himself to plant seeds of doubt in the magistrate's mind, Chukka's flawed testimony almost single-handedly led to his brother's wrongful conviction.

'He's a natural born liar!'

'So I gather, and due his comeuppance.'

'There's an understatement!'

'Once we've established that he appropriated Rashid's vehicle without his consent, I've every confidence your brother will be cleared of any wrong-doing,' Vihaan said. Digging into his briefcase he retrieved an A4 photocopy, in the centre of which was the image of a torn piece of paper:

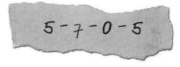

'Rashid's call alert,' Khal acknowledged.

'And, perhaps more importantly, the security code to the Gold property,'

'You lost me…'

'The image reinforces our argument.'

'In what way?'

'It was taken from a scrap of paper which slipped out of Amir Mistry's pocket.'

'By whom?'

'His father... Dipak,' Vihaan replied to Khal's utter astonishment. 'Take a closer look at the bottom right of the image.'

He held the copy up to the skylight, his eyes squinting to make out a light smudge underneath the untidy scrawl, its squiggly lines brought into focus by a narrow shaft of light visible through a crack in the blind.

'A fingerprint or thumbprint?'

'Yes... which he kindly forwarded on to me.'

'Six years after his son's death?'

'He mistook it for a pilfered credit-card PIN code!'

'Which Amir memorised?'

'It appears so.'

Vihaan snapped his briefcase shut and expressed his regret at being unable to attend the impending ID parade, promising faithfully a trusted young paralegal would be on hand to keep an eye on things in his absence.

'One more thing?' Khalid asked, briefly stalling him.

'Go ahead... please!'

'The thumbprint?'

'Uh-huh,' Vihaan acknowledged, his head tilting.

'Can it be used as evidence?'

The lawyer turned back towards him and straightened his tie, his suave, relaxed manner presenting an air of self-assuredness. Softly he spoke in a smooth and rational tone, the words sounding like music to Khalid's ears.

'Sufficiently to corroborate Rashid's statement!'

*

Curry Mahal, Leicester

They sat opposite each other at a corner table with red-velvet-covered chairs, quietly discussing the impending ID parade in between stabbing their forks into a mouth-watering plateful of curiously red tandoori chicken.

'It's time for you to come clean, baby bro.'

'For fuck's sake, Khal!'

'Come on, Rash... I want the whole truth!'

'Which part of "I've been totally honest with you" don't you understand?'

Khalid halted to take a slurp of his watery pint of lager, before finally bringing up the matter of the Ford Mondeo sighted outside the Gold estate's gates shortly after the break-in.

'Were you or were you not the vehicle's driver?' he demanded, his eyes like a predator on its prey.

'No... no, and no again!'

'So you knew nothing of the impending robbery?'

'Not a goddamn thing!'

Reaching out to place a reassuring hand on his brother's arm, Khalid felt him stiffen and then pull away from him. For a moment he hated himself for misjudging him so unfairly. In reality, though, he wasn't out of the woods yet.

'Drink up, little bro,' he said, raising a hand to summon the waiter for the bill. 'You've got a busy morning ahead of you!'

FIFTY-TWO

2.30a.m., Friday May 13ᵗʰ 2011
Raigmore Hospital, Inverness

JON SHAMBLED FORLORNLY along the empty corridor, his downbeat demeanour not helped by the foul whiff of urine wafting from a nearby ward, mingled with the pungent odour of disinfectant permeating the whole building.

Fatigue spread throughout his body, a heavy exhaustion that caused his bones to ache. He fought against it, but the need for sleep tugged at his eyelids. As he wandered aimlessly he constantly mumbled under his breath.

'Number one in the album charts…? I should be elated!'

Initially, he failed to notice the two brutish police officers bringing up the rear. He jumped aside to allow them to pass, only to feel his legs taken from under him courtesy of a size-twelve Magnum patrol boot.

Too stunned to speak, he flailed his arms furiously in protest, his efforts to shake off their clutches immediately thwarted by the sharp snap of handcuffs ratcheting over his wrists, the metal cutting into his skin.

Jon screamed out in agony. His dewy eyes glared up at the hateful-looking, sturdily built officer towering above him, who barked at him authoritatively in a southern English accent.

'Consider yourself nicked, sunshine!'

'But I've done nothing!'

'Disorderly behaviour on NHS premises!' the cop snarled, digging a knee into his back to jerk him upright again.

After a moment's pause they thrust their hands under his armpits and dragged him across the floor. They were ushering him towards the main exit when the harsh squawk of a walkie-talkie brought them to a shuddering halt.

They exchanged glances back and forth, and promptly dumped Jon down onto a row of low-backed chairs. Visible through the glass sliding doors, a meat wagon tore at full throttle into the adjacent ambulance bay.

'Well, I'll be damned!' one of the officers gasped, his mouth falling agape. 'Rock 'n' roll's answer to O. J. Simpson!'

'Oh, how the mighty fall!' his companion sighed.

In a matter of seconds the place was swarming with police, their strapping black-clad bodies bearing down on Jon's defenceless figure before hoisting him up onto their shoulders and carrying him head first out to the bay.

Amid a series of grunts and curses they piled him into the high-sided vehicle. Seemingly oblivious to his protests, a female guard sat him down and readjusted his cuffs to secure his left hand to the inner cage.

From his lowly perch he caught a glimpse of the chill, dark sky, his heart sinking and eye sockets welling up with tears. In a last desperate moment he screamed deliriously, but nobody took the blindest bit of notice.

'*Agne...e...e...es!*' his pained, rending voice echoed to the heavens, before it was cruelly hushed by the sudden slamming of the doors.

*

3.00a.m.
Leicestershire

Melanie Philpott was a light sleeper. She was lying awake staring at the ceiling as usual, her muddled thoughts preoccupied with the arrangements for an upcoming dinner party, when unexpectedly the bedside phone sounded.

'One moment, please,' she politely told the caller, gently nudging the DI. 'Darling, there's an urgent call for you.'

'Uh... what?' he gasped, disorientated. 'What time is it?'

'Shortly after three o'clock.'

'For Christ's sake... tell him to call back!'

'He was most insistent, darling.'

He grumpily repositioned the pillows to prop himself up against the headboard, reaching his hands into his stiff lower back muscles, before rudely snatching the cordless phone from her and barking into the mouthpiece.

'Philpott... Who is this?'

'James Wilson, of the Northern Constabulary in Inverness.'

'Ah yes, Superintendent,' he softened. 'I must apologise for my abruptness!'

'No offence taken... You'll be interested to learn that, at two-thirty a.m. today, two officers investigating a complaint received from the city's hospital apprehended an individual fitting Jonathan Gold's description.'

'In a hospital? Was he suffering in any way?'

'It would appear not.'

'So, what was he doing there?'

'He was fast asleep in the waiting room,' Wilson grunted. 'And didn't take too kindly to being woken by a security guard.'

Philpott's eyes lit up at the sight of a steaming cup of coffee placed at the bedside by his ever-dependable better half. He paused mid-conversation to take a sip, trying to get his head around the startling heads-up.

'Did the guard recognise him?'

'No... he mistook him for a homeless tramp!'

'And tried to evict him?'

'With some difficulty, or so I'm led to believe,' Wilson said. 'Along with a couple of other unkempt down-and-outs.'

Again the DI paused. Something was amiss. A multi-millionaire rock star sleeping rough in a hospital waiting room, mistaken for a penniless vagrant by a night guard doing his rounds? Something didn't add up.

'With any luck I'll have an officer up there by late lunchtime,' he vowed. 'A seasoned detective named Dan Hackett.'

A creepy silence ensued, the only discernible sound coming from the light rustle of paper amplified in the earpiece.

'Bear with me,' Wilson asked, busily scrutinising his notes.

'What've you got?'

'Something in the night guard's report...'

'Read it to me!'

'"As I approached him and attempted to evict him from the building, the trespasser became agitated and even threatening, and made reference to a lady friend fighting for her life on the ICU ward..."'

'So Gold was there legitimately?'

'Without any mention in the admission notes.'

'Why would he lie?'

'I don't know!'

For some reason unknown, Philpott felt Jon's pain. A superstar who, having made a fatal mistake, turned his back on a brilliant career to condemn himself and his significant other to a life of self-imposed exile.

'And there's no record of any critically ill patients recently admitted to the ICU?'

'Not a damn thing.'

'Thank you, James.'

'Not a problem... I'll be in touch!' the Scot said, instantly ringing off.

3.30a.m.

Not even thinking, his head once more hit the pillow. Drifting back towards semi-consciousness he began babbling half-audibly in his sleep, his muttered words slurring together, much to the chagrin of his wife.

'What was that, darling? JJ Gold homeless?'

He shot bolt upright in the bed, totally disoriented, frantically reaching for the phone to punch in Hackett's number.

'Dan… drop everything, and pack an overnight bag!' he panted in relief. 'I need you to leave for Inverness right away!'

FIFTY-THREE

RICHARD TURNER THEATRICALLY WANDERED to and fro, solicitously poring over the eight-strong line-up captured in numerical order on the projection screen before him. His evident sense of self-importance was gradually getting under the duty officer's skin.

'The majority of the participants are volunteers,' the PC advised, 'some of whom have full-time jobs to return to...?'

'I'm not an idiot, constable,' Turner contemptuously answered back, 'so please refrain from treating me as such!'

The cop, who already had good reason to think otherwise, drew a long, inward breath.

'Sir, please... we haven't got all day!'

'Have patience!' Turner shot back. 'I'm torn between two of them, but under the lights they all look rather alike.'

Seated at the back of the room, Khalid wagged his head in disbelief. His feelings were clearly shared by the equally flustered paralegal; wearing a look of pure frustration, she gestured towards him with her palms raised.

'Simply study each individual's features and give me the corresponding number should anyone resemble the vehicle's driver.'

'Numbers three and seven have shifty eyes...'

'Okay everyone, show's over!' the officiator announced, at once sparking a mini-stampede towards the exit.

Turner stubbornly stood his ground, steadily working himself into a temper tantrum. Almost comically he found himself abandoned in the room, gesticulating and stamping his feet on the floor like a wronged spoilt brat.

'Sir... come, come, now!' a young PC said, backtracking through the door. 'Please make your way to the reception desk.'

'But I'm not finished!' he snapped, indignantly.

She spoke in a calm, non-patronising voice, placing a persuasive hand into the small of his back. Deftly, she coaxed him out into the hallway, edging him closer to the reception area seemingly immune to his protests.

'You can voice your concerns to the officer at the desk,' she said, self-assuredly. 'Enjoy the rest of your day, sir!'

*

Holly's Coffee Shop, Leicester Centre

The spotless café's state-of-the-art coffee machine came to the boil like a mini-volcano, its steaming contents spewing out into two bowl-shaped cups and duly brought to the table by a pretty-faced teenage waitress.

'Eyes right, Rash!' Khal said admonishingly, alert to his watchful glance following her curvy rear back to her post.

'Just window shopping, that's all!'

The morning's ordeal had left Rashid's nerves frayed and ragged, yet somewhat relieved at the outcome he voraciously tucked into a house special tuna melt, feeling so much better than he'd dared to hope.

'It seems you're finally off the hook, little bro!'

'Hmm, maybe,' he said reflectively. 'Though I may still be called to give evidence if the case goes to trial.'

'True... and then there's the small matter of Chukka.'

'He's bang to rights... facing a long stretch!'

'How do you know?'

'Let's just say that I keep my ear to the ground!'

Khalid gave a wry smile, gently raising the frothy cappuccino to his lips. Looking up he noted a change in Rashid's attitude, his body language conveying a newfound maturity far removed from the mischief-maker of old.

'You're on a roll!'

'No thanks to the guy at the ID parade,' Rash said. 'I caught sight of him at reception, making a right song and dance.'

'He's a psycho... a drama queen,' Khal said, chuckling.

'What's tickling you?'

'He fingered two of the volunteers... one of whom waits tables at the Pride of India round the corner, and the other who works as a part-time special constable! Lena, your paralegal, was in fits when she told me.'

Almost choking on his food, Rash gulped down a mouthful of coffee to try and compose himself, the hot contents seeping from the corners of his mouth, much to the disgust of a group of lunching ladies.

'I'm sorry,' he said, rising to his feet, the embarrassed look on his face twisting into a boyish smile. As he took his seat once more his gaze strayed towards the serving hatch, his heart lifting at the sight of the cute little lady.

'What's up, little bro?'

'She's making eyes at me!'

'Who is? C'mon, let's hit the road.'

'You go on ahead, big bro,' he said, trying to hide an impish grin. 'I have some important business to attend to!'

*

The Scottish Borders

The black-and-white façade of Gretna Green's famous blacksmith's shop stood flickering in the early-morning sunlight, drawing a half-interested glance from the weary DS parked up across the street taking a moment's rest.

To the rear of the building a gaggle of happy-snapping Japanese tourists took turns posing beneath a statue symbolising a giant pair of clasping hands, in front of a café displaying a closed sign in the window.

Ignoring his continuously aching back, Hackett took a little more time out to put in a call to his girlfriend, Sheila. She tiredly clutched at the bedside phone, mistaking the call for a request to help out on a dangerously understaffed ward.

'Hey sweetheart… you'll never guess where I'm phoning from!'

'I'm too exhausted to be playing games, Dan.'

'Gretna Green!'

She gasped. 'What in God's name are you doing up there?'

'I'm about to get hitched.'

'To a sixteen-year-old bimbo, I don't doubt.'

'No, to a vicious manslayer, by means of a pair of handcuffs!'

She picked up on the close-knit harmonies of American band the Fleet Foxes purring away sweetly in the background, their latest offering *Helplessness Blues* providing the accompaniment for much of his journey.

'So you're in Scotland?'

'Midway through a trip up to Inverness.'

'To read a man his rights!' she exclaimed. 'Namely JJ Gold!'

'How could you possibly know?'

'It's on every news channel going,' she revealed. 'Turn your radio on!'

'Shit... the gaffer begged me to keep it under wraps!'

A vibration close to his ear alerted him to an incoming text message, sent from the self-same DI Philpott:

> Dan, the media got wind of Gold's impending arrest. Speed is of the essence!

It succinctly confirmed what he already knew: the rumour-mongers had been working overtime again, and would doubtless be heading north in their droves. He needed to move fast to keep a step ahead of the pack.

'Must fly, sweetie!'

'Danny, just before you go...'

'Be quick!'

'Take a listen to his *Angel of Death* CD,' she told him. 'And particularly the song called "Soldier of Misfortune".'

'I will, I promise,' he vowed. 'Toodle-oo, sweetheart!'

*

For the first time in months Rashid slept like a baby, the events of the previous day still fresh in his memory. He had dropped off the moment his head hit the pillow, as if transported to a wonderland of pleasant thoughts.

His mind wandered time and again to his chance encounter with the stunning young waitress, her porcelain-white hands scribbling her contact number onto her order pad, sending his heart pounding like a drum.

His stretching fingers fumbled around at the bedside in an effort to switch off the cheeping alarm clock. As it fell silent, he realised his phone was ringing too. He twisted onto his arms and grabbed the device displaying his brother's name.

'Khal... what's up?'

'I received a call from Jon at one o'clock this morning!'

'Uh-oh... something's wrong?'

'He called from the hospital in Fort William,' Khal said, hoarse with concern. 'His partner Agnes is fighting for her life!'

'He's one of your closest pals... haul your ass up there!'

'You're right... maybe I should.'

'Go for it, bro... Vihaan's got everything under control.'

A burst of static interference sounding in Khal's ear caused the signal strength to plummet to a single bar, before moving to the window and tapping on the touchscreen he noticed a flurry of incoming texts and emails.

'Rash… you still there?'

'Yeah… what's happening?'

His voice cracked uncharacteristically, as flipping his finger across the screen his worst fear came to life before his eyes.

'It's Jon…'

'Khal, speak to me… what is it?'

'He's been apprehended,' he squeezed out falteringly. 'And taken into custody for the murder of Amir Mistry!'

*

Utterly spent from the seemingly never-ending journey, Hackett entered the Cairngorms National Park, shortly veering off the main drag onto an elevated strip of wasteland. He stopped a while to dote on the endless majesty of the landscape, as a soulful wail spilt forth from the chassis-mounted loudspeakers:

'Oh lord what have I done, oh-oh-oh lord my course is run.'

The haunting refrain rang out repetitively, its melody delivered with rousing gusto by a sixty-strong gospel choir, soaring close to fever pitch in glorious, reverberant harmony amid a perpetual backdrop of pounding cellos.

And suddenly, as though quelled by a sweep of the conductor's baton, the mighty outpouring subsided into near silence, as the delicate pitter-patter of muted pizzicato set the tone for the soul-crushing vocal:

'Under a cloak of darkness, poised like a crouching tiger about to seize upon its prey,

A blood-red mist descends before my eyes as I jump into the fray.

A crushing blow meets solid flesh and bone, striking a deadly chord

I am a soldier of misfortune, and I must fall on my sword.'

He froze, completely gobsmacked, promptly hitting the seek/search button to pinpoint the exact same section, listening intently as realisation dawned: *'A blood-red mist… A crushing blow meets solid flesh and bone…'*

'God, what a killer line!' he muttered. Aware of the unintentional faux pas, he added, 'In every sense of the phrase!'

He tweaked the volume. The unremitting sub-bass synth rocked the car on its suspension, intermixed with a cannonade of kettledrums and

238

crashing cymbals, spiralling like a rabid tornado into a frenzied crescendo of symphonic strings in so many ways evocative of Tchaikovsky's *1812 Overture*.

A rush of muddled thoughts began to swirl around in his mind, sending a cold prickle of fear running down his spine. This was an act of revenge; rash, vindictive and heartless. How could he have so badly misjudged Gold's character?

And then, in a gaping canyon of decaying reverb, the mighty wall of sound crumbled into a vast nothingness, displaced by the poignant strains of a solitary violin, fading slowly like dying embers to a stunning conclusion.

FIFTY-FOUR

Two days later
Raigmore Hospital, Inverness

AGNES FELT GROGGY, not knowing quite where she was or even how she got there. She pulled herself up the bed and yanked at the surrounding curtain, panting half-breathlessly to try and attract a young RN's attention.

'Nurse... where am I?'

Her ears pricking up midway through making her morning rounds, the sister twisted round towards Agnes wearing an incredulous look, and briefly put her chores on hold to scamper across the ward to her bedside.

'Goodness me, what a turnaround!'

'Have you seen Jonathan?'

'Jonathan?' she asked curiously.

'My partner!'

'You were brought in by a crew of paramedics, my darling,' the nurse said amiably. 'Approximately thirty-six hours ago.'

Aggie spoke in a fragile, semi-breathy voice, animatedly describing Jon's appearance to a tee, the untrimmed facial hair and long dishevelled locks. By chance she caught sight of the ID band strapped around her wrist.

FORENAMES: UNKNOWN   SURNAME: UNKNOWN
DOB: 04/01/1918

'You don't even know my name!' she gasped.

'We've been trying to track down the pre-alert information provided by the paramedics, but seem to have come up short.'

'And I'm in the hospital's Intensive Care Unit, presumably under the care of a pulmonary disease specialist... yes?'

'That's perfectly correct.'

'With no record of my identity, or how I got here?'

Just then a small posse of medical personnel entered the ward via the double swing doors, prompting the young nurse to wheel a screen into place to allow them a smidgen of added privacy.

'Good morning, miss; my name is Anwar Choudhury.'

'Agnes Ryan,' she replied, throatily.

'So you do have a name?' he said semi-humorously. 'My team and I have been monitoring your quite remarkable progress!'

'My condition's hereditary… through my mother's side.'

'Hmm, interesting,' he mumbled thoughtfully. 'How frequently do you suffer from attacks of respiratory distress?'

'At irregular intervals, often many months apart.'

The expression on her face deepened and her eyes grew watery, so much so a rogue tear slid down onto her cheek.

'My dear young lady… what's wrong?' Choudhury asked, with a look of concern.

'He would never have left my side!'

'Who, my dear?'

'My lover… Jonathan!' she answered piteously. 'Something's not right, I just know it!'

He unhooked the clipboard from the foot of the bed to check her notes, irritably squeezing his chin between his forefinger and thumb, and pored aghast over the scraps of information staring up at him on the page.

'It would appear you slipped under the radar, Agnes.'

'How so?' she asked.

'The hospital's PAS* has no record of an Agnes Ryan, or the consultant in charge at the time of your admission.'

'It's as if I don't exist!'

He cleared his throat, apprehensively flipping the page not quite knowing how to respond. Once again he frowned deeply, horrified at the lack of information submitted to the A & E reception staff during Agnes's handover.

'I can only apologise profusely,' he said, clearly ill at ease. 'It seems the crew omitted to prepare an ambulance trip sheet!'

She swivelled onto her belly, slid down beneath the tightly layered sheets and buried her head deep in the pillows, from where she let out a muffled, anguished wail.

'Jon… my Jonathan!'

---

* PAS – Patient Administration System

He sought to console her, caringly placing a hand on her outstretched arm, his voice both soothing and reassuring.

'I'm recommending that you be transferred to a more relaxed medical-surgical ward,' he said, gently gripping her wrist. 'Where the healthcare team and myself will continue monitoring your breathing patterns.'

'I lost the ability to breathe the day he came crashing into my life!'

'You love him very much, don't you?'

'More than life itself!'

'The most painful scars are often those that no one can see,' he softly uttered. 'We must find him, one way or another!'

Agnes glanced back to meet his dark, purposeful eyes, the compassion replaced with a look of grim determination. He nodded, backing away towards the swing doors, to leave her in the capable hands of the medics.

*

Three hours later
Zone 10, Ward 11

Agnes rested back against the bunched pillows, peacefully luxuriating in the fresh spring air wafting in through the half-open window, its joyous sweetness partially overriding the sharp, persistent odour of antiseptic.

'Good afternoon, Miss Ryan!'

She spun around and found herself face to face with a sturdily built woman squeezed into a starched blue uniform, her square-shouldered, oddly intimidating figure rooted to the spot, hands akimbo on her hips.

'Hello?' Aggie mumbled, warily.

'Are you okay to talk?' the woman asked, a little brusquely.

'Yes... sorry, I was miles away!'

'I'm Deborah McKay, the senior nurse who assessed and assigned you to ICU during the small hours of Friday morning.'

Aggie sighed deeply. 'Thank God!'

'First of all, I owe you my most sincere apology,' Sister McKay said, hanging her head. 'There's simply no excuse for such shoddiness!'

Aggie perked up, her hopefulness giving rise to a strange fluttering in her stomach. Impulsively, she reached out to grab the Sister's arm, the desperation in her voice obvious despite the hoarseness of its tone.

'Jon... my partner?'

'I'm afraid we drew a virtual blank.'

'He must've been here!' Aggie said insistently.

'I coordinated the handover myself,' the Sister rallied. 'I remember it vividly; the chief paramedic appeared somewhat distracted...'

'The handover?' Agnes said, looking up questioningly.

'You were admitted to Belford in Fort William shortly before midnight,' the nurse said, briefly glancing down to scrutinise her notes. 'And subsequently transferred to the care of our emergency department by ambulance.'

The piercing sound of a smashing teacup triggered something in her mind, its shrill crash at once sending her memory into a rush of spinning thoughts: the sudden tightness in her chest! Falling! It all came flooding back. She'd grown dizzy midway through a bout of spring cleaning, and paused awhile to grab a coffee and a light bite to eat. Minutes later she re-entered the living room, only to collapse in a heap as the mug flew from her grasp.

'There's only one possible explanation!'

'For what, dearie?'

'How I got to Belford!'

Subconsciously, she recalled the *Hummingbird*'s gentle rocking motion, its bow cutting smoothly through the water's surface. The night had been peaceful, save for the rhythmic plodding of Jon's feet, at some point brought to a halt by the squeal of tyres pulling in to the side of the road, and the sound of a kindly voice:

'Do you need a ride?'

Just outside the double doors, a workman's hammer drill noisily penetrated the upper wall, his feet precariously balanced on top of a wobbly stepladder. He appeared to be engaged in relocating a badly positioned surveillance camera.

'I have an idea!' the Sister said, snapping her fingers and striding to the door, mumbling, 'Why didn't I think of that before?'

'Nurse... nurse... wait!' Aggie cried out weakly, before finally drifting towards sleep through a haze of misgivings.

*

Post-afternoon tea

Agnes inched forward to grab her beaker from the bed-tray, hindered slightly by a pressure sore developing on her lower back. To her left she observed an open-mouthed elderly woman snuffling between each laboured breath, exhausted from her efforts to wrestle a Sunday broadsheet into some semblance of order.

Bored half-senseless, Aggie eased herself carefully onto the edge of the bed and stretched over to clutch at the crumpled pages. Her expression turned to frozen disbelief at the headline splashed boldly across the front page:

Vagabond Gold arrested for brutal murder

Unable to move, an overwhelming feeling of impending doom gripped her heart, swelling in her chest and larynx as though suffocating the last wisps of life out of her body. She stared, transfixed with absolute horror, ripping away the tube attached to her nose and screaming out hysterically in gasping fits and starts.

The harsh sound of an emergency two-way radio only enhanced the general aura of chaos, its sharp clack slowly rousing the majority of patients from a semi-comatose state in the midst of the rush of scampering feet.

A young medical orderly tried to calm her, scurrying in great haste from the far end of the ward to wrap a steadying arm around her quivering shoulders, before step by step coaxing her back towards the bed.

'Sweetie, what is it?' Sister McKay's voice resonated chidingly. 'We don't want you upsetting the other patients!'

'I hate myself… and want to die!'

'Agnes… whatever it is, we can fix it… Are you experiencing a repeat of the lung pain? Do you need some painkillers?'

'Nothing can take away the pain I'm suffering right now!' she sobbed, burying her face deep into the mound of pillows, pining over her special someone, in the knowledge her world was damaged beyond repair.

PART TWO

FIFTY-FIVE

Late August 2011 – one week before trial

THE GUTTURAL BARK of the neighbour's Great Dane had awakened him several times during the night, its nervous disposition stirred by the high winds constantly rattling the plastic wheelie-bins lined up along the abutting fence.

The irritating buzz of his silent cell phone vibrating on the bedside table caused him to finally stir.

'Dan... it's Marty!' barked a familiar male voice. 'I've been trying to get hold of you for the best part of a month!'

Hackett let out a sardonic laugh.

'I thought you'd emigrated,' he taunted him. 'To Bangkok!'

His old pal's wince was practically audible as he recalled the drunken bender the previous summer, when – out looking to paint the town red – he had experienced an embarrassing encounter with a Thai ladyboy.

'Jesus... I'll never live that down!'

'It's all in the Adam's apple, or so I heard!'

'Beer goggles more like,' Marty freely admitted between gritted teeth. 'I have a small favour to ask of you.'

'I might well have guessed!'

'I'm in line for a hush-hush move up to Manchester, to take up a position as Production Exec for the BBC's *Breakfast* team.'

'Congratulations... but where do I come in?'

'Doubtless you've been reading the papers, in the run-up to the JJ Gold trial?'

'And you're fishing for some inside info?'

'Everyone on the planet's drawing their own conclusions... and you've actually rubbed shoulders with the guy!'

'Go on,' Hackett urged, putting aside the pleasantries.

'I'd like to speak to him… face to face.'

Hackett's chin dropped, his mouth falling open. He knew only too well about Evans's clever tactics, often used to startling effect on a number of high-profile interviewees to extract information not normally given.

'You're asking me to swing an interview with a man detained on a criminal charge. The big guns would have my guts for garters!'

'The gutter press already hung him out to dry,' Evans said, imploringly. 'His side of the story deserves to be heard!'

'He loathes the press, Marty!'

'And quite rightly so. A majority of the rags have shown no mercy,' Evans persisted. 'Yet despite that there's a huge wave of sympathy sweeping the nation… It's happening right now, even as we speak!'

'I don't know, Marty… I barely got a peep out of him in nine hours during the journey south from the Scottish Highlands,' Hackett contended. 'So what possesses you to think he'll come clean to an infamous gossipmonger?'

Evans immediately leapt to Gold's defence, arguing that most law-abiding citizens would have reacted in exactly the same way given the same circumstances, backed up with a mini-archive of persuasive facts and figures.

'Take a look at the stats; his "Endless Heartache" single's been perched at the top of the chart for the past five weeks, not to mention his *Meltdown* album, which has shifted an incredible seven million copies worldwide!'

'The guy's on trial for the unlawful killing of a fellow human being! There's no way I can be perceived as taking sides!'

'Oh well, perhaps it was a long shot,' Evans finally backed down. 'Bang goes my prestigious "Scoop of the Year" gong!'

Out of the corner of his eye Hackett spotted a mobile number recently scribbled at the top of his jotter pad. The messy, childlike handwriting jumped out from the page, setting his thoughts on a different tack.

'I've got an idea… but don't hold your breath.'

'I'm all ears!' Evans gasped, excitedly.

'Give me half an hour tops. I'll get back to you,' Hackett said, relocating to the corridor to search for a modicum of privacy.

*

Richard Turner's online bank statement didn't make for good reading. The abbreviation 'REV' next to a monthly standing order clearly showed that his salary payment had, for reasons unknown, been reversed.

'It must be a scam!' he boiled under his breath, rapidly heading upstairs to scurry along the landing to his aunt's bedchamber.

Through the slightly open door he picked up on the soft strains of her voice, tunelessly vocalising the lyrics to John Paul Young's seventies classic 'Love is in the Air'. His knock brought her efforts promptly to a halt.

'Come in, Richard!' she called out, twisting round towards him, her face wearing an unusually stern expression.

'I'm sure it's an oversight, or perhaps even a bank error,' he said jumpily, 'but my salary hasn't yet reached my account!'

'No, it isn't an error… I've been meaning to have a little chat with you.'

'Really… about what?'

'The company finances, Richard. There's been an increasing amount of suspicious activity in recent months,' she said, cutting to the chase, 'including an alarming number of unauthorised withdrawals!'

He fidgeted nervously, feeling the palms of his hands becoming sweatier by the millisecond. Not quite sure how to respond he glanced sheepishly at her, half-hesitantly muttering his reply in a deeply unconvincing tone.

'I b–borrowed a small sum, to kit myself out in a n–new suit and shoes, w–well ahead of the JJ Gold court hearing…'

'To the tune of four thousand pounds!'

'As a key witness I could well find myself on TV,' he jabbered. 'I had every intention of paying the money back!'

He'd run out of excuses, and made for the door, his foot snagging under the rug to send him tumbling onto his knees.

'Don't you dare turn your back on me!' she viciously snapped. 'You'll stay right here until I'm damn well finished with you!'

'I'm sorry,' was the best he could muster.

'I took the liberty of consulting a local accountant,' Phoebe stressed, laying down the law. 'Who strongly advised me to freeze the account with immediate effect. As a result, you are no longer on the payroll, Richard!'

'But I've worked tirelessly to keep your affairs in order!' he said, becoming desperate. 'We're family – flesh and blood!'

'Your dishonesty disgusts me!' she angrily countered. 'I'll put a roof over your head until you get fixed up with a job elsewhere!'

'Where will I go… what will I do?'

'And that's my final word!'

He slunk back out onto the landing, smarting under his humiliation. Tears blinked in his eyes amid a series of grunts and gasps brought on by the rage boiling inside him. How dare she accuse him of cooking the books, when she, after all, was nothing more than a shameless hussy running a house of ill repute!

His face contorted into a malevolent scowl. He'd worked all hours God sent and deserved every penny he got, only to find himself on the receiving end of a vicious tongue-lashing. Contemptuously, he swore to get even and bring her sordid little empire to its knees; but first and foremost he'd bide his time until the trial was over.

FIFTY-SIX

Two days later
HM Prison Leicester

THE HALLWAY RESOUNDED with the clank of metal upon metal, ending with the grating whirr of the security door's electric release. It opened into an oval-shaped holding area manned by a motley crew of duty orderly officers.

Rudely summoned forward by a finger-wagging female warder, Agnes found herself subjected to an unnecessarily rigorous rub-down, testing her mettle to the limit as the virago's wayward hands explored every orifice in her tensed body.

Finally given clearance to enter the stark visit room, she found herself encircled by a cluster of heavily made-up WAGs, their necks craned towards a laminated glass window. On the opposite side, a phalanx of grey-clad inmates shuffled forward in single file under the supervision of a thickset, loud-mouthed guard.

'Come on, move it!' he barked in the general direction of a small bunch of stragglers seemingly sharing a joke at his expense. The chief culprit's straggly locks and animated profile provided her first glimpse of Jon.

'Huh, typical!' she snickered into her hand, swiftly rising from her seat to vie for his attention, only to become caught up in a surge of bodies practically climbing on top of one another to make for the opening door.

The guard's efforts to restore some semblance of order proved futile, serving only to provoke a fresh bout of pushing and shoving. His burly frame was cast aside by the captives bulldozing past him to reach their loved ones.

Agnes's heartbeat quickened, her eager gaze peering through the crush of canoodling couples. Her view was obscured in a flash by the arrival of a uniformed backup unit, whose actions cruelly cut short the happy reunions.

She hadn't really bargained on how she would feel when she saw him, at last meeting his gaze with her own.

'*Jonathan!*' her voice resounded in the ceiling space above.

'*Aggie!*' he responded, rushing forward. His attempt to embrace her was nipped in the bud by an over-officious warder, who ushered them to a Formica-topped table. Seated opposite one another, her knees clasped between his while their fingers entwined. Speechless, their eyes locked longingly, until softly the words began to flow.

'How are you?' she asked uneasily, her attention distracted by a large discoloured bruise high on his cheekbone.

'All the better for seeing you,' he replied, almost apologetically. 'You look ravishing; talk about a sight for sore eyes!'

'Bloodshot, more like… What happened?'

'Nothing more than a little spat,' he reflected with an indifferent smirk. 'There are a few head cases in here!'

All week long he'd rehearsed the things he wanted to say, but just looking at her took his breath away. She leaned forward, smiling at him just inches from his face. He found his voice, and unleashed a barrage of questions.

'Did you keep the appointment with your specialist?'

'Yes, I met with Mr McGregor at the Nuffield in Glasgow, on my way down yesterday.'

'How about the results of your MRI scan? Did anything show up?'

'Everything was just fine; the scarring's minimal.'

'How are things on Knoydart? Are you planning to return soon?'

'Lonely! And no…I booked into a B & B not far from here.'

'Are those bastards still bothering you…? And what about money?'

'Jon, Jon, for heaven's sake… one question at a time, please!' she said, tightening her grip on his hand, all the while fighting the urge to leap up from her chair and enfold him tightly in her arms.

Belatedly dragging his eyes away from her, he punishingly slapped himself on the wrist and managed to calm down a little. Before long they were chatting in a much more relaxed fashion, just above the subdued hubbub surrounding them throughout the room.

'Have you seen the papers?' he half-laughed, half-scoffed.

'They nicknamed you "The Decapitator",' she said, shivering uneasily. 'Along with a few other choice noms de plume!'

'The knives are out for me… big time.'

'I spoke with your counsel, James, only this morning.'

'James, eh?' he replied, semi-jokingly. 'You've never mentioned your fetish for men sporting horsehair wigs!'

'He passed on the number of a freelance journalist who'd like to interview you, ahead of the trial's opening arguments.'

'They're all the same, Aggie – anything to get an exclusive.'

'This guy believes you should be acquitted.'

'I'm dead to rights, Ag!'

'Nonsense; Hillier's adamant you should enter a plea of not guilty.'

'Get real, Aggie… Take a look at what I've become. I'm no better than the moron I knocked the living shit out of!'

Taking a quick shufti at the clock on the wall, he became aware that their animated verbal exchange was drawing interested stares in their direction.

'Stubborn you may well be, but a cold-blooded killer? I don't think so!' she quibbled. 'Talk to the guy… what harm can it do?'

'They're about to lock me up and throw away the key,' he said, despairingly. 'For between fifteen and twenty years!'

'So speak to him… we need all the help we can get!'

'You need to move on, Aggie,' he said, disconsolately. 'It isn't as if you'll have any problem finding someone else…'

'Have you completely lost your mind?'

'I'm done for, Aggie. What I did was indefensible!'

Her eyes widened and her mouth dropped in astonishment. She felt the urge to scream out loud, to grab hold of his shoulders and try to shake some sense into him, but the suffering in his eyes made her heart melt.

'I waited a lifetime to find you, Jonathan, and I'll go on waiting for a hundred lifetimes if that's how long it takes!'

Jon noisily shuffled his chair forward, much to the annoyance of the testy chief warder. Like an actor waiting in the wings to take his cue, he strode into the middle of the room to holler out a high-handed announcement:

'Two further minutes, ladies and gentlemen, if you please!'

Amid a flutter of activity Jon stood, placing the palms of his hands on the tabletop and staring tearfully down at her.

'You're a beautiful woman, Aggie; don't put your life on hold. Take off somewhere, at least for the duration of the trial!'

She remained seated, her face filled with high resolve, her tone defiant as she delivered her parting shot. 'Each day without you is like a prison sentence of my own. I'm in this for the long haul, Jon, and I'm going nowhere!'

The metallic clank of the door signalled an end to the allotted time. A chorus of moans and groans mingled with the discordant racket of tables and chairs scraping over the scuffed vinyl floor.

Little by little the gathering began to disperse, helped in bullish fashion by the small posse of warders, one of whom caught Jon and Agnes out of the corner of his eye and acted swiftly to break up their animated discussion. In macho fashion he lurched forward in a frenzied attempt to drag them apart, his vice-like hands powerfully forcing Jon's arm up into the small of his back, before shoving him mercilessly towards the alternative exit.

Jon gritted his teeth through the pain, unflinchingly rotating his neck to cast one last lingering look over his shoulder, his ears just able to pick up on her impassioned plea echoing buoyantly along the stretched passageway.

'Speak to him, Jon... his name's Martin Evans!'

He stopped dead in his tracks, much to the warder's exasperation, heedless of his request to 'get an effing move on'. Spinning back round, he unleashed a passionate cry wrung from the very depths of his soul.

'I love you, Aggie!'

For an instant she appeared dazed. Her brief reverie was broken by a hulking guard, keys jangling from his bulging waistline.

'Madam... please, I'm waiting to lock up!'

She glanced up at him, then away. 'But of course!' she said obligingly, making a speedy exit towards the main door.

*

7.10p.m.
Belmont Guest House, Leicester

She awakened, a little groggy from an unscheduled catnap, totally disoriented by an ambulance siren loudly blaring in the near distance. With her body submerged up to her shoulders in a bath full of lukewarm soapy water and half-stifling a yawn, she relaxed her head back, gradually piecing together the thoughts and images flitting across her mind's eye, the recollections coming thick and fast to trigger a wide range of feelings and emotions.

For a moment she envisaged her life without him, questioning whether or not she'd ever see him again. In the next, she visualised their eyes meeting across a courtroom, caught in the crossfire of a see-sawing legal shootout.

They would come through this, no matter what difficulties lay ahead, and what obstacles they found in their path. Time apart would only deepen their love, and they'd come out on the other side discovering they were stronger.

FIFTY-SEVEN

Saturday September 3rd – three days before trial

JON'S NOT INFREQUENT VISITS to the prison governor's office provided him with some light relief from his range of humdrum daily activities, their often in-depth parleys on occasion extending well beyond the accepted norm.

A proficient clarinettist himself, Graham Bancroft's love for music transcended the challenges of his professional life, his eclectic tastes ranging from classical to contemporary, not forgetting a passion for old-school R&B.

He greeted his guest with a smile and a warm handshake, courteously nodding to him to take the vacant seat opposite.

'How's life treating you, guv?'

'Never better, Jonathan,' he replied, leaning back in his chair. 'Though I admit to having had one over the eight last night!'

'A family celebration, sir?'

'That's a good way of putting it,' he chortled good-humouredly. 'My daughter Jennifer is pregnant with her first child.'

'Wow… congratulations, guv!' Jon responded with a hopeful glint in his eye. 'Let's crack open a bottle and celebrate!'

Bancroft brushed off the comment with a hearty guffaw, instead rummaging in a drawer to ferret out a copy of a national daily. He unfolded it and set it out under Jon's nose across the polished surface of the desktop.

'I thought you might like to see this.'

Jon cautiously pulled his chair forward to cast an eye over the splash headline. His mouth curled cynically at the unflattering image plastered beneath the eye-catching bold type spread the full width of the front page:

Writer of wrongs

**Inside the tortured mind of singer-songwriter JJ Gold
by Martin Evans (See pages 4&5)**

'Huh… perhaps I'd be more at home in a nuthouse,' Jon said derisively. 'Never mind banged up in a penal institution!'

'Take a peek inside, and give the article the once-over,' the governor urged. 'You may be pleasantly surprised.'

'What difference is it likely to make?' With an oddly indifferent air Jon folded the newspaper in half and slid it back across the desktop.

His attitude clearly rubbed the governor up the wrong way. Jumping up instantly he stared him directly in the eye.

'Aren't you going to read it?'

'I'm just anxious not to get my hopes up,' Jon said miserably, 'only to be shot down in flames when we go to trial.'

Bancroft's face contorted into a sympathetic frown, his agitation subsiding considerably as he slowly retook his seat.

'Never underestimate the power of public sympathy, young man.' he growled. 'Only days ago most of the dailies wanted your head on a spike… but look now, the worm's turning. Read the piece, Jon, I implore you!'

'If you say so, guv,' he finally assented.

'Don't give up hope, Jonathan. I've read the pathologist's report several times; his findings are nothing short of remarkable.'

'Is that so?' Jon gulped. 'Then why is my QC quaking in his shoes?'

'That will be all for today,' Bancroft said tetchily, at once radioing a warder. 'And take the newspaper with you!'

*

Once back in the confines of his cell, Jon took the guv's hint. Sitting back languidly on his bunk, he nimbly flipped through the pages to the two-page spread, adorned with a pastiche of snapshots taken at various stages of his career.

He'd never much cared for journalists, in particular the dirt-digging gutter press with whom he'd locked horns on several occasions. Yet Evans was different from the underhanded tabloid hacks he'd known, possessing an ability to draw his readers into an argument in a way that his own words could never have done.

He read on, constantly questioning why a respected journalist would offer him a chance to tell his side of the story, much less a virtual stranger willing to fight his corner and subsequently put his reputation on the line.

In conclusion Evans quoted a brief passage from the second book of the Bible, boldly set apart from the main body of the text:

'If the thief is found breaking in, and he is struck so that he dies, there shall be no guilt for his bloodshed.' Exodus 22:2-3

He shot upright, staggered by the aptness and power of the words. For a wonderful fleeting moment the negative thoughts that had haunted him for so long seemed to melt away, replaced with just a tiny glimmer of hope.

He read the piece through one more time, feeling his eyelids becoming heavier and heavier. Once his head hit the pillow he was asleep within seconds; but instead of drifting into a lucid dream, his demons came calling again.

FIFTY-EIGHT

The trial – Day One

A PLUVIAL, INHOSPITABLE MORNING-TIDE greeted the multinational raft of sodden reporters and paparazzi assembled on the steps of Leicester's imposing red-brick crown courthouse. This colony of drowned rats were eagerly waiting for the arrival of JJ Gold in advance of the trial's highly anticipated opening statements.

'It seems Gold was transferred to a holding cell at the crack of dawn,' Channel Four anchor-man Terry Davies griped loudly, pulling his phone away from his ear and stabbing his forefinger at the red button to end a call.

'The sneaky, conniving bastards!' head cameraman Tom yelled bluntly. He passed the word along to his technical colleagues, the majority of whom began to turn the air blue with a similarly rude and offensive reaction.

'How can you be sure?' producer Ivan cut in, removing his glasses to wipe off the droplets of rain with a crumpled hankie.

'I just put in a call to Evans,' Davies replied. 'The jammy so-and-so somehow managed to worm his way inside!'

Ivan huffed out a humourless laugh and turned tail to wander back to his van, his partial sneer revealing his true feelings.

*

Inside the deserted justice building an oddly chirpy Jon stood admiring himself in a free-standing mirror, reinvigorated from a sluice and wet-shave under the watchful supervision of a blue-uniformed court employee.

'Your hair's a mess, son,' the old guy scolded him. 'In my experience it doesn't pay to rub the jurors up the wrong way.'

Jon stepped away from the sink, carefully buttoning up a starched cotton Gant shirt, purchased at the eleventh hour from an old-fangled men's clothing store, together with a tasteless extra-wide paisley tie which the court official was now holding out to him.

'Uh-oh, no way. I wouldn't wipe my backside on that!' Jon said vehemently. 'It's what's called a wardrobe malfunction!'

'Don't be so vain,' the official shot back. 'No one will even notice.'

All at once he became alert to the presence of a suave figure hovering in the doorframe. Smartly attired in his silk gown and wig, James Hillier stood quietly observing the 'goings on', his smile quickly dropping into a scowl at the sight of the stickler's instant change of tone and body language.

'Thank you, Monty. That will be all!'

'Very good, sir,' the old toady acknowledged, promptly taking the hint and backing deferentially out of the door.

Jon's mood brightened considerably. As he fumbled into the trousers of his two-piece suit, the QC offered him a friendly slap on the shoulder, helpfully pulling the jacket from its peg and holding it up for him to slip into.

'Hugo Boss, no less!' Hillier commented.

'How do I look?'

'Very stylish,' he said, nodding graciously. 'I'd wing it without a tie.'

Jon picked up on a noise from afar, oddly resembling the clip-clop of horse's hooves. It was accompanied by a hubbub of muffled voices, reminiscent of a large outdoor gathering of fans awaiting the opening of a rock festival.

'What's going on out there?' he inquired.

'You might well ask,' Hillier reflected. 'A crowd estimated at between two and three thousand have brought the city to a standstill.'

'Why all the fuss?'

Hillier alluded to the massed ranks of spectators and international media outlets lining the streets, all under the keen supervision of a small cavalry of mounted policemen, attempting to maintain peace and order.

'It's absolute bedlam,' he said, puffing out his cheeks. 'It's bizarre. I've never seen anything quite like this before.'

'A rowdy mob baying for my blood!'

'Not a bit of it,' Hillier contended. 'There are scores of banners and placard-waving protestors, mostly in support of your innocence.'

Jon sank into a trance-like stupor, warmly calling to mind the extra-ordinary bond he'd forged with his ardent army of fans, a large number of whom had stuck with him throughout the many highs and lows of his career.

'Their loyalty never ceases to amaze me!'

Suddenly mindful of the clock ticking towards ten a.m., the QC turned his attention back to the matter at hand, swiftly dragging two chairs into the middle of the room and beckoning to Jon to park his backside.

He touched on the 'ground rules' of trial procedure which he'd be required to follow, urging him to remain calm at all times no matter what course the prosecution may pursue, or how aggressive the arguments may be.

'Rupert's a fearsome adversary,' Hillier said, sucking air through his teeth. 'I'll have a battle royal on my hands, that's for sure!'

'You're friends?' Jon asked, narrowing his eyes.

'After a fashion,' he snuffled, half-amused. 'I somewhat fortunately outwitted him in a rollercoaster murder case last year!'

A light knock sounded, followed by the appearance of a court usher's head poking round the door.

'I'm sorry to bother you, Mr Hillier, but Mr Justice Alderman arrived a short while ago and would like to see you in his chambers,' he advised in a fawning tone, his bent-over figure somewhat reminiscent of Uriah Heep.

The QC rose from his chair like a prize fighter leaping off his stool, his shoulders flexing as he prepared for battle. He grabbed Jon's hand and pulled him into a man hug, before bellowing out an impassioned war cry.

'It's showtime! The gloves are off!'

*

Scarcely half a mile from the besieged law courts, an attractive, casually dressed brunette toyed with a bowl of stodgy porridge in the breakfast room of her upmarket B & B. She was eavesdropping on a distracting conversation spewing mainly from the lips of a bolshie guest in between gorging on a full English fry-up.

'Obviously as a key witness I'm not at liberty to disclose any information relevant to the case,' he yapped above the general din. 'But then again, until I'm actually sworn in I fail to see what harm it could do!'

Agnes shifted discreetly in her chair to get a closer listen. She was immediately mindful of the guy sitting opposite the blabbermouth hanging on his every word, his right hand scribbling on a notepad in the fastest shorthand scrawl he could muster.

She gasped, then took a second glance, her hand shooting over her mouth to keep from calling out his name. 'Turner,' she muttered, heaving an anguished sigh, conscious of a sick feeling in the pit of her stomach.

'And you're one thousand per cent certain the body was still in one piece when the getaway vehicle fled the crime scene?' the reporter asked excitedly, again grabbing Aggie's attention as she tried to gather herself.

'Absolutely, unquestionably,' Turner said smugly. 'I tracked his every movement with my Sky-Watcher telescope.'

'And saw him dragging the corpse towards the woodshed?'

'Damn right I did!'

Rudely snapping his fingers, Turner summoned the busy waitress, then twisted his neck to move on to the next question.

'So in spite of his claims to the contrary it could only have been Gold who decapitated and dissected the body?'

'Bang on!' he said, picking up where he left off. 'And I'll be testifying as such!'

The reporter had all he needed, exuberantly finishing off with a final flourish of his pen. The story was absolute dynamite and he knew it, to such an extent he could barely wait to start writing it up in the privacy of his room.

'Thank you,' he uttered, preparing to stand.

'But there's more!'

'I'm sorry – I need to meet the editor's deadline!' he said, dodging around the waitress to make a run for the door.

'More coffee, sir?'

'Yes,' Turner snivelled. 'And about time too!'

Her stainless-steel dispenser at the ready, she moved in from his blind side and hovered close to the table. A feigned toppling motion towards him sent the scalding brown liquid spurting uncontrollably onto his lap.

'*A-a-a-argh!*' he shrieked deafeningly, his body keeling over onto the floor. Almost comically he writhed in pain, clutching with both hands at his private parts whilst kicking his bent legs in the air like a baby.

Agnes pulled her hands to her mouth to stifle a fit of the giggles, twisting her chair around to distract herself by looking out of the window. On the road outside she spotted two teenage girls carrying a 'FREE JJ' banner; and, taking a moment to catch her breath, her thoughts drifted to Jon's first day of reckoning.

*

'*All rise!*' the wiry, black-gowned clerk announced. The rumble in the courtroom diminished to an uneasy silence, interrupted only by the ungainly footsteps of the Honourable Mr Justice Hans Alderman, widely known in legal circles as 'The Hangman', slowly ascending the wooden stairway to his lofty perch.

He paused for a second to clear his throat and then, knees creaking in protest, eased himself down onto his seat. With a flap of his hand he gesticulated to the floor and gallery who, having been watching intently, promptly followed suit.

After an exchange of nods with the barristers for both the defence and prosecution the judge stared grim-faced towards the public gallery. At long last he broke the awkward silence with a snarling and hostile rebuke:

'To the fathead who attempted to use flash photography, one more such indiscretion and you will be removed from my courtroom!'

People shifted uncomfortably in their seats, every eye turned towards the wrongdoer at the end of the row, who hastily stashed the offending camera behind his legs and remained stooped forward with his head hung low.

Mr Justice Alderman fell back in his chair and peered down his nose over the rims of his glasses, finally nodding his assent to both the prosecution and defence counsels to begin their arguments with their opening statements.

'Thank you, My Lord,' the learned Rupert Watts led off, over-dramatically springing to his feet. 'Ladies and gentlemen of the jury, the statement of facts I am about to set out dates back to a November night in the year 2005, when a maniacal egoist saw fit to exact the most violent retribution against an impecunious Hindu boy found trespassing at his luxurious country estate in the dead of night.'

Hillier glanced to his side, conscious of the stunned expression on Jon's face. It was instantly picked up on by the eagle-eyed members of the press, who frantically scribbled away as if their lives depended upon it.

'Be still. It's early days yet!' Hillier whispered, placing a finger to his lips.

Jon shut his ears to the advocate's scathing address, preferring to lean back and drift into a deep and pleasant trance, almost oblivious to Watts's overblown attempts to vilify his character in the grossest manner.

As though magically transported to a fantasy land, an image of Agnes formed in his mind: her roseate cheeks glowing with life beneath her limpid dark-brown eyes, her knees pinning his chest to the smooth wet sand, her lips covering his face in a flurry of kisses while the waves sloshed against their wriggling toes.

The high-pitched sound of feedback abruptly snapped him out of his fugue-like state, Watts's harsh words all at once replaced by a cacophony of whistles and squawks boomeranging to every corner of the courtroom.

A short recess was taken, fortuitously providing Jon with a chance to question the prosecutor's bludgeoning attack on his character. His already frayed nerves were set further on edge by the background rumble of discontent.

'I'm no racist!'

'Rupert came down particularly hard on you,' Hillier said perceptively. 'But that's exactly what he does, Jonathan.'

'I never did like bullies!'

'Have no fear, he thrives on toying with the jurors until he sees the shock registering in the whites of their eyes.'

'Like a lion teasing its prey?'

'A rather apt analogy. Though his statement was riddled with inaccuracies, not to mention a sprinkling of improper comments.'

One loud rap of the bailiff's gavel brought an immediate hush, as given the go-ahead to reconvene Watt's shrill announcement rattled the whole room into watchfulness with all the subtlety of a pneumatic drill.

'The prosecution wishes to call Detective Sergeant Daniel Hackett!'

'Hey, I know that guy!' Jon said confusedly, his attention diverting to the witness skipping up to take the stand.

'So I believe,' Hillier nodded, admonishingly raising a finger to his lips.

*

Back outside on the street the dwindling throng meandered hither and yon, many clutching fast-food containers and rippled cups of frothy coffee, ears pricked for any scraps of information leaking out of the courthouse.

At the top of a narrow pedestrianised alley, Agnes found herself confronted by the court's imposing red-brick façade. She was suddenly distracted by a riotous altercation developing at the foot of the steps leading to the main entrance.

CORPORAL PUNISHMENT FOR RACIST CRIMES! a raised placard splashed in bold lettering, sent teetering from left to right by a knot of angry JJ aficionados garbed from head to toe in official merchandise.

A loud volley of choice expletives and insults rang out in the midst of a furious tug-of-war, the Anglo-African protestor giving as good as she got despite being seriously outnumbered by the feisty band of incensed teenagers.

Just then a pair of would-be Samaritans stepped into the fray, arms waving wildly to try and break up the fracas, joined moments later by a yellow-jacketed policeman menacingly wielding a rubber baton.

Not to be denied the plucky ringleader slipped sideways, avoiding his grasp while lashing out with her boot at the rickety support stave, spurred by the crack of splintering wood as the billboard clattered to the ground.

Agnes snaked her way through the encircling crowd to mingle amongst the onlookers and lend her support. Within moments she was gleefully pumping her fist, buoyed by the sight of the rabble-rouser beating a hasty retreat.

In one last act of defiance the woman turned and spat, almost inevitably launching into a profanity-laced rant, her biased, ill-chosen words straight-away drowned out by a thunderous chorus of boos and catcalls.

Belatedly, a police backup unit arrived, the tooled-up officers branching off in different directions to persuade the throng to disperse. Tagging along behind a small group of fans, Agnes listened to their lively chitchat.

'Crazy bitch. JJ's not a bigot!'

'He idolised Nelson Mandela!'

'And what about the African kids he sponsored?'

'And then there's his fling with the black supermodel!'

She spun around instantaneously and accidentally collided with a hun-kered-down paparazzo. Her heart-stopping nosedive was somehow captured in mid-flight in the oversized zoom lens of his precious Nikon camera.

'I'm truly sorry!' he cried out, energetically dashing across the tarmac to help her back up onto her feet. 'Are you hurt?'

'A little shaken, but I'm fine,' she panted, soon gathering herself. 'Did you happen to get any news from Court Four?'

'Not a dickie bird, ma'am.'

'Surely there must be something?'

'Only that the case could drag on for months!'

Trying to hide the shock that must have been written all over her face, she dusted herself down and bade him goodbye. Pausing momentarily, she craned her neck back to take one last look at the towering court building.

'A supermodel, eh?' she chuntered, half laughing, half incredulous. 'You little tinker... what a dark horse you are!'

*

Inside the airless courtroom a curiously attentive Jon silently cursed the prosecutor's compassionless approach, while inwardly acknowledging the detective's unshakeable self-control during the course of a ferocious interrogation.

'Detective Sergeant, I'm merely trying to establish that the mutilation and dismemberment of the cadaver commenced during the immediate aftermath of the fatal bludgeoning, for the sole purpose of disposing of the evidence to prevent identification,' Watts asked, cunningly rephrasing his previous question.

'And I reiterate: although the blood spatter points towards that, there's no way I could be a hundred per cent certain.'

'Did you or did you not uncover a trail of the deceased's blood beneath the pebbles scattered on the estate's front courtyard?'

'Indeed I did. I rather fortunately stumbled across an untidy heap of decorative gravel on the pathway, which meandered round towards the woodshed, very close to where the defendant's gardener was re-raking the drive.'

'And you can confirm that the blood samples collected at the crime scene exactly matched the deceased's DNA?'

'Yes, the swabs were a direct match, as verified upon closer inspection by the forensics manager, James Erskine.'

'And using your "copper's nose" would you say the bloodstain trail led back towards the house or in the contrary direction onto the forecourt?'

'I really couldn't say.'

'Not even by hazarding an educated guess?'

'Surely you'd be better served posing the same question to the pathologist, assuming he'll be taking the stand?'

'Thank you, Detective Sergeant – I'll give your advice careful consideration!'

An uncomfortable silence followed, so strong that you could hear the proverbial pin drop. Watts glanced up at the clock and then down at his notes, breathing in sharply to psych himself ahead of the lunch recess.

'Let us now go back to your initial visit to the defendant's country estate, focusing for a moment on his state of mind just hours after the deed was committed, and whether or not his demeanour changed as the weeks passed?'

'I'm satisfied he was of sound mind, both on the night of the crime, and during each of my subsequent visits to the house.'

'Which, would it be fair to say, extended to an increasing number of social calls... Please correct me if I'm wrong?'

'What are you implying?'

'That you struck up an unusually friendly rapport with him!'

Tired of being browbeaten, Watts's words stuck firmly in Hackett's craw. He recognised at once that his professional conduct had been called in question, yet gritting his teeth he somehow managed to keep a cool head.

'You failed to mention that I was investigating an attempted aggravated robbery!' he said, slapping down Watts's efforts to interrupt. 'And further-more that I tried to comfort him following the tragic loss of his parents!'

The QC froze, his nose clearly put out of joint by the tone of Hackett's reply. As though deeply wronged he turned to face the jury with his palms upraised, then strode into the middle of the court to look the witness straight in the eye.

'I put it to you that your better judgement was in fact clouded by a preoccupation with the defendant's celebrity status!'

'What?' Hackett exclaimed.

'Are you or are you not an ardent admirer of his music?'

'It could be said,' he fired back. 'But if owning a couple of CDs makes me a nutty fan, then you are sadly misguided!'

'On how many occasions did you visit the property?'

'Four, possibly five times at the most,' Hackett said off the top of his head. 'Like you, it's my job to ask questions!'

'A job in which you were assigned to the role of acting Senior Invest-igating Officer very shortly after the killing. Which with all due respect is quite a shift up the ladder for a Detective Sergeant, wouldn't you agree?'

'The role of an SIO is based purely on past experience.'

'Can you honestly say that you were comfortable in this capacity?' Watts continued. 'Particularly on such a grisly case?'

'I acted as the temporary SIO on a much-publicised drug-ring case towards the end of last year, which led to a series of subsequent convictions. Five of the six traffickers are now behind bars where they belong!'

'Bravo, officer,' Watts said mordantly. 'Yet you were overlooked for promotion in the aftermath of the prosecutions, in a blatant snub from the selection board. Can you attempt to explain the reasoning behind their decision?'

'They offered me a senior position in Barrow-in-Furness. But I expressed a desire to remain in the East Midlands, for personal reasons.'

'The notes in front of me stress that during the preceding five years you have been passed up for promotion on no less than four separate occasions. Which surely raises questions about your professional competence?'

'I made it perfectly clear to successive promotion boards that I wished to remain out in the field, and not stuck behind a desk. I love my job, and I've never been afraid of getting my hands dirty, no matter how my CV reads!'

'So, in effect, you admit to displaying a notable lack of ambition, which clearly hasn't gone unnoticed by your superiors.'

'Objection!' Hillier roared, springing to his feet. 'The witness is being badgered in a concerted effort to discredit him.'

'Sustained!' Alderman instantly responded.

'My Lord, I'm attempting as I believe is necessary to develop what has thus far unfolded as a rather ambiguous testimony.'

'Mr Watts, please don't push your luck!'

'My apologies, My Lord,' he said, sneakily glancing at his watch.

All eyes turned towards the clock on the wall, and then to the judge and back to the clock again. Hackett fidgeted in his seat, only too aware the lunch recess was imminent. His stupor was broken by the judge's hoarse tones.

'Mr Watts? Do you have anything to add?'

'Yes, My Lord... Detective Sergeant, the keynote of any investigation must be care and thoroughness, would you agree?'

'Yes, unquestionably!'

'And you're satisfied you performed your duties with the utmost proficiency?'

'I left no stone unturned.'

'Other than a scattering of pebbles on the defendant's driveway concealing crucial biological evidence!' Watts added, almost contemptuously. 'Upon which the outcome of this case may ultimately be decided!'

Again a stony silence fell upon the courtroom, the only sound the sharp clang of a distant church bell leaking in through the open skylight. It was mercifully followed by the words DS Hackett had waited so long to hear.

'I have no further questions, My Lord!'

FIFTY-NINE

IN A DESERTED FAST-FOOD OUTLET specialising in piri-piri chicken, a motionless young-middle-aged woman lay nose down to the tiled floor, her prone figure obscured by a formation of fixed Formica-topped tables.

Behind the main serving counter a hook-nosed Iranian employee, busily washing down the grease-smeared worktops adjoining a piping hot stainless-steel grill, was suddenly alert to an unkempt youth peeping through the door.

'Clear off, for Christ's sake!' he yelled scathingly. 'I'm trying to run a business here, not a food kitchen for the homeless!'

'Dial 999... quickly!'

'And why would I want to do that?'

'Because there's a body crashed out over by the toilet entrance!'

'And I'm the frigging Pope!'

'For crying out loud man, call a fucking ambulance!'

At that moment he caught sight of a dormant walking boot jutting out into the aisle between the tables. Anxiously he fumbled for the phone on the wall, his nerves all aquiver and his eyes as wide as dinner plates.

The ragamuffin scurried to her side and dropped to his knees, his hand grabbing her wrist to feel for a pulse. With no little skill he placed the heels of his hands on her chest, and lowered his head to perform CPR.

'Is she dead?' the attendant snivelled.

'She's barely breathing,' the guy half-panted, 'but alive!'

She lay stone still, her dishevelled locks like a dark shroud on the floor. He gently stroked her forehead with his calloused fingers, his admiring gaze focused on her porcelain-white features, ears listening to her faint breathing.

'I apologise. I mistook you for a beggar!'

'No matter.'

'You brought her back to life!'

'A little trick I learned… in Afghanistan.'

'You were a soldier?'

'Yep, before the wheels came off,' he said sadly.

The sound of a siren and sudden screech of brakes signalled the ambulance's arrival, the agile band of paramedics scrambling at a near frantic pace out of the rear doors and directly into the building.

'I'll rest easier now, knowing she's in safe hands,' the ex-squaddie said, turning towards the exit.

'Stick around!' the Iranian asked, eager to atone for his rudeness. 'I can rustle up some meatballs – on the house, naturally!'

'Thanks buddy, but no thanks,' he retorted, grinning from ear to ear. 'I wouldn't eat that crap if you paid me!'

*

Oadby, Leicestershire

Beads of sweat oozed from Hackett's pores following a long, relaxing soak in a hot steamy bath. A huge fluffy towel rubbed them away, but fell short of erasing the harsh words echoing in his head.

He fumbled into a loose-fitting tracksuit and traipsed downstairs to take his place at the dinner table, almost forgetting to acknowledge the lovely Sheila busily adding the final touches to a dish of lasagne.

'Nothing personal, sweetie, but you look awful.'

'Thanks a million,' he murmured, somehow able to force a smile. 'Just a little ragged around the edges, that's all!'

'A bad day at the office?'

'Huh, so to speak!'

'You poor thing. What happened?'

'Don't ask,' he said, puffing out his cheeks. 'Though if I never see the inside of a courtroom again it'll be too soon!'

She topped his wineglass up to the brim in an effort to placate him, then gazed across the table until their eyes connected. In a gentle, peaceful moment their fingers intertwined, her voice adopting a sympathetic tone.

'Was it really so bad?'

'The prosecutor's a Rottweiler!' he opened up. 'You'd have thought it was me standing trial from the grilling he gave me.'

'What's he trying to prove?'

'That my testimony doesn't carry much credence.'

'How ridiculous!'

He quietened, silenced briefly by a mouthful of piping hot minced beef blazing a fiery trail up to the back of his tongue, clearly glad of the chance to air his grievances in the company of someone willing to listen.

'He even suggested I was star-struck!'

'That's downright disrespectful!'

'On the plus side, the defence barrister turned the tables on him.'

'Thank the stars!' she exhaled, comfortingly gripping his hand. 'Will you have to take the stand again first thing?'

'Fortunately not,' he said, calmed by the alcohol's effects. 'There's still some unfinished business to attend to.'

*

Mallaig, Lochaber District, Scotland

His filthy boots resting on the arm of the sofa, Jimmy Logan took some time out to sleep off a weekday morning hangover, blissfully ignorant to his nephew Duncan bursting into his bungalow laden with a bag of groceries.

'Uncle Jimmy, wait till you see this!' he shouted excitedly.

'Piss off and let me be,' Logan mumbled, half-stirring. 'Can't you get it into your thick skull that I'm taking a wee nap?'

Duncan cheekily nudged his heel, and stood dangling a morning paper in front of his face, its distorted headline displayed in bold lettering:

FOOL'S GOLD
JJ fans in pitched battle with race protestors

Logan lifted his head and rubbed at his eyes, his gonads visible through a gaping hole in the crotch of his jeans. He squinted to focus on the images beneath the caption, the second an unusually grim-faced shot of Jon.

'The Sassenach!' he half-spluttered. 'Who the fuck is he?'

'The rock singer, JJ Gold!'

'You're shitting me, son!' Logan purred, grinning devilishly. 'And he's famous, you say? Rich? A rock star?'

'An international megastar, no less!'

An evil glint sparked in Logan's eyes, soon displaced by a series of loaded questions mostly centred on how valuable an asset Jon might prove to be. In a flash of inspiration he had all he needed to hatch a devious masterplan.

'One more question, son,' he said, pausing for thought. 'Why would a millionaire rock star hole up in the Highlands?'

'Simple – he's running away.'

'From what?'

'Take a look at the inside pages!' Duncan implored him.

Logan reached inside a drawer to lay his hands on his age-old glasses, promptly sliding the tarnished wire frames around his ears and scanning through the article with his nose virtually pressed against the page.

'Shit! He caved some Indian kid's head in with a baseball bat!'

'You got it!'

'Fire up your computer, son,' Logan said, abruptly.

'Uh-oh!' Duncan said suspiciously. 'What are you up to?'

'Draw me up a list of the editors of every daily rag under the sun,' he replied. 'Along with the numbers of their direct lines!'

*

Royal Infirmary, Leicester

The small gathering of nurses and crew fastidiously rummaged through Agnes's few paltry belongings, desperately trying to uncover some form of ID to give them an idea of who the mystery patient might be.

'Not a single credit or bank card,' senior nurse Martha said, with a disheartened sigh. 'It's as if she doesn't exist!'

'She very nearly didn't,' chief paramedic Rhiannon reflected, puckering her lips. 'For a moment I thought we'd lost her.'

Slumped on a solitary stool towards the rear of the staff room, a young medic cut a pathetically sad figure. Shoulders hunched, he stared at the floor, as if his whole world had come crashing down around him.

'The young chap looks pretty shaken up,' the nurse commented.

'That's what we call a baptism of fire,' Rhiannon said pensively. 'He watched her flatline for a full ten seconds.'

'Poor kid. He'll get used to it in time.'

With a friendly tap on her knee, Sister Martha rose up and bade the medic a brisk goodbye, duly making her way to the Brain Injury Unit, hoping against hope to organise a scan to check for any signs of permanent damage.

In the ICU a young nurse kept a constant vigil by Agnes's bedside, gently stroking her face, praying she'd live to fight another day.

SIXTY

Day Three

Jon awoke to the baffling flutter of wings, seemingly emanating from the metal support joists above his head. Closer inspection revealed the source to be a rogue swift that had somehow breached the prison's security system.

Hillier's masterful cross-examination of DS Hackett during the opening day's final arguments had at least provided him with a slight glimmer of hope. That optimism had been tested throughout the following day by the ramblings of pathologist Michael Letterman, on top of a tedious testimony courtesy of an eccentrically garbed DNA expert.

He quickly freshened up prior to skipping into the meat wagon for the short hop to the court. Pretty soon he was once more in the confines of the holding cell, staring into a shaving mirror handed to him by an ageing staff member.

Much to the old stager's distaste he started plucking sadistically at the hairs in his nostrils. Within seconds he had succumbed to a violent fit of sneezing, fortunately nipped in the bud shortly ahead of Hillier's early arrival.

'Good morning, Jonathan,' he chirped, almost giving him a start. 'You clearly needed to get something off your chest!'

'Yeah, I must be allergic to prison food.'

'Did you sleep well?' the QC asked.

'I slept like a baby,' Jon replied, adding with a smirk, 'I cried half the night!'

'Very droll!' the QC snickered, placing his briefcase on the table. 'It seems the tabloids are stirring up a real hornet's nest...'

'In what way?'

He placed his pricey leather document case onto the cell's shabby table, and withdrew an infamous gossip-rag from among a bundle of letters and printed-off emails, setting it down for Jon to give it the once-over.

WORLD EXCLUSIVE: JJ TEEN SEX SCANDAL SHAME
Startling new evidence uncovered

'Pray tell me whether there's any truth in this story, Jonathan?' Hillier stated earnestly. 'The timing couldn't be worse!'

Jon read on, readily sniffing a rat the size of a capybara. '*Lascivious private life… Homemade porn movies… Sexploitation…*' the degrading text alleged, choosing, without valid reason, to 'expose' him as a sexual predator.

'It's absolute bollocks, James,' he said, lugubriously. 'Every single word of it!'

'Sprung from a dubious source, do I detect?'

'Batman and Robin!'

Hillier glanced up at him and smiled, his expression changing in a flash owing to the dark humourless look on Jon's face. It was clear that he wasn't joking, and that the article was nothing more than a pack of lies.

'The Dynamic Duo?' he said, shooting him a curious look. 'Perhaps you'd care to enlighten me?'

'I've been sold down the river, by a pair of morons,' Jon replied despondently. 'What else could possibly go wrong?'

He shook himself down and let his story unfold, his words flowing more easily once the swell of anger began to recede. For a surreal moment he found himself transported back to Lochaber, his mind visualising Logan's nephew suspended from a staircase, swathed from head to toe in cling film. He saw his fist connecting with Logan's angular jaw, and CJ, his friend in need, battling it out with an unruly and drunken mob.

And then he saw Agnes, waving to him from the dockside over a backdrop of skiffs and frigates chugging unhurriedly into the busy little harbour, her deep chestnut locks blowing freely, caught by the cool salt breeze.

'Jonathan? Are you okay?'

'I'm fine,' he responded, allowing himself a smile.

'We'll sue for libel.'

'Go for it, James!' he said half-dozily. Thumbing the page, he suddenly found himself staring transfixed at an eye-catching quarter-page snapshot.

'Aggie, my Aggie!' he exclaimed.

He picked up the paper to study the picture more carefully, marvelling at the photographer's skill in capturing her tossed in mid-air, juxtaposed against a gun-toting police officer merged to the fore of the court building.

'What's wrong? What is it?' Hillier inquired.

'Agnes – she was here!'

He gazed in awe at the image, and gently traced his finger around her frozen figure. Her eyes fixed directly into the camera's lens, as though beckoning him forward to break her fall and sweep her up in his arms.

Hillier remained silent, merely gesturing towards a metal clothes peg mounted on the wall, where Jon's sprucely ironed jacket and trousers were draped over a wooden hanger.

He glanced at the QC and then back down, unable to drag his eyes away from the picture. Maybe, just maybe, she was out there somewhere among the throng of spectators, so close she was almost within touching distance.

'Jonathan… chop-chop, dear chap!'

He snapped abruptly out of his reverie.

'Yes, James. Sorry!' he replied. 'Just a daydream!'

*

Belmarsh Prison

Perched on the edge of his bed, CJ carefully bound a makeshift dressing around the bloodied knuckles of his right hand, watched with puzzled interest by a chummy warder known affectionately as Big Fat Ron.

'What do you mean, you need medical attention?'

'I think I've broken a bone.'

'How?' Ron grunted apathetically.

'I had a little spat with the wall!' CJ admitted, a touch embarrassedly.

'You belong in a nuthouse, not a bloody nick!' the screw wisecracked. 'Take five and I'll give the prison doctor a shout.'

He lingered a while longer in the doorway, his tall, broad figure casting a shadow over the entire cell. Sternly and inquisitively he glared over at CJ, wondering what could have possessed him to do such a thing.

'A penny for your thoughts, Ronnie?'

'What the hell got into you?' he questioned with a baffled expression. 'You're out of here in a matter of days!'

'I saw red,' CJ said, nodding towards the tabloid headline.

'You lost the plot, due to a newspaper report?'

'I guess so,' he admitted.

'Jesus Christ, son!' the guard gasped out loud. 'Mind you, they stitched him up good and proper, like a prize kipper!'

'Eh? What did you say?'

'The singer – what's-his-name?'

'Jon! JJ Gold!' CJ blurted, shooting to his feet.

'That's the guy. It seems some conniving bastard knifed him in the back.'

'Stitched him up…' CJ said, pausing. 'Like a kipper!'

He pumped his unbound fist and leapt up from his bed, spontaneously lunging forward to plant a sloppy kiss into the centre of Ron's forehead. The warder frantically backed away, lashing out with his hands, elbows and knees.

'What the fuck's got into you?'

'Ronnie, you're a goddam genius!' CJ said jubilantly. 'I urgently need to make a call, to a pal up in the Scottish Highlands!'

SIXTY-ONE

Mallaig, Lochaber District

THE USUAL DREGS OF SOCIETY were gathered outside the doors of the Marine Hotel, impatiently anticipating a Friday get-together to blow off some steam at the end of the working week.

Boisterous cheers from his pals greeted Jimmy Logan's overdue arrival, his recent stroke of good fortune made perfectly clear to all and sundry from his uncharacteristic willingness to thrust a hand into his pocket.

'A wee dram for the lads, Neil!' he asked, eyeing the top shelf for a moment before thinking again. 'The bog standard Bells will do!'

'Did your lottery numbers come in?' the barman enquired.

'Wouldn't you like to know?'

At the sound of the squeaky door hinges all conversation died away, every head turning in the direction of young divorcee Marnie. Hips gently swaying, she sashayed over to a stool at the opposite end of the bar.

'What'll it be, sweetheart?' Neil asked.

'A G&T with a slice, please.'

'Make it a large one!' Logan interrupted. 'On my tab, son!'

She raised a hand of thanks and coyly fluttered her eyelashes, but politely declined the invitation to join him, mostly in view of the intimidating gang of half-drunk locals gathered around him hanging on his every word.

He wasn't taking 'no' for an answer. Hooking his toecap around a vacant stool to drag it closer to the bar, he patted the upholstered cushion with his mitt to finally entice her into his motley circle of friends.

'You're looking lovely tonight!' he commented. 'Dazzling even, darling!'

'Thank you,' answered Marnie, being ultra-cautious. 'You seem to be splashing your money around this evening?'

'Let's just say I came into an unexpected windfall!'

'Lucky you!' she said, with mock surprise.

His beady eyes lowered to her V-neck top and lingered unashamedly on the swell of her ample cleavage. She glanced to one side to conceal her embarrassment, sipping self-consciously at the ice-cold liquor.

'Whatever happened to the English thug you took up with?'

'You mean Carl?' she asked warily.

'Aye, the shaven-headed action hero,' Logan growled, baring his yellowed dentures. 'What a fucking headcase!'

'Ah, he's a real pussycat at heart,' she said, ignoring the remark. 'He moved to Australia to experience life Down Under.'

'Best place for him,' he snarled. 'With all the other wild animals!'

Again distracted from the conversation, he continued to undress her with his lust-filled eyes. Then, with a snap of his fingers, he summoned the barman who was midway through replenishing the tankards of a sulk of thirsty fishermen.

Unsettled, she put her hand over her glass and refused his offer of a refill, instead uncrossing her legs and preparing to move to a table full of like-minded acquaintances, convinced some ulterior motive must be afoot.

'Sit your shapely butt down!' he said gruffly, quick to see the error of his ways. 'Now, now, don't be so unsociable!'

'Surely you're not trying to hit on me?'

'Me? Get real, sweetie, I'm old enough to be your dad!'

'So, what's the catch?'

'We were discussing my nephew Duncan,' he half-choked, cackling like a hen. 'Who just so happens to be unattached!'

'Isn't he a little young?'

'He's a big, big boy now!' he said, slurring his words. 'Hung like a freaking donkey!'

Her patience stretched to its limits, she again attempted to raise herself up. Moving swiftly from his stool Logan tried to block her path, his efforts to grab her in part thwarted by the confused tangle of bodies.

'Get your filthy hands off me!' she cried out.

'You ungrateful little bitch!' he roared crassly. 'You should swing by for a nightcap and take a wee look for yourself!'

At that instant he staggered clumsily onto the size twelve boot of a gargantuan seaman, who responded by lifting him up from the floor with consummate ease and sending him hurtling backwards onto the seat of his pants.

Stars flashing before his eyes, Jimmy stumbled to his knees, just in time for yet more humiliation to be heaped upon him in the form of a freshly pulled pint which Marnie doused with vengeful glee over the top of his head.

Infuriated by his brazen antics, barman Neil rushed to jerk him upright and manhandled him to the exit, his arms flailing wildly amid a tirade of four-letter expletives, ultimately silenced by the thud of the slamming door.

SIXTY-TWO

Day Four

THE CLOCK TICKED ROUND to eleven-thirty on the hearing's fourth morning, heralding the arrival in the witness box of Richard Turner. Kitted out dapperly in an expensive charcoal-grey Hugo Boss suit and tie, he was scarcely recognisable from the psychopathic fuddy-duddy who had stalked Jon's movements for so long.

'Please be seated,' Mr Justice Alderman ordered, briefly acknowledging the witness. 'And that includes you, young man!'

Turner seemed disorientated and gave the judge a nervous nod, finally taking a seat and speaking in a tremulous voice.

'Yes, Your Majesty,' he said.

A hushed burst of incredulous laughter spread to every corner of the court. The clerk stared at the judge open-mouthed, while heads turned this way and that, mostly covering their faces to hide their embarrassment.

'Simply "Sir" will suffice!'

'But of course, sir,' he responded fawningly.

Alderman hid his exasperation well, lightly rapping his gavel to quell the continuing murmurs. All at once his nose began to twitch, his irritation further aggravated by the overpowering smell of a cheap brand of aftershave.

'Mr Watts,' he announced, discreetly wiping his glasses to shield his nostrils. 'Would you kindly take the floor?'

'Yes indeed, My Lord,' Watts responded with enthusiasm. 'For the record, would you please state your full name?'

'Richard Anthony Turner.'

A high-pitched snigger which turned into a chortle yet again interrupted the proceedings, much to the prosecutor's annoyance. Glaring over at the defence counsel's row, he stopped mid-sentence to show his displeasure.

'My Lord, this is intolerable!'

'Mr Hillier!' Alderman intervened. 'A quiet word, please!'

Jon stiffened, only too aware that every eye in the room now rested on him. He leaned across the table and jotted Turner's initials onto the middle of the QC's notepad, still holding back the urge to laugh aloud.

Hillier strutted back to the bench and shot him a chastising look, then gazed down at the scrawled letters leaping out at him from the page, his hand rushing to his open mouth to conceal the beginnings of a smile.

R.A.T.

An admonishing finger wagged in Jon's face sparked a near frenzy of activity amongst the press. In their eagerness to tap frantically at the keys of their laptops, they failed to pick up on Turner's icy glare at the accused.

'My most humble apologies,' Hillier finally avowed, offering a deferential bow to both the judge and his learned friend opposite, who half-turning in his direction returned the gesture with a brief nod of acknowledgement.

'I trust there will be no further interruptions,' Alderman said sternly. 'Mr Watts, pray begin, if it so pleases you?'

*

By the day's final session a taut air of uncertainty permeated the clammy courtroom. It was etched in the faces of the disillusioned onlookers shifting nervously in the public gallery, each ruffled by the details of the witness's damning testimony, and sensing the noose may already be tightening around the star defendant's neck.

Eager to run through the fateful night's events with a fine-tooth comb, Watts reeled off a whole sequence of questions, fired at Turner like an artillery barrage, in an effort to give the jury something to ponder overnight.

'At the risk of repeating myself, I saw no evidence of any human remains, or for that matter of any human-sized packages, removed from the defendant's property between the hours of midnight and five in the morning!'

Spent with the toil and fatigue of the day, Alderman glanced down discreetly at his wristwatch and then, much to everyone's astonishment, rapped his gavel to curtail the session almost forty minutes ahead of schedule.

As he beat a lumbering retreat, he paused to summon Watts and Hillier to his chamber, amid a cacophony of bickering voices raining down on the departing witness from high up in the public gallery. Shouts of 'Lying scum!' and 'Perjurer!' reverberated above a hullabaloo of catcalls and hissing, backed up with further calls of 'Turncoat!' and 'Judas!', which hastened Turner's departure through the double exit doors.

Hillier performed an about-face to grab Jon's arm and pull him to one side; and questioned the true motivation behind Turner's malicious attack, the sordid details of which had only served to strengthen the prosecution case.

'The guy's nuts, James. A fickle fan turned rat.'

'In keeping with his rather unfortunate initials,' Hillier said, half-jokingly. 'No personal vendettas, or long-term grudges?'

'Not that I'm aware of,' Jon said thoughtfully. 'He was stalking me and I kept him at arm's length; that's all there is to it.'

They veered off in different directions, Jon towards a side door leading to a corridor snaking along to the holding cell, and the QC to the rather more pleasant surroundings of the judge's chamber, still with more questions than answers.

Something wasn't right, he could feel it in his bones. Something in Turner's hostile demeanour and his offhand manner of communication. Something urgently needed to be addressed, even if it took him all night.

*

Day Five

Notwithstanding Hillier's best endeavours to discredit him during an intensive hour-long cross-examination, the unshakeably confident Richard Turner somehow held firm. He snapped back at every carefully posed question with irritating assurance, to all appearances revelling in the spotlight at being centre stage.

His somewhat theatrical exit again triggered an undercurrent of murmuring voices, mostly venting their anger with a string of muffled obscenities amid growing concerns the defence case had fallen on stony ground.

In the ensuing hiatus people sipped at plastic bottles of Highland Spring to cool off, while others cheerlessly propped their chins up on their hands, all adding to the sense of uncertainty permeating the air.

With a sharp rap of the gavel Mr Justice Alderman succeeded in restoring some semblance of order, his guttural voice urging Watts to call his next witness, announced in a loud, powerful tone by the overly officious court clerk.

'The prosecution calls Rashid Shah!'

He stepped up to the witness box and was sworn in, his uneasiness apparent from his hunched shoulders and trembling hands. He nervously coughed to compose himself, glancing at the defendant and looking back.

'Good morning, Mr Shah,' Watts led off courteously. 'I understand you were friendly with the deceased, Mr Amir Mistry, and that you shared a city-centre apartment together in the period leading up to his death?'

'We weren't close, not really.'

'But close enough to move in together?'

'His previous landlord kicked him out on the street,' Rashid replied. 'And he somehow persuaded me to take him in.'

'As a philanthropic, or kind-hearted, gesture?'

'You could say that.'

The prosecutor's sardonic tone started to get his back up and set his already frazzled nerves even more on edge. He felt a burning sensation rising up into the back of his throat, realising the worst was still to come.

'Are you familiar with the Leicestershire village of Granby, Mr Shah?'

'Not really, I'm just a townie.'

'Then perhaps you can explain to me why a dark blue Ford Mondeo registered in your name was seen both entering and departing the very same village on the night of November the eleventh, 2005?'

'I wasn't in the car!' Rash said emphatically. 'Neither as the driver nor a passenger!'

'But Mr Shah, you were positively identified in a subsequent identification parade by a member of the local community?'

'Nonsense! He fingered two Asians immediately following the parade, only to change his mind the next morning!'

'So you believe the witness's judgement should be brought into question, Mr Shah?' Watts said, probing a little deeper. 'On account of his inability to distinguish between people from different cultural backgrounds?'

'Huh, you said it!'

Watts fumed, his posture becoming rigid at the cockiness of the reply. He briefly referred to his notes and decided to take a different tack, eager to establish some form of link between the witness and the defendant.

'How well do you know the accused?'

'Barely at all,' Rashid said coyly. 'Although I was privileged enough to rub shoulders with him on a couple of occasions.'

'Sufficient to procure the security code to the electronic gates at his country estate?'

'Code? What code?'

'The four-digit PIN code used to gain access to the driveway of the accused's mansion!'

'I've never been to his home!' he responded crabbily. 'And I haven't the faintest clue what you're talking about!'

'We have sworn testimony that the gates opened and closed at regular intervals before and after the break-in.'

'I'm not aware of any such code, or for that matter the gates you're referring to!'

'I put it to you, Mr Shah, that not only did you gain access to the property, but that you witnessed the vicious, repetitive bludgeoning of your accomplice Amir Mistry before fleeing the scene in the said motor vehicle!'

'And I repeat, I wasn't there!'

In a low, dirty attempt to discredit Rashid, the scheming Watts unsurprisingly broached the subject of his prior criminal record, slowly but surely tightening the screw to use it as bad character evidence against him.

'Mr Shah, did you or did you not memorise the said cipher for the sole purpose of gaining access to the defendant's property?'

'What part of "I wasn't there" don't you understand?'

Watts paced the floor like a caged animal, his arms waving erratically from the space below the judge's bench. With his nose in the air Alderman looked down for a moment, before his head inclined urging him to continue.

'One more question, Mr Shah,' he said, collecting himself. 'Where were you on the night of Amir Mistry's untimely death?'.

'At home, studying for an exam!'

'I have no further questions, My Lord!'

*

The post-lunch session got under way on the dot of two p.m. when, given the nod to take the floor, a refreshed-looking James Hillier strode to the front of the witness box and greeted Rashid with a polite half-smile.

'I'll do my best to keep things brief, Mr Shah,' he commenced. 'I understand you work in the field of health and social care?'

'That's correct.'

'A far cry from a life of crime, wouldn't you say?'

'Absolutely right!'

'Mr Shah, do you often rub elbows with the likes of celebrities and famous musicians?'

'Fat chance, sir. I tend to move in different circles.'

'So how did you come to meet the defendant?'

'My brother Khalid was writing his biography, and offered me a pair of VIP tickets to a charity bash he was due to attend.'

'And when such an opportunity presented itself, you couldn't pass it up?'

'Word for word!'

'A charity function, you say?'

'Yes, for children with spina bifida.'

'A worthy cause indeed. So he struck you as being a benevolent, kind-hearted sort of fellow, scarcely capable of inflicting inhuman cruelties as described in such detail by my learned friend for the prosecution?'

'My Lord, I must object in the strongest terms!' Watts yelled furiously. 'My learned friend is leading the witness!'

'I'm terribly sorry, My Lord,' Hillier said, with a semi-apologetic smile. 'I have no further questions for this witness!'

SIXTY-THREE

Day Six

A LEGION OF ARMED SECURITY PERSONNEL blocked off the mortared steps winding up to the court's main entrance. Meanwhile, a glut of yellow-clad overseers officiously checked the credentials of those granted access to the building via a narrow network of metal barriers crisscrossing towards a revolving door.

Behind the red-brick walls, the fuzzy-headed defendant slumped into his seat alongside an oddly bright-eyed James Hillier. He half-interestedly looked up to check out a sports-jacketed, cravat-necked forensic psychiatrist stepping rather unsteadily up to the witness box, his withered right hand clutching an antique walking cane.

Roughly an hour into his testimony, Jon's rounded lips breathed a muted sigh. His apathetic frown was noted by the ever-alert QC, who moved to jab him in the lower ribs courtesy of his pricey Montblanc rollerball pen.

'Focus, Jonathan, please!'

On the face of it unbothered by the analyst's dreary, drawn-out deposition, Watts pinched his chin studiously and nodded his head in accord, his true feelings laid bare by a shifty glance down at his wristwatch.

'The range of emotions a PTSD sufferer feels during a flashback can be a contributory factor to rage-induced aggressive responses. Indeed, studies prove we're all capable of committing acts of minor or major atrocity.'

'So, Professor Hunt, you're suggesting that the defendant's thoughts may have been impaired at the time of the murder?' Watts said, stopping him mid-flow. 'And that this resulted in loss of control of his faculties?'

'Disassociated states such as DID generally occur in response to severe trauma, and frequently take control of a person's behaviour and consciousness. A perpetrator often can't recall particulars about the moment of attack.'

'DID, Professor?' Watts asked, confusedly.

'Dissociative Identity Disorder.'

'And how long can these periods of dissociation last?'

'Hours or days, sometimes much longer; there's no set pattern.'

He prattled on in a soporific monotone, giving careful thought to every considered response. Eventually he paused to catch his breath, the words almost seeming to stick in his throat.

Instantly seizing on the opportunity, Watts politely thanked him for his invaluable cooperation, at last bringing an end to the overlong attestation, marked with a collective sigh of relief from the majority of those present.

*

Fifteen minutes later

As though aping a boxer jumping up from his stool, Hillier sprang out of his chair to preside from the centre of the room, hell-bent on wrapping up the morning's arguments prior to the scheduled one p.m. lunch break.

'Professor, during your earlier testimony, my learned friend Mr Watts focused rather heavily on the psychological impact of post-traumatic stress disorder, in short PTSD, claiming that when the defendant returned to the outhouse during the aftermath of the alleged killing, his brain may have shut down.'

'That hardly constitutes a question,' the professor said, aloofly.

'Sir, if you'd please let me finish…'

'But of course.'

'Professor, on the assumption that dissociation is a symptom of PTSD, approximately what percentage of sufferers experience memory impairments or blackouts following exposure to a traumatic or terrifying ordeal?'

'High, I'd say. Evidence suggests that a majority of PTSD patients have problems transferring short-term to long term memory.'

'One in ten individuals, according to NHS statistics.'

The expert witness took this in. 'Hmm… significantly lower than I thought!'

'Indeed. Thank you, Professor Hunt,' Hillier said, authoritatively. 'My Lord, that concludes my cross-examination.'

With the clock ticking towards twelve forty-five, the wily judge called for an early halt, and rose to his feet. Before making tracks to the safety of his chamber he passed a handwritten note to the court clerk, who duly made the announcement in his best stentorian voice:

'This court will reconvene at thirteen forty-five… at which time the doors will be closed to the public!'

He could not have even half-expected the hostile reaction this drew from the gallery. In the act of fleeing he lifted his briefcase to shield his head from a deluge of flying debris, his short legs scurrying like a frightened mouse to escape the barrage of catcalls and insulting gestures.

*

The testimony of Jonathan Jacob McGoldrick

From a high-rise apartment block on the opposite side of the street a white flag-cum-bedsheet undulated in the breeze, daubed with a red painted slogan:

GOOD LUCK JJ
WE LOVE YOU
CARLA & JENNY

A bivouac of media tents and shelters were lined up along the kerbside. One of a gaggle of roving reporters waxed lyrical into an ITN newsreel camera, providing an unbiased account of the early-afternoon proceedings, fed via email directly from a fellow hack present in the court's press gallery.

'A relaxed-looking JJ Gold, garbed in a jacket, open-necked shirt and chino slacks, responded with confidence and conviction to brush aside the prosecuting counsel's opening flurry of questions,' she affirmed approximately two hours into the arguments. 'Stay tuned for further updates!'

Back inside the courthouse, Watts's leather-soled shoes slipped precariously on the polished hardwood floor, bringing him to an unwished-for standstill midway through the act of unleashing his coup de grâce:

Rupert J. Watts, Crown Advocate: I have in my possession a copy of *Q* magazine, a monthly publication specialising in rock and pop music. I'd like to quote a passage from a recent article focusing profoundly on the accused's talents as a writer of songs – should it please you, My Lord?

Mr Justice Alderman: Very well, Mr Watts.

RJW: 'Gold's brutally honest lyrics provide an emotion-packed insight into the joys and misfortunes of a utopian troubadour constantly striving to break new barriers.' What do you make of those observations?

JJ: Hmm. A little bit long-winded for my liking; music journalists are renowned for talking out of their backsides!

286

RJW: The piece was written by my niece, who also happens to be my god-daughter... I take it you disagree with her sentiments?

James Hillier, Defending QC: Objection, My Lord. I fail to see the relevance of my learned friend's line of questioning, not to mention his attempts to embarrass and discredit the respondent.

Mr Justice Alderman: Overruled, for now. Mr Watts, would you kindly care to come to the point, on the double please?

RJW: With all due respect, My Lord, I'm merely trying to establish that the accused's poetic licence extends to an openness that leaves little to the listener's imagination, prior to reciting a short extract from one of his compositions written in the aftermath of the fatal incident, which clearly defines a malicious intent, at the time of killing, wilfully to take the life of a fellow human being!

Mr Justice Alderman: Get on with it, Mr Watts!

RJW: Mr McGoldrick, would it be fair to say that the lyrics to your songs often tackle what may be termed as sensitive issues?

JJ: Yes, and then again no. My songwriting undoubtedly gives me the opportunity to get a few things off my chest, and if that means ruffling a few feathers along the way, then what will be will be!

RJW: And exacting revenge in callous and wanton disregard of the consequences to human life would in your view be categorised under 'getting something off your chest'? Let us explore the significance of the extract to which I previously referred:

'Under a cloak of darkness, poised like a crouching tiger about to seize
    upon its prey,
A blood-red mist descends before my eyes as I jump into the fray.
A crushing blow meets solid flesh and bone, striking a deadly chord
I am a soldier of misfortune, and I must fall on my sword.'

'A crushing blow meets solid flesh and bone' doubtless refers to the part-wooden, part-metallic baseball cudgel swung with a total lack of concern for another's life towards the skull of a powerless petty larcenist!

JJ: I scrawled down those lyrics on an old sheet of A4 only hours after the accident, when I was totally out of whack. They'd not long taken my Dad away in a box. I wasn't thinking straight!

RJW: A few scrawled lines which amount to an acknowledgement of guilt. A confession from which guilt is directly deducible, characterised in the language of a callous and egocentric individual bent on retribution!

JJ: I struck him on the side of the head. One single blow. I didn't mean to kill him. I didn't even realise he was dead. And when I returned to the woodshed the body was missing. It just doesn't add up!

RJW: Unlike the collection of severed body parts you disposed of at a variety of illegal dumping grounds!

Watts's unrelenting attack left Jon browbeaten and mentally fatigued. Close to tears, he slumped low in his seat with his chin on his chest. His thoughts ran uncontrollably, flayed by a merciless whirlwind of words, rendered in gruesome detail to tilt the pendulum of justice heavily in the prosecution's favour.

'And so, on the basis of the evidence laid before you on the part of the Crown, in the name of justice, I implore each and every one of you to come back from your deliberations with a unanimous verdict of guilty!' Watts concluded, mopping his brow with a hankie and shooting a knowing glance in the direction of Hillier.

*

The defence summation

'Most distinguished ladies and gentlemen of the jury, I will now follow my learned friend's brutal character assassination of the hapless defendant, whose previous brushes with the law amount to nothing more than a half-dozen points on his driving licence,' Hillier proceeded, in a vastly different tone. 'A devoted son, utterly overwhelmed by grief, reacting instinctually to the unforeseen loss of his beloved father, fomented by an outrageous and contemptible act of violence against his defenceless mother!'

In an impassioned and persuasive closing argument, Hillier's last-ditch defence met with many a raised eyebrow. Several jurors shifted uneasily in their creaking bench seats, examining the bemused expressions of their fellow members, while a sour-faced Rupert Watts exhaled showily towards the ceiling rafters.

'The defendant openly admits an intention to strike down the intruder, due to an abnormality of mind which substantially impaired his mental responsibility at the time of the crime. My learned friend the prosecutor has attempted to overwhelm you with testimony and evidence of the accused's guilt. However, I implore you to consider the irrefutable evidence that the defendant Jonathan McGoldrick acted under severe emotional stress, and thus return a verdict of not guilty, by reason of emotional disturbance!'

SIXTY-FOUR

Thursday September 29th 2011

Crises for Gold & Euro the Tory-biased broadsheet led, accompanied by two extraordinary mugshots of a bedraggled Jon sharing the spotlight with an image of Angela Merkel, the German Chancellor.

The hoary old court usher peeked over Jon's shoulder and attempted to lighten the mood with an unkind wisecrack about the portly Deutsch-lander's curiously masculine features, before wheeling away to laugh at his own joke.

'Shouldn't be long now,' he said, his face becoming more serious. 'It's not often a jury deliberates for more than three days.'

'Qué será será,' Jon replied, ponderously.

Upstairs in the empty courtroom a sleep-deprived James Hillier checked the clock function of his Samsung cell phone and allowed himself a moment of quiet reflection. In just a few minutes, the press gallery would be filled with a flock of hungry media vultures, ready to feed on the scraps of news the world had waited so long to hear.

Content that he'd given it his best shot, but prepared for the worst, he traipsed off, head bowed, to bid Jon good morning.

Only metres away in the adjoining chambers a quietly confident Rupert Watts measured out the room's perimeter, not at all impressed by the jurors' lack of response to his summation of seventy-two hours prior.

He looked up at a gilded frame suspended on the wall, and engaged in imaginary dialogue with the esteemed dignitary whose likeness peered down at him. 'What could possibly be keeping them?' he muttered, semi-audibly. 'This is an open and shut case if ever there was one!'

Then came a light tap-tap-tapping at the door.

*

'All rise!' the court clerk boomed, his unnecessarily loud voice coinciding with the punctual arrival of Mr Justice Alderman.

The judge remained on his feet for a short time, his eyes scanning the largely unoccupied courtroom and fixing on the group of grim-faced jurors, deftly reading their body language to tell him exactly what he needed to know.

'Please be seated. Foreman of the jury, I would ask you to remain upstanding.'

'Yes, My Lord.'

'Have you reached a verdict on which you are all agreed?'

'Indeed we have, sir.'

'Do you find the defendant guilty or not guilty of the murder of Amir Mistry?'

'*Guilty*, My Lord!'

'Very well. Ladies and gentlemen of the jury, I wish to thank you all sincerely for your time and service. You are now free to go. The court will reconvene at ten o'clock tomorrow morning, at which time I will pass sentence.'

No one moved a muscle, save for 'The Hangman' lurching out through a side door which abruptly slammed shut. Out on the street the news leaked out to a hue and cry of gasps, moans and wailing, more comparable to a public outpouring of grief at the loss of a revered spiritual leader in a far-flung foreign land.

The unthinkable had happened. In the span of a few seconds a single, vengeful action had changed Jon's life and stripped him of his liberty. Stunned and devastated, he leant his weight on Hillier's arm and mustered a whispered 'Thank you!'

Flanked by two police officers he left the court, his thoughts focused only on Agnes.

*

Friday September 30th 2011
Leicester Crown Court

A brooding, impenetrable silence hung over the closed courtroom, broken simultaneously with the judge's arrival by the melodic chimes of the nearby Catholic Church, repeatedly ringing out the same descending pattern.

'Will the defendant please rise?'

Resigned to his fate, Jon stood erect and met Alderman's gaze, his lips twisting into a sad, rueful smile. In return the judge offered him a compassionate nod, then concluded his morning's work with a Parthian shot.

'The mandatory sentence for murder is life imprisonment, but I have to decide the length of the minimum term you must serve. Over the last two weeks the court has listened to compelling evidence of your guilt. However, the equally cogent defence put forward by the defence counsel casts doubt on the issue of premeditation, pointing instead towards a partial abnormality of mind in the minutes leading up to the killing on account of the attack on your parents. In conclusion, you will go to prison for twenty-five years, and will serve a minimum term of twelve years prior to consideration for your release by the Parole Board.'

PART THREE

SIXTY-FIVE

February 2012
Knoydart

A STYGIAN PALL of unshifting cloud cover hovered malevolently above the white-coated slopes of the icebound peninsula. It afforded a joyless homecoming for the solitary female passenger aboard the mid-afternoon ferryboat, chugging its way discontentedly towards the heavily sanded, algae-stained jetty steps.

Eyes squinting through the persistent granulated mist, the shivering Agnes made out local resident Cara's beaten-up Land Rover skidding to a halt midway along the slush-ridden pier. Her face cracked into a rare smirk as the dizzy headscarved woman almost came to grief upon leaping out from the driver's side.

'*Cara – I'm over here!*' Aggie shouted, gliding uncertainly on the patchy surface in her sheepskin-lined Ugg boots.

'I barely recognised you, lovey; are you okay? Goodness, you've shed so much weight since last summer!' Cara said, half concerned, half light-heartedly. 'You look so thin and tired, darling, like a bag of bones!'

'I've been travelling since the crack of dawn and I'm out on my feet,' Agnes said, passing off the remark with a flick of her wrist. 'I'll be right as ninepence once I get a roaring fire on the go over at the croft.'

'Not a word of it, sweetie!' Cara said insistently. 'You need a bellyful of wholesome Scottish cooking inside you!'

Agnes wrestled her haversack onto the Jeep's rear bench seat, and glanced at her blanched complexion in the rear-view mirror, only too aware of how badly she'd neglected herself during the period of Jon's incarceration.

'The rooms will be colder than the hinges of hell!' Agnes whined. 'I desperately need to make the place habitable again!'

Cara ignored her complaints and skated round to the driver's side, gripping onto the roof-rack to remain on her feet. Little more than a stone's throw away a tureen of lamb stew stood simmering on the stove, which accompanied with a flagon of hot mulled wine would surely help bring the glow back to Agnes's cheeks.

*

Thirty minutes later
Inverie

'Ted and Bobby have offered to ship your stuff over to a lock-up in Fort William,' Cara gabbled, in between busying herself in the kitchen. 'They'll keep it in storage for you until they receive word to shift it southwards.'

'How much will that set me back?'

'Free of charge – Ted insisted,' Cara said chirpily. 'As a token of his appreciation for the quad bike Jon gifted to his lad!'

Aggie said nothing and casually wandered towards the bay window as if in a daze. Her eyes lingered sorrowfully over the dark grey mass of clouds hovering threateningly over the gloomy, windswept hinterlands.

'How kind!' she eventually mumbled.

'That man of yours has a heart as big as a bucket!'

'Yet as cold as the frozen emptiness I'm gazing at right now,' Aggie sadly reflected.

Cara spun towards her and paused, her hand placing down the breadknife in utter confusion, her jaw falling slack.

'My ears must surely be deceiving me! You always worshipped the very ground he walked upon. And yet here you are wallowing in self-pity, bereft of hope. Just remember, he won't be under lock and key forever!'

'We used to walk upon these shores hand in hand, and I truly believed I'd found paradise. How mistaken I was. Just look at it now, the image of a Siberian labour camp. I won't be sorry to see the back of the place.'

'Just listen to yourself!' Cara snapped back. 'Come and sit yourself at the table, and let's not hear another word!'

They sat in silence for a short time, but for the slurping of hot broth from their soup spoons. Agnes seemed to be carrying the weight of the world on her shoulders, very soon made clear in a single heartfelt sentence.

'He refuses point blank to see me. It's been more than five months now – a hundred and sixty-one days to be exact!'

'I had no idea… Oh, you poor darling!'

'I've tried showing up at the prison unannounced,' she said openly. 'But it's almost as though I no longer exist.'

'Have you tried writing?'

'Countless times,' she confessed. 'Almost until my arm was dropping off.'

'Did you receive a reply?'

'Just one,' she half-sobbed. 'Which was short and to the point.'

'Share it with me.'

Agnes fumbled for an envelope tucked into the back pocket of her jeans, and withdrew a crumpled sheet of paper which she slid across the table, its handwritten ink smudged by a dozen or more dried tear stains.

My dearest Agnes

There's so much I'd like to say to you but putting words to music seems a whole lot simpler than trying my hand at composing a letter, so please forgive me for keeping this brief.

During my time in here something inside of me has changed, I'm not entirely sure why but all I know is it is not about you.

As I write my firm of solicitors in Edinburgh will by now have transferred the ownership of the croft to Agnes Hilary Ryan, along with drawing up a mandate for my name to be struck from our joint account, following which the assets will be assigned to a new account set up solely in your name. There may be a few forms to sign but all the necessary paperwork will be mailed to you on Knoydart.

So long Aggie, be strong

Yours

Jonathan

Cara laid down her spoon to pore over each line, then going back to the beginning to read it over again. She bowed her head low in an effort to hide her surprise, unable to come to grips with the brevity of his words.

'And there you have it. No "I miss you", or even a single kiss!' Aggie said with understandable bitterness. 'He may as well have said kiss my backside. Six months, that's all, and he's already given up on me!'

'You need to read between the lines, to connect the dots,' Cara pleaded. 'He's looking to provide for you, in his absence!'

'Absence! He's facing a minimum of ten years. And if the letter's anything to go by he'll have been sectioned by then!'

'It's merely a cry for mercy!'

'He's losing the plot. I'm told he sits crouched like a mad monk on the cell floor staring into space reciting mantras!'

'His flights of fancy will soon pass,' Cara stressed. 'And he'll need you there to pick up the pieces when he crash lands.'

A strange emotion bubbled up inside of Agnes, like a force pulling her away from him. He'd admitted that some part of him had changed, just as though something was broken and maybe damaged beyond repair. The road ahead of her would be long and hard, but she needed to free herself for the sake of her sanity.

'I have to move on,' she said, fighting back the tears.

'You can't just run away!'

'The butterflies that once fluttered in my stomach have morphed into a swarm of angry killer bees, fleeing the hive to start anew,' Agnes said pensively. 'Somewhere, somehow I lost my way, and now I have to find my way back.'

They replenished their wine glasses and relocated to the sofa, the tone of their conversation becoming more relaxed from the effect of the alcohol. They recalled the wild weekends spent together, flitting back and forth across Loch Nevis to enjoy one another's company, and the hangovers which often lasted for days.

Predictably, Cara turned the subject back to Jon, half amusedly making mention of the charismatic stranger she'd met on the train, and how her eyes were glazed with passion during an impromptu afternoon coffee.

'You were utterly smitten – it was plain as day!'

'It all seems like a dream.'

'Hold on to it!'

'For how long? Ten, maybe eleven years?'

'Forever, if necessary. He loves you more than life itself!'

'Take me home... please!'

She rose up a little too quickly and became wobbly on her legs, her head turning woozy and her sight momentarily blurred. She leaned against the sofa's arm to catch her balance, her ears alert to Cara's incessant chatter.

'I played dumb until now. But something about him resonated with me when he stopped me on the street to ask about the ferry times. Something I couldn't quite put my finger on... as if I knew him from a previous life.'

'Spare me the spiritual mumbo-jumbo stuff!'

'If you'll let me try to explain…'

As if out of nowhere a sudden downpour began lashing heavily against the window pane, followed by a lightning bolt slicing through the darkened sky. In her wisdom, Agnes decided to stay a while longer.

*

4.30a.m.
Brightwater Croft

Afflicted by spasmodic bouts of a discomfiting sleep-wake disorder, Agnes thrashed beneath an assortment of throws and weighted blankets, her mind in utter turmoil over Cara's strange and fantastical pipe dream.

'Believe me, I'm under no illusions it was Jon I saw, arms and legs pumping through an onrush of rolling waves!'

From the first moment they met she noticed something different about Cara, from her kooky, free-spirited personality to her curious penchant for bohemian clothing, reminiscent of a late sixties flower child.

Could it simply have been the booze talking, or was it that her mind was playing tricks on her? No matter what it was, her bizarre ramblings certainly stretched the imagination way beyond the bounds of credibility.

'He came out of nowhere, his tanned upper body glistening in the sunlight, thrusting through the blue-green current up onto a white sandy beach,' she'd continued, seemingly lost in her own little world.

'But you hardly knew him!' Agnes had bickered. 'His skin's been the colour of snow ever since I first set eyes on him!'

She'd blown a fuse, and stormed into the hallway to reach for her hat, coat and gloves. However well-intentioned they may have been, Cara's words rang hollow, replaying inside her head like a recording stuck on repeat.

On their way back neither of them uttered a word, but for a subdued 'bye-bye' when the Jeep halted at the bottom of the drive. Agnes then trudged off without looking back, knowing that she may never see Cara again.

*

10.15a.m.
Loch Nevis

'Farewell Knoydart, my little chunk of heaven,' Agnes muttered touchingly, leaning over to gaze out into the mist from the ferryboat's stern. 'You brought me back to life, and for that alone I'll be eternally grateful!'

She recalled the untold number of similarly inclement winter days and nights, thawing out by a roaring fire snuggled in the arms of the man she loved, his warm body against hers as his whiskery chin tickled her cheek.

'You'll catch your death of cold out here, missy,' a friendly voice carried on the wind. A young deckhand was busily hauling in a thick mooring-line. 'Go inside the cab and warm yourself with the other passengers.'

'I came over a little queasy,' Aggie yelped, wiping away an icy teardrop. 'I could do with some fresh air.'

'Well, it doesn't come much fresher than this!'

'Quite right!' she said, trying a smile.

With any further chitchat hampered by the engine's clattering pistons, she shuffled back around to catch one final glimpse of the icebound peninsula dissolving into the wintry haze, aware of him watching her closely.

As he diligently continued with his work he couldn't help but notice the dark circles round her eyes, coupled with a distressed, almost haggard expression on her face, suggesting that all was not well.

'Are you okay, missy?' he called out above the racket.

'I'm just hopeless at saying goodbyes.'

'Saying goodbye doesn't mean it's forever,' he said, moving closer. 'I don't blame you for getting out at this time of the year.'

'I doubt I'll ever be out this way again,' she vowed, expressionlessly. 'I've a long and difficult journey ahead of me.'

'To sunnier climes, perhaps?'

'Somewhere far, far away from here!'

'Well, good luck missy!' he said, cheerily making ready to secure the headfast. 'I hope the angels are watching over you!'

As they chugged towards the pier head, she thanked him and headed for the vessel's bow, her supple figure stooping down to heave her rucksack onto her back. Within seconds of docking she clambered up to the top of the ramp, and stopped, at that moment feeling more lost and alone than she could ever remember.

SIXTY-SIX

IRISH ÉMIGRÉ EAMON DUFFY lived for the outdoors. He had craved his own breathing space in which to pursue his avid fascination for the animal world the very minute he cut loose from his mother's apron strings.

'You were such an independent little boy, Eamon,' mum Maggie often mentioned to his discomfiture. Time and again she reminded him of the injured frog he once rescued from the side of the road, patching the critter up in the garden shed utilising a matchstick and cotton strands to fashion a minuscule splint.

'Amphibians suffer as well,' the boy upheld, almost contemptuously dismissing his mum's much-recycled tale.

Shaken to the core by the inexplicable disappearance of schizophrenic husband Hubert, Maggie indomitably returned to full-time nursing. Almost immediately she secured a plum post at Galway's University Hospital, and entrusted the eleven-year-old's care to retired headmistress and family friend Maeve Nagle.

Outwardly unmoved by his father's disruptive vanishing act, the budding naturalist poured himself into his studies. Under the heedful tutelage of his kind-hearted guardian he progressed in leaps and bounds, sufficiently to set his sights on a career in animal biology, or perhaps more realistically as a veterinary surgeon.

Footloose to explore the neighbouring hills and hollows from the outset of summer's lengthy school hiatus, the arrival of Maeve's granddaughter temporarily forestalled the growing lad's wanderlust. Instead, he was compelled into assuming the role of a protective elder brother, fostered by a soft spot for the young lassie.

'Granny, it's not fair…! *Please* let me go with Eamon today. I'm bored of baking cakes and scones – I want to go on an adventure!' little Agnes pleaded, proving hard to resist with her button nose and glowing brown eyes.

'It's perfectly okay, Mrs Nagle; it'll make a change from going it alone. She can help out by carrying the lunch box!' he acknowledged with a whimsical smile, before vowing faithfully to keep a watchful eye on her.

*

Juxtaposed by their respective parent's onerous workloads, the callow twosome quickly became inseparable, sharing a like-minded passion for the bucolic surroundings encircling Maeve's comfortable country home.

Although polite and responsible for one so young, Eamon's body language soon began to reflect the many physiological changes that were taking place within him. With the first stirrings of sensual attraction, his curiosity became noticeably keener.

'Have you ever kissed a boy?' he asked diffidently, unsnapping the water canteen from his belt. 'You know, properly?'

'I did, yes, but only once!' Agnes replied, a little taken aback. 'And anyway, why would you want to know a thing like that?'

'I'm just curious, that's all. Did you like it, and who was the lucky lad?'

'Tyrone Oliver. And yes, it was quite nice; but promise me faithfully you won't breathe a word of it to my granny!'

'I cross my heart and hope to die, Ag,' he vowed a little enviously, looking at her with a miffed, sheepish expression.

She reminded him that her granny only allowed her to stay out until dusk; and, scrambling to her feet, suggested they begin to make tracks. Then, for some reason, she stooped down to plant a light peck in the middle of his forehead.

'What was that for?' Eamon gasped, his mouth falling open.

'Because you're my best friend in the world,' she said sweetly, picking up her backpack. 'I just wanted you to know!'

*

Some two and a half years later, mother Maggie successfully applied for a senior nursing post at Sydney's historic St Vincent's Hospital, and young Eamon found himself uprooted from the Emerald Isle in search of greener pastures Down Under. A touching send-off ensued, inflamed by Eamon's heartfelt parting shot.

'I'll come back for you some day, Ag,' he pledged, doing his utmost to put on a brave face. 'I give you my word!'

She tottered forward, her handkerchief rubbing away the tears, and handed him a small tinsel-wrapped gift.

'I'll keep a place warm for you in my heart,' she said, feelingly. 'And promise me faithfully that you'll write!'

'You'll always be the only girl for me!' he yelled from the cab's window, not taking his eyes off her diminutive figure.

His mother held him close to ease his pain, going on to explain there'd be plenty more fish in the sea Down Under. He could look forward to endless sunny days, and most of all a new home that offered a perfect outlet for his inexhaustible passion for wildlife.

'Koalas, emus and kangaroos,' she enthused. 'How exciting is that?'

'Poisonous snakes too!' he added, finally perking up. 'The venom of the taipan is the most toxic on the planet!'

'That-a-boy!' Maggie said, encouraged by his apparent change of heart. 'You're going to absolutely love it!'

'But I will miss her, Ma. She's like a part of me!'

*

Australia

Heartened by the mild climate and outdoor lifestyle, his homesickness soon began to fade, enabling Eamon to once again knuckle down to his studies. He was justifiably rewarded with the offer of an international scholarship to the University of Queensland, helped in no little part by his mother's unflagging efforts.

It meant relocating to the cosmopolitan city of Brisbane, contiguous with both the Gold and Sunshine coasts, where the vast array of attractions strewn on the campus's doorstep made for an exhilarating change. Lured in by a like-minded circle of freshmen, the frequent letters to his first love became fewer and further between.

He had taken up an invitation to tag along on a weekend blowout to the aptly named Surfers Paradise, little more than fifty miles west of campus. A pair of hazel eyes shining across the waterfront set his heart aflutter, stimulated further in but a matter of minutes by a serendipitous intro-duction, courtesy of a friend's friend.

'I love your accent; are you visiting from a parallel universe?' the bronzed beauty joked. Eying the heart-shaped locket dangling in the vee of his open-necked shirt, she went on to introduce herself. 'I'm Sandra, from Battery Point, near Hobart, Tasmania.'

'I not long landed from Planet Galway, in the west of Ireland,' he chuckled. 'I'm an undergraduate at the university in Brisbane.'

'A long way from home! What are you studying?'

'Veterinary medicine. I've harboured a fascination with wildlife, pretty much since I was knee-high to a praying mantis.'

'A "pet" subject, you might say,' Sandra half giggled, seemingly taking a shine to him. 'If ever there was one!'

'Ha, no one's ever said that to me before,' he said, inwardly attempting to suss her out. 'Can I buy you a drink?'

'Yeah, why not? What say we crack open a bottle of Bollinger, accompanied by a couple of dollops of beluga caviar?'

'Are you being serious?'

She backed off, aware of his half petrified features. 'It'd be great, but a lime and soda will do nicely, with plenty of ice if that's okay! Do you have a name, or should I stick to College Boy? Or just plain old Paddy?'

'Eamon! Eamon Finnian Duffy to be precise, from a little dot ten thousand miles away in the northern hemisphere. It's really lovely to meet you... Sandra!' he smiled, civilly excusing himself to make towards the bar.

*

Through countless telephone conversations and handwritten missives, in addition to the odd romantic interlude nestled in the attic room of mother Maggie's downtown apartment, the relationship blossomed into something lasting, marred only by the Bass Strait separating them during the triad of prolonged semesters.

'Sandy, this may be a long shot,' he said from out of the blue, dropping down onto one knee in the middle of a bustling Sydney burger joint. 'But once I've graduated, would you do me the honour of becoming my wife?'

'Eamon, get up, you're embarrassing me!'

'So that's a resounding no?'

'Why would I want to marry a man who's not been up front with me?'

'Huh...? I've always been honest with you!'

'Then what about the girl in the silver locket?' she said, accusingly. 'That you hid from me, in the bedside drawer!'

He raised his chin and tilted his head up towards the ceiling, his frown lines adding to the gloominess of his expression.

'It was Agnes... dear sweet Agnes!'

No sooner had she questioned his sincerity than an awful possibility dawned on her.

'Oh no! Me and my big mouth!' she said, full of anxiety. 'Not your little sister? Please tell me she didn't die young!'

'She was like a sister to me,' he opened up. 'The pendant was a going-away gift she handed to me when we left Galway.'

'That's all I needed to hear.'

'So will you reconsider?'

'What was the question again?' she teased, flitting away.

He chased her around the table and caught up with her close to the exit, his arms wrapping around her shoulders to pull her into his embrace. From back inside the diner a wave of hoots and hollers resounded out onto the street, right away recognised with a smile and a fist-pump, before they legged it out of sight.

'I'm really not very good at this stuff,' Eamon admitted, stopping for a moment.

'Hmm... Sandra Duffy has a pretty nice ring to it...'

'You bet it does!'

'And try as I may, I can't think of anyone else I'd rather spend the rest of my life with!' she said, finally easing the tension.

'Can I take that as a yes?'

'I'm all yours, Mr Duffy!' she vowed, showering his face with a deluge of kisses. 'Body and soul, and whatever else!'

*

April 2011
Galway, Eire

'Agnes... is it really you?' the clean-cut charmer said, tenderly pecking her on the cheek. 'Wow – you look absolutely amazing!'

'It must be all of twenty years... and just look at you – what a hunk!' Aggie responded in kind. 'I barely recognised you!'

'Where does the time go? I often think back to the day the cab pulled off the drive, watching you wave goodbye. For weeks I cried myself to sleep, thinking I'd never see you again. I'm so glad to be proved wrong!'

Immediately relaxing and enjoying one another's company, they chatted idly about everything and anything: his marathon journey, the ideal climate Down Under, and above all their time spent together as kids.

'Eleven thousand miles, phew!'

'Wild horses couldn't have kept me away. Aunt Maeve meant the world to me. The pastor described her to a tee: "a caring and wonderful woman". Without her, I could never have been inspired to fulfil my dream.'

'A big shot veterinary surgeon, whoa!' Agnes ribbed him impishly. 'Australia's answer to James Herriot, perhaps?'

'To tell the truth, there's not much resemblance to the North York moors. I've treated wombats, kangaroos, snakes, you name it… even a tiny little bandicoot a local nature-lover once rescued from the jaws of a native wildcat!'

'That's a new one on me!'

'They're pretty cute!'

Recalling his long-standing marriage, mentioned fleetingly in a letter from her gran soon after the event, she broached the subject thinking to offer her belated congratulations. Instantly she detected a shift in his demeanour.

'Did I hit a sore point?'

'Sandra sadly passed away,' he answered, totally unexpectedly. 'Following a short bout of small-cell lung cancer.'

'Oh Ea, I had no idea… Come here, let me hug you!'

They deftly sloped off to a tucked-away chintz-curtained snug, to discuss in private the many twists and turns their lives had taken, from Eamon's recent tragic loss, through a jumbled heap of cherished childhood memories.

'She passed the day before our fifteenth wedding anniversary. I felt so helpless, but there was nothing I could do.'

'To have gone through such an ordeal alone, and still be sitting here with your head up takes enormous strength of character!'

'Onward and upward, as the saying goes. No clever turn of phrase could ever describe how I truly feel… and now with Maeve's passing, I only thank God for bringing you here to make everything a little more bearable!'

From the crowded veranda within earshot of the snug, the tinkling ivories of Elton John's 'Rocket Man' leaked in through the slightly ajar roof light, paving the way for the flamboyant star's Americanised velvety tones: '*I miss the earth so much, I miss my wife. It's lonely out in space!*' the ill-timed lyric bled out.

'It must be lonely as hell stuck out there in Tasmania.'

'I can't say it hasn't been tough, Ag.'

'Why don't you up sticks and come home?'

'It *is* my home,' he said, defensively.

'But you're right here, right now, where you belong!'

'No Ag, I'd never leave!'

He waxed lyrical about the unspoilt green fields and stunning scenery, and the true friendliness of the native Apple Islanders, not forgetting his ranch perched at the top of a hill, overlooking a sandy beach known as Wineglass Bay.

'It sounds idyllic!'

'You should come visit. I mean it!'

'Grab your coat, Mr Duffy,' she said, sidestepping the invitation.

'Why? Where are we going?'

'Do you remember when we snuck off into town behind Gran's back?'

'And she called the Garda... how could I forget!'

'Well, there's no stopping us now!'

He dashed off to the cloakroom at breakneck pace, and returned seconds later clutching their overcoats. Like a pair of naughty schoolkids they slipped off into the night, set on giving Aunt Maeve the send-off she deserved.

*

The Crane Bar, Galway City

'*And it's so sad to be alone-o-o-o-one. Help me make it through the night!*' the pub songstress thundered out, warbling the stirring finale to Gladys Knight's classic seventies hit to an appreciative, packed house.

'She's breaking my heart, Ag!' Eamon yelled above the din.

'A real powerhouse!' Agnes enthused.

Suddenly she felt goosebumps rise all over her body. 'Jeez, I don't believe it!'

'What is it, Ag? Tell me!'

'This song!' she gasped, dumbstruck.

'Then what have I got? Why am I alive anyway?

Yeah, what have I got? Nobody can take away?

Got my hair, got my head, got my brains, got my ears

Got my eyes, got my nose, got my mouth... I got my smile.'

'Nina Simone, if I'm not mistaken.'

'And also my Mum's favourite ever song!'

Without further ado she took his hand and dragged him onto the dance floor, where swaying in rhythm under the pulsating lights, they pulled at one another's hands and belted out the lyrics in sync with the music.

'I got my arms, got my hands, got my fingers, got my legs
Got my feet, got my toes, got my liver, got my blood
I've got life, I've got my freedom, I've got life.'

For the first time since Sandra's death he felt truly alive. His veins coursed with raw energy and his heart pumped fast in his chest, quickening further at the sight of Agnes leaning herself forward into his embrace.

The marked change of tempo almost at once cooled his ardour, until for one brief instant their cheeks brushed together and her head rested on his shoulder, eyes closed while they floated lightly across the floor.

The singer's gravelly voice softened to a velvety purr, effortlessly pouring out a cover of Nora Jones's mellow signature tune. Its slow, poignant melody gently sent him into a dream he wished would never end.

'Come away with me in the night; come away with me and I will write you a song!'

He felt the warmth of her breath against his skin, and his emotions began to run away with him. With his mouth all but touching her ear he inhaled deeply and whispered the words he felt compelled to say.

'Come away with me, Aggie!'

'Huh? Where to?' she said, nonchalantly.

'To the opposite end of the globe!'

At first she said nothing, resolved to put her thoughts to the back of her mind, and slipped away from his grasp to leave him stranded in the middle of the floor. Her finger beckoned him to join her back at the table.

'Don't look so glum, Ea.'

'Forgive me, Ag.'

'Just forget it.'

'It was just a crazy notion that came out all wrong.'

'I said forget it!'

They ordered another beer from an aproned glass-collector skipping around the tables, duly acknowledged with a friendly thumbs-up and promptly putting an end to Eamon's long-drawn-out apology.

Fresh from a short break, the well-built songbird returned to the stage to take up where she had left off. Her piano player adroitly carved out a familiar-sounding intro before her opening line instantly caught Aggie's attention.

'My heart's all aflutter like the wings of a hummingbird…'

'Where do I know that song from?' she said, wracking her brain.

'It's by JJ Gold… the long-lost tortured genius.'

'Silly me!' she said, sighing longingly.

*

Two days later
Shannon Airport

Eamon parked the hired Vauxhall Astra directly outside the terminal building and piled their baggage onto a trolley, vowing to meet Agnes by the Aer Lingus desk once he'd safely returned the vehicle.

She walked inside and paused for a second to scrutinise the giant departures board, then hurried to the appropriate bank of check-in desks eager to tag on to the shortest queue and collect her boarding pass.

'Good morning, madam,' the ultra-efficient attendant greeted her. 'Now where would you be flying to today?'

'Inverness, via Dublin.'

'Are you travelling alone?'

'That I am, with one piece of hand luggage.'

'I have a window seat available by the emergency exit at no additional cost, if you'd prefer a little extra legroom?'

'Perfect. Thank you!'

She made towards the desks marked 'LONDON-LHR' and caught sight of Eamon sprinting frantically across the reception area, his leather-soled brogues coming to a precarious halt on the polished marble floor.

Urged to step forward to the console, he plonked his suitcase on the conveyor and presented his passport. Very soon he was dogging Aggie's footsteps to join a chain of bodies slowly wending through the security gate.

'Coffee, madam?' he suggested, on the far side.

'Excellent idea!' she agreed.

They veered off to a much quieter place away from the main thorough-fare, where having ordered a large espresso and a cappuccino they killed some time sat on their backsides indulging in a spot of people-watching.

All around them people rushed hither and thither with confused looks on their faces, mostly scampering in the direction of the busy departure gates, their suitcase wheels squeaking and dragging on the tiles.

He tilted his chin upwards to the information screen above his head and once again ran a keen eye over the status of their flights, before standing to gaze down at her with a look of solemn resignation.

'My gate's up on the board.'

'What can I say?' she responded.

He moved to embrace her and was almost knocked off his feet by a briefcase-carrying businessman zipping past him to make a mad dash for his plane, hastened by a shrill announcement bursting through the tannoy system.

'My invitation still stands.'

'Maybe someday, eh?'

'I'll always love you like a sister, Ag!'

'God bless you, Eamon.'

He slipped a white vellum envelope into her hand and leant over to plant a farewell kiss in the centre of her forehead. And he was gone.

SIXTY-SEVEN

March 2012
Granby, Leicestershire

ON THE BACK OF A PROMPT eight p.m. start, jobbing builder Tom Kettle and his lackey Kevin seemed to make light work of digging out the footings to a new extension, until pausing for a second the senior man screwed up his nose.

'Easy does it, Kev, there's an odd patch of soil just under your nose that's a different colour to this gooey crap!'

'How about I give it a wallop with the pickaxe?'

'Don't be so hasty,' Tom said dubiously. 'What if it's something valuable?'

'Like a treasure chest, you mean?'

'You never know, lad!'

One by one they dropped into a crouch and began burrowing through the soil with forked hands, wisely opting to use a pair of hand trowels duly grabbed from their kitbags to help scoop out the surrounding earth.

'Nearly there, boss,' the lad grunted, stretching even lower to at last lay a glove on the side of the mystery object.

'Can you get it to budge?'

'No chance, boss. It's rock solid!'

With grim determination he removed his gloves and dug his fingernails deeper. Finally he managed to grip on to a smooth-surfaced object, which felt something like an old fish-tank or perhaps an antique sink of some description.

'Any joy, son?'

'No. It's huge – much bigger than I thought!'

Tom urged the lad to pick himself up and run his hands under the tap, content to knock off for a cuppa and discuss their next move. His eyes were drawn to a durable-looking plank leaning against the wall by a heap of firewood.

'I have a cunning plan!' he said, smiling and looking satisfied with himself. 'Sit yourself down and let me explain…'

*

Leicestershire Police HQ

The phone call from newly crowned DCI Matt Philpott caught Hackett napping on the job. His body was spent from a twelve-hour stint of round-the-clock surveillance, made worse when it was revealed that the suspect had long since done a bunk.

'I just came off the blower to Gavin Chambers, the new DI,' Philpott said zealously. 'He wants to borrow you for a while.'

'Oh yeah – congratulations guv!'

'Cheers!' he said, gloatingly. 'Where are you right now?'

'Uh-oh. Why?'

'There's been a development at a site out in the back of beyond,' Philpott unfolded. 'He's eager to pick your brains.'

Worn out and exhausted, Hackett only half listened to the guv'nor's overlong summary of events – the cowboy builders, the grisly discovery – until, almost inadvertently, he thought to mention the village's actual location.

'Did you say Granby?'

'I figured that might grab your attention!'

He cast his mind back to the row of quaint terraced cottages directly over the road from the sprawling Gold estate, and the odious Richard Turner, whose court testimony single-handedly put the singer behind bars.

'What exactly did they unearth?'

'Use your grey matter, Dan.'

'A severed human skull?'

'You got it in one!' the chief said. 'Luckily Butch and Sundance managed to exhume the sodding thing in one piece.'

'From someone's back garden?'

'Yep, but it gets worse.'

'Try me, guv.'

'The fucking monstrosity was sealed in a giant glass jar. Preserved in formaldehyde, like something out of a Frankenstein movie,' he explained, retching in disgust. 'Chambers has got a SOCO unit at the scene as we speak.'

'Turner!' Hackett growled. 'I can smell it a mile off!'

'The guy who torched the cottage?' Philpott inferred.

'On the nose, guv.'

'Get your arse over there, Dan!'

Minutes later Hackett was twisting his VW around a network of quiet country lanes, his mind kicking into overdrive almost in sync with the accelerator. Could it be Gold had used Turner to carry out his dirty work – and in the aftermath the creep had sold him down the river and vanished into thin air? Just as before, nothing seemed to stack up.

SIXTY-EIGHT

Kingston upon Hull

THE SUDDEN RAP of the door knocker found Phoebe sitting in the middle of the floor painting her toenails. Her suspicions were immediately aroused by the sight of a youthful-looking police constable caught on the security camera.

Not even thinking to cover herself she rose to her feet and sashayed out onto the landing, scooting down the staircase without touching the rails to finally unbolt the door and confront the fresh-faced PC.

'I'm sorry to bother you, ma'am, but I'm informed on good authority that this is the last recorded address for a Mr Richard Turner, who I understand is related to you. We've been trying to track him down for some time.'

'I'm afraid I haven't seen Richard in months,' she said respectfully. 'We didn't exactly part on the best of terms.'

'What a shame. I was rather hoping you may be able to provide some useful information as to his current whereabouts.'

'Come in out of the rain, please,' she said hospitably. 'Perhaps I could offer you some light refreshment?'

'Thanks, but no thanks, ma'am,' he said, quickly averting his eyes from her negligee. 'All I need is a forwarding address.'

'He left without a word, officer.'

'In which case, I'd best be on my way.'

'Slow down. What is it with the younger generation these days? I may not be in possession of a forwarding address, but there's something in my study that may be of interest to you, if you'd care to come in?'

He finally went inside and traipsed behind her along a dimly lit passage. Ducking into a side closet she grabbed a housecoat from a hanger, slipping it over her underwear to protect her modesty.

'I gather Mr Turner is your nephew, ma'am?'

'That's correct,' she replied. 'Is he in some kind of trouble?'

'At this stage we're merely following up all lines of enquiry, ma'am.'

'That wasn't what I asked!' she snapped at him. 'I'm merely implying that his life must have taken a wrong turn.'

'Based on what, ma'am?'

'Just call it feminine intuition!'

She stopped midway along the hallway and bent forward to unlock an ill-fitting door, its hinges creaking spookily as they stepped into a fusty-smelling wood-panelled study filled from top to bottom with clutter.

'Please pull up a chair, officer.'

'Thank you, ma'am.'

She booted up her large-screen Apple computer and logged her personal banking details into the boxes of a vivid blue-and-white-etched home page, astutely aware of his eyes straying towards her half-exposed cleavage.

'Are you sitting comfortably, officer?' she said, teasingly.

'Um... yes, ma'am.'

'Then let's waste no more time!'

*

Twenty minutes later

She dragged the mouse over a transaction marked 'Apex Property Holdings', quickly drawing his attention to a BACS transfer made not long before her nephew's departure, and processed without her prior consent.

'Any idea where the company's based?'

'They act as residential letting agents in Doncaster,' she said with certainty. 'I took the liberty of Googling them.'

'And you're a hundred per cent sure it was Mr Turner who accessed your account?'

'Unquestionably.'

She then alerted his attention to a partially splintered desk-drawer lock, its misshapen front plate showing clear signs of having been forced, more than likely by use of a flat-tipped screwdriver or some kind of jemmy.

'And the log-in information was presumably kept in the drawer?'

'Precisely. I saw it had been tampered with some time ago, and as a result changed both my password and PIN code.'

'But where there's a will there's a way, eh, ma'am?'

'Indeed, officer!'

She assisted him by printing off the details of the unauthorised transaction, and then handed the sheet to him in a small brown envelope. As she did so she became alive to a change in his demeanour, shown by a new-found spring in his step.

'Please accept my gratitude, ma'am – you've been extraordinarily helpful!' he said, buoyantly. 'I'll see myself out!'

*

Humberside Police

'Good work, Priestley. You could be in for a Chief Constable's commendation,' the Superintendent lauded. 'This pig-headed individual's been leading us a merry dance for far too long. I'll get on to South Yorkshire right away.'

'Thank you, sir.'

'You're dismissed. Well done, lad!'

Without further delay he scanned through his little red book and located and dialled the private number of his long-time associate and former golfing buddy, the esteemed Deputy Chief Constable Gerald Markham.

'Gerry, it's Roger Fleming.'

'Podgy Rog? Well, I'll be damned!' the DCC responded, a little unkindly. 'To what do I owe this pleasure, dear fellow?'

'Let it be known I've shed two stone since your calamitous round at Sutton Park last summer,' Fleming shot back in a similarly sarcastic tone. 'Which needless to say begs the question, how is the handicap these days?'

'Don't ask!' Markham said, keen to avoid the subject. 'What can I do for you, old chum?'

Fleming broached the matter of the fly-by-night arsonist, who over a lengthy period of time had managed to give his department the slip, more recently rumoured to be laying low somewhere under Markham's jurisdiction.

'A certain Mr Turner, unless I'm mistaken?'

'How could you know that?'

'I received a call from Matt Philpott down in Leicestershire.'

'How so?' Fleming said, slightly put out. 'We didn't receive the tip-off until approximately half an hour ago.'

'Wheels within wheels, Roger!'

Markham smugly informed him of the gruesome discovery exhumed from a patch of ground close to the elusive Turner's former home, his tell-it-like-it-is account propelling a surge of sour bile up into Fleming's throat and larynx.

'Lord above, Gerry!' he said, his stomach churning wildly. 'This could turn the Gold case on its head!'

'Undoubtedly, dear fellow,' Markham acknowledged. 'But mum's the word, eh?'

'Indeed, we digress!' Fleming replied.

He moved on to Turner's uncanny ability to seemingly vanish off the face of the earth at will, alluding to the ambitious young constable's astuteness in narrowing down his whereabouts to an address in South Yorkshire.

'Did he obtain the exact location?'

'Doncaster, old boy.'

'The penny drops,' Markham said broodingly. 'Smack bang in the middle of my patch!'

He hurriedly jotted down the letting agent's details, and, on the assumption Turner was still in residence, vowed to take swift and decisive action by sending a couple of his prized assets to pay him a visit.

'Thanks, Gerry. I never once doubted you!'

'Only too happy to help,' he said, shiftily. 'Doubtless I'll see you at Tinsley Park, for the charity four-ball in May?'

'I hadn't realised you were playing?'

'But old chum, we've been paired together!' he sniggered, immediately hearing the click of the line go dead.

SIXTY-NINE

KHALID AWOKE RESTLESS, confused and disoriented. His phone's musical tone warbled from among the pile of clothes dumped at the end of his bed, caught under the light seeping through the blind of his high-rise Manhattan hotel.

For a moment he considered rolling over and burying his head in the pillow to shut out the noise, but coming to his senses he threw aside the duvet and hopped across the room on one leg to finally salvage the offending device.

'Do you know what the time is?' he answered abruptly.

'Oops... don't tell me you're still in LA?' Rashid's voice yapped.

'Duh, no – I'm in New York!' Khal articulated wearily. 'Tucked up in the snore-bag, five hours behind the sodding UK!'

'You mean it's four in the morning?'

'You learn fast,' he grouched. 'I was up half the night working. I'll call you back later!'

'Don't hang up, Khal!' Rash pleaded. 'Do you have Sky News?'

Khal fumbled in the semi-darkness for the remote, and flicked rapidly through the channels before spotting the familiar face of an auburn-haired news presenter melodramatically jabbering into a foam-covered microphone.

'Human remains!' he gasped. 'They must've unearthed the missing skull!'

'They're referring to it as "excluded and undiscovered evidence" which could ultimately lead to JJ's acquittal!'

'And that he was deprived of a fair trial!'

'I'll probably have to testify again!'

'How so?'

'I bumped into Chukka's ma.'

'You don't say!'

'She made out he's a completely reformed character.'

'Elephants might fly!' Khal said cynically.

'He's eligible to apply for parole next month.'

'I wouldn't lose any sleep,' Khal sniffled wryly. 'The law's pretty uncompromising when it comes to drug traffickers.'

At the mere mention of the word 'sleep' he felt an overwhelming urge to lie back and let his head drop down onto the pillow. His handset slipped from his grasp and slid down to the floor with a mighty crack.

'Khal... *Khal!*' Rashid yawped. He was interrupted by the announcement: '*The number you have called is currently unavailable...*'

*

A slow, numbing tiredness crept through Hackett's exhausted limbs, mollified in part by an urgent newsflash hitting his brand-new HD TV screen. **Former trial judge renders Gold conviction unsafe**, the rolling caption read.

His thoughts were disrupted by the pet name 'POL POT' flashing intermittently on his cell phone.

'What's the latest, guv?' he inquired. 'Any word from forensics yet?'

'Jim Erskine asked for a second opinion. I just signed off a request to bring in a senior pathologist from Scotland Yard.'

'And what about grounds for a retrial?'

'Anybody's guess!' Philpott said, hoarsely. 'However, that isn't the reason for my call.'

'You sound awful, guv!'

'Bloody hay fever!' he said, sneezing and wiping his nose. 'Get your bag packed, I have an assignment for you.'

'Somewhere exotic?' Hackett asked, more in hope than expectation.

'Doncaster!'

'You're kidding me,' he said dejectedly.

'Just a sec, Dan,' Philpott said, suddenly distracted. 'I'll call you back in five.'

Somewhat taken aback, Hackett ambled up the stairs and threw a small pile of belongings into a leather holdall. Feeling his mobile vibrating again in his pocket he quickly gathered himself to take command of his faculties.

'That was quick, guv. I have my pen poised!'

'The day of reckoning has finally arrived.'

'How do you mean?'

'Get your butt up north, son,' Philpott snarled, 'and bust his arse once and for all!'

'I'm not with you, guv?'
'Your old mate – Turner, who else?'
'Richard Turner…? Shit! You just made my day, Matt!'

SEVENTY

March 2012

'Hello, is that the Coles Bay Veterinary Practice?' Agnes asked, her fuzzy voice battling above the atmospheric static hampering the connection. 'I've been having nightmares for an hour or so trying to get through!'

Clearly the receptionist had lots of time on her hands, and offered up a whole range of excuses for the unseasonal weather conditions prevalent on the island, eventually getting round to dealing with her enquiry.

'That aside, dearie, how can I help?'

'Is Mr Duffy available please?' Agnes asked courteously, anxious not to be put on hold. 'I'm calling from the UK!'

'He's out completing his early morning rounds, sweetie.'

'When is he due back?'

'Ordinarily he'd be back by now…'

She considered hanging up, but then heard voices in the background. The conversation was at first dominated by the receptionist's unrefined line of chatter, but very soon gave way to a melodic and familiar lilting tone.

'Just putting you through, dearie!'

'Eamon Duffy speaking,' he finally announced. 'Please excuse the awful connection!'

'Eamon… it's Agnes!'

'I beg your pardon? You'll have to speak up!'

'It's me… *Agnes!*'

The line appeared to go dead, her efforts further discouraged by an acoustic shock in her ear. In her frustration she came very close to giving up the ghost, when through another burst of static she made out his voice.

'Are you still there… Aggie?'

'Eamon,' she said hesitantly. 'I leave for Sydney tomorrow evening!'

'Kingsford Smith?' he asked breathlessly.

'Yes, that's the one!'

'How long are you planning to stay?'

'My ticket is open-ended, for up to three months.'

Eamon couldn't believe his ears, scarcely able to contain the excitement rippling through his body, while aware that something inside her had changed. In haste he scanned his diary to shuffle his appointments around.

'What's your plane's ETA?' he asked.

'05:05 the following day.'

'I'll meet you there, at the airport.'

'That's really not necessary!'

'No Ag… I insist!'

He wanted to know everything, but more than a little bewildered by the suddenness of her decision he sensibly opted to keep his thoughts at bay. Was it a silent cry for help, or had her perfect match suffered an irreparable rift? Or perchance, just maybe, their coming together in Galway had somehow turned her head?

'Are you sure?' she said meekly. 'I don't want to be a burden to you.'

'I've never been surer in my life!'

He raved about Sydney's wealth of attractions: the giant bridge overlooking the bustling harbour, the stunning beaches just a short hop from the ferry terminal, and last but not least his passion for Darling Harbour.

'I can't wait!' she said enthusiastically.

'Will you come to Tasmania?'

'If the offer still stands.'

Her words stunned him, so much so he felt the need to unfasten the top button on his shirt. Not quite knowing how to respond, he made mention of an ex-colleague's swanky three-bed apartment in the city's fashionable Rocks district, perfectly located within easy walking distance of the central sights and nightlife.

'Will you fly back with me?' he asked half-expectantly. 'To Hobart?'

'If you have room.'

'I'll make room!'

He jumped up and danced around in a circle. 'Sit tight,' he said, and promised to take care of everything and get back to her.

His mind twirled into a jubilant tailspin. 'Stay calm,' he chided himself, and set about reorganising his diary.

SEVENTY-ONE

Somewhere south of Doncaster

'THERE I WAS, a-digging this hole, hole in the ground, so big and sort of round it was, and there was I, digging it deep…'

The novelty song blared out through the car's equally antiquated stereo system, receiving a once-in-a-blue moon airing on Brian Matthew's nostalgic Saturday-morning *Sounds of the Sixties* radio show.

'How fitting!' Hackett laughed heartily. 'From what I gather you're a dab hand when it comes to digging up the dirt!'

'They say sarcasm is the lowest form of wit,' Turner yapped from the rear seat.

'Yet it remains the funniest!' Hackett countered, making ready to exit the main drag at the upcoming intersection. At that juncture a maniacal white-van man swerved sharply in front of him in his blind spot, causing him to yank violently at the steering wheel and unleash a string of obscenities from the open window.

'Perhaps you should keep your eyes on the road,' Turner reacted scathingly, 'as opposed to making snide remarks?'

'And perhaps you'd be wise to keep your mouth shut!'

His eyes scanning left and right, a sprawling area of tall trees beckoned, accessed via a bridleway rutted with potholes and puddle-filled hollows. It led eventually to a clearing bordered by a train of hefty tree trunks.

'Where the hell are you taking me?' Turner panicked.

'Sherwood Forest!' Hackett replied. 'Where, if you're a good boy, you can take a leak up against Robin Hood's favourite tree!'

The vehicle rocked crazily on its suspension, tossing the captive from side to side like a possessed rag doll. Undeterred, he continued retaliating to the detective's all-out assault of merciless ribaldry.

'You're pathetic!' he snarled, hatefully.

'That's rich, coming from you.'

'You've got nothing!'

'Is that a fact?' Hackett sniffed, pulling to a halt.

He flipped to the relevant page on his pad and proceeded to read out the damning laundry list: 'Arson; perjury; a laptop on which child pornography was stored; and last but not least, aiding and abetting a wilful murder.'

'I have no idea what you're implying!'

'That you're well and truly in Shit Street!' Hackett growled. 'Now put a sock in it while I relieve myself in the bushes.'

'You can't leave me here!'

'Why not?'

'I also need to use the loo!'

Hackett stared at him suspiciously, and then reached into his pocket to bring to light a small ring of keys. Quietly circling back he opened the rear door and stretched his upper body across Turner's to unlock his cuffs.

Suddenly yanking a hand free, Turner immediately lashed out, the loose cuff still attached to his wrist smashing pitilessly against the detective's temple. Hackett saw stars and toppled backwards onto the damp brown earth, making a last-ditch effort to cling onto Turner's ankles before a size nine boot caught him smack on the jaw.

Not finished yet, Hackett bravely crawled onto his knees. His gaze followed Turner's hunched body round to the hatchback's tailgate, from where moments later he returned gripping a long-handled scoop shovel.

'Don't even think about it!' Hackett said, somehow staggering to his feet, his head within striking distance of the blade.

'Hand me both sets of keys,' Turner snarled, the shovel blade raised menacingly. 'To the cuffs, and the car!'

'Don't do something you'll regret!'

'Do as I say!'

'They'll throw the book at you for assaulting a police officer.'

'Huh, call yourself a policeman,' Turner said mockingly, edging towards him. 'Now, hand over the keys, or else!'

Hackett could sense his patience running thin, and in a reckless moment threw himself at Turner like a human battering ram. Turner reacted quickly and sidestepped him, before slamming down the shovel on his unprotected skull.

*

Blurry-eyed and still half dazed, Hackett slouched into a seated position. He found himself surrounded by a trio of aged ramblers, one of whom leaned forwards to offer him a cup of tea poured from her flask into a plastic cup.

'I need to borrow a cell phone,' he said weakly. 'I'm a police officer.'

Their heads swung tentatively back and forth, looking to one another for some kind of reassurance. Sticking a hand in her pocket, the elder of the group somewhat reluctantly passed him her black leather phone case.

He rose unsteadily and meandered at a snail's pace back towards the main drag. Taking a breather on a decaying tree stump, he filled the chief in with a sketchy account of his catastrophic misadventure.

'Easy now, son. Do you feel dizzy?'

'My head's throbbing!'

'At a guess you're suffering a mild concussion,' Philpott said, with some concern. 'Do you know your exact location?'

'In the middle of nowhere, close to an area of parkland, just off the A614 roughly thirty miles north of Nottingham.'

'I'll put out an emergency red call to all units in the area,' the chief said decisively. 'Sit tight, and don't go anywhere!'

'I'm not likely to, guv,' Hackett said glumly. 'He nicked the sodding car!'

'Phew!' Philpott heaved into the handset, urging him to stay strong and assuring him that help would soon be on its way.

*

One day later
King's Mill Hospital, Sutton-in-Ashfield

His wounds patched up following a number of tests and an overnight stay, Hackett wandered to the reception to formally discharge himself. He was happily surprised to see Philpott's familiar figure loitering in the waiting area.

'Guv, I am honoured!'

'I thought I should make an effort.'

'Much appreciated, guv!'

The chief took his arm to steady him, and led him out through the automatic doors to his C-Class Mercedes-Benz, anxious to hear first-hand his tale of woe, and how Turner could possibly have escaped his clutches.

'There's no way you can blame yourself,' the chief encouraged him. 'The bastard left you for dead out cold on the ground.'

'Outwitted by a snivelling cry-baby,' Hackett said, nursing a seriously bruised ego. 'I'll never live this one down, guv!'

'Mum's the word, eh?' Philpott said, reassuringly. 'And besides, Dan, it seems he's pretty handy with a shovel!'

Around forty minutes later they drew up outside Hackett's home, the chief worriedly checking over his bruised and scabbed features before waking him from an exhausted catnap with a light tap on the shoulder.

'Uh, cheers Matt,' Hackett said groggily.

'Rest up son, for as long as you need,' the boss said caringly. 'And as soon as you're able – bring me his balls on a plate!'

*

One day later

Hackett parked Sheila's loaned Renault in the shade of a giant Lombardy poplar, and ambled to the door of the quaint B & B. His movements were observed by the curious landlady from the window of the dining room.

'Mr Harris, if I'm not mistaken?' she said, presumptuously. 'We have you down as staying with us for two nights.'

'That's correct, Mrs Grainger,' he replied. 'I was rather hoping to recharge the batteries in the wake of a recent accident.'

'How awful!' she said, eyeing his complexion with a degree of mild suspicion. 'Were you involved in a motor accident?'

'Skydiving,' he fibbed. 'I crash-landed in a disused airfield.'

She winced, and wished him a speedy recovery, then launched into a well-worn sales pitch doubtless borrowed from the pages of a local travel guide, followed up with a short lecture about meal times and house rules.

'Sounds just the ticket!'

'Room nine is at the end of the passage,' she said, handing him a key. 'Ring the bell if there's anything more you need.'

'I will. Thank you!' he bade, grasping his duffel bag. 'Just one more thing: is there a decent pub within staggering distance?'

'The Fox and Goose, in the next village,' she obliged, making mention of the regular smattering of oddball characters.

'Sounds like fun!' he snickered, his boots dragging on the creaking plank floor. 'I'll catch you later, Mrs Grainger!'

*

Under the cloak of darkness Hackett crept out to the car, grabbing a rucksack full of goodies from the boot to gear himself up for an unauthorised spell of late-night surveillance duty, based purely on an intuitive hunch.

He finally came to rest in a quiet corner overshadowed by an avenue of tall red cedars, from where he pondered his target's most likely moves. He found himself rendered slightly uneasy by the hoots and squawks emanating from a whole range of nocturnal critters scurrying backward and forward on the matted forest floor.

Behind a dense thicket of hedge-tree a loud rustling noise further set his nerves jangling, swelling into a rumbling thud of footsteps drawing ever nearer by the second. The source of the sound was captured at the flick of a wrist in his Maglite beam.

Like a flash he sprang out of the path of a colossal, luminous-eyed red deer, bolting at frightening speed out of the pitch-black darkness, its powerful hindquarters thundering past him in a salvo of airborne mud.

He panted hard, and rummaged in his bag for a travel blanket he had thrown in. His body had still not fully shaken off the after-effects of his recent ordeal. As if wise to his presence, the sound of the night creatures seemed to vanish into the light mist as, nestled against a grassy knoll, tiredness overcame him.

SEVENTY-TWO

Eastern Tasmania

'IT'S A HUNDRED TIMES more beautiful than I could ever have imagined,' Agnes stressed, staring open-mouthed from a viewpoint not far from Eamon's home. 'Just what the doctor ordered. If you'll pardon the pun!'

Standing side by side they gazed down over the deserted crescent-shaped stretch of sand, its pale cream surface shimmering in the morning sunlight, lapped by the endless turquoise waters rolling in to the shore.

'That, dear Aggie, is Wineglass Bay, regarded as one of the world's most magnificent beaches,' Eamon gushed, carving out a path through a jungle of overgrown flora. 'I never get tired of looking at it from up here.'

Further in from the shoreline a young couple took time out shaping their footprints in the moistened sand, reminiscent of the rare, precious sun-soaked summer days when as kids they frolicked under a balmy northern sky.

'I may not be the best company right now,' Agnes opened up. 'I've been stuck in a fog of darkness since we last met.'

'Talk to me,' he urged. 'I'm a good listener.'

She explained how she'd acted on a sudden emotional impulse: the envelope in her coat pocket... an old song playing on the radio that sparked her imagination... but perhaps worst of all the constant nagging loneliness.

'It's as if I need a little time to readjust to the light.'

'I said I'd always be here for you.'

They wandered on, shielding their eyes with their hands as they descended to the blinding expanse of sand. Lightening up in a jiffy, she threw off her trainers and galumphed off to paddle in the rippling water.

'It reminds me of where we used to play, in Dog's Bay,' she shouted upwind. 'Take off your shoes and join me!'

He galloped towards her, his rubbery legs resembling a clumsy cartoon-character. Hooking his foot behind a grass-tufted sand dune, he hurtled head first down into a heap right in front of her.

'The song?' he asked, rolling onto his knees grinning.

'Which song?'

'That reminded you of me!'

'KT Tunstall,' she said, and burst into song. 'You're the other side of the world to me!'

She kicked up her heels and raced off, her feet showering him with a drizzle of seawater and loose sand. Undeterred, he gave chase but she playfully upped the pace, eluding him, laughing, her smile beaming like the sun.

'Hang a left, Aggie,' he yelled, half-breathlessly, 'and make for the sheltered ridge alongside the giant rocks.'

They headed up the beach and collapsed beneath the ridge, catching their breath.

'You look sad,' she observed, perched beside him.

'I've cried buckets whiling away the hours on these sloping sands.'

'Sometimes we need a good cry.'

They fell quiet and leaned their heads back against the hillock, tuning into the waves tossing against the shore. Each had a unique voice of its own, as if whispering softly that everything would be okay.

'For a moment there I was transported back to the old Candy Store sweetshop,' Eamon softly reminisced. 'The very day Mrs O'Connor passed away, and I dabbed at your eyes in a failed attempt to console you.'

'How could I ever forget?'

'The handkerchief was dripping wet!'

'And covered in gunge and slime,' Aggie recalled disgustedly, 'from a dormouse you dissected the same morning!'

'Sometimes I wish we could press rewind, and go back to being kids forever.'

'Or simply gather up our troubles and toss them into the sea.'

'If only!' he said dreamily.

She cuddled next to him and settled her head on his chest, for a moment communicating silently. He stroked her hair and eyed her roseate cheeks glowing in the sunlight, his heart warmed by her comfort in his arms.

'I feel so at home here,' she whispered.

'Then stay,' he said, faintly. 'And let your heart heal.'

'Can you fix me, Ea?'

'I can treat a lame horse, or cure a puppy dog with distemper,' he said, reflectively. 'But I can't mend a broken heart.'

She pulled her head away and stared back into his eyes, then wrapped her arms around his neck, and drew him close. His chin dipped forwards and his lips lowered towards hers, and in a spontaneous moment they kissed.

*

South Leicestershire

Ten thousand miles away in the chillier confines of the East Midlands countryside, a hooded figure, overburdened by a kitbag full of assorted horticultural implements, trudged furtively onto a patch of land favoured by local airheads for fly-tipping, his wellington boots squelching into the boggy black surface.

He ran a sceptical eye over the accumulated earth, swearing blind to himself that he'd revisited the very same spot. Then, all psyched up, he thrust a garden pickaxe at the outer rim, oblivious to anyone else's presence.

From behind an overgrown thicket of gorse, Hackett stared into the clearing through the eyeholes of his balaclava, then edged his way forward on the balls of his feet, gripping a fearsome-looking monkey-wrench.

He ducked beneath a low-hanging tree branch and by accident put his foot in a rabbit hole. With his ankle in part trapped he clutched at the boughs of a nearby bush, its leaves rustling loudly to stifle his pained cry.

Still smarting under his recent humiliation, Hackett fearlessly took off like a charging bull, his head ramming solidly into Turner's lower stomach, followed with a crushing uppercut to knock the wind out of his sails.

His figure flat out next to the rotting debris, Hackett dragged him by the collar to the foot of an old oak tree, then bound him to its trunk with a roll of silver duct tape before standing back to admire his handiwork.

Both stupefied and winded, Turner tried to speak, his voice gasping in fits and starts. In no mood for his histrionics, Hackett stuffed a balled-up sock in his mouth, sealing the deal with a strip of tape across his lips.

Content to leave him to the mercy of the abundance of night creatures, Hackett made off into the gloom, briefly glancing back at his pathetic figure before signing off with a short and to the point 'Sleep tight!'

*

Granby

The age-old church clock struck two, and roused light sleeper Beatrice Watson from an intermittent slumber. Her ears were alive to a muffled whimpering sound, emanating, she assumed, from the abutting back o' beyond.

She nudged her husband. 'Darling, wake up!' she urged.

'Lord above, Bee. What is it?'

'I swear I can hear a voice, or voices even!' she flapped. 'Somewhere out in the hedgerow, Billy – there it is again!'

He leaned up on his elbow and cupped his other hand to his ear, then grumpily lowered his head back on to the pillow, inclined to think it may be the hoot of an owl, or a fox's yap, or perhaps even the chitter of a badger.

'Bill, darling, listen!' she said insistently.

This time he shot upright, and stepping into his slippers rushed straight to the window. His interest had been aroused by a muted cry of despair, presumably emitting from the public footpath running adjacent to the house.

'Uh… uh… plea'… heb… 'umon, plea'!'

'It's more than likely some drunken fool on his way back from the pub,' he deduced. 'But better safe than sorry!'

'Thank you, my darling,' she said, watching him don his clothes. 'And Billy, I want you to promise me you'll be careful!'

*

King's Meadow Woods

> Boss I just received a tip-off as to Turner's whereabouts.
> My source tells me he returned to his old gaff in Granby this evening.
> By the time you read this message I will have put out an alert.
> Sorry if I woke you… Danny boy.

Hackett tapped out a text message from the driver's seat of his salvaged VW, which he had found dumped on the far side of a secluded woodland car-park within spitting distance of a buzz of activity transpiring in a nearby glade.

He stepped out of the car and slyly crouched behind a tree, training his binoculars on a half-dozen or more spectators, all assembled, eyes agog, in a ragged circle around a semi-naked blonde exhibitionist. Her voice shrieked with pleasure while her body writhed like a contortionist.

Hackett watched for a moment, flabbergasted by her extraordinary prowess, before turning disgustedly away, yearning for a few hours in a nice warm bed.

*

A mile away

Drawn towards the muffled voice, Bill Watson quietly crept through an opening in the hedgerow, squelching on his toes towards an infamous dumping ground abhorred by the large majority of law-abiding villagers.

Unable to recognise him under his torch's yellowy beam, Watson squatted down to remove his gag, almost instantly springing back upright and glaring into his eyes with a look of pure astonishment.

'*You!*' he boomed.

'Cut the tape!' Turner whimpered. 'Where's your humanity?'

'Humanity!' Watson roared hatefully, somehow or other resisting the urge to inflict grievous bodily harm on him.

'Please… for Christ's sake!'

Just the sound of his voice made Watson's skin crawl. Its low, unctuous tone emanating from twisted, thin lips was further exacerbated by the shifty-eyed and insincere look on Turner's face, forcing his temper to its very limit.

'You expect my sympathy, after spying on my daughter!'

'It was a stupid mistake!'

He'd never considered himself to be a violent man, but Turner's inability to apologise in some way caused him to temporarily lose control of his senses, his right foot thrusting into his chest just beneath his ribs.

'You'll pay for this!' Turner said defiantly, startled by a numbing right cross raining down smack on his cheekbone.

'Will I now?' Watson said, stooping down to reseal the tape across his mouth. 'The second blow was for JJ Gold!'

Turner squawked something unintelligible, his eyes widening in horror as Watson unzipped his flies before, taking a pace forward, he hovered over him to take a leak, his parting shot formed in a puddle right beside him.

*

Hackett's phone alarm woke him at six o' clock, its bleeping tone almost in synch with the clang of the church clock, still pealing in the near distance while he hopped across the carpet to thread his legs into his jeans.

'Good morning, Mr Harris!' the lady of the house bade him. 'And what might you be doing up at this unearthly hour?'

'I'm a notoriously light sleeper, Mrs Grainger!'

'I'm afraid breakfast isn't served until seven,' she said apologetically. 'I'm awfully sorry for any inconvenience.'

'Not a problem, ma'am!'

He searched in vain for his boots on the shoe rack in the hallway, before being redirected to the outside porch by the landlady's pointing finger. A distracting message alert forced him to check his phone screen.

> Got him. Give me a call the minute you're in the land of the living!

He stepped out of the door in his stockinged feet and parked his backside on the porch's low wall before punching in Philpott's number, unmindful of the morning chorus chirruping tunefully in the nearby woods.

'Danny Boy, how are you son?'

'Pretty much fighting fit, guv,' he answered.

'Where are you?' the chief asked, a mite suspiciously.

'Resting up, guv,' Hackett fibbed. 'Just like the doctor ordered!'

'At home?'

'At Sheila's place. I spent the night here.'

Largely unconvinced, Philpott moved to the subject of Turner's extraordinary arrest, his exact location having been pinpointed by a caller named Watson, whose address was given as The Manor House in the nearby village of Granby.

'Gold's former abode,' the DCI reminded him.

'Nothing more than a coincidence, guv.'

'I smell a rat, Hackett!'

'What do you mean, guv?'

'He was found gagged and bound to a tree!' Philpott said furiously. 'Assaulted by a masked brigand in the still of the night!'

'But... I received word,' he faltered, 'a tip-off...'

'What do you take me for?'

Hackett choked as he made to speak, his mouth dry and his tongue sticking to the roof of his mouth. He'd known all along his mission was potentially foolhardy, and as his father would say he'd been 'sussed to a crust'.

'Guv, I need to lie down!' he finally said.

'What's a balaclava made of, son?'

'Cotton? Acrylic?'

'Wool, son. Like the wool you're trying to pull over my eyes!' Philpott raged. 'I should have your head on a plate for this!'

SEVENTY-THREE

Spring 2012
Leicester Prison

His copy of *The Classic Yoga Bible* spread out on the floor next to him, Jon completed his morning ritual by raising his body into a vertical handstand. His movements were observed by key-jangling prison warder Kevin.

'Chop-chop, Goldilocks!' the screw barked. 'The guvnor's requested the pleasure of your company at ten o'clock sharp.'

'Just two more minutes, Kev?'

'C'mon, put a stop to that bollocks,' he said coarsely. 'It's ten to already.'

Disgruntled beyond words, Jon dropped down and rolled over onto his feet. His head a little light from an onset of dizziness, he calmed himself with a series of long deep breaths resembling a train letting off steam.

'You should try it sometime.'

'Yoga?' Kevin said, sniffing disdainfully.

'Yeah, why not?'

'You sound just like my missus!' he retorted, clenching his teeth. 'Now get your arse in gear, and get a bloody move on.'

*

Ten minutes later

Even the wide open window couldn't blot out the unpleasant sewage-like odour permeating the governor's office, as rising up from his chair he extended a hand across his desk and gestured for Jon to take a seat.

'Please excuse the smell, Jonathan,' he apologised. 'An incident in the shower block seems to have clogged up the system.'

'Shit happens, sir!' Jon jested, laughing.

'Quite, Jonathan, quite!'

Gathering up a bundle of papers littering his desktop, he laid his hands on an official-looking document, then grabbed his reading glasses from his inside jacket pocket before looking Jon squarely in the eye.

'I had a lengthy chat over dinner with your QC Mr Hillier last night.'

'I wasn't aware the two of you were acquainted?'

'Jimmy and I go back a long way.'

'He's a good guy,' Jon murmured. 'We hit it off from the word go.'

'Far too handsome for my liking,' the governor remarked. His face became serious. 'However, we digress slightly.'

Unable to relax, Jon rolled his shoulders in an effort to relieve some tension, and interlocked his fingers while cracking his knuckles. Then he peered down at the back-to-front letter and spoke in a somewhat sombre tone.

'If I look confused sir, it's because I am.'

'Be still for a moment, please,' Bancroft pleaded. 'What I'm about to tell you could prove to be a game changer.'

'Sorry, sir... Please go on.'

He read aloud a key extract from the senior pathologist's report, and then unfurled a subsequent petition to the House of Lords, its contents filing for leave to appeal Jon's case on the grounds of an unsafe conviction.

'In layman's terms, Jimmy's preparing to call for a mistrial.'

'Just as I was beginning to feel at home!'

'Very droll, Jonathan.'

'As a consequence of the new evidence James spoke of?'

'I'm not at liberty to discuss anything further with you, but this I will say: of all the prisoners serving out their sentences in this institution, your behaviour has been exemplary. There are no blameless individuals in our prisons, since each and every inmate will at some time have been lawfully convicted by the courts, no matter how vehemently they protest their innocence. You, however, belong to a small minority prepared to accept the inevitable in spite of any extenuating circumstances. I wish you well with the appeal!'

All the way back to his cell Bancroft's words seemed to echo inside Jon's head, hanging over him like the fetid stench. An unsafe conviction... a file for leave of appeal... and, perhaps worst of all, the notion of a new trial.

'Bad news, Goldilocks?'

'Best not to get my hopes up, only to have them dashed.'

'You sound confused.'

'Something doesn't smell right, Kev.'

'That, my son, is an understatement,' he said, wrinkling his nose in disgust. 'Keep your pecker up. I'll see you later!'

The door slammed shut behind him to finally leave Jon alone with his thoughts. Stretched out on his bed his mind began to play tricks, and for the second time in little more than an hour his world turned upside down.

SEVENTY-FOUR

Granby

THE HOSTILE ELEMENTS bit into Hackett's complexion like a swarm of invisible bees, slowing his pace to a crawl. He gazed up at the sturdy edifice of scaffolding poles rising to the summit of Turner's one-time country retreat. Turner... why on earth would a rock-'n'-roll icon like Gold have befriended such a lowlife piece of scum? Beats me, he thought, as he took a shifty peek through a replacement window to the front of the cottage's open-plan living area.

'Good morning!' a rather la-di-da voice greeted him from a stationary BMW. 'Aren't you a tad early, dear chap?'

'I'm sorry?' Hackett replied, confused.

'The nine o'clock viewing?' the man said bluntly. 'The agent's a good pal of mine!'

'I was having a good nose, that's all,' Hackett shot back. 'I'm staying at the B & B on Back Lane for a couple of nights.'

'Oh! Must dash. Enjoy your sabbatical!'

The guy unnecessarily toed the accelerator while his electronic gates slowly clunked together. Oddly, the resulting spray of mud and slush was accompanied by a shower of loose mortar rushing down from the cottage's rooftop.

Hackett wandered into the middle of the lane and craned his neck upward. He was able to make out a cockeyed chunk of brick working its way loose from the chimney stack. It aroused his suspicions enough to warrant a closer look; and he began energetically to scale the weatherworn structure.

All at once he was besieged by a further cascade of powdery rubble raining down onto the top of his head, albeit insufficiently to deter him from the task at hand. His better judgement muddled by a feeling in his gut, he swung ape-like up onto an overhanging supporting bracket, and somehow

337

managed to gain an adequate foothold, thankful for a moment to stop and catch his breath.

A shaft of sunlight flashed in his peripheral vision, drawing his attention to a protruding metal object glinting through an enlarged gap in the crumbling masonry work ostensibly supporting the slope-mounted stack.

Suddenly his phone began vibrating in his top pocket. Too wrapped up in what he was doing, he allowed himself only a half-glance at Philpott's curt, unequivocal message:

> My office in thirty minutes!

Hackett shuddered slightly, his eyes raising to bring the concealed fragment into focus. At first he figured it to be a sawn-off vent pipe or the remains of a twisted old TV aerial bracket, in part sheared off its rivets and bolts.

Hemmed in by the jagged framework of braces and runners, in a concerted effort he forced himself up towards an arrangement of wooden toe-boards stretching laterally above his head. This gave him enough room to hook his boot around an access ladder coupled to a transom running parallel to the pavement below.

A further lusty heave transferred his weight onto the knurled top rung, enabling him to grip his hands around the rusted upper guardrail very close to a large gaping hole in the brickwork, from where his eyes locked in horror onto the broad serrated edge of a lengthy spiked cutting implement jutting out at an oblique angle.

All caution thrown aside, a pull at the silvery shaft uncovered the bloodstained guide bar of a chainsaw blade, loosely fixed to the mechanism's housing among a sooty mess of clay lining and cracked roof-tiles.

Cleverly, he looped a finger over the dislodged chain, watching the front handle gradually slide into view amid a rumble of noise, until a further hefty tug brought the whole thing crashing down in an avalanche of dust and debris.

Hackett's spine-chilling scream seemed to linger in the still, moist air. Its shrill echo was superseded by a sickening, stomach-wrenching thud, his motionless, bloodied body sprawled on his back face upwards in the gutter.

Her eyes witnessing the whole episode from her bay window, an elderly resident struggled up from her armchair to grasp the house phone, her trembling fingers managing to punch in the digits 999.

'Emergency, which service do you require? Fire, Police or Ambulance?'

'Ambulance, my dear!' she croaked above the background din. 'There's a dead man lying at the side of the road!'

SEVENTY-FIVE

Tasmania

'I'm sorry Eamon, but I honestly can't do this!' Agnes cried self-reproachfully, her semi-naked figure perched on the angle of the bed as she embarrassedly fumbled to refasten her bra strap. 'It just doesn't feel right!'

'It was a bad idea, Aggie,' he said disappointedly, head in hands. 'I felt like a scared kid, as if it was my very first time!'

He danced on one foot while he pulled on his jeans, slyly peeping at her dressing through the corners of his eyes. Longingly, he gazed at her goddess-like figure silhouetted under the glow from the overhead skylight.

'Maybe I should be thinking about packing my bags…'

'I'll hear none of it!' he said, spinning round impulsively. 'I promised I'd always be there for you. No matter what!'

From the moment she had arrived things had been different between them, almost as if he was on a mission to move on from their past, hoping in time to transform their relationship into something more permanent.

'I'm damaged beyond repair, Eamon,' she said softly.

'But adorable nonetheless,' he sighed. 'Stay Ag. Forever if you so desire!'

'You're such a selfless, sweet, kind man,' she said, slipping on her top. 'I don't know where I'd be without you!'

He leaned forward to peck her gently on the cheek, then grabbed her hand to hold her in a light hugging grip. She caught a glimpse of his wistful smile and felt him pull away from her before making for the door.

'Somewhere in the Scottish Highlands!' he said, grinning mischievously. 'In all likelihood freezing your tits off!'

*

For what felt like the umpteenth time in the past days Rashid punched in the number of his brother's cell phone. He sensed that something wasn't right, almost as though he was intentionally trying to avoid him.

On this occasion Khalid picked up: 'Little bro, how's it going?'

'Hmm, so-so.'

'What seems to be the problem?'

'I'm considering jacking in my job,' Rashid said, surprisingly. 'To take a six-month sabbatical and go off travelling!'

'Are you for real?' his brother reacted, distrustfully. 'I thought you loved your job?'

'I'm midway through a sixteen-hour shift, Khal. It's been like this for months, and I'm ready to throw in the towel.'

Sometimes Khalid thought he knew his brother better than he knew himself. He could tell from the tone of his voice that something underlying had got under his skin, made clearer by his unwillingness to confide in him.

'How could you even contemplate leaving?'

'I need to get out of here Khal, and go back to my roots.'

'Go back where?'

'To Pakistan!'

'Have you lost your mind?'

'I can stay with Aunt Laila.'

'In some rat hole in Lahore?' Khalid said, becoming irate. 'Please spare me the bullshit and give it to me straight!'

The silence at the other end of the line spoke volumes, to such an extent that he could almost hear Rash thinking. Not ready to let it go, he pushed him a little harder, until backing down Rash uttered a solitary word:

'Chukka!'

'He squealed to the cops?' Khal gasped out loud.

'Like a fucking pig!'

Once he started he couldn't stop, and tore into the group of armed police who'd paid an impromptu visit to the Centre, all tooled up like an SAS hit squad and inexplicably led by an officer sporting a bulletproof vest.

'Did they have an arrest warrant?' Khal inquired, gobsmacked.

'I didn't think to ask,' Rash said, panting. 'They were freaking half the patients out. I had to ask them to leave.'

'They're sure to come knocking again.'

'Hence the need to keep my head down for a while!'

Khalid warned him against doing anything too hasty, and puzzled over the police's heavy-handed response. Chukka's baseless accusations had surely stirred up a hornet's nest, but to come forward and perjure himself in a court of law was another matter, and his testimony would be laughed out of the room.

'The court cleared you of any wrongdoing at the original hearing, which implies that unless they've recently uncovered a raft of new evidence, it's by no means certain you'll be called to the stand at all.'

'Try telling that to the cop who read me the riot act!'

'A ringtone, which he most likely overheard; a security code to trigger a set of gates… They've got nothing on you, Rash!'

'I recorded the whole thing on my cell!'

'The cops?'

'Every single word!'

'Clever boy! Hold it up to the receiver, and let me hear it…'

'**Police:** *I took some time out to read up on these ritualistic Taliban beheadings and Muslim sacrifices, but what's with the preserving of the head? Do you keep it stashed away somewhere to admire like a trophy?*

Rash: *Firstly the large majority of Taliban extremists come from Afghanistan, not Birmingham where I was born, and secondly I just so happen to be a Catholic and not a practising Muslim, in spite of my exotic skin colour.*

Police: *And what brought you to Leicester? Was it to blend in among the large Asian population based in the city?*

Rash: *I moved here when I was two years of age.*

Police: *With your parents I presume?*

Rash: *No, I flew in on a magic carpet with Ali Baba and the Forty Thieves!*

Police: *Are you taking the piss, Abdul? Mind your manners, son, you've got some serious explaining to do!*

Rash: *I don't have to put up with this. You're upsetting the residents. If you want me to come in to the station to make a statement then I'll do my best to cooperate, but as of now I'm going to have to ask you to leave!*'

The conversation halted and made way for the clomp of heavy boots pounding across the floor, mingled with the sound of male voices ringing in an uncoordinated fashion all along the passageway.

'And that was it. Not a murmur of apology for the intrusion, nothing but a trail of mud all the way to the door.'

'They must have something on you,' Khal reflected. 'Relevant to the new info uncovered by their in-house forensics unit.'

'And how do I get them off my back?' Rashid said anxiously. 'The vultures are circling, and I've got no credible alibi!'

'Listen up, and listen good. You're my brother, Rash, and I love you. We'll get you through this, I give you my word. But with Dipak out of the picture you're going to need a top new lawyer. And I think I know just the man!'

'And if my new pals show up again?'

'Lie low for a couple of days,' Khal suggested. 'I'll be out of here at the crack of dawn on the very first train.'

'I'll meet you at the station!'

Rashid strolled into the day room to search for his assistant Alex, spotting him playing the referee in a semi-heated political discussion. He was distracted by the beep of his phone alerting him to a text message from Khalid.

> Check out the visiting hours at Welford Road clink, and while you're at it, the place where Chukka's under lock and key.

> I'll log in to the centre's computer in a jiffy. As for Chukka, he's banged up at HM Rye Hill near Rugby.

> Second thoughts, I'll bring the car, and an extra-long coil of rope!

> What's with the rope?

> If I give him enough, he may try to hang himself!

SEVENTY-SIX

A GRIM-FACED MATT PHILPOTT crept quietly through the doors of the Intensive Care Unit, his shoes squeaking on the sheet tile floor. He was hoping against hope for a substantial improvement in the DS's near-fatal condition.

'What's the latest, Sheila?' he whispered.

'Not good, I'm afraid,' she said tiredly, following an all-night bedside vigil. 'We're awaiting the results of his brain scan.'

She mopped her man's brow with a wet wipe. Her mind, already befuddled from lack of sleep, was swimming with the conflicting opinions and risks set forth by the various hospital consultants.

'Let me watch over him for a couple of hours,' the DCI suggested. 'Get yourself off home and catch up on some shut-eye.'

'My place is here by his side,' she said dauntlessly.

Philpott cast her a rueful smile, and leaned his body over the bed, his gaze locking on to Hackett's battered and bruised face. His every sense strained for a flicker of movement, or even a faint twitch of his hand.

'He's a fighter, he'll pull through.'

'He was supposed to be convalescing,' Sheila reflected. 'Not risking life and limb on some ivy-covered rooftop!'

'I'm guessing he spotted something out of the norm,' the DCI surmised. 'Probably at the top of the scaffolding tower.'

She moved to the bed's opposite side and threaded her fingers into Hackett's palm beneath the complex entanglement of wires and catheters, dipping down to kiss him among the swathe of bandages covering his head.

'He can hear you,' she said lovingly.

'He can?' the DCI puzzled.

'The nurses frequently whisper in his ear, whenever they're about to take his blood pressure or give him an injection.'

344

In a rare show of emotion Philpott dug deep into his pocket to pull out a handkerchief, and dabbed surreptitiously at the corners of his eyes, before clearing his throat and faking a weak, suppressed sneeze.

'What were you doing on that housetop?' he sniffled. 'You'll get some stick from the lads when you come back into the fold!'

'In a desk job. If he's lucky,' Sheila said, swallowing hard. 'The neurosurgeon said it's unlikely he'll ever walk again!'

'Dan Hackett a pen-pusher? Not on your life!' the chief said boldly. 'He's an all-action hero, aren't you, my old mucker?'

'But he sustained injuries to his head, neck and spine!'

Philpott exhaled a long, drawn-out sigh, his head tilting downwards to recite a silent prayer. After a moment he glanced over at Sheila, who was lovingly listening to every breath; and, nodding her goodbye, slid out of the room.

*

Leicestershire Police – Interrogation Room

'Police brutality! You've got a nerve!' DS Jeff Wade raged irately, minutes into a showdown with Richard Turner. 'I'll have you know the officer you singled out is at present comatose in a local hospital fighting for his life!'

He stormed out into the corridor in an attempt to calm himself and keep from doing something he'd live to regret, making off towards the staff kitchenette to take some time out and consider his next move.

'Cup of tea, Jeffrey lad?' desk sergeant Joe greeted him. 'You look a little flustered, son; a tough nut to crack eh?'

'Don't even go there, Joe!'

The sergeant popped a couple of teabags into a pair of chipped mugs, and snuck out of the ajar fire door to sneak a crafty ciggy, quickly nipping back inside as the kettle roared to the boil to eventually hand Wade a steaming cuppa.

'You're a lifesaver, old pal!'

'Get it down you, son,' he said, hacking coarsely. 'A bit of a smart arse, eh?'

'Worse, Joe. A fucking psycho!'

'Hmm, tricky,' he inferred, slurping the remains of his tea. 'Get your arse back in there and give him both barrels!'

Wade's resolve strengthened upon re-entering the room. His glare met the suspect's deep-set eyes leering back brimming with pure loathing and contempt. It was all Wade needed to wind him up for the confrontation ahead.

Arms folded, he picked up where he had left off in a no-nonsense tone. He was braced for the latest bout of verbal diarrhoea, which duly arrived by way of a vicious tirade of insults spouted unceasingly from Turner's snarling lips.

'I'll thank you not to speak until you're spoken to!'

'Oh, I haven't even started yet!' Turner snapped back, at once quietened by the upturned table crashing to the floor.

Wade's intimidating figure seemed to tower over him, his fists clenched in balls while the volume of his voice escalated to a thunderous crescendo, strenuously reading aloud a laundry list of damnatory misdemeanours:

1) Suspected arson.
2) Assaulting a police officer in the execution of his duties.
3) Theft of a motor vehicle belonging to a law enforcement task force.
4) Threatening a police officer with physical violence while under arrest.
5) Assault occasioning actual bodily harm to a police officer.
6) Criminal conduct under the Sex Offences Act Section 67, file under Voyeurism.
7) Suspected possession of extreme pornographic images stored within a computer hard drive.

Turner's uncooperative attitude persisted, and not surprisingly he exercised his right to remain silent, thus creating something of a conundrum for himself due to an issue which had arisen in the course of his interrogation.

'I was about to come to that,' Wade said, gloatingly. 'During a call to the offices of the esteemed Mr Marcus Davies, we were informed he no longer represents you. Would you like us to appoint an independent solicitor?'

Turner stared up at the ceiling and, close to tears, squeezed out his response. 'It would appear I have precious little choice!'

SEVENTY-SEVEN

Four days later

As Chukka's almost indecipherable lingo spilt from Khalid's new Android handset, the man himself, with his Rastafarian tresses tied together behind his neck, was bizarrely captured on video, evidently without his prior knowledge.

'*Hey fam, I bin chin-wagging like forever with the man 'ere. We cut this deal dude, and he's like promised to write one of them character preference things, which should cut me some slack with the payroll board!*'

'I told him I was testing out a new app on my phone!' Khalid laughed.

'And he swallowed it?' the advocate gasped.

'Hook, line and sinker!'

'Ping it over to me as an email attachment, and I'll give the matter my undivided attention in my study this evening.'

As Khalid produced the appropriate USB cable from his briefcase, its open lid revealed a newspaper on top of a stack of assorted documents. The headline instantly caught the lawyer's eye:

GO FOR GOLD
Court decision likely to be overturned

'The recording,' Khal said. 'Do you think it'll hold up in court?'

'Hmm? I'm sorry, I was a little distracted by the paper's front page.'

'Things are happening… maybe a little too fast.'

'So speed is of the essence!'

'It could be argued.'

'I'll need a statement from your brother Rashid without delay, to acknowledge receipt of Mr Allen's video message.'

'I'll get on to it right away,' Khalid promised. 'And I can't thank you enough for fitting me in at such short notice.'

'Not at all. One more thing, Mr Shah…'

'But of course!'

'I get the impression this malefactor Chukka models himself on some kind of pseudo-Jamaican gangster-rapper?'

'He's of mixed origin,' Khal snickered in amusement. 'An English mother, West Indian father.'

'And presumably the word "preference" refers to a character reference, and "payroll" is a Freudian slip for parole?'

'So you're familiar with the lingo, Mr Davies?'

'Hmm, not quite my thing,' he replied, half-smiling. 'Let's chat again tomorrow.'

*

London, W1

'I thought you should see this, boss,' press secretary Dawn informed fat-cat record chief Miles Templeton, alerting him to a text message doing the rounds from the white-collar wing of James Hillier's East London chambers:

> Retrial ordered by Court of Appeal following an order quashing a conviction under part IV of the Criminal Justice Act 2003

'This is gold dust babes, twenty-four carat!'

'An unintended pun, boss?'

'What'd I say?'

'You referred to the text as *gold* dust?'

'That's it!' he exclaimed, almost bursting a blood vessel. 'A definitive "Very Best Of" box set, entitled *Twenty-Four Carat Gold*!'

'Excellent timing!' she acknowledged. 'Especially as the pendulum of public opinion is swinging back in JJ's direction.'

Conceitedly, he beat his chest and praised himself for the flash of inspiration, as Dawn placed in front of him the transcript of a BBC news bulletin aired that same morning.

'Huh… they'd have had him hanged, drawn and quartered this time last week!'

'I'll prepare an updated statement.'

'How 'bout News International, what's their take?'

'I'll check online.'

'Well get your sweet ass moving!' he said domineeringly. 'And bring me the morning papers, the second they arrive!'

At her desk her fingers sped across her computer keyboard, pinging emails hither and yon to her extensive list of media contacts, in between chattering into her speakerphone and preparing an up-to-date press release.

'All systems go, boss,' she said, dashing back to Templeton's office. 'And Marcus in A and R is already on the case.'

'Nice job, sweetheart!' he said, lauding her efforts. 'This has the makings of the most spectacular comeback since Lazarus!'

*

Ahmed's Café, Leicester

The brothers Shah met up for breakfast in a cheap and cheerful greasy spoon. Peering above the rim of his reading glasses, Khalid sat brooding over a selection of morning papers spread on the table in front of him.

'What time do you call this?' he moaned.

'Good morning to you too,' Rash said sarcastically. 'My assistant Alex had a problem with the Centre's alarm system.'

He squeezed his body into a chair and nestled his backpack between his legs. Reaching forward to grab a knife and fork, he caught a glimpse of a familiar mugshot gracing the front page of an eminent broadsheet.

Angel of Death conviction quashed
Court orders retrial, set to take place within months

Khalid slid the paper across the table and urged him to run an eye over the accompanying article. The light was abruptly obscured by the host's burly figure as he plonked down two platefuls of food, blotting out Jon's bristly features.

'Cheers, Ahmed!' Rashid said, skewing his eyes up at him. 'Any chance of a slice of bacon, or even a pork sausage?'

'Just shut up and eat, you moron!' the devout Muslim said wryly. 'And count yourself lucky you're not barred!'

They wolfed down their food in between slurping from their coffee mugs. Pulling a notorious gossip-rag from underneath their plates, Khalid's free hand dangled another splash headline right under his brother's nose.

SENSATIONAL NEW FINDINGS DEEM GOLD VERDICT UNSAFE
Early release beckons, turn to page 5

Early release beckons, turn to page 5

'Incredible!' Rash said tersely.

'And there's more!' Khalid indicated, carefully tugging a print-smudged tabloid from the bottom of the pile.

'VAGABOND KILLER' CASE GOES TO RETRIAL
Questionable new evidence offers multi-millionaire rock star second bite at cherry

'Huh, there's always one,' Rash said scathingly, wrinkling his nose. 'I wouldn't wipe my arse on that blab sheet!'

'You seem ill at ease,' Khal observed.

'The meeting with the solicitor,' he snuffled. 'You haven't said a dicky bird!'

Khalid threw him a smug, knowing smile and dug deep into his jeans pocket to scoop out his mobile. He was clicking onto his downloaded images when, like a hot potato, he juggled the suddenly chirping device in his hands.

'Khalid Shah,' he answered, pulling it to his ear. 'Yes, he's with me right now... No problem, Mr Davies, ten-thirty it is!'

*

Leicestershire Police HQ

Off in his own little world, DCI Philpott at first omitted to acknowledge desk clerk Maureen as, vying for his attention upon his entry into the building, she hurriedly squeezed out into the foyer to waylay him.

'Good morning, Chief!'

'Sorry Mo, I was miles away!'

'You asked specifically to be kept up to speed on any developments concerning DS Hackett?'

'What've you got?' he blurted, coming to a stop.

'An officer working the graveyard shift logged a call from an elderly Granby resident, in regards to Dan's nasty tumble.'

'Stop beating around the bush, Mo!'

'It would appear her husband retrieved some items from the roadside, not long after the ambulance sped off.'

'Get her on the line, Mo!' he urged, striding purposefully towards the privacy of his office. 'You just never know!'

Once ensconced behind his desk he instinctively flicked on the speaker-phone, and suddenly turned away to shield his ears from a penetrating high-pitched whistle which drowned out any possible chance of conversation.

'Hello... hello!' a frail voice echoed.

'Ma'am, can you hear me?' Philpott screeched, alert to the problem. 'If so, please turn down your hearing aid!'

'My apologies, constable!' she managed to say clearly.

'Detective Chief Inspector Matthew Philpott speaking,' he said, slightly taken aback. 'How can I help you, ma'am?'

'I'm afraid I'm in something of a dilemma...'

'Please calm yourself and speak clearly into the handset, ma'am,' he gently urged her. 'Can you tell me your name?'

'Harriet Grainger,' she said, in a tentative tone. 'I've a feeling my husband may have dropped an awful clanger...'

'In what way exactly?' he asked, his biro poised at the ready.

She plunged into an elaborate account of her husband's passion for all things mechanical, spilling forth rather engagingly from her lips with the silky smooth intonation normally associated with a skilled storyteller.

'Engine parts, you say, ma'am?'

'Yes, officer. Knick-knacks!'

'What kind of knick-knacks specifically, ma'am?'

'Coiled springs, an assortment of nuts and bolts, even a small carburettor. Oh, and a badly stained blade of some variety, which we deduced may well have been used to cut through the carcass of a dead animal!'

'Mrs Grainger, I'm truly grateful,' he said, inhaling deeply. 'I'll have a car over there pronto to bag everything up.'

'Not necessary, constable, I have them here next to me within my grasp, neatly packed in a Sainsbury's shopping bag.'

'Detective Chief... oh, never mind!' he said, piqued.

'One more thing, constable...'

'Fire away, ma'am.'

'Your colleague, Mr Harris. Will he pull through?'

'Hackett, ma'am... Daniel Hackett,' he said, frowning. 'He's relatively stable, ma'am.'

'How strange!' she wavered. 'He signed in as D. Harris…'

'Did he now?' Philpott growled, instantly joining the dots. 'Sit tight, ma'am, someone will be with you very shortly.'

Seething, he handed her back to the main desk to leave her details, wishing he could have strangled Hackett when he had the chance.

*

Ahmed's Café, Leicester

'Speak of the devil,' Khal said, terminating Davies's call.

'Well… talk to me!'

'Do you have your laptop handy?'

'It's right here in my backpack… why?'

'Switch it on. I need to Bluetooth something to you from my mobile.'

'This'd better be good.'

Ignoring his brother's continual gripes, Khalid scrolled through his stored data and promptly enabled the tethering option on his phone, then pinged the video file as an email attachment before jumping to his feet.

'Where the hell are you going?'

'For some fresh air,' he said, shaking his head. 'Sit back and enjoy!'

SEVENTY-EIGHT

London, England

A MIGHTY WALL OF SOUND pulsated through the ajar door of the studio's console room. Creeping inside to dump his stuff an hour ahead of schedule, in-vogue producer Rik 'Gonzalo' Mendes froze in his tracks.

'What and who the heck is that?'

'JJ Gold, no less,' engineer Klaus Schelling said proudly. 'His record company asked if I had any unfinished or unmixed tracks lying around from a session we worked on together in Montreux a few years back.'

'What a stunningly original piece of music!' Mendes eulogised. He felt the hair stand up on the back of his neck as he listened, visibly moved, to the achingly passionate vocal, draining every last drop of emotion out of the tune's lyrics.

'But sadly incomplete,' Schelling commented.

'The percussion sounds are mind-blowing; what did you use?'

Schelling laughed, providing a rundown of the hours experimenting with contrabass flutes, Moog synthesisers and a heavily detuned Japanese gong bass drum to cook up the most earth-shattering note possible.

'And you say the track needs some work?' Mendes said excitedly. 'I'd give my right arm to have a crack at it!'

Nudging up the faders to fill the room with a surging wave of glorious noise, Schelling offered him his empty seat to give him the chance to lend a more critical ear, whilst adding his input with a few inspired adjustments.

'The working title we used was "The Void",' he unveiled, making reference to JJ's crazy notions to widen the track's scope utilising a military band complete with musket, fifes, drums and bassoons, concluding with the resounding boom of cannon fire in a grand finale reminiscent of Tchaikovsky's *1812*.

The producer sat stunned and silent, as if mesmerised by the power and majesty of the track. Leaning his head back, he closed his eyes to try to piece it all together, his mind absorbing the poignancy of the lyrical content.

There's a void in my life, a yawning, aching hollow,
Shadowed beneath a rocky crag,
Where the truth's too hard to swallow
In the valley below lie the broken shards of a jillion shattered dreams.
As a voice in the distance screams:
'Don't let me fall'.

There's a hole in my heart where but once there was you,
A gaping wound within my soul
Where an ill wind whistles through
But with a leap of faith I swoop into the unknown
Where swirling rapids cleave the canyon walls
And again the lonesome voice calls:
Ah-ah-ah-ah

So reach for your soul and touch me with your light
And on wings of hope together we'll take flight
Defying the gravity constantly pulling us down
Far above the unforgiving rocky ground
There's a void in my life that only you can fill
But I have faith that somehow, someday I will.

*

Belmarsh Prison

The cumbrous, rotund figure of prison warder Jed 'Podge' Randall burst into CJ's cell, his eyes almost popping out of his head at the sight of the inmate washing his smalls and carefully draping them over the radiator.

'Skid marks, eh Jenks?' he said, laughing throatily. 'Which do you want first son, the good news or the bad news?'

'Stop pissing about, Podgy. What is it?'

'There's an error on your PSI Discharge form!'

'You what?' CJ snapped, his muscles tensing. 'A fuck-up?'

'Apparently it's only half-completed.'

'Says who?'

'The snotty-nosed cow in the governor's office.'

'Perhaps she'd like to see my Charlie Bronson* impersonation!'

Podge was acutely aware that CJ was on the verge of throwing a fit and pleaded with him to remain calm. Plonking his backside down on the unmade bed, he produced a two-page form from a pink document wallet.

'Let me finish, please.'

'What's the good news?' CJ asked, sullenly.

'The governor overruled her!'

'He did?'

'But even so, you can't be formally discharged until your B79 has been processed and issued.'

'Too much red tape, Podgy!'

His pen poised at the ready, the warder busily scanned down the page, diligently seeking out the missing information required, dotting some i's and crossing t's here and there, before casting a quizzical glance CJ's way.

'All that's missing is a forwarding address.'

'Why? It's not as if I'm high-risk!'

'So your Offender Manager can contact you during the coming weeks,' he explained. 'Come on, you know the rules.'

'The Scottish Highlands,' CJ said guardedly.

'That's a start... go on?'

'To see a man about a boat.'

'If you want to get out of here, I need an address!'

'Knoydart,' he replied.

'That's a new one on me,' Podge uttered, pausing his writing. 'And does this fictitious backwater have a postcode?'

Quickly rearranging his dampened undies, CJ rummaged through his holdall full of possessions and searched out his tattered little red book. He located the page marked 'K' and shoved it into Podge's line of vision.

Oak Tree Cottage,
Knoydart
PH41 4PL

'Fictitious my arse!' he said sneeringly.

'I stand corrected!' the tubby guard conceded, lumbering to his feet. 'Geography never was my strongest subject.'

---

* Charles Bronson – referred to as 'Britain's most violent prisoner'

'You know Podge, I'll miss waking up to your ugly mug first thing every morning,' CJ mumbled with genuine warmth.

'One wrong move and you'll be back!' Podge sniffed, before loping onto the landing, hard pressed to choke back his emotions.

SEVENTY-NINE

Two days later
Glasgow Queen Street Station

THE SWARTHY-LOOKING STRANGER on the platform immediately aroused CJ's attention, his silky-smooth voice busily chattering into his gleaming white iPhone to outline the details of his backbreaking northward trek.

'Excuse me for being nosy,' CJ said, approaching him. 'I overheard you mention you were heading out to Knoydart?'

'I most certainly am,' Khalid replied, a mite cagily.

'Via Fort William?'

'Yes, on the Jacobite steam train.'

'I know it well,' CJ reminisced.

'How so?'

'I used to live nearby.'

'A pretty spectacular journey, from any perspective.'

'Jaw-dropping!' he said, nodding. 'Anyway, sorry to have bothered you.'

They boarded the train, and by coincidence plumped for the same 'quiet' carriage, soon finding themselves with only the aisle separating them and almost simultaneously closing their eyes to take a short nap.

'Good afternoon, ladies and gentlemen. This is the 15.36 train to Fort William. Stopping at Helensburgh, Ardlui, Crianlarich, Upper Tyndrum, Bridge of Orchy, Rannoch, Tulloch and Spean Bridge. Arriving in Fort William at 19.30.'

'Now there's a tongue-twister!' Khalid laughed, looking over at CJ.

'A proper mouthful!' he acknowledged, rubbing his eyes. 'By the way, I didn't mean to be rude on the platform.'

'Blame me, I was a little bit abrupt!'

'Not a bit of it; I'm happy for the company,' he countered. 'So you're no stranger to the "bounds" and its rough terrain?'

357

'This'll be my fifth trip,' Khal said, beginning to relax. 'Though sadly on this occasion I also have a funeral to attend.'

'A relative?' CJ pried.

'A friend, who retired to the Isle of Skye.'

CJ gave an apologetic little shrug and again shut his eyes, his head rocking in rhythm with the train's gentle motion while the flickering light through the window seemed to highlight his unshaven, scar-faced features.

'Carl Jenkinson,' he mumbled, waking suddenly and stretching his arm across the aisle. 'My friends call me CJ.'

'Wait a minute... CJ... Jon's pal?'

'Jon who?'

'Jon... more famously known as JJ?'

'Well, I'll be jiggered!' he gasped. 'You must be Khalid!'

'How would you know that?'

'From a framed photo hung on the wall of the croft!'

A lengthy conversation ensued, with both men whiling away the time swapping stories back and forth, mostly centred upon their mutual friend's chequered existence, interspersed with a handful of amusing anecdotes.

'I heard all about the saloon bar dust-up in the harbourside pub.'

'It's impossible to keep anything secret.'

'He likened you to Rambo!' Khal said half-jokingly.

'He was heavily outnumbered.'

'Say no more!'

To the accompaniment of clanging buffers and the squeal of brakes, a small chain of conical mountains jutted into the horizon like saw-teeth, before being partially obscured by a cluster of shabby-looking buildings lining the track at the next port of call.

'Where are we now?' CJ asked a passing attendant,

'Bridge of Orchy, sir... Can you no see the Munros over yonder?'

'What's your tipple?' Khalid cut in, eyeing the drinks trolley. 'On me, naturally!'

'Just a Coke, ta!'

'Something stronger, perhaps?'

'I haven't touched a drop in eighteen months.'

'By choice?'

'By order of a court judge!' CJ snuffled.

'But of course,' Khal said, embarrassedly. 'The boat... the arrest...'

He ordered up two colas and listened intently to CJ's reminiscences. His chequered past… the friendship he'd forged with Jon… and lastly his burning desire to up sticks and reconnect with his sister Down Under.

'Australia… which part?'

'Tasmania,' he said somewhat pensively.

Khal gasped in horror.

'The Port Arthur massacre!'

'How could you remember?'

'I wrote a piece for the *Mail*,' he sighed.

'My brother-in-law Gordon got caught in the firing line.'

'He was shot by Martin Bryant?'

'The bastard confined him to a wheelchair!'

A gory image of the mass slaughter came rushing back to Khalid's mind, made all the more horrifying by CJ's description of his sister's first-hand experience, playing dead on the coach floor while literally all hell broke loose.

'And miraculously, she survived?'

'They planted a memorial garden next to the crime scene,' CJ said sadly. 'I vowed that some day I'd take her there.'

For reasons unknown Khalid's thoughts turned to the lovely Agnes, her dark, glossy locks flowing on the stiff northerly breeze, wandering lonely along the deserted shoreline, her heels dug deep into the damp sand.

'Will you be staying at the croft?'

'Brightwater?' CJ said, startled. 'She sold up, and took off without making so much as a whimper. She wrote to me.'

'Sweet mother of mercy!'

CJ crouched low to unzip his rucksack's front pocket and slipped a single-sheet letter from a buff envelope, then slid it across the tea-stained tabletop and sat back with his arms crossed awaiting Khalid's response.

My dear CJ

I write to bid you goodbye with an aching heart.

Warm thoughts of you will always surround me. You helped me laugh, and offered a shoulder to cry on to help me face life's uncertainties. 'In readiness to serve and protect' Jonathan once joked.

Yet here I sit by the seashore scared and alone, haunted by the fear that the man I live for may be lost to me forever. The man who taught me how to love, and sent my desires soaring towards the stars.

He bequeathed me everything, save for the ray of hope I need to guide me through the dark days ahead, taking time to readjust, knowing his presence in my life will forever be missed.

Soon after dawn breaks I will close the door to the past, and bid a sad farewell to Brightwater, the little paradise I called home. To journey far and let go of what was, and put my faith in what will be.

What the future holds I cannot say.

But I remain forever your friend.

Agnes

Khal stopped to breathe deeply and then slowly read it through again, stunned by the honesty and poignancy of her words, still more saddened that she was undoubtedly making the biggest mistake of her life.

'Jon could be acquitted.'

'I visited him,' Khal said, dumbfounded. 'He never said a word!'

'Recently?'

'Ten days ago.'

CJ's demeanour became ultra-serious.

'You and I need to get busy.'

'How so?'

'We have to find her,' he said resolutely. 'They belong together!'

EIGHTY

April 2012
Tasmania

A LITTLE BLEARY-EYED from a late night of putting the world to rights on the terrace, not to mention the effects of a bold Shiraz, with the clock's second hand ticking round to nine Agnes seized upon the morning's first call.

'Good morning, Coles Bay Veterinary Practice!'

'Uh, who's that?' an unrefined Aussie accent rasped, before enquiring as to the whereabouts of her predecessor Martha.

'Sad to say she's currently laid up in the Royal Hobart Hospital.'

'What's up with her?' he barked, unsympathetically.

'She's recovering from a punctured lung,' Agnes said, slightly taken aback. 'And will be out of action for a while.'

'Huh! Is Pretty Boy Macduff in yet?'

'I'm sorry. We don't have anyone here by that name!' Aggie said disobligingly. 'To whom, or what, are you referring?'

'Macduff... your boss!'

'Oh, you mean Mr Duffy!' she said mockingly. 'I'll just check and see if he's available. Who shall I say is calling?'

'Digger Marsh. It's urgent!'

His harsh, brusque manner disconcerted her, so much so that she stuck him on hold to let him stew for a while. She peeped through a crack in the door to Eamon's office only to find him engaged in deep conversation.

'I'm afraid his line's busy,' Aggie resumed, while locating Marsh's file in the customer records. 'I'll get him to call you back.'

'I said it was urgent!'

'And you expect him to drop everything?'

'The bloody chestnut mare's struck down with laminitis, and she needs to be X-rayed – meaning without delay, missy!'

To one side, an historic wall map identifying the island as 'Van Diemen's Land' colourfully displayed a set of landmark points spread far and wide, mostly relating to the late eighteenth and nineteenth centuries.

'Do you hail from the island, Mr Marsh?'

'Born and bred. Unlike you!'

'Then try casting your mind back to when Tasmania was a penal colony.'

'What are you on about?'

'Try and cast your mind back to a time when your forefathers settled on the island, in the early eighteen hundreds.'

'What is this crap?' he snorted, his irritation obvious.

'The scores of convicted felons and shysters who arrived by the boat-load,' she continued. 'It's clearly in your blood!'

'What the hell's gotten into you?' he raged.

Totally ignoring him, she rose up and bounded back towards Eamon's office. Flushed from a lengthy exchange with his previous caller, he couldn't fail to notice the misplaced, cranky expression on her face.

'Ag, is something amiss?'

'There's a cantankerous pig named Marsh on the line.'

'Uh-oh. What's rattling his cage today?'

'His chestnut mare.'

'Bertha!' he tutted. 'Laminitis, at a guess?'

'Ea, he hasn't settled a bill in more than two years!'

'Crikey, Ag, you don't miss a trick!' he spluttered. 'How much does he owe?'

'More than two thousand dollars!'

Eamon considered this for a moment. 'He's a regular client, plus I know he's good for the money.'

She tapped the side of her nose and shot him a knowing glance before scurrying back to the reception desk, in no mood to put up with any more of the sourpuss's nonsense.

'Do you have access to a credit card, Mr Marsh?' she took up again. 'If so, we can set about unblocking your account.'

'You blocked my account?' he boiled over, threatening nastily to take his custom elsewhere. 'Put me through to Macduff!'

'It'll be my pleasure,' she chirped, 'once the outstanding balance of two thousand and eighty dollars has been cleared!'

After years of bucking the system he'd finally come up against someone able to hold her ground. Bringing his card to hand, he grudgingly proceeded to read out the sixteen-digit number running across the middle.

'I suppose you're satisfied now?'

'Indeed I am… Now, where were we?'

'Macduff!' he said bluntly.

'Just one moment, and I'll put you through…'

*

Mallaig Harbour

'I'm sick to death of working the graveyard shift,' smokehouse assistant Dougie Burns grumbled to himself as he battled his way through a tempestuous easterly gale towards the rattling shutters of the dockside depot.

Keys jangling as the door unlocked, a familiar humming sound greeted his ears, emanating from the vicinity of the fire-pit and kilns located to the building's rear, whilst oddly throwing off a repulsive, sickly odour.

He put two and two together and concluded that his boss had left the main chamber on. Diligently cranking the kiln's rotating handle, he snapped open the door and reeled back at the hideous spectacle awaiting him.

His heart racing, he yelled out in absolute panic, his hands trembling above the screen of his lifeless cell phone. Cussing, he hurried outside into the lashing rain and sprinted across the courtyard to the nearest payphone.

'Mr Robertson, it's Dougie!' he shrieked, between quick gasping breaths. 'There's been a break-in at the depot!'

'Check for any missing items,' the boss said, thrusting his legs into his overalls. 'I'll be there as soon as I'm physically able.'

'Should I call the cops?' the lad jabbered.

Robertson warned him not to be too hasty, and rang off before scuttling out to his van in utter disbelief, questioning who in their right mind would even consider going out of their way to pilfer a job lot of smoked kippers.

*

Coles Bay, Tasmania

Heavily laden with a stack of bulky record books and journals, a radiant-looking Agnes swaggered across the half-empty car park, making a beeline for a gap in the hedgerow skirting the practice's perimeter.

'Off to the beach again?' Eamon shouted from his car window, on his way to a callout. 'Some light reading, I see!'

'Your company ledgers more like,' she said, raising her eyebrows, 'which haven't been updated in a month of Sundays.'

'Oops!' he said a tad sheepishly.

'I spoke with your accountant, just this morning.'

'Martin Frobisher?'

'That's him.'

'Do I detect a problem?'

'Only that the company's on the verge of bankruptcy!'

'God, since when?'

'Since you've been operating as a charity!'

She proceeded to tear strips off him in a schoolmarm-like tone, making clear how his account had been overdrawn for months, then going easy on him and vowing to work day and night to put his affairs in order.

'Where would I be without you, Ag?'

'Down on your uppers!'

'Marry me, Aggie!' he begged her, throwing open the car door and dropping onto one knee. 'We can make it work!'

'Me, marry a pauper? Not likely!' she kidded. 'I'll catch you later, once I've soaked up some of this glorious sunshine.'

*

Mallaig Harbour

Allie Robertson gaped up in astonishment at the pair of stark-naked carcasses left dangling in the kiln, both hoisted upside down by way of two steel lifting-chains, akin to sides of beef in a butcher's refrigeration store.

With the simple press of a button Dougie began winching them towards the ground, his nose twitching in disgust at the rank-smelling odour when the locking chain clattered to a sudden halt in the cogwheel.

'Perhaps you'd care to explain how you got here?' Robertson snarled. 'And for fuck's sake put some clothes on!'

They stood staring at one another, gormlessly huffing and puffing like the two main characters from the movie *Dumb and Dumber*, hands covering their private parts in a pathetic effort to make light of their predicament.

'I found a bundle of old rags smouldering out back in the incinerator, Mr Robertson!' young Dougie butted in.

'The expression "done up like a kipper" springs to mind!' the boss man howled facetiously. 'Well? I'm still waiting!'

'I have no idea!' Logan muttered with a vengeful look.

'He snuck up behind us, and cracked our heads together!' nephew Duncan pitched in. 'And then the lights went out!'

'Who? King Kong?' Robertson roared, his patience stretched to the limit. 'What kind of cock and bull story is that?'

He threw them a pair of overalls apiece and sauntered off to take a good look around, wracking his brain to narrow down exactly who could have accessed his premises to set about wreaking such a humiliating revenge.

'The Sassenach!' Logan mumbled under his breath.

'Uncle, no!' Duncan whined, mindful of the potential repercussions. 'There's no way you can be absolutely sure!'

'I may've been mistaken.'

'In which case, we're done here!' Robertson said. 'Now get your scrawny arses off my premises, before I call the boys in blue!'

*

The driving rain had mercifully abated as, wending their way onto the main drag, Duncan stalled at the staggered crossroads. He was steeled for his uncle's anticipated reaction as he prepared to unleash his bombshell.

'We need to talk, Uncle!'

'What's ye problem, laddie?'

'You and I have become a standing joke among the local community.'

'Don't talk such crap, son!'

'It's true. We're a laughing stock!' Duncan confessed. 'It's time to move on!'

'Fat chance – I've hardly a pot to piss in!'

'Not you... *me!*'

Stunned into momentary silence, Jimmy climbed out of the car and paced the pavement. Faced with the realisation that he might soon be left to fend for himself, he reverted to type by going back on the offensive.

'You ungrateful little bastard!' he said scathingly. 'I should take you over my knee and thrash the life out of you!'

'I'm not a kid any more!' Duncan countered. 'And furthermore, I'm not your skivvy!'

Struggling hard to repress his rage, Logan inched threateningly towards him, before finding himself toppling backwards into the middle of the street, stunned by a flurry of punches to his head, stomach and arms.

'But we're family!' he whimpered. 'I taught you everything you know!'

'That's what I'm afraid of!'

'Where will you go?'

'Inverness,' the lad said, shortly. 'I leave on Tuesday, along with my new flatmate.'

'Who?' Logan asked pitifully.

'Marnie!' he replied, flitting off into the blackness.

EIGHTY-ONE

Leicester district

CAUGHT UNAWARES IN THE MIDST of her daily chores, the name 'PAM ICU' flashed up on Sheila's phone screen, motivating her to screech into the nearest lay-by much like a Formula One racer entering the pits at a Grand Prix.

'Miss Wilson?' the Sister's familiar voice stated.

'Pam!' Sheila replied, breathlessly.

'I've been trying to get hold of you all morning. For a moment there I thought you'd given me the wrong number.'

'What is it?' she said, trembling. 'This is unbearable!'

'Stay calm, lovey!'

'How's Dan?' she sniffled.

'I'm calling with some encouraging news. Your hubby-to-be regained consciousness at six-thirty a.m. this morning!'

'Sweet Jesus!' Sheila said, going rigid.

Her heart leapt inside her chest, almost bursting with joy. She imagined the corner of his mouth curling into one of his trademark wry smiles, and pushing her foot on the accelerator sped off excitedly in a whirlwind of mud.

*

His mind consumed in the quietude of his office, busily working his way through a never-ending pile of paperwork, the disorienting ringtone of his desktop phone caused DCI Philpott to almost jump out of his skin.

'Matt, it's Sheila, Dan's fiancée,' she panted. 'Are you free to chat?'

'Of course, sweetheart.'

'I'm on my way to the hospital.'

'For heaven's sake, woman, don't keep me on tenterhooks!'

'He regained consciousness early this morning!'

Philpott tried to talk but the words seemed to stick in his throat, the only sound to leave his lips an unrestrained shriek of delight. He inhaled deeply and managed to speak, but what he intended to say came out all wrong.

'God damn it!'

'Matt, what the hell?'

'Forgive me, Sheila darling,' he said exasperatedly, 'but I'm just about to go into a meeting with the new DCC!'

She joked that her fiancé wasn't going anywhere any time soon; and then recalled a previous conversation, stating she'd checked through his personal documents and files, none of which bore any significance to the Gold case.

'I don't understand it, though. Something was stressing him out.'

'Sheila, forget it,' Philpott urged her, his voice cracking. 'Your place is at his side!'

*

Forty-five minutes later
Royal Infirmary

Hackett's crimson eyes stared blankly forward, his head tilted slightly to one side. From the corner of his drooping mouth a tiny drop of spittle leaked onto his pyjama top, dabbed away at once by the ever-watchful Sheila.

'Miss Wilson?' the duty doctor asked, squeezing by her to check on the ventilator. 'We've been observing Daniel's respiratory pattern for the past three hours, which pleasingly has settled into a smooth rhythm.'

'Sister Walsh… she said he regained consciousness!'

'So he did, for just short of an hour.'

'Might he have seen or heard anything?'

'Quite possibly,' the medic said, nodding. 'Although he was so heavily sedated I very much doubt he remembers a thing.'

Eager to keep track of the task at hand he checked Dan's blood pressure and pulse for what seemed to be the umpteenth time, then lifted both eyelids to check his pupils, before leaving the room with a courteous nod.

She felt utterly powerless; but all she could do was be there, hoping, praying for a faint glimmer to light his eyes.

*

His left arm clutching a spray of flowers, Matt Philpott galloped towards the ICU. His entry to the ward was annoyingly blocked by a small gathering of medics seemingly engaged in some sort of collaborative discussion.

'Allow me to explain the nuts and bolts of the procedure,' a bespectacled specialist rattled on, animatedly holding court before a rapt throng of junior colleagues, mostly making notes inside their work folders.

Before long they dispersed, allowing him to push through the swing doors. He was greeting Sheila with a gentle peck on the cheek when in a fleeting moment something clicked in his brain.

'Nuts and bolts!' he bizarrely exclaimed.

'Matt… are you okay?'

'I need to contact the forensics lab, urgently!' he said, heading off as quickly as he came. 'I'll be back in five, sweetie!'

Her head began to spin, exacerbated by a further flurry of activity in the shape of a four-man ambulance crew surging in with an accident victim strapped to a trolley pursued by the indomitable Sister Walsh.

'Sheila, my darling,' she said, holding back for a second. 'You look exhausted!'

'I guess I got my hopes up just a little too much!'

'Not a bit of it, lovey. Doctor Carmichael, the paraplegia specialist, would like a quiet word when you have a minute, in regards to a new procedure the Americans are trying out on patients with spinal cord injuries.'

Ever hopeful, Sheila nodded zealously and watched her disappear behind an L-shaped screen, then sidled back up to Dan's bedside and slumped into a chair.

She was just on the verge of closing her eyes when he uttered a faint, miraculous grunt.

*

Thirty minutes later

Poised apprehensively at the bottom of the duvet, Sheila's tired eyes fixed onto her man's whiskered cheeks, her heart pumping nineteen to the dozen, desperately searching for the merest flicker of recognition.

From under the sheets a prolonged rumble of flatulence broke the silence, succeeded right after by a breathy snort rippling from his nostrils, promptly greeted with a howl of delight from the recently arrived DCI Philpott.

'He's trying to tell us something,' Philpott said, breathing a tiny chuckle. 'Talking through his backside as per usual!'

'Matt, really!' she tutted. 'Though I swear he's trying to communicate…'

They moved closer to his parted lips to heed his every breath, each tiny burst of air firstly rising and then fading away. The hushed stillness was broken by the sound of scampering feet announcing Sister Walsh's arrival.

'Sorry to break up the party,' she said, setting about her hourly routine. 'Now, how's my star patient this afternoon?'

'He's been making some rather peculiar noises, Pam,' Sheila let on. 'Along with the odd sharp intake of breath!'

'Uh-oh!' the Sister said, her nose twitching. 'Perhaps you could make yourselves scarce for a minute or two?'

They took the hint and wandered off in search of the nearest vending machine, shortly located in the nearby stairwell where they quietly chewed the fat over a KitKat apiece washed down with a can of San Pellegrino.

'He could hear what we were saying!' Sheila said, optimistically. 'He even managed some semblance of a smile!'

'Dan won't give up the fight; he's a warrior!'

Their heads both turned towards the parting lift doors, from where a sprightly-looking elderly couple emerged onto the landing, immediately setting their eyes on her and rushing in her direction with open arms.

'Mum! Dad!' Sheila cried out joyously, swept into a three-way hug, oblivious to Philpott furtively slipping away.

*

One hour later

Her mood lifted by the unforeseen family reunion, Sheila bade her parents a fond goodbye and re-entered the side room to crash out for a while in the leather-upholstered armchair. She had all too briefly closed her eyes when the tap-tap of footsteps announced Sister Walsh's arrival, along with a tall blue-suited stranger.

'Sheila… darling?' she whispered, crouching to pat her on the knee. 'I'd like to introduce you to our chief neurologist.'

'Doctor Philip Carmichael, at your service,' he announced ultra-politely, courteously extending his right hand.

'Sheila Wilson… the patient's fiancée,' she responded, attempting to gather herself. 'I'm delighted to meet you!'

Instantly cutting to the chase, he explained the basics of a state-of-the-art ultrasound scanner which used a system of high-frequency pulses to evaluate the blood flow in the central hub of the brain.

'Known in technical terms as the thalamus!' he said enthusiastically, before referring to a roll of printed-off data.

'And are the signs encouraging?'

'It's not my wish to raise your hopes unnecessarily,' he said cautiously. 'But the results are nothing short of remarkable.'

'That's amazing!' Sheila gasped.

'As previously mentioned, he's by no means out of the woods,' Carmichael said. 'The nerve damage may be irreparable.'

'Will he ever walk again?' she asked, sombrely.

He pinched his chin between his thumb and forefinger and reeled off a list of common complications which occurred after a majority of spinal cord injuries, then checked his notes and flashed her an optimistic smile.

'There is, however, evidence of musculature recovery.'

'You mean there's a possibility that…?' she said, clamming up.

'Daniel's made such great strides, which would suggest he'll be able to walk independently at some stage in the future.'

She somehow restrained herself from throwing her arms around him, and chose instead to let out an ecstatic whoop, then perched her bottom on the edge of the bed before tenderly pressing Dan's hand to her heart.

'Did you hear that, my love?'

And, as though by magic, his eyelids slowly began to part.

EIGHTY-TWO

August 2012
Hobart, Tasmania

THE BRIGHT LIGHTS OF Elizabeth Street flickered intermittently through the rear windscreen of Eamon's Range Rover, casting a medley of shapes over Agnes's long, flowing locks, oddly in sync with the engine's guttural roar.

Aware of the repercussions from being caught while driving above the legal limit, he carefully weaved around the expanding capital's outskirts, strewn every which way with an attractive array of executive and urban homes.

'What a delightful city!' Aggie said, revelling in the leafy surroundings. 'I can't believe we haven't been before.'

'It truly is,' he agreed, flushed from the effects of the zesty Chardonnay. 'But in truth I really shouldn't be driving!'

'What was the name of the fish I ordered?'

'Striped Trumpeter, Ag!' he replied, slowing to steer the vehicle through the gated entrance to a roadside hotel.

He parked close to a set of steps leading to the ornate front entrance, from where a trio of waistcoated porters at once flitted down towards them, grabbing their overnight bags and bounding back to the lobby.

'Gosh, this is all very grand!' she said tipsily. 'Do we have separate rooms?'

'I booked a suite with a queen-size bed,' he answered reassuringly. 'And a sofa bed in the sitting-room area!'

'You're so delightfully old-fashioned, Eamon!' she slurred between hiccoughs. 'And to what do I owe all this?'

'I thought I'd spoil you!'

'Why, may I ask?'

'You rescued me from going under!'

'Oh yes. I did, didn't I?'

They trailed behind a tall brass-topped trolley being wheeled along the corridor to their suite by a middle-aged bellboy, who stooped to unlock the door, unloaded their luggage inside the room and dashed off, contentedly clutching a twenty-dollar bill.

'A nightcap, perhaps?'

'Why not?' she agreed, giggling. 'After all, I'm the best receptionist-cum-bookkeeper-cum-beach bum on the planet!'

'Can't argue with that, Ag!' he laughed, courteously opening the door, desirous of popping the cork on a bottle of fine champagne.

*

Two hours later

She left the bedroom door slightly ajar and clambered between the silky sheets, distracted by a shaft of light cutting through the slatted blind. As she flopped her head back onto the pillow the room began to spin.

'Are you still awake, Ea?'

'Semi-conscious,' he grunted from the sofa bed.

'The entrée we shared. It was exquisite!'

'Moreton Bay Bugs, Ag,' he said drowsily. 'Try and get some sleep, please!'

'One more question!'

'Okay, shoot!'

'Does it bother you that I spend so much time at the beach?'

'Not in the least.'

'It's as if the waves talk to me, Ea!' she purred romantically. 'Almost as though they're trying to tell me something!'

Utterly wiped out, Eamon didn't answer and rolled onto his side, within moments succumbing to the overwhelming desire to sleep. Tiptoeing out of bed, Agnes closed the door to shut out his loud, sonorous snore.

*

Port Arthur Historic Site, Tasmania

Visible from the side window of the garden-side café, an endless horde of sightseers wandered sombrely through the landscaped grounds, each with their own grim tale to tell of the most terrifying and tragic day in the island's history.

'We don't have to do this, Becky,' CJ insisted, busy playing mum. 'I can barely imagine what it must be like for you.'

'I have to, Carl, if only for Gordon's sake,' she replied, rooting in her handbag. 'Damn, I must've left it in the car!'

'What've you lost?'

'My camera!'

Put into a tizzy she began to empty the contents onto the table, frantically fumbling in her handbag and coat pocket before yelling out in frustration and giving up the ghost, her head slumped forward into her hands.

'Becks, take it easy!' he said coolly. 'Stay put, and I'll nip back to the car!'

He hurried through the door and sprinted athletically towards the parking lot, lithely squeezing his torso through a small gap in the fence. The ear-piercing whirr of a car alarm caused him to reel back in surprise.

'Whoops, sorry if I startled you!' a voice from the driver's side yelped. 'The old gal can be a little over-sensitive at times!'

'No problem. Do you need a hand?'

'It's just a slow puncture,' the guy acknowledged, peeping his head over the bonnet. 'But thanks all the same!'

'Okey-dokey; best of luck, fella!' he said, pausing and muttering to himself. 'Now where did I park the bloody car?'

He meandered back and forth and eventually laid eyes on Becky's faithful little runabout. Quickly grabbing her camera from beneath a raincoat dumped on the rear seat, he scampered back in the opposite direction.

'All sorted!' Mister Fix-it shouted, slamming down his Range Rover's boot lid. 'And thanks again for offering to help.'

'Not at all,' CJ replied, giving him a thumbs-up and doubling back whence he came. 'Have a safe onward journey.'

He quickened his pace to a light jog and spotted a nimble-footed woman scurrying along the pavement, her head and shoulders partially obscured by a row of young eucalyptus trees lining the grass verge.

With a quick backward glance he pushed on ahead. Suddenly alert to the weightlessness of the camera case in his hand, he halted momentarily to clip open the back cover, only to find the film compartment empty.

He half-silently cursed and instead made for the gift shop, catching sight as he did so of the 4x4 idling towards the exit. The man's attractive other half perched in the passenger seat, sweeping the hair from her face.

He stood riveted to the spot, and then caught a clearer glimpse of her profile through the half-open window. Just for a short-lived moment he was dumbfounded by her uncanny resemblance to the long-gone Agnes Ryan.

Ten minutes later

CJ found Becky seated at a coveted outdoor table. Happily leaning back soaking up the sun's warm rays, she was savouring a scrumptious-looking lemon cheesecake, outwardly oblivious to her solemn surroundings.

'That's my girl!' he said, sitting himself down and beckoning for the waiter. 'I stuck a new roll of film in your camera.'

'Oops, silly me!' she said, sheepishly. 'I plum forgot.'

He ordered a beer and closed his eyes to indulge in a few moments' contemplation, his mind wandering back to the brunette in the guy's car. Something about her bugged him, something he couldn't quite put his finger on.

'Sup up, lovey!' she said, summoning up what courage she could. 'I thought we might take a stroll to the memorial garden.'

'Are you sure you feel up to it?'

'Stop fussing!' she admonished him. 'You can take my picture by the plaque they erected in honour of the dead.'

He took her arm and they exited the busy Visitor Centre, soon finding themselves confronted by the huge penitentiary building, its austere exterior set to the rear of a swarm of day-trippers picnicking on the grass.

'I don't get it,' he said vaguely. 'I thought it would be a sad place.'

'Me too,' she replied. 'Are you okay?

'I'm fine. Why?'

'You look a little off-colour,' she observed, concernedly. 'As if you saw a ghost!'

He raised his head and smiled wryly, again immersing himself in his thoughts, thinking that maybe, just maybe, he had.

EIGHTY-THREE

September 2012 – three days before the retrial

A JUMBLE OF ITEMISED DOCUMENTS organised in chronological order lay spread over the desktop of QC Rupert Watts's home study, tinted by the ochre hue diffusing from the low-wattage bulb affixed to an antique table lamp.

He thumbed open the flap to a case-note folder, in which the image of a deceased man's disfigured cranium showed itself in the goriest detail, encircled by a clutch of Post-it notes depicting the extent of the wounds.

He lugubriously grasped at a half-full bottle of Jack Daniels from a nearby trolley and replenished his tumbler for the third time before glancing through his leather Filofax to locate the learned James Hillier's number.

'Jimmy, my old pal!' he said fawningly. 'Please accept my profuse apologies for calling at such an inappropriate hour.'

'Not at all,' Hillier warily replied.

'I figured that, not unlike myself, you'd most probably be hard at it poring over the pathologist's recent findings?'

'That's correct, Rupert.'

'I have to say the photographic evidence has to be the most brutal I've ever seen, specifically the mindless gouging out of the poor bastard's left eye. I just needed to take a timeout, old chap; I hope you don't mind?'

'Your uncanny ability to read your adversaries like a book is well documented in legal circles,' Hillier responded. 'And before you ask, I'm convinced beyond a reasonable doubt my client would in no way be capable of committing such a heinous crime. So bang goes the theory that I'm about to cave in, dear fellow!'

Barbed words flew hither and thither as the exchange grew more and more heated. Watts's tongue in particular became looser and quarrelsome, for the most part fuelled by the effects of the excess of Jack Daniels.

'I know exactly what you're up to!'

'Do tell, Rupert.'

'You're about to argue in favour of loss of control and diminished responsibility.'

'Is that so?'

'Hmm. As ever, you're keeping your cards close to your chest.'

'But who is holding all the aces?' Hillier said, in a curiously confident manner. 'Let battle commence, old boy!'

*

Tuesday September 18th 2012
Leicester

A less frenetic level of activity permeated the lucent city's central hub, as for the second time in only months a flood of representatives from the world's media converged on the unprepared East Midlands conurbation.

Beneath the elevated atrium of the much-photographed courthouse, a burning shaft of bright sunlight refracted into the busy foyer, close to which yet another day's opening arguments laboriously began to get under way.

Present in the stand for the third consecutive session, youthful-looking forensic pathologist Tarquin Rees-Hubbard painstakingly chronicled the succession of blows delivered with egregious malice to the luckless victim's skull, which undoubtedly played a major role in the individual's premature and untimely death.

'Professor Hubbard!' Mr Justice Alderman burst in, sneaking an indiscreet shufti at his antique desktop timepiece. 'I fear you may have previously covered this aspect of the case during the latter stages of yesterday's hearing?'

'At the risk of repeating myself, My Lord, I'm merely working backwards with the aid of the video recordings to reactivate the likely chain of events which were ultimately fatal, and may help identify the actual cause of death.'

'Very well,' Alderman conceded. 'Let's crack on.'

'I would now ask the jury to turn to their copies of the image currently displayed on the screen, as we examine the contusion located directly beneath the patchwork of lacerations spread over the victim's cerebellum.'

'In layman's terms, please!'

'Forgive me, My Lord. Perhaps I should explain that the brain is made up of three main functioning parts, these being the forebrain, midbrain and latterly the hindbrain, which is where the cerebellum is located.'

'In the rear of the brain?'

'To some extent, though more specifically it comprises the large lower posterior of the brain,' the pathologist answered, eyeing his briefcase. 'I have some detailed diagrams in my document wallet if you'd care to take a look?'

'That won't be necessary.'

He seemed a little put out, and turned his focus to what he believed must have been the first injury, depicted by the discolouration found at the base of the skull, inflicted by a blunt instrument prior to a secondary attack.

'The original autopsy report omitted to touch on the possibility of a time lapse between the occurrence of the initial injury and the deranged act of savagery which ultimately brought about the victim's death.'

'Professor Hubbard,' Hillier interceded, jumping to his feet. 'How great a time lapse might you be referring to?'

'The original contusion undoubtedly caused immediate trauma to the brain, followed forthwith by loss of consciousness.'

'And the subsequent mutilations?'

'In my estimation the lacerations inflicted by the resultant, more frenzied attack ensued some forty-five minutes later, most likely employing a medieval cudgel not dissimilar to a mace or a barbarian Viking club.'

'Thank you, Professor,' Hillier said in closing, hearteningly sensing a turning of the tide. 'Thank you very much indeed!'

EIGHTY-FOUR

London

A BOTHERSOME ECHO on the line made conversation difficult, but in any event the squeaky southern English accent caught Khalid by surprise, sufficiently for him to conclude he must have punched in the wrong digits.

'Francis Fine Furs,' the voice strangely resounded. 'How can I help?'

'I received a missed call from this number around an hour ago,' he informed her. 'I guess I must have been mistaken!'

'Where are you calling from?'

'London, England.'

'The old home country!' she said, half-sentimentally. 'How's the weather holding up?'

'It's bucketing down. And dark as hell!'

'Nothing much changes, eh?' she laughed. 'This call must be costing you a small fortune, so I won't keep you!'

Just as he was about to ring off something clicked in his head. Her gentle, almost cockney twang; the mouthful of F's carrying over the air-waves, most likely from some distant part of the globe, such as Melbourne, Australia…

'Did you say furs?'

'That's right.'

'And you have a brother named Carl?' he said eagerly. 'Who's currently over there visiting?'

'How would you know that?'

'We're friends!'

'Is that Khalil?' she said, as the penny dropped.

'Khalid… with a D!'

She tittered embarrassedly and apologised for the faux pas, then recalled CJ's late-night Skype call from her tablet, hastily curtailed on a

379

miscalculation of the time-zone difference between the UK and Down Under.

'He phoned you on the landline this morning!'

'And I'm returning his call,' Khal said, a little bemused. 'Could you please ask him to Skype me back? I'll be waiting up.'

*

Twenty-five minutes later

The descending beep and swish of the ringtone literally caught Khalid napping, when on the dot of one a.m. CJ's slightly pixelated, unkempt whiskery features became visible in the centre of his computer display.

'Mahatma!' CJ greeted him with a mocking smile.

'Typically non-PC, as ever!' Khal responded, his head shaking. 'Did you forget to pack your shaver before you left?'

'It's designer stubble,' CJ claimed. 'Have they set a date for Jon's retrial yet?'

'The second instalment gets under way next Tuesday.'

A long, pregnant pause ensued. Clearing his throat and lowering his voice, CJ stared apprehensively into the iPad's screen, fidgeting uneasily in his chair in anticipation of dropping his bombshell into the mix.

'I swear I saw her.'

'Who? When?'

'Agnes! Only yards away from me, plain as day!'

'Where?' Khal gasped.

'Port Arthur,' he said quietly. 'I saw her through the window of a clapped-out Range Rover, pulling out of the car park.'

'In Tasmania?'

'At the scene of the massacre!' he chattered. 'We touched on it soon after we met, on the train to Fort William!'

As though numbed by a rush of blurred flashbacks creeping into his head, Khalid's mind went back to a freakish conversation in the Knoydart pub, spent in the company of an eccentric, albeit engaging, local psychic.

'A sandy beach where the waves came crashing in… a bronzed Adonis dashing from the water's edge to sweep his lover off her feet…'

'Cara!' CJ cooed. 'Her finger on the wineglass's rim, making it sing!'

'The local called her a witch,' Khal recalled.

'I did some research online,' CJ said excitedly. 'You won't believe this!'

'Try me!' Khal said.

He was looking back at CJ in a semi-disbelieving stare when the screen fell away into a dull, inert blankness.

Skype can't connect

*

One hour later

Zonked out on the sofa, his mouth agape, the ping of an incoming message alert abruptly brought Khalid to his senses. His hands groped in the dimness to bring the screen to life, revealing an unknown email address ending with the letters '.au'.

With a right-click of the mouse onto the highlighted attachment a blaze of colour smacked him right between the eyes, etched in the form of an idyllic crescent-shaped beach, accompanied by an eye-catching heading:

WINEGLASS BAY – TASMANIA'S HIDDEN JEWEL

CJ had signed off his email with the tantalising words:

It's no more than a couple of hours drive from where I spotted her. Together with the new man in her life!

EIGHTY-FIVE

Leicester Crown Court

A SEA OF NONPLUSSED FACES looked towards one another, their wide, disbelieving eyes sizing up the gaudy yellow-tracksuited figure swaggering ungracefully into the courtroom before plodding up into the witness box.

'Would you begin by stating your full name, please?' defending advocate James Hillier asked, in a dubious tone.

'Ugh. Me what?' he mumbled, vacuously.

'Your given birth names,' Hillier said, a hint of a smile crossing his lips. 'As in your first, middle and last names!'

'Charles Winston Allen,' he murmured. 'They is all like first names, but everyone what knows me calls me Chukka!'

'So I gather. Mr Allen, I understand you've a confession to make, in addition to an overdue apology to the court?'

'Yeah, man. It's like I couldn't let Rash take the rap again, not for something he never done!' he babbled semi-incoherently. 'He's innocent, man; and besides, neither of us went nowhere near that dude's crib!'

'Which dude, Mr Allen?'

'The rock-star geyser, sat over there!' he said, nodding his head in Jon's direction.

'And the apology?'

'Yeah. It's like I never meant to waste nobody's time when I couldn't make it here last time out. I'm sorry and everything!'

'Thank you,' Hillier curtly responded, his neck twisting round to acknowledge Mr Justice Alderman with raised eyebrows.

'Very well. In moving on from your friendship with Rashid Shah, I wish to examine your relationship with the deceased man, Mr Amir Mistry,' he said, cutting to the chase. 'Were the two of you on friendly terms?'

'We weren't besties,' he grunted, 'you know what I mean?'

'Did you accompany Mr Mistry on a car journey to the village of Granby on the night of November eleventh, 2005?'

'I don't remember no exact date, man.'

'Really; but you recall paying a visit to the "rock-star geyser's" home, together with your accomplice, the late Amir Mistry?'

'Yeah, man,' Chukka said gormlessly. 'And it was me who drove Rash's banger!'

A little distracted by a murmur of amusement emerging from the public gallery, Hillier paused and paced the room, his chin drooping thoughtfully onto his chest, oddly to the annoyance of the irritable Mr Justice Alderman.

'You parked the car outside on the lane, is that right?' he resumed. 'In advance of entering the defendant's property?'

'The both of us climbed up a tree round the back, and went in over the wall, the same way as I got my ass out, man!'

'Succinctly put,' Hillier said, half-choking. 'Let us consider the probability of the deceased's body being removed.'

'I never seen no dead body!'

'Not following the attempted robbery?'

'I seen a shitload of dead dudes when I worked in the Infirmary's morgue. But I dint see jack shit that night, man!'

Mr Justice Alderman furiously rapped his gavel and in no uncertain terms instructed the witness to curb his language. His stern dressing-down hit home with such venomous gusto as to reduce Chukka to a cowering wreck.

'Recommence, Mr Hillier!'

'Thank you, My Lord. So, concerning the removal of the cadaver. Did either you or Mr Mistry at any time activate the property's gates using an electronic security code, as shown in the photograph marked Exhibit G?'

'I don't know nothing about no electric gates!'

'Then please explain how the cadaver was removed from the property. Was it via the gates or by some other means?'

'What's one of them, man?'

'A human corpse, Mr Allen!' Hillier said, his brows raising in pure astonishment. 'The mortal remains of Amir Mistry!'

A collective gasp spread throughout the courtroom, by and by lapsing into a swell of lightly derisive sniggering, made worse by the witness's almost comical efforts to conceal his embarrassment behind his designer sunglasses.

'He was alive the last time I seen him.'

'Inside the grounds of the defendant's property?'

'Yeah, that's it, man!' Chukka grunted dismally. 'But when he started kicking off, I was outta there like a shot!'

'Kicking off, Mr Allen?'

'I clocked him through the window,' he blabbed. 'Smacking the old lady hard in the face, like some kind of fruit loop!'

'And so you did a runner?'

'I was over that wall like an Olympic high-jumper, man!'

'I'm truly grateful, Mr Allen,' Hillier said a touch hollowly, staring incredulously at him. 'Your witness, Mr Watts!'

The prosecutor waved his hand dismissively and cast a brief, contemptuous glance at the witness. 'I have no questions, My Lord,' he eventually stated, looking at the judge, who immediately called for an impromptu break.

*

Leicester Royal Infirmary

The TV screen of the new-fangled bedside unit stretched over Hackett's stomach in front of his face. His narrowed eyes were pinned to a windswept news reporter performing to camera from outside the Crown Court.

'*And with not enough new evidence brought to the table for the original verdict to be overturned, the picture once again looks bleak for the ill-starred rock musician JJ Gold.*'

'*So how much longer is the hearing expected to last, Phil?*' the studio anchorman asked, a tad indifferently.

'*We're edging ever closer to the closing arguments, Hugh. At a guess, roughly forty-eight hours.*'

'*After which the jury will retire to deliberate?*'

'*That's right, Hugh. I'll provide a further update later.*'

'*Okay, many thanks Phil!*'

The anchor withdrew and disinterestedly handed the reins to his loquacious co-host who, placing down her water tumbler and crossing her legs, welcomed a swarthy-looking celebrity chef onto the sofa beside her.

Hackett somehow forced his body upright, his trembling right forefinger jabbing furiously at the screen, much to the amazement of the young orderly who broke off from her routine and looked at him with utmost concern.

'Nuss... phone...caw... now!' he stammered.

'A call... is that it?' she latched on.

384

'Sh… eela!'

'Sheila? She'll be here any time soon!'

'*Now!*' he gasped. '*Caw, now!*'

At that moment an elderly patient appeared in the doorway. Naked from the waist down, a trail of loose stool stretched behind him to the foot of his bed, where his pyjama bottoms lay discarded in a soiled heap on the floor.

The nurse screeched aghast and spun on her heels before scurrying off as fast as her legs would carry her, totally oblivious to Hackett's blissful expression, his nose twitching and his voice able to articulate the word 'Shit!'

*

Crown Court

Behind the closed oak doors of Alderman's chambers a heated exchange ensued between the two advocates, inflamed by the line of argument spouting forth from Watts's lips, to the clear annoyance of the uptight Hillier. He pushed aside a cream cheese bagel, his nose put seriously out of joint by his opposite number's unshakeable intransigence in strongly opposing his eleventh-hour petition to recall a key witness to the stand.

'Ordinarily I'd have no problem with such a request,' Watts said loftily. 'But based purely on a hunch? Not likely!'

'Climb down off your high horse,' Hillier raged. 'The pathologist's modified findings prove he has a case to answer!'

Little by little he was inching towards the end of his tether; but, keeping his cool, he unzipped his briefcase to uncover a bundle of photos, duly dispatched in an untidy heap across a pile of papers covering the Judge's desktop.

'Huh, a scattering of immaterial images,' Watts huffed obstinately. 'Wholly irrelevant to the issue being tried.'

'Turner wilfully destroyed vital evidence, Rupert!' Hillier contended. 'The whole crux of the case lies with his testimony!'

'Calm yourselves, please!' Alderman interjected. 'Rupert, dear chap, the odds remain heavily stacked in your favour.'

'Which implies what, dear fellow?'

'That on the basis of the attester's previous testimony, which could hardly be described as conclusive, I hereby give my consent.'

EIGHTY-SIX

September 25th 2012

THE ENDLESS FLOW OF PEOPLE rushing back and forth resembled a large colony of giant rats, busily sidestepping a snarl of wheelchairs and mobility scooters, twisting and turning in the corridor like dodgems in a funfair.

A familiar cry caught Sheila's attention, and through the throng she caught sight of Sister Walsh. The nurse's text message remained fresh in her mind, received against all expectations midway through the weekly morning meeting, and greeted with a yelp of delight much to her colleagues' surprise:

> He walked the entire length of the hallway this morning on a pair of elbow crutches

'Pam!' she bawled out, weaving through the confusion. 'I dropped everything and got here as quickly as I could!'

'Go straight to the ICU, sweetie!' the Sister urged her. 'I need to pick up Dan's rehabilitation programme notes.'

They scampered in opposite directions, Sheila's nostrils pinching at the pungent odour of strong disinfectant. It was thankfully replaced by the soft fragrance of calla lilies as she veered off into the calmer side ward.

She quickly took off her coat and stretched up onto her toes to adjust the plastic air-vent, and then gazed across at Dan's motionless figure, oddly concealed beneath a humongous pile of pillows, sheets and blankets.

'Who's a clever boy then?' she said, to a strange silence. 'You could be walking unassisted in a matter of months!'

She moved in closer and patted her hands down on the bedclothes. Sensing something was off, she tugged back the sheets in haste and promptly threw a minor fit, fearfully tossing the bed linen onto the floor, tensed with terror, too afraid to scream.

'Sheila, sweetheart!' Sister Walsh said, edging through the door barely able to believe her eyes. 'What is it?'

'He's gone, Pam!'

'Gone? But that's impossible!'

'Alert the security staff, Pam. For God's sake!'

Within a short time a throng of nurses and guards cluttered the hall, each receiving their own set of instructions and scattering every which way to any exit route that could provide a possible means of escape.

'Check the loos in the outer lobby, while I contact the house supervisor,' Pam urged Sheila. 'He can't have got far!'

Sheila reacted quickly, slipping out through the double doors and following the corridor round to the right. Her hopes soared instantly as she caught sight of a red 'engaged' sign flipped across on the disabled toilet.

'Dan...? *Dan!*' she shrieked. 'If it's you, please say something!'

'How bloody rude. Go away!' a hoarse voice barked, thick with bitterness. 'Can't a man even take a dump in peace?'

She sank to her knees and clasped her hands together in pitiable despair, deaf to the flushing loo and opening of the door, succeeded by a cantankerous rant spouting from the lips of a dressing-gowned patient.

*

Thirty minutes later

Near the nurse's station a group of earnest-faced staff members animatedly put forward their own theories, eager to provide any information in regard to the whereabouts of the invalided detective.

'So he just nipped out for a little stroll, is that it?' the wrathful supervisor growled. 'Without any assistance whatsoever?'

'He left one crutch behind,' CNA Sarah astutely added. 'So someone entering the building must've helped him!'

'What about CCTV footage?' a young doctor chipped in.

The charge nurse nodded her head gravely. 'We already checked the immediate area, without any sightings.'

'Take Nurse Jeffries with you and check in all the surrounding wards, toilets and bathroom facilities,' the super barked. 'And Pam, put the police on standby, while I organise a workforce to search the public areas.'

'But he *is* the police, ma'am!'

'Good thinking. Which means they won't need a description!' she responded snappily. 'Notify them regardless of his profession!'

*

Hackett felt his exertions begin to catch up with him, and sorely in need of some respite propped himself up against a grease-spattered wall, his body camouflaged by an accumulation of wheelchairs and trolleys.

Notwithstanding his fatigue, he keenly observed a service elevator concealed behind a pillar in a shadowy recess. Its parting doors revealed a cleaning operative slothfully lugging a mop and bucket. In no apparent hurry she trudged slowly and miserably along the corridor, absent-mindedly leaving a slimy trail of soapsuds in her wake.

Slapping his face lightly to keep himself alert, Hackett painfully manoeuvred himself onto his backside while pondering his next move. An unexpected rush of blood coursing through his veins revitalised him sufficiently to slither across the floor in time to prevent the lift doors from reclosing. He hauled himself inside and hit the button for the lower ground floor.

The full weight of his exhaustion hit him suddenly, creeping over his entire body. Stubbornly, he fought to keep his heavy eyelids from closing, helped in no small measure by the short sharp clunk of the elevator's arrival.

He got down on all fours and crawled through a rubbish-strewn loading bay to a battered skip dumped close to the access road. Gripping both hands onto the sloped bin wall, he forced himself into an upright position.

Able to raise his head above the spiked metal fencing, he at once spotted a dark-complexioned cabbie parked in an emergency lay-by, peering back at him through the railings, his eyes filled with a look of deep concern.

'Are you okay, buddy?' he asked.

Hackett nodded affirmatively and gesticulated wildly towards the yellow cab. He was acutely aware that he needed to act fast, and that by now his disappearance must have set the alarm bells ringing.

'You need a taxi?'

'Mm!' he grunted, giving him the thumbs-up.

'Give me half a minute!'

He stopped momentarily to regain his breath, his knee joints locking in an oddly flexed position. Slowly but surely he again hoisted himself up, and one step at a time began to work his way along the high-sided skip.

Literally seconds later the cab screeched to a halt dangerously close to his feet. The young Asian sprang agilely out from the driver's side, seeking to prevent Hackett from toppling forward onto the bonnet.

'*Home... den wait!*' Dan laboriously articulated.

'Are you sure you don't need an ambulance?' the driver said mistrustfully, helping him into the cab. 'You look to be in pretty bad shape!'

'No!'

'It's your call, buddy,' the kid ceded. 'Where to?'

'*Cubby Feels... den... back town!*'

'Kirby Fields?' he said smartly. 'And then back into town!'

Still struggling to articulate, Hackett leaned forward to acknowledge him with a friendly pat on the shoulder, before he was jolted by a sudden burst of acceleration which sent him hurtling backwards onto the rear seat.

A short apology and a quick glance between them suggested he was okay. The mood lightened further at the sound of a golden oldie pumping out of the radio speakers which aptly summed up Dan's current debilitating limitations.

'*I'm in pieces, bits and pieces; I'm in pieces, bits and pieces.*'

'They're playing your song, buddy!' the driver chuckled. 'Hold on tight, and for heaven's sakes fasten your seatbelt!'

He skilfully weaved in and out of the traffic, abruptly braking to steer clear of a zigzagging motorcyclist and checking his rear-view mirror as the full weight of the passenger's body thudded into the back of his seat.

Hackett screamed out more in fright than pain. Forcibly pushing his paralysed right hand against the padded leather, he was instantly startled by a tingling sensation radiating from his shoulder down to the tips of his fingers.

'Sorry, buddy... nearly there!'

Too stunned to make a sound, Hackett's gaze fixed elatedly on his gently arcing fingers, miraculously flexing and balling into fists right in front of his eyes, rather as if he were a piano maestro warming up before a performance.

'Kirby Fields coming up. Which way?'

'*Lef... lef!*'

'Roger that. Left, and left again!' he said perceptively. 'And the house number?'

Hackett held all ten fingers aloft, the sudden movement of the car causing him to teeter sideways onto the seat. A little shaken, he managed to manoeuvre himself upright, more than happy to be back on familiar territory.

'Fourteen… twelve… whoa!' the cabbie deliberated, slowing almost to a halt. 'Bingo – Cameron's den, number ten!'

He pulled onto the drive behind Hackett's mud-spattered Golf, and scampered round to the rear to help him onto his feet, then guiding him one step at a time towards the cottage-style portico over the front door.

A well-aimed kick at a mound of decorative gravel brought a silvery Yale key glinting into view. It was quickly retrieved by the crouching Good Samaritan, who sprang to his feet and hunched forward to unlatch the door.

Once inside the cramped hallway Hackett gesticulated towards a set of keys dangling from a wooden holder affixed to the wall. He was eyed with deep suspicion by his new pal, who admonished him with a wag of his finger.

'Not dive… boot… oben!' Hackett slowly articulated.

'Open the boot. Is that it?'

'Mm… mm!'

Patently relieved, the young cabbie unhooked the zapper and raced outside. On lifting the Golf's rear hatch, his eyes fell upon a fluorescent yellow jerkin, its rear panel and shoulder straps marked with the words 'LEICESTERSHIRE POLICE'.

'You're a cop!' he said, startled.

'Uh… Get bag!'

Without further delay he pulled the black refuse sack from the boot, cautiously setting it down at the side of the cab, then twisted on his heels to dash back for Dan, who astonishingly hobbled towards him unaided.

'Do you need me to help you get dressed?'

Hackett shook his head and continued to stumble onwards, observed by the cabbie like a child taking its first steps. Almost at the car, his legs began to buckle, at which the hero of the hour rushed to save the day.

'Go… now!' Hackett urged. *'Plea!'*

The driver flashed him a trusting smile and stooped forward to help bundle him into the back seat of the cab. Then, checking the sun's direction, he raised his hands and dropped down to his knees, still as stone in whispering prayer.

'O Allah, grant this man the courage and strength to keep on going; and grant him from yourself mercy.'

EIGHTY-SEVEN

Leicester

THE THRUM OF HEAVY TRAFFIC tripping in and out of the busy city centre pulsated in the eardrums of a reflective James Hillier. He was poised by the window scanning a notepad full of bullet points, akin to an actor rehearsing his lines.

A cold, eerie chill all at once swept down his spine, filling him with a discomfiting sense of foreboding, yet somewhat peculiarly strengthening his resolve to go for broke and take the case by the scruff of the neck.

*

2.05p.m.
Crown Court

Hillier rose to his feet after the hour-long lunch recess, and psyched himself up for one final hurrah. His announcement drew gasps of disapproval from the majority of onlookers spread throughout the courtroom.

'I wish to recall Richard Turner to the stand!'

Every eye fixed upon Turner as he trudged reluctantly across the floor, pausing unnecessarily to adjust his tie. Eventually scaling the steps, he took a Bible in his right hand, and aloofly sat back in his seat, arms folded.

'Mr Turner,' Hillier began. 'In your previous testimony you alluded to the gates at the defendant's property opening and closing several times under your watch. Did you at any time desert your post in the observatory?'

'Only to replenish my coffee cup,' he lied.

'And, without going into too much detail, how powerful was the telescope that you trained on the property's driveway?'

'It's a Leica spotting scope with a 1600 millimetre lens. Reputedly the most powerful on the market!'

'And doubtless powerful enough to focus clearly on an electronic keypad situated roughly thirty metres away?'

Rather than fanning the flames with a vitriolic attack, Turner surprisingly remained cool and shot him an insolent, vindictive look, his teeth baring slightly when his lips parted to unleash a furious scathing reply.

'If you're implying I entered the property either before or after the killing took place, then you're well wide of the mark!'

'So you refute the suggestion that you made a note of the four-digit code required to gain access to the gated complex?'

'One hundred per cent!'

'Then perhaps you'd care to explain why your fingerprints were found all over the keypad's metallic outer casing?'

'The postman mistakenly dropped some of his mail into my letterbox,' he snarled. 'And I was simply being neighbourly!'

'How chivalrous of you,' Hillier said, throwing up his hands in frustration. 'I put it to you, Mr Turner, that not only did you make a note of the said code, you punched in the very same digits to access the accused's property!'

'That's utter nonsense!'

'Armed with an offensive weapon!' Hillier roared. 'Acquired from the macabre collection on display in your observatory!'

'You couldn't be further from the truth!'

'Let me remind you, you are still under oath,' Hillier retaliated, waiting like a hungry lion preparing to move in for the kill.

*

Leicestershire Police HQ

DCI Philpott paced the office floor, sickened with worry at the news of Hackett's inexplicable disappearance, disclosed in the middle of his coffee break courtesy of a sallow-faced investigating police constable.

'It seems that DS Hackett became rather animated during the coverage of the Gold trial on the early news, and took a particular dislike to a photograph of a key witness flashing up on the screen during the bulletin.'

'Thank you, Watkinson. That will be all.'

His throat felt dry. He knew he was feeling the strain, and waved his arms wildly through the window to catch Maureen's attention. Already sensing that all was not well, she scurried from her desk to heed his call.

'Is it true?' she asked. 'About Dan?'

'The gospel truth!' he said, glancing sternly in her direction. 'Get me the Officer in Charge at the city's crown court!'

*

Crown Court

Amid the cacophonous knell of the court's fire-alarm system, a rabble of panic-stricken bodies rushed to evacuate the building, thoughtlessly leaving the Honourable Mr Justice Alderman cut adrift in his elevated position.

Hillier became aware of the Judge's predicament and vaulted up onto the platform beneath him, then pressingly urged him to lean forward onto his shoulder before setting him down to usher him towards the main exit.

'Bless you, dear James. What a calamity!' he said, almost breathlessly. 'And coming at such an untimely moment!'

'Indeed, Hans,' Hillier reflected. 'This case seems to have left me battered and bruised, both mentally and physically!'

'All is not lost,' Alderman said, wagging a finger in his face. 'My instincts tell me you're barking up the right tree!'

'Hacking at a rotten branch I fear, trying to convince the jury,' Hillier retorted.

He was interrupted by a blaring announcement:

'Apologies for the interruption, ladies and gentlemen, which we now understand was due to an intermittent fault in the building's fire detection system!'

He graciously took the Judge's arm and led him back to the open fire door, where waiting at the top of the stairs a grovelling court bailiff intervened to take up the reins. His spirits were strangely lifted by Alderman's words of encouragement.

EIGHTY-EIGHT

HALF DEAD TO THE WORLD, Hackett lay sprawled out across the back seat, somewhat discomfited by the young cabbie's grim-faced expression fresh from slamming down the boot lid and bouncing into the driver's seat.

'*You okay?*' he mouthed vaguely.

'My sweatshirt got snagged on something sharp!' the young man grumbled. 'Pardon my French, but what the fuck is that thing?'

'*Bag?*' Hackett asked, his eyes wide.

'Damn right!' the cabbie said agitatedly. 'I caught a glimpse of the bloodstained handle sticking out of the polythene covering!'

'*Ne'er mind... it okay!*'

'You're the boss... Where to next?'

'*Cown Cut... Jay... Jay!*' Hackett articulated with some difficulty.

'You got me this time, buddy,' the driver smiled. Something registered in his mind. 'Wait a sec... did you say JJ?'

'*Tile!*' Hackett mumbled, frantic.

'JJ the rock star? The retrial?' he said, swallowing hard and slamming the gearstick into first. 'Brace yourself, buddy!'

*

Crown Court

'All rise! This court is now in session, the Honourable Mr Justice H. Alderman presiding,' the bailiff announced in a haughty tone, eager to get the disrupted session under way. 'Everyone please be seated.'

'Good afternoon, ladies and gentlemen,' Alderman cordially bade. 'I thank every one of you for your understanding... Mr Hillier?'

'And so, Mr Turner, picking up where we left off... I broached the possibility of a second act of unlawful entry to the defendant's property,' he resumed, confidently. 'Which you dismissed out of hand as "utter nonsense".'

'I did indeed!' Turner brazenly replied.

'Then let me put it to you this way: did you by way of deception obtain the electronic passcode to your idol's home?'

'My "idol"? Huh! Get your facts right!'

'Are you the same Richard Turner who received a hospital visit from your self-confessed hero in 2003?'

'I was seriously concussed,' Turner said fictitiously. 'And in an effort to cover himself in glory he appeared at my bedside!'

The response left Hillier almost dumbfounded. Shaking his head in disbelief, he decided to let him stew for a while, deliberately sauntering back to study his notes, sufficiently to keep the whole room on tenterhooks.

'Did you live in close proximity to the defendant?' he took up again, completely unfazed. 'At two separate addresses?'

'Purely by coincidence,' Turner said, unconvincingly.

'Would you care to enlarge?'

'I moved offices with my employment.'

'But, Mr Turner, I have it on good authority that you requested a transfer from the Leicester office shortly after the accused vacated his city-centre apartment. Is that correct, or perhaps once more just a coincidence?'

'Whose authority?' he snapped.

'A Mr James Bradley,' Hillier slowly drawled, 'whose sworn affidavit can be found in a bundle on the defence table.'

'That fat idiot doesn't know his backside from his elbow!'

'You appear to see things from a different perspective than your former colleagues, who described your preoccupation with celebrity culture, and in particular the musician known as JJ Gold, as a worrisome distraction.'

'Tittle-tattle!' Turner said belligerently. 'I couldn't wait to get out of there!'

'Ah, so you did request a transfer?'

'Purely of my own volition!'

As Hillier's merciless examination continued a pall of uneasiness hung over the court, intensified by the sharpness of Turner's devious ripostes, put forward in such a manner as to raise doubt in the minds of the rapt jurors.

'Mr Turner, I again put to you that you unlawfully entered the defendant's property during the aftermath of the incident in question, where you subsequently discovered the body of a man you believed to be dead!'

'You have no evidence to support these allegations!'

'A forced lock on the woodshed to the side of the house,' Hillier hit back. 'Which once again bore your fingerprints!'

'Hogwash!' Turner said defiantly.

'And moreover, upon losing your nerve as the corpse began to stir, you took matters into your own hands,' Hillier said, approaching the dock like an animal moving in for the kill. 'And bludgeoned Amir Mistry to death!'

A collective intake of breath circulated around the courtroom, as those present watched the witness intently, awaiting his response.

At that point a quite extraordinary and unexpected intrusion brought the proceedings to a startling halt.

Every head turned towards the entrance, from where a cudgel-wielding maniac lurched perilously in the direction of the witness stand, hotly pursued by a dusky-skinned accomplice and flanked by a unit of uniformed officers.

'*Stop!* This man is a police officer!' the plucky Asian cried.

All at once Hackett's feet disappeared from under him, his arms thrusting forward to send the terrifying spiked bastinado thudding into the bench's panelled façade.

The court bailiff screamed out in terror and, in moving to protect the Judge, collided with the witness who, quick to take advantage of the ensuing pandemonium, had fled the stand and was peeling off towards the jurors' exit.

'Seize that man!' the Judge bawled. His call appeared to fall on deaf ears, until leaping from underneath him like a karate black belt, the cabbie sent his extended right leg smashing brutally against the side of Turner's jawbone.

In the central aisle close to the prosecution's table a pile of writhing bodies pinned the intruder spreadeagled to the floor, observed in horror by the slack-jawed Hillier.

'Unhand that man at once,' he thundered, weighing in, clenched fists flailing, to try and break up the melee. Meanwhile the petrified cabbie crashed onto his knees and grabbed at Dan's wrist to check for a pulse.

'Somebody please call an ambulance, *now!*' he screeched, finding Dan's skin cold to the touch. 'He's fading fast!'

Hillier switched on his phone and danced anxiously on the spot until the operator picked up. 'Ambulance. Crown Court, Wellington Street. Now!' he barked. His eyes were drawn to the murder weapon lying beneath the pews. 'Where the hell is Richard Turner? The witness on the stand – the true slaughterer?'

'He must've done a runner, sir,' a passing security guard informed him. 'While we were apprehending the interloper!'

'He was within your reach, yet you allowed him to escape?' he said, incensed. 'Don't just stand there – find him, you idiot!'

Adjacent to him the young Asian knelt by Hackett's recumbent body, the sockets of his eyes wet with tears. Tenderly, he caressed Hackett's icy hand, his gaze never straying from his face, deeply touched by his extraordinary courage.

'Keep fighting, my friend!' he spoke softly, gazing up to the heavens empty of hope, drained of every last drop of emotion.

*

Outside in the foyer the heavy footsteps of a backup alert force ground to an abrupt halt, their faces etched with disappointment at arriving on the scene too late to quell the riot emanating from the floor of Court Four.

Accompanied by a distraught-looking Sheila, DCI Philpott led the way through the busy main foyer, his eyes focusing on a gun-toting black baseball-capped cop purposefully strutting past him in the opposite direction.

'Officer – a moment of your time please. The name's Philpott… Detective Chief Inspector Matt Philpott to be precise.'

'How can I help you, sir?'

'Can you fill me in on what's been going on in there? I hear an axe-wielding madman tried to attack the judge!'

'Chinese whispers, sir. The truth is there's an injured detective flat out on the floor, who rose out of his hospital bed to unmask the true killer,' he startlingly unveiled. 'Excuse my language, but the man's a fucking hero, sir!'

'A detective! Did you get a name?'

'Afraid not, sir,' he responded, exhaling sharply. 'Though I suspect his name will soon be on everyone's lips!'

Philpott thanked him and spun round to face Sheila, who was already taking matters into her own hands by flitting off towards the court door. Just then he caught from the corner of his eye a shady-looking character limping across the lobby.

A gang of onrushing paramedics briefly obscured his view, but a second glance revealed a glimpse of Richard Turner, who was moving shiftily behind a giant vending machine while he hesitated to figure out an escape route down to the ground floor.

All at once he made a break for the main staircase and began descending the steps. His movements aroused the attention of a gum-chewing armed PC, who briefly wavered from his position outside the court's exit doors.

'*You!* Arrest that man!' Philpott roared, flashing his badge. 'And take him to a holding cell, where I'll deal with him later!'

The officer moved swiftly and in seconds flat had Turner pinned up against the wall, before tugging him aside to make way for a white-sheeted gurney rolling through the lift doors, accompanied by a group of EMTs and grievers.

'Hell no!' Philpott cried out in anguish and despair. His gaze fixed on the inconsolable Sheila, her head and shoulders nestled against the chest of a swarthy stranger, an indescribable pain pervading her heart.

His strength deserting him in one final selfless act, Detective Sergeant Daniel Hackett had uttered his last breath.

EIGHTY-NINE

September 26ᵗʰ 2012

IT HAD BEEN a fitful night's sleep for Hillier, finally curtailed at the crack of dawn by a call from an associate at the Complex Casework Unit. Traipsing downstairs he wearily waited for the kettle to boil and pored over an in-depth forensic report, produced upon request at the eleventh hour by a crack team of DNA analysts.

The clatter of the letterbox jolted him back to full awareness. With the toe of his shoe he sifted through the pile of bills and junk mail littering the doormat to uncover the morning broadsheet's headline.

Luckless white knight makes final stand
Rock star retrial takes unexpected tragic twist

The accompanying sob story almost moved him to tears. It was recounted in heartrending fashion below a collage of deeply poignant images, mostly centred on the lion-hearted cop posing arm-in-arm with his smiling fiancée.

His thoughts harked back to his father, riddled with lung cancer, lying in a hospital bed. 'Get a grip on yourself,' he'd said, noticing his son's tears streaming down his face – advice he'd do well to heed now.

He opened the window to breathe in some fresh air, and found himself warmed by a short burst of sunlight upon his forehead, its rays reflecting off the marble worktops to imbue him with the promise of a brighter day ahead.

*

Behind the towering walls of the prison building a melancholy dawn chorus echoed upward to the topmost landing, spilling into the clammy lock-ups where the inmates gradually stirred into life.

Sparked by the plucked strings of a solitary ukulele, Jon's modulating tones purred achingly into the drab silence, ebbing and flowing like smoke rings in the air, and falling captivatingly on the ears of those listening in.

'And so, by now you know, that trouble will find me wherever I may go
But to leave without a word, let alone a kiss goodbye
A nagging pain, will we ever say hello again
Maybe you're more trouble than you're worth, but I will travel this earth
Until I find you.'

A series of fingerpicked triplets tearing up and down the fretboard further showcased Jon's uncanny ability. The sound was interspersed with the thud of boots on the stairs, drawing ever closer to Jon's cell to cut short the impulsive performance.

'Tear down these walls that quell a million cries
The impassable barriers that shut out every new sunrise.'

As he paused in the doorway ready to let rip, SO Iain Harrison's words trapped in his throat, his ears tuning to the captivating falsetto finale soaring effortlessly up to the rafters of the cavernous main wing.

Abruptly, the music stopped. Perhaps predictably it prompted a deafening roar, amplified a hundredfold by the clatter of tea mugs clanking incessantly in appreciation. The ruckus was sufficient to rouse Harrison from his dreamy abstraction.

'Okay, show's over, you lot!' he shouted hoarsely, reverting to character as he acknowledged the governor's presence. 'Calm down, every single one of you, and let Mr Batty speak, you ignorant rabble!'

'We want more... we want more!' the collective murmur began to escalate, merging into one tumultuous uproar of steadily increasing intensity, whilst ultimately drowning out the supervisor's apoplectic tirade.

'Quiet chaps, *please!*' the governor bellowed, his hands raised pleading for calm. 'Unlike our self-confessed Susan Boyle fan, Mr Harrison, I pride myself on being able to appreciate real talent when I hear it!'

The whole place rang with derisive cheers and laughter, much to the embarrassment of the incredulous SO, who looked daggers at his senior, clearly taking deep exception to his attempts to openly ridicule him.

'Shut it!' he snapped viciously, his words swallowed by the pandemonium erupting all around him. 'And I mean *now!*'

'Men... settle down,' the governor took up. 'In light of yesterday's unfortunate events at the city's Crown Courthouse, our incumbent minstrel has a more pressing engagement, for which he urgently needs to smarten himself.'

'Kick their arses, Jonny boy!' a chirpy cockney voice yawped. It sparked a spate of similarly raucous good-luck cries from every which way as, duffel bag in hand, Jon skipped down the steps flanked by the governor and SO.

'Goodbye JJ, goodbye... goodbye JJ, goodbye,' a solitary lag's voice echoed into the stairwell, sung to the tune of Ruby Murray's timeless pop song.* Pretty soon it was boosted by a near four-hundred-strong male voice choir:

'Goodbye JJ, goodbye... Goodbye JJ, goodbye.

We'll see you again, but we don't know when.

Goodbye JJ, goodbye.'

'I'll be back, lads... one way or another!' Jon shouted, wiping the tears from his eyes.

All at once his mind filled with an image of the late Johnny Cash's legendary San Quentin concert. 'Governor Batty? I've got an idea... What if...?'

*

11.20a.m. – final morning
Leicester Crown Court

'Please be upstanding,' the court usher announced, rising from his pew to cue the arrival of the crookbacked judge, followed not far behind by the animated counsellors, their heads close together in deep conversation.

'Be seated,' Alderman opened. 'Ladies and gentlemen, further to the tragic events witnessed in this courtroom yesterday, I firstly on behalf of all those present wish to express my deepest sympathy to the nearest and dearest of Detective Sergeant Daniel Hackett, to whom the court owes an enormous debt of gratitude.'

'Hear, hear!' the rapt gathering concurred.

'The detective's complete disregard for his own pain and injuries went above and beyond the call of duty, motivated by his selfless determination to uncover a key piece of evidence relative to the outcome of this case.'

Emotion croaking in his throat, Alderman sat back in his chair to take a moment's respite. His thumb and forefinger tugged lightly at a wad of documents crucial to the final result, tucked inside a loose-leaf folder.

'This morning I received an amended report from the senior forensic pathologist acting on behalf of the defence, which by means of scrupulous

---

* 'Goodbye Jimmy, Goodbye' by Ruby Murray/Kathy Linden (1959)

DNA testing proves beyond all reasonable doubt the cause of death occasioned on the night of November eleventh, 2005. Upon further scrutiny of the findings together with the prosecutor and defence counsel in my chambers prior to this session, I have determined to accept a proposal put forward by the learned Mr Watts, who has agreed to drop the prosecution.'

A collective gasp of astonishment spread across the courtroom floor, amid the tap-tap-tap of fingers on the assembled press's laptops, relaying at lightning speed their own version of the sensational breaking news.

'Ladies and gentlemen of the jury, you are dismissed forthwith. I thank you all, not only for your time but your invaluable service,' Alderman continued, perceiving a sense of disappointment amongst the departing panellists.

In summary he turned to address Watts; and, alluding to a statement regarding the possibility of dropping the charges from murder to a count of aggravated assault, asked: 'Do you need more time to reconsider your position?'

'My Lord, I move to acquit the defendant on the grounds of the information set out in the report received this morning,' he conceded, bowing out with the utmost grace. 'The prosecution wishes to rest its case!'

PART FOUR

NINETY

October 2012
Melbourne, Australia

HER STYLISH RAY-BAN SHADES perched atop her perspiring forehead, Agnes gazed in admiration at Oz's progressive 'Garden City', blown away by the diversity of sports facilities shimmering beneath her in the scorching heat.

A sudden twist to cling on to the cone of her fast-melting ice cream diverted her gaze towards the imposing, state-of-the-art Convention Centre where, ensconced in the main exhibition hall, Eamon Duffy was whiling away the hours attending a world conference on breeding endangered species in captivity.

She strolled along the promenade to a small circular news kiosk, adorned from top to bottom with an array of glossy magazines displayed in wire racks amongst a selection of global daily rags.

'Do you sell pocket packs of tissues…? Anything'll do,' Aggie asked. As she was licking the sticky tips of her fingers clean, her attention was drawn to a bold headline splashed in heavy type across the *Herald Sun*'s front page:

GOLD RUSH
Ex-con rock star's
whistle-stop tour dates
sell out in thirty seconds

'A dollar please, possum,' the vendor pulled her up. 'For the Kleenex?'

'Sorry. Yes… I was distracted!'

'You want the paper too?' he asked, noting her flushed expression. 'And how's about a bottle of water, on the house?'

'How sweet, but it's really not necessary!'

'You need to stay hydrated, sweetie,' he warned her with a semi-playful wink. 'It's an absolute stinker out there!'

A skip and a jump away, an elderly couple were just leaving a riverside bench, bathed in the shade of a high-rise building. It was snapped up in a nanosecond by the fatigued Agnes, who parked her curvy rear and unfurled the paper.

A rogue tear escaping from her chin formed a light smudge in among the sooty newsprint. Alongside the article, as if staring longingly into her saddened brown eyes, a recent mugshot of a clean-shaven Jon took centre stage.

'You lost weight, my love,' she muttered to herself, scrutinising the accompanying hot-off-the-presses announcement:

FRI DEC 14th SUNCORP STADIUM, BRISBANE – **SOLD OUT**
SAT DEC 15th ALLIANZ STADIUM, SYDNEY – **SOLD OUT**
SUN DEC 16th DOCKLANDS STADIUM, MELBOURNE – **SOLD OUT**

'Do you mind if I join you, poppet?' a kindly-faced woman of the cloth enquired as she shuffled her backside along the wooden seat, aware of Agnes's sorrowful disposition. 'Phew, it's a hot one. Are you suffering, my dear?'

'That's one way of putting it!'

'Far be it from me to interfere, but if you need a shoulder to cry on, look no further,' the woman said, taking hold of her hand.

'It's just… I'm punishing myself for deserting the one person who ever truly meant the world to me!' Aggie opened up, her head hanging pensively on her heaving bosom, her tears creating small rivulets on her cheeks.

'The path of love can be long and tortuous, my dear, never trodden devoid of snares and pitfalls,' the woman poeticised, taking a slow, deep breath. 'You must have faith to overcome the obstacles that confront you.'

'He's coming to Melbourne,' Aggie sighed, again glancing down at the double page. 'In just a matter of weeks!'

'I know. Isn't it exciting?' the priestess enthused. 'Are you a fan?'

'Huh, he's touched the hearts of millions the world over,' Aggie replied, staring off into space. 'Mine is but one!'

'All aflutter like the wings of a hummingbird… isn't that what the song says?'

'Aflutter! Broken into little pieces, more like!' Aggie said gloomily. Her lips parted to mouth her favourite tune:

'If only you'd believe in you, the way that I believe in you; you'd look at me and say that everything will be okay!'

'How pretty! It isn't one I know,' the woman observed. 'Does it have a title?'

'"Song for Agnes".'

'How sweet. I'll put a search into iTunes.'

'He never recorded it,' Aggie sighed. Suddenly she found she was running short of breath, her chest heaving as if she were drowning.

The woman put an arm around her shoulders to try and comfort her, at the same time fumbling in her handbag for her phone before punching in three zeros. 'Ambulance please. Crown Promenade, in front of the Convention Centre!'

*

West Hampstead, London

'I could murder an Indian,' Jon said, polishing off the dregs of his third tankard of ale during an early-doors libation, hidden away in the wood-panelled snug of a rambunctious picture-postcard London pub.

'Don't look at me, I'm half-Pakistani!' Khalid joked, to an outbreak of bawdy laughter. 'We can send out for a takeaway?'

'The Viceroy!' CJ threw in, coming up for air from a frothy pint of Guinness. 'Just round the corner from the Tube!'

Khalid waved a schoolmasterly finger in their faces and reminded them both of the true purpose of the get-together, throwing in the terms 'Google Earth' and 'technophobes', to try to keep their minds focused.

'Lighten up, Khal!' Jon beseeched him, hands upturned, arms out-stretched. 'CJ and I only just fell off the wagon!'

'Do you want to find her?'

'But of course!' they said, almost in unison.

'I thought as much…now drink up!'

*

Their evening's entertainment put temporarily on hold, the men sat rapt in front of the oversized computer screen, taking it in turns to rotate the earth from top to bottom, before touching down on a map of Australia.

'Tap "Tasmania" into the search box,' Khalid urged Jon, offering his expert guidance. 'And drag the map downwards.'

'Got it!' Jon said animatedly. 'How do I zoom in?'

'Use the button on the right-hand side of the screen. There it is, Port Arthur prison. Now follow the south eastern coastline.'

406

Piece by piece the pixels merged to form a sharp and clear image, in seconds depicting an aerial shot of an idyllic horseshoe-shaped bay, its powdery white sand stretching from end to end in a haze of shimmering heat.

'That's the craziest thing I ever saw!' Jon whispered, his jaw dropping to the floor. 'Wineglass Bay... wow!'

*

A spicy interlude in the semi-plush surroundings of the Viceroy provided further food for thought, nestled around a circular table munching their way through an assortment of tandoori specialities fit for a maharajah.

'It's still a long shot,' Khal mumbled, quickly adding a note of caution. 'There's every chance they were sightseeing.'

'You said the car was a banger,' Jon pointed out, loudly crunching into a poppadum. 'So it wouldn't have been rented.'

'An old Range Rover, caked in mud,' CJ said, with his mouth full. 'A workhorse, from a rural area, at a guess.'

They polished off the remnants on their plates and relocated to another hostelry where, eyes squinting in the dim light of the lounge bar, they took turns to pore over a map displayed on Khalid's iPhone.

'So if the island's population is anything to go by, there's roughly a one in half a million chance of finding her!'

'Don't be so negative, Jon,' Khal said sternly. 'Check the area between Hobart and the bay, there'll be farms dotted everywhere.'

'Maybe she got hitched, to a gentleman farmer?'

'She wouldn't have – couldn't have!' Khalid said, his mouth agape. 'Not even on the rebound!'

Jon slid his backside along the padded bench seat and slumped over a separate table, supping his beer reflectively. Already it seemed as if he was on the verge of giving up, borne out by his increasingly dejected tone.

'All I ever wanted was for her to be happy,' he said, heartbreakingly. 'Even if that happiness doesn't include me.'

'Don't give up, Jonny boy, don't even think about it!' CJ said, casting him an evil eye. 'She's somewhere out there!'

NINETY-ONE

SOMEWHAT COERCED INTO attending a reunion with chief exec Miles Templeton, Jon reluctantly swung by his record company's plush West End offices. Having greeted him overzealously with man-hugs and sloppy kisses, the gushing reception committee escorted him up to the penthouse suite perched on the top floor.

'What an amazing view!' Jon gasped, peering over the city's rooftops. 'You must be shifting some serious units!'

'Welcome back to civilisation, son!' Templeton replied, grabbing a magnum of Bollinger from his customised wine-cooler.

'Heaven forbid, Miles, not at this hour!' Jon crustily declined. 'Can't we just cut the crap and get down to business?'

'And spurn a flute of God's nectar? Get your shit together, son. I missed you, much more than you could ever imagine!'

'I'm truly touched, Miles!' Jon said, sarcastically.

Templeton cut straight to the chase and broached the subject of new material. 'You must've written some cracking tunes while you were caged up,' he said with great enthusiasm, urging him to get back into the studio.

'I've booked some time at Metropolis next week, to record two new concept songs with a string quartet I came across,' Jon unveiled. 'After that I go into rehearsal with the band ahead of the Australian mini-tour.'

'Speaking of which, you'll need to reschedule.'

'No way, Miles!'

'Everyone wants a piece of you, son; we received an approach from NBC over in New York City. They're looking to record an in-depth profile on your life. Once it hits the screens you'll be the hottest property on the planet!'

'But I already postponed twice!'

'Delay it again!'

Tentatively, Jon referred to the matter of the contract extension that landed under his lawyer's nose just hours after his release, which remained on his desk unsigned, awaiting the last dotted i's and crossed t's.

'Never mind the agreement. Think of the fans!' Templeton said cunningly. 'Don't you think they waited long enough?'

'I'm damaged goods, Miles. I just spent a year of my life cooped up in a box, so why would I want to commit to another six-month stretch climbing up the walls of a studio? I need time to reset my boundaries, to heal!'

Templeton scratched his chin thoughtfully and sank into his chair, his sideways glance examining the strain etched in Jon's hollow cheekbones, camouflaging the invisible battle-scars of loss, heartbreak and incarceration.

'Put the album on hold!'

Jon fell silent, and heedless of his words shot Miles a troubled look. Uncharacteristically, the exec kept his cool and allowed Jon to have his say, well aware that to push him too far may ultimately prove counterproductive.

'Music's been the dominant force in my life for as long as I can remember. I never once made time for anything or anyone, not until I met a woman different from any human being I'd ever known. And what did I do?'

'You messed up big time!'

'I lost my mind and pushed her away!' he reflected agonisingly. 'Out of my life and into someone else's arms!'

'Tell me about the new project,' Miles said, subtly changing the subject. 'And we can stick out a press release to tide us over.'

Templeton summoned PA Jenny, who entered the room with a swagger and greeted Jon with a hug and a kiss, instantly rekindling memories of a steamy one-night stand some years previously tucked up in a Cannes hotel.

'You look amazing, Jen!'

'You don't look so bad yourself!' she said, sultrily. 'What is it, boss?'

'Jot down the details of Jon's latest masterpiece, honey!' Miles said snappily. 'And get a statement out ASAP!'

*

'Let's go through it once more; three new songs comprising a mini-album, including your own take on Vivaldi's Lute Concerto, featuring the London Symphony Orchestra. Are you able to confirm the other two titles?'

'Yep, "Song for Agnes" and "The Room Downstairs".'

'Wait a minute!' Jenny paused, wildly flicking her finger across the screen of her iPad. 'Did you say "Song for Agnes"?'

'Uh-huh... why, what's up?'

'We received a long-distance call listed at the crack of dawn from the Reverend Dorothy Smith of the Anglican Diocese in Melbourne, Australia. She mentioned something about a chance meeting with a lady named Agnes!'

'Agnes Ryan?' Jon said, bolting upright.

'She asked if a tune entitled "Song for Agnes" by JJ Gold existed. I fobbed her off, assuming it to be a crank call!'

As if in a trance he stopped to collect his thoughts, the colour slowly returning to his face. From the bird's-eye view he watched a jet plane soar above the London skyline, and knew she was out there waiting for him.

'No ifs, no buts. I'm going to Australia!'

NINETY-TWO

December 2012
Docklands Stadium, Melbourne

THE OPENING BARS of the explosive introductory fanfare were greeted by a tumultuous roar, modulating into a prolonged chant of 'J-J... J-J... J-J... J-J,' rising up in the twilight's semi-darkness to add to the feeling of anticipation.

Her face and arms deeply tanned following a period of missionary work in Moorea, French Polynesia, collarless cleric Dorothy Smith clung tightly on to loving hubby Joe, engulfed by the enthusiastic, fist-pumping fifty-thousand-plus throng, stretching up onto their tiptoes to catch the first glimpse of the emancipated hero.

'Take a look through my binoculars and you'll see Stef crouched down among the medics gathered by the brow of the stage,' Joe observed, proudly aiming a finger in the direction of his son. 'He's a jammy so-and-so!'

The temperature soared to a stifling forty degrees centigrade, the excitement rising to a near fever pitch. A pair of giant Super Troupers flooded the stage in a garish blaze of light, at last picking out JJ's lithesome figure.

'I am a vagabond, driftwood, no good... I am a vagabond and no one knows me,' he belted out, feeding off the energy of the sweat-soaked crowd, accentuating each memorable line in vigorous, joyous delirium.

Back-to-back megahits resounded into the star-studded blackness, complemented by a rhythmic blitz of laser beams dancing zigzag patterns above the animated throng, cooled by the contents of two giant water cannons.

'Hey all you vagabonds, how's it going?' Jon roared to a deafening kickback, removing his Fender Telecaster to slurp from a plastic Evian bottle, ahead of emptying the remainder over his shaggy blonde locks.

The mesmerised audience pushed forward at every opportunity, screaming out their approval at each gyration of his hips. Soft-pedalling, he strapped on his best-loved Martin guitar and wandered casually back to the mic.

'Here's a couple of lovey-dovey new tunes I wrote during a sabbatical I took in the Scottish Highlands a while back!'

A respectful hush greeted an improvised passage of skilful fingerpicking, each plucked harmonic floating enchantingly into the balmy air, prompting a majority of the onlookers to lock into a far-reaching embrace.

'We all need someone to cling to, even my tour-manager, Dingo! But who'd want to cuddle an ugly brute like him?' Jon snickered, reacting in kind to a middle-fingered response from the wings. 'But I guess the only way I can reach out and touch someone is through the words of a song. This tune's called "Song for Agnes"!'

'Oh, dear God!' Dottie exclaimed out of nowhere. 'It was him…! He came to St Paul's, trying to track me down!'

'Who, sweetheart?' Joe asked, deeply concerned.

'Him!' she said, pointing. 'The poor young thing I met at the promenade. How could I ever have doubted her?'

'Dottie, what's got into you?'

'He's singing about her – listen to the lyrics!' she said bluntly. 'I have to get backstage, to get an urgent message to him!'

'Are you being serious?'

'Deadly, my love!'

*

As Dottie regained consciousness stretched out on a makeshift gurney, her eyes were able to make out the kindly features of her stepson's face. Carefully Stefan helped her into a seated position and tilted a plastic beaker towards her lips.

'You've been out cold for twenty minutes!'

'Where are we?' she asked confusedly. 'Is the concert over?'

'We're in a sector allocated to the St John's staff,' he explained. 'JJ's playing his third and final encore as we speak.'

She tugged lightly at the sweat-soaked clothing stuck to her body like a second skin and then gamely lowered her feet to the floor. Still feeling more than a little disoriented she steadied herself with the help of Stefan's arm.

'Did you get to meet him?'

'I patched up a blister on his thumb on the opening night in Brisbane,' he said proudly. 'We got on like a house on fire!'

'You lucky boy!'

'It's my job, Aunt Dottie... Dad mentioned something about passing a message to him? We can linger awhile in the corridor until he comes off, and who knows I may be able to catch his eye. If you feel up to it, that is?'

She nodded emphatically, her efforts to speak drowned out by the vociferous cheering of the ecstatic crowd, accompanied by the blast of fireworks erupting high in the sky to bring down the curtain in a rousing finale.

*

Ten minutes later

They skulked in the passageway at the rear of a large posse of photo-hungry paparazzi, half-blinded by a whirlwind of dust created by a gravity-defying police chopper hovering perilously close to the tunnel entrance.

Shortly afterwards Jon and his entourage strutted backstage, stopping to acknowledge a group of dallying dignitaries who temporarily delayed their getaway to sidle up next to him and pose for a handful of snapshots.

Amid a dazzling blaze of flashing cameras Stefan grabbed Dottie's hand and skirted around the crush of media people to where Jon was lingering for a few seconds prior to making a move towards the heavily guarded dressing room.

'How's the thumb, Mr Gold?'

'Stef, isn't it? Thanks to you the thumb's brand new!' Jon replied, shooting a smile at the puffed-out Dottie bringing up the rear. 'Give me five to towel off and come and join me for a beer – bring your Mum too!'

'I saw Agnes!' she blurted out, stopping him dead in his tracks. 'Here, in Melbourne, towards the end of October!'

Quick as lightning Dingo stepped out in front of her with the intention of blocking her path, his canoe-paddle-sized hands gently manhandling her to one side, under a large black shadow cast by his hulking, muscular frame.

'No, Dingo, let the lady speak!' Jon swiftly intervened. 'And you called my record company in London, is that right?'

'Yes, I'm so sorry!'

'Did she mention my name?' he asked, his face taut and anxious. 'How did she look...? Please tell me she was okay!'

Dottie's face took on the look of a troubled angel, her expression shifting to real concern. Tongue-tied, she tentatively reached out and clutched his hand, and drawing in a huge breath finally managed to find her voice.

'We chatted together, on a bench overlooking the river, until suddenly she began to struggle for breath,' she unfolded, hands flapping nervously. 'Forgive me, but I flew into a panic and called the emergency services!'

*

His right hand cupping a large gin and tonic, a sullen-faced Jon dallied pensively on his hotel-room balcony, gazing into an endless, glittering sky, repeating the cleric's unsettling tale over and over in his head:

'As I entered the hospital the next day, I caught sight of Agnes being ushered into a cab under the watchful gaze of the charge nurse who'd admitted her. It appears her partner arrived late on the scene, before whisking her off to the airport to catch a flight to Hobart!'

He felt so close to her, and yet so far away, knowing that somewhere beyond a stretch of water she may be finding comfort in the arms of another man.

All at once he became aware of a hulking presence behind him in the room.

'Shit, Dingo, you gave me a start!'

'You didn't answer,' he grunted. 'So I borrowed a pass key.'

'You look all hot and bothered… what's up?'

'The post-tour festivities are in full swing downstairs,' he said, clapping a hand on Jon's shoulder. 'With one notable exception!'

'All that backslapping… I'm just not in the mood.'

In spite of their widely differing personalities, over the past weeks they'd forged an unusually strong bond, born out of a deep appreciation for one another, complemented by an equally sarcastic sense of humour.

'Some cocky English bastard was asking after you,' Dingo said, slightly discomfited. 'He tried to gatecrash the party.'

'Did he give you a name?'

'TJ… or was it CJ?'

'You're shitting me…! Which crew member knocked him back?'

'Feedback Phil, the monitor engineer.'

Jon let out a wicked guffaw, and undergoing a sudden change of heart disappeared into the bathroom to sluice himself down before slipping into his jeans and flip-flops and turning towards Dingo with upturned palms.

'How do I look?'

'Like a nob,' Dingo said disparagingly. 'Now get your scraggy ass downstairs!'

At the bottom of the stairs they took a short cut across the lobby. From a seat close to the function room, CJ sprang to his feet and rushed towards Jon, oddly planting a sharp wet kiss right in the middle of his forehead.

'You managed to get a visa…! When did you arrive…? Did you make it to the gig…? Shit, why didn't you call me?' Jon asked, breathlessly.

'The probation service granted me special permission to travel, on account of Gordon's ongoing health issues!'

Unable to hear themselves talk above the DJ's patter, they relocated to a quiet corner on the mezzanine level. As they cackled like hens over a bottle of Shiraz, CJ switched gears to put forward an unexpected proposition.

'What's on your agenda tomorrow?'

'A full day just chilling out and relaxing,' Jon said, letting loose a huge sigh. 'Did you have something else in mind?'

'A short hop across the Bass Strait!'

'To Tasmania?'

'Hobart. I took the liberty of reserving two seats!'

'You crafty son of a bitch!'

'Get ready for a bumpy ride,' CJ said, staring him in the eye. 'We're on a mission to find her, come hell or high water!'

*

Twelve hours later

A piercing announcement from the flight deck temporarily scuppered CJ's chances of narrowing down his search. His finger was tracing a detailed large-scale map, focused chiefly on the coastal region known as Freycinet.

'Good morning, ladies and gentlemen, this is the co-pilot speaking. I'm delighted to inform you that we've begun our descent into Hobart International Airport, and should be landing in approximately fifteen minutes.'

'We're almost there,' Jon said, lightly nudging him. 'Buckle up.'

'Khal texted me; there are just two Ryans on the island – a shopkeeper in Hobart and a chiropractor in Launceston.'

'Agnes Anonymous, the name tag on her hospital bed read,' Jon reflected. 'Omitting to mention her mystery man.'

'That's it!' CJ cried out, excitedly snapping his fingers. 'She was admitted to a hospital… was it the Royal Melbourne?'

'Yeah… that's the one.'

'Do you have any idea when?'

'A couple of months ago.'

'This could be just the break we need!'

The plane rocked and juddered on the eddying air currents and cut CJ short in mid-flow. Briefly perturbed, he gripped the armrests of his seat, then glanced across at Jon with a strange glow of satisfaction.

'Do you mind telling me what's going on?'

'Becky, my sister!' he said, euphorically. 'She worked at the RMH as a registrar, shortly after she arrived in Oz!'

'I'm at a complete loss!'

'Think about it,' CJ explained. 'Aggie's significant other must've accepted full responsibility for her early discharge.'

'And he most likely signed her release papers?'

'You got it in one!' he whooped, offering Jon a high five. 'I'll get Becky to do some digging the minute we arrive!'

NINETY-THREE

One week later
Freycinet Peninsula, Tasmania

UNDER THE SUMPTUOUS HUES of the eastern sky the craggy granite peaks stretched pink and grey down towards the lower ledge of the distant shore, where the foamy sapphire waters lapped enticingly into the silica sand.

Briefly taking time out to dote on the sweeping bird's-eye view, Jon's mind drifted, likening the mountain air to the surrounds of the Highland hideout he once shared with the woman he let slip through the cracks.

'Make haste, Jonny boy!' CJ bawled, forging relentlessly ahead. 'I'd like to check out Coles Bay before we call it quits!'

'My legs feel like lead weights!'

'A couple more miles, that's all,' he yelled back. 'Stick at it!'

Down in the adjacent valley an area of woodland loomed in the nearby distance, its tall she-oaks drooping as though encumbered by the sapping heat while casting shadows over an expanse of lush green grass.

'Can't we rest awhile in the shade of the trees?' Jon hollered, desperately. 'I can feel a blister developing on the back of my heel!'

CJ dropped his pace and, lingering for a second to feast his eyes on the panorama unfolding before him, began backtracking up the hill to where he had started down, conscious of Jon's slight hobble and waning determination.

'The scenery's to die for,' he said, stirringly.

'Isn't it just?'

'One last roll of the dice, yeah?' CJ said, urging him on. 'I can almost taste a cold beer slipping down my throat!'

Jon patted his shoulder and kicked forward. 'Let's do it!'

*

Coles Bay, Tasmania

Agnes fought back a giggling fit, sparked off by Eamon's risible efforts to erect a spindly-looking Christmas tree in the corner of his office, its threadbare branches sprouting out at an angle from a fire bucket filled with sand.

'Ea, what in tarnation are you doing?'

'Hi, Ag. I thought I'd make an effort this year.'

'A little late in the day, isn't it?'

'Better late than never, Ag!' he reflected. 'What've you got on today? Doubtless you'll be heading off to the beach?'

'First things first,' she said, raising a finger. 'I have a date with Percy Jarvis.'

'The farmer?' he answered, mystified.

'Yes, at eleven 'o' clock sharp.'

'He's older than time itself, Ag!' Eamon commented, exasperatedly trying to wrestle the tree into an upright position.

'I'm picking up the turkey, you numpty!'

'Silly me!'

He finally gave it up as a bad job, and lifting himself up leaned over his desk to grab the chirping phone. His expression softened at the sound of fiancée Priscilla's voice, calling to check the arrangements for the evening ahead.

'Prissy wants to know if you decided on a dress for tonight's knees-up?'

'A light green little number.'

'Hmm, nice. I'll tell her!'

'The colour of a gooseberry!' she tittered. 'And before you say anything, she's adorable. I'm truly happy for you both!'

An appreciative smile spread on his face. 'What are you like, Ag?' he said, with a good-natured shake of his head. 'Don't forget your sunscreen, and hat!'

*

The sound of a man's voice rumbling from behind a thicket of tangled branches startled Jon and CJ awake. Its slightly hostile tone emerged from an elderly hayseed, who expressed himself in a gruff Aussie accent.

'What are you pair of layabouts up to?' he grumbled, facing them down. 'Other, that is, than trespassing on my land?'

'Easy does it, old feller!' CJ retorted, springing agilely to his feet. 'It's a scorcher, and we needed to take a breather.'

'Sit yourself back down, son!' the rustic said, immediately alive to the torment in his eyes. 'I'm joshing with you boys!'

He stepped tentatively backward and produced a leather-covered hip flask from his rear pocket; and then, bending forward, joints cracking like the snapping of kindling, kindly offered them both a nip of home-distilled grog.

'Do you know a guy named Duffy who resides in these parts?' CJ asked. 'We've been hunting high and low for him.'

'Rory Macduff? The horse doctor?'

'Duffy... not Macduff!' Jon corrected him.

'His practice is on the edge of town,' the oldster said unmindfully. 'Overlooking the Great Oyster Bay.'

'And he's a vet, you say?' CJ said inquisitively.

'You got it, son.'

'Has he practised there for long?'

'Ten years. Maybe more.'

Their sagging spirits lifted tenfold by the fiery libation, Jon and CJ exchanged glances and stumbled back to their feet, their attempts to make tracks hampered by the man's playful and over-friendly sheepdog.

'Ah well, we'd best be on our way,' Jon said, taking pains to sidestep the mutt. 'And many thanks for the tipple!'

'My pleasure. Have yourselves a merry little Christmas!' the rustic said, throatily. 'Oh, and watch out for the Scottish lass on reception!'

'What was that?' CJ called back.

'Macduff's receptionist... she's a feisty little madam, if ever there was one!'

*

A little more optimistic after their short recess, a renewed surge of energy sped them both to an undulating coastal path. Winding their way up to a signposted observation point, they stopped once again to gaze down at the crescent-shaped bay.

All of a sudden a thought entered Jon's head.

'Rory Macduff!' he exclaimed.

'Huh? You lost me.'

'My Dad's old *Lion* annuals!'

'What the hell?'

'The comic-book superhero! Dad idolised Rory,' Jon gasped. 'The old boy back there would've been a similar age!'

'Enlighten me, please?'

'Macduff! It's most probably a nickname… for Duffy!'

'Holy shit!'

NINETY-FOUR

London, England

'I MUST SEND MY COMMISERATIONS to the smug Mr Cowell,' Miles Templeton said gloatingly, raising his glass aloft to toast JJ's chart-topping Christmas single. 'He'll be gutted we outstripped his latest talentless wonder!'

The celebratory chink of glasses momentarily eclipsed the outpourings of the notoriously foul-mouthed celebrity chef at another table, who was playing up to a rapt cluster of high-profile guests by turning the air blue.

'Where the fuck is the golden boy?' he ranted. 'I reserve the best fucking table in the house and he doesn't show up!'

'He sends his regards from Down Under!'

'Number fucking one, eh?' he said, referring to the chart-topping single 'Song for Agnes'. 'And who the fuck is Agnes?'

Not waiting for an answer, he redirected his attention to a Premier League footballer taking his seat at a nearby table, promptly greeting him with a further string of unnecessary F-words together with an over-the-top man hug.

'Michelin stars? The place should be X-rated!' Templeton quipped, to a roar of laughter. 'Thank fuck the food's top notch!'

*

Coles Bay, Tasmania

Her knees almost buckling from the weight, Aggie lugged the meaty eighteen-pound bird into the house and up onto the kitchen island, her movements carefully scrutinised by the ever-dependable home help, Manawa.

'Isn't she a beauty?' Agnes half-sputtered, rapidly running out of puff. 'Big enough to feed the whole town, I reckon!'

'A monster, Miss Agnes!' the char said, reaching up to grab a giant roasting tin from the top shelf. 'Fit for a king!'

'Run along home now, Manny!' Agnes urged, rooting inside her handbag. 'Have a wonderful day with your family tomorrow!'

'And you, Miss Agnes. Are you off to the beach?'

'How did you guess?' she laughed, slipping on her floppy hat and shades. 'I hope Santa brings you everything you wish for!'

*

They came to an unavoidable halt to briefly gather their bearings, then decided in their wisdom to split up and circumnavigate the area, Jon opting to take the downward path in the direction of Wineglass Bay. Faced with the steeper, more tortuous route, CJ took off towards the minuscule town centre.

Beads of sweat forming on his forehead trickled in rivulets into his dazzled eyes, obscuring his view of a bespectacled, sylphlike woman tripping furtively over the pedestrian crossing into an unseen passageway.

He lifted his shirt to mop his brow and then continued along the pavement, soon spotting a pair of hobnailed boots sticking out from beneath a weathered jalopy.

'Excuse me, mate,' he said amicably, dropping onto his knees. 'I can see you're busy, but I'm looking for the veterinary surgery?'

'Hang on a tick!' a high-pitched twang sounded. A moment later, its owner's body slid into view attached to an under-car creeper.

CJ found himself confronted by a tomboyish grease monkey, rubbing at her grubby hands with a filthy scrap of rag, looking oddly winsome in a Metallica T-shirt and cut-off denim shorts.

'Oops, I didn't mean to be rude,' he said apologetically.

'No worries!' she laughed. 'Just follow the road round for roughly half a mile and you'll see the practice on the right.'

'Thanks a million!' he said enthusiastically.

Just then he froze to the spot to tune into the song blaring out of the car radio:

'And so this is Christmas, and what have you done?
Another year over, a new one just begun."

'John Lennon… "Happy Christmas (War is Over)"!' he cooed, tunelessly mouthing the lyrics. 'What a timeless classic!'

'The best Chrissie tune ever!' she said glowingly. 'So what's the problem? A horse, maybe a dog, or a pet bandicoot?'

---

* 'Happy Xmas (War is Over)' by John Lennon and Yoko Ono/Plastic Ono Band – 1971/72

'A bandy what?' CJ asked, looking perplexed.

'You're looking for the vet, right?'

'Absolutely!'

'Eamon Duffy, yeah?' she urged. 'Who I hear is about to pop the question, if the moment presents itself tonight!'

'To whom?' he gasped.

'Priscilla!' she answered. 'My big sister!'

His mouth dropped agape, the realisation hitting him with the impact of a hammer blow. He felt helpless and slumped forward to prop himself up against the bonnet, his head lifting to holler out to the heavens.

'Agnes, where the hell did you go?'

'Eamon's half-sister?' she asked, eyes narrowing. 'She ducked into the alley across the way, around five minutes ago!'

'Agnes Ryan?' he said, gasping. 'Brunette, attractive, big brown sparkling eyes?'

'Sounds like a fair description to me!'

Unable to help himself, he grabbed her and dragged her towards him, unthinkingly planting a kiss onto her grime-covered forehead before darting back across the street and disappearing from sight into the alley.

'You're amazing!' he called back.

She froze, startled beyond words. Something about him sent her pulse into overdrive, as if stirring some long-lost emotion inside her. She felt the urge to cry out, but her throat tightened; and in a trice he was gone.

NINETY-FIVE

Wineglass Bay, Tasmania

THE TANGY AROMA of barbecued meat wafted aimlessly into the cloudless sky, tickling the noses of the scores of reunited kith and kin taking turns in observing their sand-dusted children frolicking excitedly at the water's edge.

'Mummy?' a cute pigtailed tot asked, splashing her awake with the contents of her bucket. 'Where is Santa now?'

'Probably resting in his grotto far away in the North Pole, while his little helpers load his sleigh for the long night ahead!'

'What if he oversleeps, like Daddy?'

'He won't, darling!' she smiled, again dozing off.

Her back propped up against a misshapen hummock to the front of a sweep of shingle stretching into the rocks, Agnes whiled away her time leafing through a trashy bestseller, leaving off for a moment to dote upon a toddling twosome dallying hand-in-hand just like marzipan miniatures on top of a wedding cake.

Nearer to the shoreline a recumbent meat-market of reddening bodies shimmered lifelessly in the blurry haze, roasting under the sun's penetrating rays oblivious to the spectacle about to play out in front of them.

No one knew what provoked the lonesome brunette into straying barefoot from her regular post, lured for reasons unknown into a disorganised huddle of oil-coated merrymakers, where she stood transfixed. As if in a wonderful dream, a sea-spattered Adonis dug his heels into the softened sand and powered his way towards her, hampered only by a caboodle of youngsters participating in a game of beach volleyball.

On the clifftop path CJ skidded over an assault course of jutting rocks and tree roots to gradually make his way down the hazardous descent, then halted to focus on the seashore below, as his lips arced into a contented smile.

Reminiscent of a love scene on the set of a romantic movie, Agnes's airborne limbs wrapped tightly around Jon's torso, pinning him to the sand in a joyful heap, her lips smothering his cheeks with a flurry of kisses.

'I've searched heaven and earth to find you!' he whispered tremblingly. 'Life's so meaningless and empty without you!'

'I thought you'd never come,' she sighed, distracted by a voice echoing from the hillside. 'This can't be true!'

'Jon...! Aggie!'

She glanced back, and swiftly rolling onto her knees caught sight of a familiar-looking shaven-headed figure gesticulating from the steps, his right fist pumping jubilantly in the air, before he sped off in the opposite direction.

'CJ! He's here?'

'As large as life!' he said, slightly puzzled. 'Lord knows where I'd be without him, regardless of his demented ramblings!'

Nestled dreamily together on a gaily coloured beach towel, Jon's brutally honest story gradually unfolded... from sitting for hours cooped up in his prison cell, feeling the walls closing in on him, through his obsessive thoughts running riot, imagining Agnes in the arms of another man, loving him as he loved her.

'Not a day went by that I didn't think of you,' she sighed. 'Gazing at the turquoise water, searching for you.'

Her jaw suddenly dropped, and she stopped and gasped. 'My God!' she finally said.

'What is it, Aggie?'

'Cara!'

'The psychic in Inverie?'

'Her dream premonition. It came true!'

'You sound just like CJ!'

She firmly pinned him back to the ground and laid her cheek to his chest, feeling her head rise and fall to the steady rhythm of his heartbeat, as though breathing new life into her in sync with the lapping ocean waves.

'Hush your mouth, and put it to better use,' she said sassily, straddling his ribcage and lowering her lips towards his.

*

'You came back. Whatever possessed you?' the freshly cleansed tomboy said wryly, answering the door clad only in a washed-linen bathrobe, outwardly mystified by the likeable stranger's unexpected U-turn.

'Pardon me for asking, but why do you constantly do yourself down?' CJ said splutteringly, his index finger wagging in her face. 'Take a look in the mirror; there's a striking young woman lurking under the surface!'

'Striking…? Have you been drinking?' she responded a mite aggressively. 'Is that some kind of backhanded compliment?'

'There you go again!'

'You're funny.'

'Funny ha-ha, or peculiar?'

'A bit of both, I guess.'

'I know this may seem a little forward,' he said cautiously. 'But I was wondering if you were free tonight?'

'To play second fiddle? You've got to be kidding!'

'Huh?' he grunted.

'She cold-shouldered you!'

'Who did what?' he asked confusedly.

'Agnes!'

He stepped backward a pace and covered his mouth to conceal his amazement, panting between breaths while trying to keep from laughing. Meeting her eyes he slapped the side of his face, and somehow managed to speak.

'Aggie… and me?' he said, oddly flattered by the idea. 'I'll explain everything later… that is if we're on for tonight?'

'You bet your boots we are!' she said, flashing him a wink. 'Get your dinger back here for eight o'clock sharp!'

'My dinger?' he said, perplexed.

'Your scrawny ass, you dumbo!' she giggled. 'The name's Diana, though everyone round here calls me Dido.'

'CJ… though my Mum calls me Carl!' he added semi-humorously, thinking all his Christmases had come at once.

NINETY-SIX

Coles Bay, Tasmania

'LOVE IS IN THE AIR... *everywhere I look around,*' John Paul Young's golden oldie boomed into the rafters, harmonising perfectly with the smitten glances passing back and forth across the congested dance floor.

'May I just say how proud we all are to have a real live superstar in our midst tonight!' the makeshift DJ babbled, cueing the dreamy pizzicato strings paving the way to the worldwide chart-topper 'Song for Agnes'.

Jon politely bowed his head and lovingly gathered Aggie up in his arms, blissfully oblivious to the phalanx of merrymakers spontaneously fanning out into a circle around the community hall's perimeter.

'Bang goes my anonymity!' he murmured with a gentle, half-rueful smile. 'I'd got used to keeping a low profile.'

'You love every minute of it!'

'You can tell?'

'I see gladness, flooding your eyes!'

And so they danced to the song she inspired him to write, gliding across the floor perfectly in unison. Jon enfolded her body into his and slipped his hand towards the base of her spine, vowing never to let her go again.

'*If only you'd believe in you, the way that I believe in you,*' the opening line poignantly quavered, its lilting melody rippling above the heads of the watching throng to interrupt the chitchat taking place in the corner.

'How's about we drink up?' Dido chirped, tugging lightly at CJ's hand. 'And head on up to the Hazards for a moonlight safari?'

'The Hazards?' he said curiously.

'Dove Mountain. My favourite spot on the island!' she purred. 'It's a beautiful starry night, and the views are to die for!'

A rapturous roar of approval greeted the song's stirring finale, prompting a mini-stampede towards the dance floor where, besieged by a

427

swarm of excited well-wishers, the musician and his muse responded with a medley of hugs and handshakes.

As midnight approached, the DJ crossfaded into a guitar-led intro and grabbing his mic began the countdown. '*Five... four... three... two... one!*' he yawped, cueing in the Slade classic, 'Merry Christmas Everybody'.

Coloured streamers rained down amid the crack of party poppers and champagne corks. Couples kissed and embraced, pulling one another onto the ever-crowding dance floor, in an atmosphere of unbridled joy.

CJ jumped to his feet and, throwing his arms around Dido, deposited a huge smacker squarely on her lips. She drew back for a moment to catch her breath, instantly picking up on a puckish smile crossing his face.

'Let's get our dingers out of here!'

*

Dove Mountain

A kaleidoscope of milky moonbeams danced over the multi-shaped pink granite formations, casting a luminous shadow onto the chilled-out twosome. Completely at ease with one another they swapped stories beneath the dappled sky.

'Who'd have thought it possible, eh?' Dido considered, looping her arm inside his and smiling mischievously back at him. 'A jam-eater and a whingeing Pom, snuggled up close together on a mountain top!'

'Tasmanian Devil, more like!' he replied, playfully wrestling her onto the gravelly earth.

His eyes were suddenly drawn upward to a shooting star streaking through the heavens. 'Wow! What the hell was that?'

'Two stars realigning in a faraway galaxy!' she cried, bolting upright. 'Hurry, and make a wish before it's gone!'

Frozen like statues they sat, legs dangling precariously over the vertiginous rock face, as a glittering fountain of light cascaded down towards the silken ocean, melting away like parachute waterfalls into the burnt ochre sky.

'You don't think...?' CJ said, quickly stopping himself to swat at an imaginary mosquito. 'No, it's nothing, forget it!'

'Spit it out!' she said, bluntly.

'I just got the weirdest feeling,' he timidly confessed. 'Two stars aligning, and all that superstitious mumbo jumbo!'

'Take another gander, only this time let your eyes adjust to the darkness... then focus on the puffy white plume floating just beneath the arc of the moon...' she urged him excitedly. 'Got it? Now tell me what you see!'

'Two silhouettes merging into one!' he said fancifully, captivated by her dreamy smile. 'But that's almost inconceivable!'

'Some things are written in the stars – though I'm more inclined to think they realigned tonight for Agnes and your buddy Jon, reunited at last under a crescent moon. As for you and me... our story's just about to begin!'

THE END

ENCORE

Jon and Agnes tied the knot in a quaint chapel on the outskirts of Melbourne, Australia. The small service was conducted by the Reverend Dorothy Smith.

JJ Gold's eagerly awaited fifth album *Eldorado* simultaneously topped the UK and American charts upon its release in early May 2014, going on to sell a staggering 25 million copies worldwide.

CJ and Dido married under special licence in early 2015, giving birth to a baby son named Callum ten months later. The family reside in Port Arthur, Tasmania, where CJ works as a tourist guide at the town's infamous prison.

Under European law Sheila Douglas applied to a Parisian court to request permission for a posthumous marriage to the love of her life, Dan Hackett. Following a long-drawn-out legal wrangle lasting in excess of two years, the application was subsequently revoked.

Richard Turner received a custodial sentence of thirty-two years for the brutal murder of Amir Mistry. He is currently an inmate in Wakefield prison.

Khalid Shah's biographical account of Jon's extraordinary life, entitled *At the End of the Rainbow*, remained on the international non-fiction best-selling lists for the entirety of 2014. The author now resides in Los Angeles, where he turns his hand to script and screenplay writing for the lucrative Hollywood movie industry.

The white beaches of Sandaig on the Knoydart Peninsula provided the setting for Gavin Maxwell's acclaimed novel *Ring of Bright Water*.

ACKNOWLEDGEMENTS

My THANKS GO OUT to the following people:

The extraordinarily resilient community of Knoydart, Scotland, for allowing me to intrude on your valuable privacy.

The drunken, foul-mouthed resident of Fort William I unfortunately happened upon in a downmarket Mallaig hostelry, who unknowingly inspired the character Jimmy Logan. (His nephew Duncan remains purely fictional.)

Doctor Luke James, for offering his invaluable input and information regarding all matters medical.

Cheryl Fixter, for her unerring assistance in explaining the ins and outs of police procedural matters.

Paul Fixter, for his additional knowledge in the workings of the police force.

Chester Stern, author of *Dr Iain West's Casebook*.

Dexter O'Neill and Paul Ballard at Fantom Publishing.

Phil Reynolds at Phil Reynolds Media Services.

And lastly to my wonderful wife Cathy, for her unwavering patience and support during the writing of this novel.